NOBLE CLAIMS

THE BLOOD & FLAME SAGA
BOOK 3

E.A. WINTERS

Paperback ISBN: 978-1-958702-03-1

DragonLeaf Press, imprint of Snowfall Publications, LLC

To chai lattes, the fuel of my writerly brain.

SOCIAL MEDIA

Connect with me on social media! [1]

- Website and newsletter: https://www.eawinters.com
- Facebook: https://www.facebook.com/eawintersnovels
- TikTok: @eawinters
- Instagram: @e.a.winters

---

1. Warning: connecting on social media may lead to exclusive content, behind the scenes snapshots, and joining a community that is way more fun than your daily to-do list. Engage with caution.

ALSO IN SERIES

The Blood and Flame Saga
Dragon's Kiss
Broken Bonds
Noble Claims
Crimson Queen

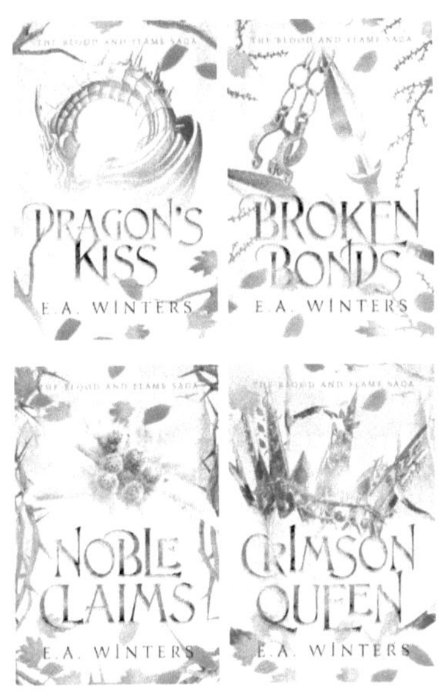

Mount Hara
Haizlin
Kalma
Carfus
Qalea
Ryden
Camar
Pillerae
N
E
S
W

Boan
Pilall
Ellix
nor
Kinlock
elera
Surion
Strip
Horen
Seddon

1

TYMETIN

Nothing about this kill was fun – no explosions, no torture, no watching as the terror in his target's eyes faded into death. Still, Tymetin supposed there was some level of elegance in the plan. After all, he'd orchestrated it himself. And all his jobs had three things in common: elegance, precision, and blackmail.

In his line of work, assurances were critical. Tymetin turned the sapphire ring twice on the little finger of his right hand, leaving the sapphire facing his palm as he crouched on the barred windowsill. The glass was open to let fresh air in, and the bars were decorative—at least, they appeared to be for anyone who didn't know how deep the king's paranoia ran.

A cool breeze played with the crescent moon reflected in a vast moat fifty feet below. Tymetin's bare toes gripped the stone sill, and he looped one arm around the bars to stabilize himself as he reached through the window with the other and plucked a letter opener in the shape of a spear off a writing desk. Jewels encrusted the spearhead of the bone letter opener—unnecessarily elaborate, like most items in the room. Tymetin doubted the spear Aurin had thrust into the Wellspring at The Crumbling all those years ago had been anything other than ordinary wood and rock. But it wasn't the materials that made the spear legendary; it was the way its wielding forever changed the world. The Melder who plunged it into the heart of magic shattered it forever.

A glorious chill ran up Tymetin's spine. It wasn't so different from what he was doing, was it? Such power. Such an outpouring of death in its wake. Known elemental melders were hunted and tested, their blood drained in hopes of clutching any scrap of remaining magic. The deed was done with ordinary materials, but it was Aurin who made the spear legendary enough to be depicted on the Jannemari flag and recreated in such ridiculous extravagance on the desks of Belvidorian kings. Tymetin also had the power to alter the course of the future, the trajectory of kingdoms, to select who lived and who died.

It was easy.

It was delicious.

Tymetin plucked the ridiculous spearhead off its shaft and produced a pen from the pouch on his belt. The pen was less gratuitous than the letter opener, identical to the many simpler reed utensils littering the bottom drawer of the king's writing box, except for the long thread secured to its tail. The gaudy things in the top drawer were far too heavy to be repurposed as a dart.

He slipped the dart inside the spear shaft, lifted it to his lips, and sent it sailing with a quick puff—one breath, the beginning of the end. The dart flew twenty feet across the room to an over-carved canopied bed stacked with furs, hitting its mark in the exposed neck of a sleeping form. Tymetin tugged lightly on the thread of the dart, and it leaped back at his command, skittering across the stone floor and back up to his waiting hand. He replaced the spearhead onto its shaft and returned it to the desk, then unwound the thread from the pen, dropped the pen into the moat below, and cast a longing glance in the direction of his mark. The king's chest rose and fell, rose and fell.

King Arnevon of Belvidore had no idea he'd just been assassinated. He never would. A pity.

Tymetin receded from the window, traversed across the face of the castle twenty feet to his left and down, and reentered the fortress through the window he'd left open. He retrieved his shoes from an apple barrel and patted the small lumpy object in the pouch on his belt, smiling to himself.

Only one thing left to do.

2

———

Semra had never wanted to end a dragon ride so badly. Zezura's great aquamarine wings beat the air and she dropped altitude and angled toward Shamaran Castle in Jannemar. For a moment, nausea threatened to take over again, but the feeling passed, and Semra felt some of her strength return. Her whole body ached, her cheeks burned, and she knew she never would have kept her seat on Zezura's back without Zephan.

Prince Zephan tightened his arms around her as they passed over the bustling city of Qalea, over the castle walls, and dove toward the courtyard below. *Slow down, Zez. If I'm going to die, I don't want anyone to say the dragonlord lost her lunch on a ride.* Dragonlord. What a ridiculous thing to call herself. The only person Semra had ever known as dragonlord throughout her life was the Framatar, the man who had his great black dragon snatch children from villages like hers in the middle of nowhere, the man who raised and trained her to be a wildly effective assassin. The man who slaughtered her real parents and used his assassin children to aid in a coup attempt that landed him in the dungeons beneath her feet. Azi Shamaran.

In reality, anyone who saved the life of a dragon opened the door to a lifelong bond with the beast, who flicked its tongue to mark its savior with the dragon's kiss—a smooth, opal-like mark on the skin that sealed the bond. Azi had told the children of the mountain that the iridescent mark on his temple was proof he was blessed by the gods. Semra stopped believing that as she grew older, but she never guessed the real story until she saved Zezura's life and became a dragonlord herself. Semra could feel Zezura's concern as she pulled up just in time to hit the ground with a little less whiplash. Zephan grunted on impact, and Semra wavered.

The wind wicked at the sweat all over her body, and a shiver ran up her spine. During the trip from the battlefield at the Surion Strip, Semra had oscillated between feeling almost decent and feeling as though death had come knocking. Movement made everything worse. Zephan helped her down as doors flung open from every direction and a flurry of heavy footsteps pounded toward them and surrounded them.

Semra's heart leaped into her throat, and the violence of the reaction brought another wave of nausea. She doubled over as the porridge she'd managed to eat last night made a hasty escape. Semra doubted she'd ever quite get used to having men with swords run at her without trying to kill her.

"Your Royal Highness! We are overjoyed to see you safely returned to us!"

Semra's stomach soured at the sound of Captain Firfell's voice, and she retched the last of her stomach's contents onto the cobbles—this time only halfway succeeding in avoiding the prince's shoes. Firfell wrinkled his nose.

"We left in a hurry. Semra was captured in Belvidore trying to save my sister, and they did something to her she hasn't recovered from. Is Coanor ready for us? You should have received word ..."

"We did, though we had little time to prepare for your arrival. We didn't realize you would be here so quickly."

"Pigeons don't need as much rest as we do, but dragons aren't half bad for speed."

Firfell pursed his lips. "I suppose not."

"What happened?" a young guard asked. He received a cutting glare from his captain and swallowed.

Semra waited for her head to stop spinning and straightened, wiping her mouth with the back of her hand and then the back of her hand on her pants. She heaved a sigh. "They tried to hurt Zez with chemicals. The same thing got in my bloodstream."

"She seems okay now," the young man said matter-of-factly, watching the dragon with cautious interest.

"Annais!" Firfell scolded.

Annais clamped his mouth shut and took a step back as if to reprimand himself.

"Yes, she's better now," Semra said. Her head swam and she reached out to steady herself on Zezura's scaly hide.

"But Semra isn't," Zephan said. "She's worse. Clearly it effects dragons differently than humans. Hence needing to see Coanor. Where is she?"

"If I may be so bold," Firfell began, "surely your family's healer should concern herself with your own health first. We have plenty of other healers that can attend to soldiers."

"I'm fine."

"Men of valor often say such things, without taking the time to properly examine—"

"Captain." Zephan squared his shoulders and leveled a glare at Firfell, and when he spoke, his clipped tone left no room for argument. "This woman nearly died and *still* pushed through to save us at the Strip. If it weren't for her efforts, you may never have received me home at all. Get me Coanor, *now*."

Firfell's jaw clenched, but he bowed. "She is prepared and waiting in the infirmary, Your Highness."

The infirmary. A place swarming with strangers controlling and handling what Semra would eat, drink, and be treated with. An assassin's nightmare. *Ex-assassin*, she reminded herself. But she knew better. *You may not be killing for the Framatar anymore, but you can't escape your history. Can you count the number of people who want you dead?*

"Excellent," Zephan answered. "We will go there now."

"Your Highness, the king requested your report on the battle and our military's status as soon as possible."

"Of course. I'll go as soon as I'm able."

Semra laid a hand on Zephan's arm, then snatched it back when the captain's eyes nearly bulged out of his head. She forced a smile. "I'm fine. You should go."

Zephan stepped in front of her and turned his back to the guards, shielding her from their glances with his body and speaking low enough that only she could hear. "You're not very convincing."

Those intense amber eyes of his seemed to search her very soul, molten-gold pools pressing in on her, pressing, pressing for answers. People often wanted answers, but this was different. Earnest, caring, vulnerable. She looked away. "I'll get some rest; I promise."

"Rest isn't cutting it. You might be poisoned."

"I'll make a list of herbs and poultices. I can treat myself."

"You're going to a healer if I have to drag you there myself."

Semra shook her head. Wrong move. Her head swam and her knees nearly buckled. She shifted her weight to cover it. "All right, fine. If it will make you happy, I'll go, but I don't need a babysitter. You need to go see your father."

Zephan examined her for a long moment, then stepped back. "It *would* make me happy. Tell Coanor she's to spare no expense in your treatment."

Semra would *not* be saying that. She nodded. "Thank you."

Zephan's mouth twisted in what could nearly have been a smile. He turned and fell in step with Firfell, heading toward the king's meeting rooms on the west side.

"Are you sure she isn't playing you?" Semra heard Firfell whisper.

"Look at her, Firfell! She's sweating buckets and can hardly stand. Are you blind?"

"I'm *fine*," Semra snapped at their backs, then whirled on her heel and plunged through a door to the eastern side of the keep, toward the infirmary.

Plunging was ill-advised. The world spun, and she shot out a hand to steady herself against the wall. Fresh sweat coated her skin, but her cheeks still felt like fire. She was decidedly not fine. Not at all. Any fool could see that, except maybe Captain Firfell, but his bias toward her made him the biggest fool at all.

Semra racked her scrambled brain. Maybe Coanor was safe. Maybe she wasn't. Even if she was, a master healer would have assistants, and it would be the easiest task in the world for any of Semra's old assassin colleagues to leverage the weakest link to their bidding. Besides, what were the chances the healer would be able to decipher what was wrong with her? Zephan had conveniently left out mention of how exactly she'd gotten sick.

If Princess Avaya was to be believed, the Belvidorian guards had dipped spears in *konnolan,* a chemical that temporarily mitigates magical essence. Because dragons held both biological and magical processes in their bodies, it was detrimental to them. When Semra intervened to save Zezura, it had gotten in her own bloodstream.

If Avaya was to be believed. After all, she'd orchestrated her own kidnapping to Belvidore, hiring Semra's old colleague Siler to do the job. Her arranged marriage to Prince Axis of Belvidore had been ruined when Zephan's mother, Queen Sharsi, was murdered and Belvidore blamed. Avaya claimed she wanted to make good on the promise to heal the relationship between the nations, working on Belvidore from the inside out, but she also stood by while Semra was beaten, and tackled her brother to the ground when he was about to kill Axis in battle. She'd willingly run off with Axis, and Semra and Zephan had failed in their mission to return the king's daughter to safety. Still, perhaps not every word she said had been a lie.

Avaya's words came back to Semra. *It shouldn't have impacted you at all. The healer said it's inert to nonmagical species.* Nearly all magic had been destroyed six hundred years ago. Magical creatures held the only remnants, and even their magic was muted compared to before The Crumbling. But then, why was Zezura totally recovered, while Semra grew steadily worse?

Semra grimaced and stumbled her way to the stairwell on her right, headed up to her chambers rather than down the hall to the outer ward and infirmary. She needed to think. Maybe she could tie herself to Zezura, and fly to some other healer, someone more obscure and less accessible. She lost her footing and rammed her shoulder into the staircase wall. Maybe she would die anyway and not have to worry about it.

Her vision blurred, and she dropped like a stone.

The sound of someone swearing and running footsteps filled her ears above the din of her own heartbeat, just before her skull should have cracked on the unforgiving rock-hewn steps. The world went black, and when Semra came to a moment later, her body ached, her head throbbed, and amber eyes were scrutinizing her.

"Semra? Are you with me?"

Zephan cradled her head in his lap in the stairwell, two fingers pressed to her carotid.

Semra tried to sit, but her limbs hung weakly at her sides. *I'm with you.* She opened her mouth to speak, but only managed a soft whimper.

Zephan brushed matted, disheveled hair from her face. "I'm going to pick you up now. If you would rather me abandon you in the stairwell, which looks mysteriously like going to your room instead of the infirmary, just say so. If you want me to take you to Coanor like someone brilliant around here recently suggested, lay there like a limp noodle."

Ha, ha. Semra wished she could muster up a blistering glare, but in that moment, it was all she could do to keep her eyes open. She blinked hard, but her eyelids were so, so heavy.

Zephan scooped her up in his arms and strode back down the stairs and to the end of the hall. *"Fine,* she says," he muttered. "Little liar. Forgive me for following you, but you're also half dead. And maybe even a little predictable."

Semra blinked again and noticed the open air and low buildings of the outer ward, and when she opened her eyes again, she lay on a cot in a small room with a dirt floor. A table on the opposite end was strewn with haphazard papers, jars, and bottles, and a straw broom and wooden bucket stood in the corner. Prince Zephan sat on a crude stool beside the bed, and a woman in her sixties sat on the edge of the bed, holding a cloth to Semra's forehead.

"If it really was konnolan, it must have been laced with something to bring on this reaction," Coanor rumbled, her voice graveled and unusually low for a woman.

"Any ideas on where to start?" Zephan asked.

"It's a gamble. I have a few guesses, but in her condition ... well, if I do nothing, she might die. And if I guess the wrong thing, she might die."

"Scourge."

"Your Highness. *Language.*"

"If ever there were a time to curse, it's now."

"If it heals her, I'll let the king know my services are no longer required. All we need to do is swear."

This woman sounded more like an up-tight mother goose than a royal family's employed healer. Semra licked her cracked lips. "Why is Zez recovered, and I'm not?"

Zephan and Coanor jumped and turned to stare at her.

"Aurin's Spear, were those supposed to be words?" Coanor rattled. "You sound like you're six bottles into a bender, darling. Let's try that again, shall we?"

Semra furrowed her brows. Zephan cocked his head. "Your words came out all jumbled. What did you say?"

"Why is Zezura recovered and not me?"

"Dragons and humans aren't built the same," Coanor said. "Dosage meant for a dragon will impact humans at a much more extreme level due to size and metabolic differences, and magical components in the blood of the dragon."

But what if your blood isn't entirely human anymore? Semra took a deep breath and cleared her throat. How would people react if they learned that Semra had survived being bitten by venomous snakes? She should have died in minutes, like Commander Ramas had when she survived the attack and turned his snakes against him. What would people say if they knew that the mark of the dragon's kiss had expanded that night in the dungeon, the night she was meant to die?

Semra reached for the serpentine amulet on her belt, the proof of Ramas' death that she'd kept with her since that day

—but no, she'd lost the amulet on the battlefield. She dropped her hand. "Can you help me?"

"I don't know, darling. But I'll give it my best."

Belvidore had been obsessively hunting for magic for six hundred years. If they thought Semra had magic, however mistaken they might be, what would they make of it? Would she be killed? Experimented on? Semra's stomach turned in knots, and she swallowed hard against the bile threatening a return trip up her aching throat. Her eyes grew heavy again, her body on fire, her head pounding. No use worrying how to find another healer now. She was out of options.

3

AVAYA

Avaya tapped her foot against the tiled floor, arranging her velvet skirts on the sofa for the hundredth time. The violet hue beautifully complemented her emerald eyes and golden hair, and the ripples of soft fabric fell like waterfalls down her slender frame. She looked good in just about anything, but she didn't wear patience well.

The door opened with a *bang* and a broad-shouldered, burly man burst through the opening. Avaya snapped her head up and leaped to her feet, cursing herself for being caught off guard. And what was the purpose of draping her skirts just so, only to pay her respects to the prince by standing when he entered? Avaya dropped into a curtsy. He snatched a goblet from an end table and hurled it against the wall. She flinched, then pulled her shoulders back and lifted her chin. She should never show weakness when she felt it.

"Something troubling you, Your Highness?"

Axis jumped, torn from his ruminations by the sound of her voice.

"Forgive me," she said. "I thought we had spoken about meeting ..."

The prince ran a hand over his face and down his dark mahogany-brown beard. The red in his face blushed pink, and he inhaled deeply, tightening the muscles of his fists before slowly uncurling his fingers. "Princess Avaya. Forgive me. My father is a fool."

"Come, sit. Tell me."

Axis clenched his jaw and paused, as if weighing the invitation for worthiness. He let out a heavy sigh, tossed his hands up, and started pacing. "He pulled our troops all the way back to our border and has avoided my meetings in favor of lazing all morning in bed. They were *weak*, they were breaking. We *had* them. We know now what weakens the dragon. We should be taking the Surion Strip while Jannemar is licking its wounds, swamped with casualties and injured men. We should be invading Kinlock and pressing north! Turian must learn precisely who he betrayed when he snubbed and falsely accused the crown of Belvidore. He—"

Axis caught himself and spun to examine Avaya's reaction.

"It's all right," Avaya said softly. "He *did* snub you. We both have cowardly fathers."

"I could have said it differently."

"No need."

"I should not have lost my temper."

Avaya took a sip of wine from her chalice to hide a smirk. Prince Axis frequently lost his temper. No reason to start apologizing for it now, particularly when he was unlikely to actually *do* anything about it. "There is nothing to forgive, my prince. Surely we are beyond formalities, since I betrayed my own family to be with you."

Axis tilted his head to one side. "Is that why you did it? To be with me?"

A thrill ran up her spine. Yes, *this* was the time to show vulnerability. When she felt strongest.

Avaya let her lashes sweep her cheek, her fingers playing with the ends of her hair. "Was I too forward? I see how lonely you are, what a great weight you carry, being a powerful king with no throne to sit on. I wanted to unite our kingdoms from the beginning, but it wasn't until after we spent time together that I knew I wanted to fight by your side."

"You dare call me a king while my father lives?" Danger edged his voice, and in a single stride he positioned himself nose to nose with her. A test.

Avaya looked up and searched his face, earnestness dripping from every word. "His Majesty the King is a great man, but mice are never equipped for glory. Only a lion can build an empire, and *you* were born a lion."

A slow smile crept over his face. "And what of your own father? You would so easily see him ruined?"

Avaya ran her hand up to the back of his neck, stretching up on her tiptoes as she pulled him down to whisper in his ear. Her free hand crushed a fistful of velvet, and her words came in a low hiss. "I hate my father."

"Do you now?" Axis yanked her against him, a bear unsure of its strength. Her breath caught, and she leaned into him. Axis pulled her head back and gripped her chin, deadly serious. "And you fancy yourself an empress?"

"*Your* empress. You and I against the world—starting with King Turian of Jannemar."

Axis's lips curled into a sly smile. He tipped her chin up and pressed his mouth to hers.

Avaya twined her fingers in his hair, pulling herself closer. The prince was precisely what she liked in a man— marvelously rich, wildly powerful, and completely enamored by her feminine allure.

When Axis broke free, he twisted a golden ringlet of her hair around his finger. "Well then, empress," he said, "there's only one problem left to sort out."

Sprinting footfalls shattered the moment as someone flew down the hall and rapped swiftly on the door.

"In a minute!" Axis called out.

The someone on the other side pounded on the door again. A guttural rumble escaped Axis's throat as he released Avaya and crossed to the door. He threw it open. "Someone had better be dead to justify this level of impertinence."

A scrawny servant paled in the doorway, shrinking back into the hall. "Y-y-your Highness ... the ... the king is dead. And I was told to bring you this. We found it just this morning."

The servant opened his hand, and there, dangling from the boy's bony fingers, swung an emerald serpentine amulet Avaya would have known anywhere.

4

———

Semra tossed and turned, her flesh on fire, her skin clammy with sweat. She would die of this heat. It would swallow her whole. Semra mustered her strength and kicked off the blankets, then gasped as the cold seized her and a chill ran up her spine.

"She's awake?"

"Nearly. She's been in and out for the past twenty-four hours. The tonic I made is helping."

"Do you know what she was dosed with?"

"Unfortunately, no. It *does* seem like she was poisoned, and the immediate nature of her reactions did narrow things down quite a bit, but none of the possibilities make sense."

"Why not?"

"Because she should be dead."

Semra reached for the edge of the blanket with her toe and winced at the ache in her joints. Her eyes were still squeezed shut.

"Semra? It's me." Zephan. "We're doing our best to keep you comfortable."

And a miserable job of it too. The blanket was lifted over her feet, and she was smothered in unbearable heat once again. Just like she'd wanted, a moment before. *Ugh.*

"Hello, darling. Can you hear us?"

Semra grunted and forced her eyes to flutter open, catching glimpses of Zephan and Coanor peering down at her in between her eyelids drooping closed again. They were so heavy.

"You've been lost to fevers for the better part of two weeks. We thought we'd lost you."

Semra bolted upright, then fell back against her pillow. Every muscle screamed its complaint. She swallowed. "Two *weeks?*"

Zephan nodded solemnly and turned to Coanor. "Do you think the mark could have something to do with it? I've never heard of the dragon's kiss preventing poisoning before, but she did survive the venomous snakes when Ramas tried to kill her."

Semra's mouth went dry. "Zephan!" she hissed, her eyes darting to Coanor.

The healer appeared unsurprised and unconcerned. "Don't worry, darling," Coanor rumbled, patting Semra's arm. "You were just as upset with him the first time he told me. But your eyes are clearer now, and perhaps you'll remember this time."

Semra's mouth dropped open. How many times had they spoken like this around her?

Coanor turned back to Zephan. "Dragons and magical species are not my specialty by any means. I don't think they're *anyone's* specialty nowadays. But from what little I know, the mark is simply a token of the unbreakable bond between a dragon and the human who saved its life. I've never heard of one this size, even in legend. It's about four inches long, across her heart up to her collarbone." She shook her head. "Remarkable."

"I'm sorry I spoiled your secret," Zephan said to Semra. "But you can trust Coanor. She is limited enough as it is trying to figure out how to save your life. Any information she can have on her patient is worth giving her."

"I'm the king's favorite healer, darling. One doesn't earn such a title by being a blabbermouth."

Unless they are good at it and want to get rich and stay alive. Semra nodded weakly.

"It's not you, Coanor," Zephan said. "She hates feeling out of control of the situation. This might be the first time she followed through with one of my suggestions without debating me about it first—all it took was for her to collapse and lose consciousness."

Semra stuck her tongue out.

Coanor smiled. "She's feeling better."

She was. Semra furrowed her brow, testing gentle movements of her arms and legs. The aches were abating. "How am I already so much better than I was half an hour ago?"

Coanor lifted a small bottle off a side table and tapped the cork on top. "Through a risky trial and error process during which you nearly died multiple times, I have developed a tonic I believe will relieve your symptoms for the time being. I'm afraid it isn't a cure, and I'm still not entirely sure why it works. I'm not sure how long it will give you, but ever since continuing this iteration of the tonic, you have been steadily improving. I sent for Prince Zephan when you showed signs of response, upon his request.

"If it *is* poison, and it certainly acts like one, it's not like any I've seen before. If you don't find an antidote soon, the poison could still overtake your system and kill you—or not. I just don't know. You need to know everything you can about what substance the konnolan may have been laced with, and any impact the dragon's kiss might have on your body."

"We need a library." Semra swung her feet over the side of the bed, then wavered.

Coanor pressed her back down to her pillow. "Perhaps we can send for some reading materials. Your best chance of survival and recovery is keeping a low heart rate and resting."

"I thought the best chance of survival was figuring out what is wrong with me."

Coanor pressed her lips and looked at Zephan. "Back me up, Your Highness."

"Coanor says you need to take the tonic twice a day. Rest here and be good. I'll see what I can find in our library, and I'll be back this evening."

Semra tilted her head. "You just regained control of the Strip through heavy casualties and have a general out of commission. You can't spend your days babysitting me. I'll take it, I promise."

Zephan rolled his eyes. "Just like you promised to come see Coanor, when we landed. I want to watch you take it."

Someone knocked on the door. "Your Highness?" Firfell's voice. Semra made a face.

The corner of Zephan's mouth quirked up, and he slipped out.

Coanor patted Semra on the arm and set a cup of water next to the bed. "I'm off to pick up some herbs from a friend so I can duplicate the formula. Some of them are quite rare. Lay back and rest, and I'll check on you soon."

Semra thanked Coanor for her care, and a moment later she was alone. Sweat beaded her brow, and she took a sip of water before sinking back into the pillows. The movement made her head throb, but it was far more tolerable than before.

I'm off to pick up some herbs from a friend …

Semra jolted upright. Her head spun, and she threw her hand out to the wall to keep from toppling over. Coanor couldn't grow all her own herbs and ingredients. Though Semra hadn't yet seen any assistants, as the king's favored healer, surely she was privy to them.

She ran a hand over her face. Who exactly was helping Coanor develop the tonic? Semra, the assassin traitor with no shortage of skilled enemies, had been incapacitated for two weeks in the most obvious location possible. All her fears of why she shouldn't go to Coanor had become reality.

Her muscles ached, but she couldn't be in the same predictable place for another instant. Semra slowly slid her feet over the edge of the bed and tested her weight, keeping one hand firmly on the wall. So far so good.

She blinked down at her toes. Bare feet. No trousers. Rats and rot, she was in a dress! A nightdress, at that. Semra glanced around the room for her old clothes. Her leather-soled boots stood next to the bed, but her tunic and trousers with built-in leg sheaths for her knives were nowhere to be seen. They would be easily identifiable, but practical and familiar. The nightdress was neither practical nor familiar and would stand out far too much. People tend to remember seeing someone in nightclothes wandering royal grounds.

Semra snatched the bottle of tonic off the table, shoved her feet into the shoes, and abandoned her little back room into what appeared to be an empty sickbay. Six cots with curtains pulled back lined the wall on the far end, and a curtain ran down the middle of the room separating the beds from the table, water basin, cabinet, and shelving. A door led outside to her right, and directly to her left, a door next to hers led to Coanor's only other interior space.

Her knees wobbled and she gripped the doorframe,

waiting for the weakness to abate. Semra hugged the wall and made her way to the second door. It must lead to Coanor's bedroom, stocked with a person's clothes and other essentials. Semra gripped the iron handle and pushed, easing the door open just a hair. She froze.

Something had moved. Semra stepped up close to the crack of the door and peered into the room. A simple bed occupied the far wall, with a small table at its head and a small trunk at its foot. Above them hung dried herbs, sketches of plants and animals, and parchments painted with beautiful, ornamented lettering. And there, gently swinging and rigged to the wall, a bow and arrow shifted backward. Semra cracked the door another inch, and the arrow drew back another inch. The bow was secured to the ceiling and cord ran from the arrow backward through a pulley and out of sight around the door.

Semra arched an eyebrow. Coanor, the king's favored healer, had a paranoid streak? An unexpected obstacle, but there must be a simple way to disengage the mechanism from outside the room, or Coanor herself would never get in. And what was she hiding? Semra reached around the door and felt along its edge with her fingers until she felt the cord on a hook. She lifted the knotted end of the cord off the hook, releasing the tension, and the arrow returned to a less-threatening position along the bow.

Semra opened the door just enough to step inside and close it behind her. The arrow wasn't aimed at the would-be intruder but at a pig-bladder balloon of some sort over the door. She shuddered. Had she almost been killed by a booby trap, after all this fuss to keep her alive?

Shelves on the wall to her left overflowed with books, bottles and jars, lotions, charcoal, paints, and parchment, spilling onto the table below. Sketches of flowers and some sort of vine climbed up the margin of one parchment. An elaborate root system was drawn beneath a half-painted verse from an open book of poetry on another:

> *We all have roots, down in the ground;*
> *strength is made, it isn't found.*

So the paranoid healer was also a philosopher. The woman was making less and less sense by the second. Torn scraps of paper littered the table amid gardening instructions and poultice recipes. A dragon drawing caught her eye, with another poetry excerpt:

> *Spearhead of an ancient spring, blood and flame and smoke*
> *Shall usher in the clash of kings, a dragon-blooded stroke.*

Semra broke out into a fresh cold sweat, and her mouth went dry. *Clash of kings...* Realization dawned. *Coanor blames dragons for the war. Dragonlords. Me.*

Her chest tightened. Semra's mind whirred in a thousand directions, but through the tumult, only two clear thoughts formed. *Get the clothes. Get out.*

Semra set down the tonic, flipped open the trunk at the end of the bed and was rewarded with stacks of blankets and clothing. She dug to the bottom for something Coanor might be less likely to miss and yanked out a simple white chemise and dusty blue overdress. Another dress, but at least it was commonplace. Semra changed, stashed the tonic in the bodice, and the nightdress under her arm, and replaced the cord on the hook of the door as she made her exit.

Two *weeks* she'd spent, unconscious, in this woman's care. Coanor was the perfect weapon. As healer to the royal family, she would have access into every royal bedroom at the drop of a hat. She could ensure a member of the royal family recovered well from injuries and ailments—or died, quickly and efficiently.

Semra wondered if one of the Framatar's old assassin children had gotten to her, or if her involvement was merely personal. Not that it mattered. Semra would need rock-solid evidence for any action to be taken against someone so entrenched in castle life. The court's mistrust of her was problematic enough as it was without her killing a trusted healer who had faithfully served the royal family for decades. Or seemed to have faithfully served.

Sunlight flooded the outer ward as mid-morning settled over Shamaran Castle. The light sandstone was so much more inviting than the deep gray limestone of Madensig Fortress, and even the curvature of the bailey as it rolled with the land seemed kinder than the rigid square in Belvidore. The clanging of the smithy nearby reverberated in her skull, and Semra wondered whose bright idea it had been to place it within earshot of the sick.

She hurried toward the storage barn and granary ahead, but then winced as her muscles cried out and her head spun at the change of pace. Semra leaned on a barrel standing outside the granary and waited for the dizzy spell to pass. She wiped sweat from her forehead and pressed her knuckles to her cheeks. Hot. Burning. And not from the sun.

Why hadn't Coanor let her die yet? Semra had been on the edge of death for long enough; it would've been easy to do. Perhaps she simply wanted the distance of getting Semra to kill herself slowly with whatever was in the tonic, or maybe someone who wanted Semra alive paid her off. That was a far more frightening option.

Still, the first dose was doing wonders. Maybe Semra had

been wrong about the healer after all. She'd seemed gruff but kind—on first meeting.

Two stableboys exited the storage barn. Semra angled away from them and adjusted the lid of the barrel. The dizziness abated somewhat, and she stuffed the nightdress into the barrel, then headed toward the back of the ward nearest the cliff. A small residence next to a cylindrical building off to one side caught her eye. A woman emerged from the residence, carrying a basket. Semra was far too exposed to avoid her. As she drew nearer, Semra realized with a start that she knew the woman—Teriv, Avaya's lady-in-waiting before the princess kidnapped herself to Belvidore.

Teriv ignored her, and Semra returned the favor, until a furtive glance over made accidental eye contact. They both jumped, then Semra gave a curt nod and tried to focus on the soft *swish* rustle of grass tread underfoot, and the feeling of trudging onward as though her legs had been forged in mud. She took a deep breath and nearly choked on the strength of the new smell.

She must be in the right place. Semra stepped into the dovecote and was greeted by an overwhelming mass of warbling birds, flapping wings, and bird droppings. Hundreds of small rectangular holes recessed into the walls from floor to ceiling housed hundreds of homing pigeons. The smell hit her like a brick wall, and Semra gagged. Her head pounded and her cheeks flushed. *You're an idiot for getting out of bed*, some corner of her mind chastised her. *I would've been a bigger idiot for staying in the woman's house another instant,* another part of her retorted.

She placed a trembling hand on the side of the dovecote, then yelped and snatched it back. Droppings, everywhere. She found a dry place on the wall to scrape her finger clean and grimaced as she reached out with both hands for one of the resting pigeons. The bird shifted its sharp talons onto her hands, unconcerned, and let out a soft coo. Semra cradled it against her chest with one hand and produced the tonic with the other. Guilt twisted in her gut—or was the nausea returning?—as she gently squeezed the beak between her fingers and dropped the tonic into the bird's mouth when it opened wide.

The bird shook its head and pecked at her hand, struggling in Semra's grasp. If she let it go, it would all be for nothing. There would be no way of telling it apart from the other birds. Semra sank down against a dry portion of wall and bent her knees, cradling the pigeon in the confines of her lap, holding it fast in one hand and stroking its soft feathers with the other. She waited there for an hour until her nose stopped bothering to inform her of the stink. The pigeon was half-asleep against her body and breathing deeply.

Breathing. That was the important part. Semra gently lifted the pigeon back to its hole and left the dovecote behind, making her way across the grass to walk along the wall. She glanced behind her and scrutinized the area. The morning sun filled the east wards, leaving her exposed, out of place, and vulnerable. Against the pleading of her aching head and muscles, Semra quickened her pace and ducked into the servant's underground network through a door in the wall, not slowing until she made it back out to the inner ward in the lower courtyard.

She smothered a cough with her arm and wheezed. One quick walk and she could hardly catch her breath! She needed her knives. And her custom-made trousers with sheaths for them. And a moment to talk to Zephan before calling Zezura and finding somewhere else to recover. Or die. Whatever the case may be.

A coughing fit made her double over against the wall, and

a massive blur hit her in the chest, knocking her off her feet. A hand clapped over her mouth and dragged her backward into an alcove. Semra's stomach dropped, and she felt as though her head might split apart. Her heart thundered against her ribs; her vision blurred. Coanor's warning rang in her mind: *Your best chance of survival is keeping a low heart rate.*

Semra made a halfhearted swing at her captor as her weakened body sagged. She gripped the meaty part of her attacker's hand and tugged. Nothing.

If the man wanted a fight, he wouldn't be getting one. She envisioned the escape—planting her feet, bending the man's thumb backward, striking an elbow to the gut as she pivoted, a hook of the leg, and her adversary tumbling to the ground. A simple thing done in the blink of an eye. She'd done it a thousand times. She could leave him there or skewer him with his own sword.

Semra's knees gave way. She had nothing left.

5

———

The hand on Semra's mouth dropped just in time to catch her under the arms and prop her up against one of the garden trees. Semra started to topple, and her eyes fluttered open and closed. The man swore and sat her down on the ground against the base of the fruit tree.

"What's the matter with you?"

She knew that voice. There was a name attached to it. What was that name?

"Whassa the matter with me?" Semra mumbled. "Whassa the matter with youuu for 'ttacking me out of thin air." She closed her eyes and furrowed her brow. Monac. Zephan's close friend and bodyguard. Monac had traveled with Zephan and Semra to Belvidore in the mission to save Princess Avaya, and after the bloodbath at the Surion Strip, he had stayed behind in Kinlock while Zephan and Semra took the dragon ride back to Qalea.

"Don't be smart. Haven't they found something to heal you yet? You look even worse than when I left you—except there's no blood on your clothes."

"Where've you been?"

"I only just got in yesterday. I left Kinlock as soon as I could after you did, but horses aren't quite as efficient as Zezura."

Semra winced as she moved to sit up a little against the bark of the tree. Her head still pounded, but the stillness seemed to have eased her symptoms. She pulled out the bottle of tonic and let a drop fall on her tongue.

"Coanor mixed this together. I think she's trying to kill me."

Monac rolled his eyes. "Naturally the only person Prince Zephan trusts with your care is *also* the person you decide is trying to kill you. That bottle from the murderess herself?"

"You have to wait until I'm dead before you officially call her a murderess. Unless I'm not the first you know about?"

"Ridiculous. So why are you drinking tonic from someone you think wants you dead?"

"Because as luck would have it, it *does* seem to help, and without it I think I may die anyway—or at least continue collapsing on the people who abduct me. Sorry about that. And because I gave it to a pigeon, and it didn't immediately keel over."

Monac chuckled, then sobered. "As fun as this reunion has been, I didn't pull you in here to hear about your paranoia."

"It's *not* paranoia when lots of people *actually want you dead.*"

Monac dismissed her with a wave. "Firfell hates you."

Semra snorted. "What keen perception you have."

"I don't mean he hates you in a concerned-for-the-king *I think she might be dangerous* way, or in a, *her dragon ruins the courtyard* kind of way, but in a deep, unyielding, and *actively trying to catch you doing something nefarious* kind of way. He wants you dead, or at the very least, rotting in a cell next to Azi."

Semra shivered. She tried to block out the image of her childhood father figure, the dragonlord who told her she was worthless and killed her best friend in front of her, as her daily companion in the dungeons. She would far rather die.

Nefarious. There was no shortage of evil in Semra's past. It didn't make sense that King Turian had treated her so kindly, despite what he knew. She deserved a tortuous death, and maybe even that eternity with Azi down below. She pulled her knees up to her chest, wrapped her arms around her legs, and rested her chin on her arm. For a moment she wished she could fade away into the walls of the alcove, into the roots of the trees, and disappear. "I was an assassin. Everybody knows I did horrible things."

"You saved the life of the king and the prince, rounded up a slew of rogue assassins, and ran off chasing an idiot princess at the behest of the crown. And oh, right, you and Zezura stopped the Belvidorian army at the Strip."

It sounded almost grand the way Monac said it. Too grand —disconnected from reality. She shook her head. "That doesn't mean I didn't do those things. I killed a lot of people for Azi. Good people." She assumed they may have been good, anyway. She never knew a thing about them, but now she knew Azi had lied to them all about what type of people they killed, and why.

"But there's no proof. Azi may have been a lot of things, but he knew how to run an operation with quality coverups. Firfell was nervous when you got here, frustrated when Zephan shirked his duties to spend time with you, and insulted when the king sent you after Princess Avaya against his advice."

Semra arched an eyebrow. "Don't be dramatic. Zephan never shirks his duties. He left me alone in the castle for weeks after we caught Azi. After the task force dwindled down, he hardly spoke to me."

"I've been back from Kinlock one day and Firfell has been drilling me, not about Belvidore, not about battle position, not about General Tallem's recovery, but about you. About when you were with us, when you were alone. You were in Madensig alone for a long stretch of time."

"Did you tell him that?"

"I had to. I spun it to sound as good as possible, but we only have your word to know exactly what happened during that time."

Semra lifted her chin. "You mean when I was dropped in the middle of a courtyard in the middle of the night and waited in a cistern for the right time to save the king's daughter? And then the king's daughter encouraged the foreign prince to beat me? *That* time when I was alone?"

"Precisely. And he also asked me how you acted with the prince. And how he acted with you. Firfell's looking for reasons to get your head in a basket, Semra. You need to keep your head down and focus on healing up for a bit, and we can find something for you to do after that."

Find something for you to do. There it was again, that subtle acknowledgment that she didn't belong, had no real place at the castle, no position, no purpose. "Coanor thinks I might die anyway, even with the tonic. She doesn't know what's wrong with me. And I'm too visible with her." *And she has weird drawings and poems about dragons and kings and blood on her table.*

"We'll figure it out. Just please, please stay out of trouble. And Semra ..." Monac leaned in close and spoke just barely above a whisper. "It's one thing to pass long glances between each other in the woods and banter back and forth. It's quite another to stand between a crown prince and the trust of his court back at home. I know, I know ... the prince does what he wants. He hates being micromanaged. He means well. But what he wants might not be wise. Also, he would kill me for saying this, so please don't tell him."

Semra's gut twisted and her chest tightened. "You're acting as though we're forbidden lovers meeting under the stars. It's not like that at all."

Monac pursed his lips. "Just be twice as careful as you think you're being. He'll have you followed soon. I'm certain of it. And he'll keep pushing until he finds something actionable. Keep taking your medicine, and I'll help you with whatever you need. I want you to be okay. I know I might sound gruff, but it's what's best for both of you. The last thing the royal family needs is another scandal—even in rumor."

Princess Avaya's staged kidnapping and failure to return home hadn't made things easy for the Shamaran family. Not to mention the queen's assassination and dragonlord attack of last year, and the kingdom being plunged into war—with its own blue dragon swirling around the capital looking after Semra. Semra gave a short nod.

"I'll focus on trying not to die. That will probably take a considerable amount of effort."

"One can only hope." Monac grinned. "Let me help you up. Remember—keep your head down. Be diplomatic. And please don't die. We've had enough tragedies."

"I'll do my level best."

Semra let out an involuntary moan as Monac helped her to her feet, her head throbbing and stomach knotting in response.

"You look pale. And also flushed. It's a weird mixture."

"Thanks for the compliment."

"Take care of yourself."

"I'll be fine."

There was no way to know if she would really be fine.

Monac and Semra both knew it, but there was nothing else to say. She had taken her next dose of tonic early, but it was already helping her feel steadier on her feet.

Semra ducked out of the alcove and walked up the courtyard toward the keep. She would have extra clothes in her room. She should make it a habit to be up and around and out of Coanor's predictable kill box of a back bedroom as much as possible. Maybe she could get into more comfortable clothes, visit the library, and then talk to Monac about finding another healer somewhere quiet.

She slowed her pace to ease the protest of her joints and pressed the back of her hand to her cheek. Warm, probably still red, but easing. Semra looked up and saw Zezura loop in the air overhead. She didn't usually hover during the day. Semra gave a small smile and felt her body relax.

You take good care of me, Zez. Thanks for always being there. A flood of warmth followed by anxiety hit her chest in response. Semra sighed. *I know you're worried. I'm not strong enough to ride yet, but I'll be okay. Visit me tomorrow on the outer ward?* Firfell would probably have a conniption. So would Coanor and the stable boys, but at least Saeb, the housekeeper, would be happy to keep the dragon away from her curated courtyards.

Semra watched as Zezura looped and dove toward her at lightning speed, the wind off her wings blowing Semra's hair back. The dragon pulled up just before landing, dipping her head down to touch her nose to Semra's hand, and arced up and away toward the river. Castles weren't good for dragons, but Semra was grateful she visited every day.

The doors of the west wing flew open and Captain Firfell stalked toward her flanked by six guards. Bitterness roiled her stomach at the sight of him. Semra also recognized two of the guards: Annais, the young one who Firfell had scolded for speaking out of turn when Semra and Zephan had returned on Zezura, and Gaulen, a stiff, solemn soldier who had been assigned to the task force to assist Semra and Siler in chasing down rogue assassins. He had not exactly been a fan of hers. Semra pulled her shoulders back and lifted her chin.

"Captain. What a distinct displeasure." *Be diplomatic,* Monac's voice whispered in her mind. She grimaced.

"Semra. It's so good to see you out and about. We all feared for your health." Firfell licked his lips and cast a quick glance to the skies. *He waited for Zezura to leave,* Semra realized. *Coward.*

Firfell looked her up and down. "You wear dresses now, like a civilized woman?"

Semra shrugged. "Maybe I've turned a new leaf."

"Doubtful." His voice dripped disdain.

Semra's voice flattened. "To what do I owe your ..." Semra cycled through her options. *Aggressive intrusion? Dreaded presence? Unfortunate reminder that you exist?* "Your visit?"

There. Monac should be proud.

"You've been summoned by His Majesty the King. We've come to escort you. We would hate to see you collapse of your illness on the way."

"How thoughtful." It was quaint, his believing these seven men could keep her contained if she wanted to be free. But then, in her current state, they could probably knock her over with a feather and string her up by her toes. Better not to let on how weak she was. She tilted her head back. "What does the king need of me?"

"I'm not the messenger. I'm the escort."

Semra gritted her teeth, but nodded and followed Firfell back through the doors of the west wing as the six guards fell in around her. Firfell set a clipped pace but slowed as he noticed Semra lagging.

"How has your recovery been progressing?"

Semra ignored him, inwardly cursing her heavy breathing. The walk was hardly heavy exertion.

They moved in silence to the tower, up the spiral staircase, down the hall, and into the grand receiving room at the foot of the throne room. Firfell spoke to the guards at the doors, and one of them slipped inside. Semra cocked her head. It must be serious to be meeting with her in the formal throne room, instead of the smaller one on the first floor.

A moment later, the doors opened and Firfell led the way across the marble floor and up the steps. Semra hadn't been in the throne room since the repairs were complete. It looked much the same as the original, with its pillars twined with delicate inlaid gold that rose to the ceiling and spread across it in continuous design overhead. The pillars stood like glorious sentinels, immovable and resolute, strong, like the king they protected. The sun poured in through huge arched windows that nearly reached the ceiling, light filling the room and sparkling along the floors and gold leaf.

Semra stared at the windows, transported back to that fateful day only last year, when the Framatar's great black dragon had smashed them in. The battle of two fifty-foot dragons had resulted in crumbling pillars and shattered glass, and the final confrontation between the king and his loyal guard and the dragonlord and his assassins had been a bloodbath.

Semra stared at a spot on the marble floor to her left. It sparkled white and perfect, but all she could see was the blood of her closest friend, Brens, where the Framatar had ordered her throat be slit and she crumpled to the floor. The echo of Semra's own scream filled her mind, mixed with the voice of the dragonlord himself.

Weakness is worthless. Weakness must be purged. And if it cannot be purged ...

A lump lodged in Semra's throat. She tore her gaze away, turning back to the windows, and wondered if they were reinforced this time somehow—and if such efforts would even matter against a dragon the size of Rotokas or Zezura.

For a moment she saw Turian, bound on his knees, with Zephan beside him; she heard Azi crooning his insults as he ordered Rotokas to unleash another torrent of flame, and demanded Tymetin whip her again and again. She could feel the scars burn on her back as if they had come alive with the memory. Her breathing quickened and a chill ran up her spine. She stumbled, and Annais caught her elbow.

King Turian sat on one of two golden thrones on the dais. The glint of its precious metal stood out brilliantly from the vibrant blue velvet against the wall behind them. To the king's left, the queen's empty throne served as a constant reminder of what had been lost. It had been suggested that only one throne be set up in the restoration process, but Turian had vehemently struck down the idea. Semra recalled his reaction.

It was the queen's compassion that softened my judgments, her wisdom that guided me, her kindness that inspired me. Without her I am not the king I want to be. My brother failed in taking her away from me, for her memory I carry always. She must remain with me still.

The designers had not dared discuss it any more after that. If only Semra had gotten to the castle sooner, if only she'd been smarter or more prepared, his wife might still be sitting beside him.

"Semra. Welcome."

Semra snapped her attention back to the moment. It was clear to see where Zephan had gotten his good looks. King Turian was a handsome man in his forties, and though he wore a beard and Zephan preferred to be cleanshaven, they had much the same athletic build.

A number of court members stood on the marble floor before the king to his right and left. Semra's heart lifted to see General Soldan, a reasonable man who was loyal to the king and present for the Framatar's attack in the throne room. Count Darbune was also present. He was friendly with Firfell and had already been antagonistic toward Semra before she went after Avaya; she could only imagine how he felt now. Several others stood on either side, and to the right of the king stood the crown prince.

It was hard to imagine Zephan as the same man she had danced with in a stable loft. She could almost feel his body close to hers, swaying to nonexistent music and surrounded by hay bales. He looked so regal standing there now, richly dressed among the rest of her betters—not just noble blood, but royal, oozing confidence and diplomacy before the court.

Firfell gave her a shove, and she nearly toppled. *Pull yourself together.* Semra cleared her throat. "It is an honor, Your Majesty."

"How are you feeling? We'd thought to bring you on a pallet, but Coanor's house was empty."

"A bit better, Your Majesty, thank you."

Turian studied her. The warmth he normally exuded toward her was curbed, and tension filled the room that Semra could not quite place.

"Aviama amuses herself by stuffing silks and satins in your wardrobe, though you are hard pressed to touch them. I'm surprised to see you without a tunic and trousers."

Semra clasped her hands in front of her to keep from fidgeting. "Coanor has been most hospitable."

"Does she know just how hospitable she has been?"

Semra opened her mouth, then shut it. His face was neither angry nor inviting. She wasn't sure how to respond, but surely admitting to theft was not the best course of action. Turian didn't wait for her answer.

"I apologize for the manner of your coming, but I'm afraid the matter is quite serious. I want you to know, no formal accusations have been made, and further investigation is warranted to uncover the truth and inform a course of action." Turian paused, and Semra held her breath.

"King Arnevon is dead. It appears he was poisoned. Our information is limited and comes from our own people. Gratefully, the newly crowned King Axis has yet to make a move, buying us time to get our feet under us."

Semra's lips parted, but no sound came.

Turian inhaled deeply. "A king had been assassinated in the same residence where my eldest daughter sleeps, and her supposed betrothed is now king. Arnevon died of long-acting poisoning only days after you were in the same room with him, and you return poisoned yourself. Since returning to Shamaran Castle, you have been attended to by our most skilled healer, and yet it appears you have stolen her clothes and fled her apartments." He spread his hands. "I have defended you many times, but this I cannot explain. Tell me now—did you kill King Arnevon?"

6

————

Semra's jaw dropped. Would the killing never end? Rats and rot, why did she seem to find herself at the center of every scheme? There were plenty of assassins the task force had been unable to find. The particularly good ones, mostly. But hearing the king's summary, even Semra would have had a hard time believing she was innocent.

"No, Your Majesty. I never touched him."

"Not touching him is not the same as not killing him, is it?"

"I did not kill him." A great heaviness sat on Semra's chest. She forced her features smooth and neutral, masking the gut-wrenching pain in her heart. Turian was one of the only men Semra had ever had true respect for. She'd often wondered what life would have been like for her, had someone like him raised her instead of someone like Avi. And now his gracious esteem had run out.

"Your Majesty, permission to address our killer?"

Turian's eyes narrowed as he turned to Count Darbune. "We are investigating, Count. No formal accusations have been made."

No, certainly no accusations, Semra thought dryly. *You've only asked me whether or not I killed a man.*

"She *is* a killer, Your Majesty. I doubt even she would contest that. The question is only whether we should add King Arnevon to her extensive list of ... career accomplishments."

Semra's lip curled and her eyes flashed. She opened her mouth to retort, but Zephan gave a barely perceptible shake of the head. His eyes were as icy as she had ever seen them. A shiver of fear ran through her. Would she have a soul on her side by the end of the hour? She snapped her mouth shut and bit her tongue.

Turian gestured for him to continue, and Darbune inclined his head in her direction. "How is it that you poisoned yourself? Has our illustrious butcher gotten sloppy? Too comfortable in the cushions of royal hospitality?"

Semra glared daggers into Darbune, her hands itching for a pair of real blades. "I did not *poison myself.* I was grazed by a spear coated with poison while trying to save Zezura."

"Because fifty-foot dragons so frequently find themselves in need of saving?"

"If dragons never needed saving, dragonlords would not exist."

Semra thought she saw Soldan's mouth quirk into a smile, but then it was gone, and she wasn't so sure.

"And what led you to such deep trouble in Belvidore that your dragon needed saving?"

"Was a report of our activities not given? Perhaps by someone you trust more than me?" *Your crown prince perhaps?*

"You were gravely ill when you landed," Turian said. His voice was even, neither angry nor friendly. Ever the reasonable assessor. "We never heard your side. We'll hear it now."

Semra took a deep breath and launched into her tale. She

explained how she had traveled with Monac and Zephan to Belvidore to save Avaya, found the house of Florin Thistle-horn the architect and found him dead, and were ambushed there while retrieving the blueprints to Madensig Fortress. She recounted how her old friend and colleague Siler had thwarted the first attempt to enter the castle, how they had gone to the annual Tabeun Tournament but their plan went awry, and how she'd been dropped into the courtyard at night and hid in the cistern until opportunity arose to sneak into the keep. She had gotten Avaya to the rendezvous point in the stable, been captured, interrogated, and beaten, and escaped saving Zezura and Avaya at the same time.

She kept her eyes fixed on the king and the nobles, but never Zephan. Semra avoided his gaze and was careful to refer to him only as "the prince" or "Prince Zephan," and never the familiar first name alone. She didn't need to give Firfell any ammunition.

"Ultimately, it didn't matter. Princess Avaya and I were focused on getting to the prince on the battlefield to tell him about the explosives in time, but the princess still ended up in Axis's hands and across the river."

She conveniently left out the part where she had demanded Zephan kiss her when the guards came, to explain away their presence near the carriages while weakening the straps connecting the chassis. No need to mention the way her heart had soared when their lips met, and the earnestness and strength of his arms. She also left out the part where Avaya had tackled Zephan to keep him from killing Axis in battle, and then fled with the enemy of her own accord.

"Who can vouch for your story?" Darbune asked when she'd finished.

"Prince Zephan and Monac can vouch for the parts that line up with them. Princess Avaya could, if she were here, but

—" Semra dropped the sentence mid-thought. *But I don't think she would.* She bit her lip.

While accused of murder and in the king's presence, it was neither wise nor diplomatic to accuse the king's daughter of being a liar. Turian scrutinized her intently. She rocked back on her heels.

"There were multiple points in your story where you were alone in the castle, or with people who are not here to corroborate," Darbune said.

"Our intelligence says your amulet was found in connection with the assassination," General Soldan said. "What do you have to say about that?"

Semra blinked. "Commander Ramas' amulet?"

Soldan nodded.

"I—I have nothing to say about that. Except that what I have told you is true, and I haven't seen the amulet since the battle on the Strip. I assumed I'd lost it there."

Firfell scoffed beside her.

"You admit then that it was yours?" Darbune asked.

Semra let out an exasperated sigh. "I haven't seen the thing that someone's intelligence supposedly said someone found. I did carry Ramas' amulet on my belt; it was emerald green and carved with serpents. Everyone who knows me well knows the amulet, and all the assassins of the mountain knew I had it. All of them are intimately familiar with it and could have it replicated."

"You always had it with you, you say. A trophy?" Darbune prodded.

Semra tilted her head and leveled a cool stare back at him. "A reminder."

Zephan shifted his weight and plucked at the edge of his sleeve. Their eyes met, then broke away. Turian rapped his knuckles on the arm of his throne.

"Thank you, Semra. I admit this brings me no pleasure, but you must remain in your quarters until your name is cleared. Zezura may not land on the grounds until the investigation is complete. Should you be found beyond the walls, we will be forced to pursue, and I think you know we cannot tolerate any bloodshed. I suggest you return to Coanor and focus on your recovery, and if you are innocent, hopefully we shall have the issue resolved before you are fully better. I am assigning a guard rotation to be with you wherever you go."

Semra's mouth went dry. Her brow beaded with sweat, and she felt her face grow hot.

The king leaned forward, locking eyes with her with inescapable intensity.

"I have been far more lenient than my court would prefer. Don't make me regret it."

Heat flooded her body, and Semra felt her knees wobble. She dipped into a curtsy deeper than she'd planned and struggled for a moment to stand. Annais extended a hand, and it took all that she had not to swat it away.

She ignored it instead and steeled herself to walk slowly and carefully down the infinitely long throne room hall. Annais and Gaulen flanked her, and she wondered how badly Gaulen hated her after seeing her in action on the task force. They had argued over how to manage the runaway assassin children, Gaulen expecting honor and chivalry and Semra knowing that such an approach would get them killed.

Their crisp footsteps against the marble floor echoed off the walls, the court deathly still behind them. Why *did* they bother making it so long, anyway? An intimidation gesture, certainly. And for the first time in a king's hall, Semra had felt exactly that.

Semra marched through the double doors, down two flights to the first floor, and through the keep toward the eastern wing. The second dose of tonic seemed to have stabilized her system. Her muscles ached, her head still throbbed, but she tested picking up the pace a bit on the way and was rewarded with no change to her balance.

How was she going to clear her name cooped up? How would Zez do, banned from the castle? What was she supposed to *do* while she was recovering, and how could she find a cure without the guards finding out exactly what was wrong with her—whatever that was?

Semra turned the corner into the empty feasting hall and spun toward her guards. "Do you really have to *follow* me?"

Annais furrowed his brow. "We ... were assigned as your guards."

"Obviously. So you have to go everywhere I go. Can one of you go in front? Can you walk next to me? I really hate being followed."

Gaulen arched an eyebrow. "Sadly for you, we aren't here to make you comfortable. We'll follow."

Semra let out an exasperated sigh and plowed through the feasting hall, through an anteroom, up another flight of stairs, and past the hall of paintings of the Shamaran dynasty through the generations. King Turian and Queen Sharsi observed her progress from their place on the wall among their ancestors, vibrantly depicted in oil paints. The unblinking gazes of their three children, Princess Avaya, Prince Zephan, and Princess Aviama, followed her too.

She quickened her pace and took in a deep breath as she finally stood outside her door. Semra hadn't been inside since before she chased after Avaya. She put her hand on the iron handle and twisted back to Annais and Gaulen.

"I'm sorry you've been given this assignment. It's either a compliment to whatever skill they think you have that you won't need to use, or punishment for something terrible you've done lately. Maybe both." Gaulen rolled his eyes, but Annais' eyes bulged just a hair. He clearly thought the latter applied to him.

"You won't be sweet talking your way out of anything, so you might as well not bother," Gaulen said. "It'll make the assignment easier on all of us."

"Annais, I owe you an additional apology. I knew Gaulen was stiff and bitter in the field, but I didn't know he was like this at home. Don't let him destroy your spirit, okay?"

"Of course not, my lady."

Semra pulled back. "I am *not* your lady. I am no one's lady. I'm not a noble."

"You're hardly a woman," Gaulen muttered.

Semra glared at him. "Enjoy your post. Annais, may your shift pass quickly, and Gaulen, may you rot in a hole as depressing as you are."

With that Semra pushed open the door to her chambers and shut herself inside. Annais chuckled on the other side of the door, then yelped. Semra smirked. Gaulen wouldn't have hit him for laughing if he wasn't bothered by Semra's words. Good. He was miserable.

Painted blue sky and mountains greeted her from the walls and ceiling of her room. Nezil Myansara flowers decorated the heights, their white petals standing in stark contrast to the rough rock of the mountains. Semra took a deep breath, but the only fresh air was from the cracked window. The breeze of the scenery could only be felt by the gently swaying flowers of the walls. For the foreseeable future, these murals would be freer than she was.

Semra crossed to the wardrobe, bypassing Aviama's hand-curated silk brocade and velvet and yanking open a bottom drawer instead. She rifled through girdles, brooches, and chemises and finally pulled out a sand-colored linen tunic and, glorious songbirds, her knife-sheath trousers. Semra quickly changed, folding Coanor's chemise and overdress and laying them on her bed. She shimmied up the post of her canopy bed and felt along the top for her bag. Out of view, but not well hidden, had been a surprisingly helpful option. She slid back down and pulled out her knives and wrap skirt.

People were disarmed by her in a skirt. They'd come to expect the crazy dragonlord woman to wear her scandalous pants, and she'd come to expect their open stares. In Coanor's dress, she'd stuck out a little less and seemed a mite less threatening. So, confound it all, she would wear the skirt. Few people knew it was custom made with hidden slits for better access to the knives strapped to her thighs.

Semra slipped the throwing knives back in their places and sighed. This was home. But she only had two. She should have six. Over the time she had been on the task force, Semra had accumulated a number of extra throwing knives and stored them in separate places, but few were left. She secured her wrap skirt over her trousers along with her belt and a leather pouch, and knelt by her bed.

Her fingers searched the wooden planks for the divot in the knot of one, just enough to hitch the cut board and wiggle it loose. Semra tugged the board up and felt inside. A bottle of oil and a cloth, but no knives.

Discontented mutterings made their way through the door, and a loud voice rose above them.

"I'll question whoever I want, and I'll do it wherever I please! Step aside or you'll spend the day cleaning the mess hall with tweezers."

Semra sucked in a breath and threw the board back in place as the door flew open with a *bang*. She rocked back on her heels just in time to see Zephan storm into her room, Gaulen and Annais peering in from the doorway.

7

"You lied to me."

Semra sprang to her feet, her eyes bulging, face hot. "Every word I spoke was true."

Zephan stalked toward her, nostrils flared, eyes hard. Semra backed away. She put her hands up.

"I've never seen you like this. You know me. I'm no stranger to accusations."

Zephan called over his shoulder, glare still boring into Semra. "Shut the door. Don't let anyone interrupt."

Semra broke eye contact to glance behind the prince to the two guards. Neither moved.

Zephan threw a punch and Semra threw a hand up to block, but his fist landed in the wall two inches from Semra's left eye. *"Shut. The. Door."*

The heavy oak door swung shut, a *click* of finality sealing them inside the room alone.

Semra flinched. Her throat closed, and she blinked back tears. He searched her face, and she swallowed. Her voice trembled. "Zephan?"

Zephan's chest heaved under his golden corded jacket,

yet another reminder of the chasm between them—gold for him, cheap linens for her. It was better that way. Semra could never wear such exquisite finery. If she ever did, she would only ever be Aviama's dress up doll, and a walking contradiction worthy of derision. Semra wasn't sure who would hate that more, Firfell and Count Darbune, or herself.

A single tear escaped down Semra's cheek, and the next thing she knew he had caught her up against him, his arm holding her tight around the waist, his face buried in her dark hair. Her arms hung awkwardly at her sides, eyes wide. What just happened? She waited, gently tried to step back, but his arms only tightened. Semra swallowed hard against a sob threatening to break free and allowed herself to slide her arms around him in return.

She was fairly certain this was precisely the sort of thing Monac had been afraid of, but could she really be blamed when he burst through the door? And could it really mean anything, with such rage in his eyes when he came in? He breathed in the scent of her, and she felt his body around her relax.

Semra felt her muscles slowly give up their tension. She was safe. He knew the truth. It was a moment of confusion when he ran into the room, a moment of pent-up emotion from the stress of the day, nothing more.

"Tell me," he murmured, his face still against her hair. "Tell me you didn't. I would understand, but I need to know."

Semra froze. She pulled back. "Even you?"

Zephan straightened. He looked like he'd been slapped, but it was nothing compared to the pit in her stomach, the ache in her bones. Semra shook her head. "I will never outrun my past. You kept telling me you believed me, you trusted me, that I am more than an assassin. That the court would come around. But none of that's true, is it? Even you ..." Semra looked away. "It doesn't matter what I do."

Zephan's shoulders drooped. His eyes misted, but he stood his ground. "I just want to hear it from you."

Semra stepped away. "You shouldn't have to. You should already know. I can't believe this. When you first came in, you said I lied to you. Don't hide it—you really think I did this."

"I'm sorry I scared you. That performance was for the guards' benefit. But in my defense, you *did* lie to me. You promised you would rest at Coanor's and be good."

"No, you *told* me to rest and be good. I *promised* to take the tonic, and I did."

"It's not like you haven't lied to me before, and you *were* gone for long periods of time. The messenger just arrived, but Arnevon died only two days after you left."

"Zephan! I've lied about how sick I felt. I've not wanted you to worry, because I didn't want you to do something crazy. Like storm into my bedroom with guards outside the door to gab about it, for example. So I said I'd go to your healer, even when I knew the healer was probably the easiest access point for someone to kill me. Plenty of people would be willing to finish me off, and after today, I'm convinced Darbune and Firfell would pay good money to see it happen!"

Zephan tugged at his sleeves and cast his eyes to the floor. "You were inside Madensig all night, and after Monac and I headed to the front, we didn't see you for days."

Semra arched her eyebrows. "Oh? And when was I supposed to have poisoned him, hmm? Was it when I covered for your escape and got captured with Avaya? When I was put in chains? Or when Axis had me beaten while your sister looked on? Ask Coanor, if you trust her so much. She put me in that nightdress. She saw the bruises when they were still fresh."

Zephan's lip curled as he stared at the floor. Angry *with* her or *for* her? He raised his eyes to meet hers, and they were soft and earnest once more. "The timeline ... it's just so perfect."

It really was. And how could the real assassin have known Semra would get grazed by that spear and get poisoned herself? Was it planned somehow or just a happy accident? It was absolutely believable that she'd done this.

Only she hadn't.

"Are you telling me you wouldn't have been able to do it? If you'd escaped sooner than you said or were kept somewhere else beside that tunnel ..."

Semra hesitated. "If things were different ..." She trailed off. If she'd had more time, if Siler had released her, if any number of other variables had come up, she could've done it. If she'd had access to the right poisons, the right materials. It would have required more planning, but it was possible.

"I could have. But I didn't."

Zephan examined her a long time, then put his hands up. "Okay, okay. I'm sorry. I just needed to hear it." He ran a hand through his hair and sighed. He looked back up at her.

"I'm going to have to keep my distance for a bit. My father won't love that I came just now. But I want you to know it isn't because it's my preference."

Semra bit her lip and surveyed his face. Her heart flopped. Those golden eyes ...

She squeezed her eyes shut and ran a hand over her face. Her weary body screamed at her, and she sagged against the wall. "I think that's wise. It's one thing to have long glances in the woods and such, but here, now ..." Semra scratched her head. What was the reasoning again? "It's ... not a good idea."

Zephan's eyes narrowed. "Why do I feel like I've had this conversation before?"

Semra swallowed. She had to change the subject. "I need to talk to you about what I found in Coanor's room. I think she blames me for—"

"Semra." Zephan shook his head. "You want me to trust you, and I will. But you need to trust me. Coanor is safe."

A knock came at the door. "Your Highness?"

"You've been in here too long," Semra said. "They're probably making all sorts of unsavory assumptions by now."

"Hmm." Zephan ran his thumb along the cut of his chin, then glanced up. He crossed the room and plucked an empty water glass from a side table.

"Do you have a particular attachment to this glass?" he asked, turning it in his hands.

"Um ... no. They're all the same."

"Excellent." Zephan stepped away from her and screamed, *"That isn't good enough!"* and hurled the crystal at the wall.

Monac burst through the door, then caught himself and gave a short bow. He pressed his lips in a flat line and eyed them disapprovingly. "Your Highness, you are needed immediately."

Zephan licked his lips and straightened his shirt. "I'm sure I am." He pivoted and swept from the room, leaving an emptiness in his wake that Semra felt like a sledgehammer to the chest. Monac followed him, turning at the last moment to shoot a glare in her direction. Her eyes widened and she lifted her hands defensively. *It wasn't my fault!*

The door swung shut and Semra climbed onto the mattress of her unnecessarily massive bed and threw an arm over her face. She let out a soft groan and pulled a pillow to her chest. Something underneath it crinkled. Semra lifted her head and pulled back the covers. A slip of folded parchment lay there. She carefully opened it and stared down at the inky scrawl:

The dragonlady feels unwell
Death to come if castle dwell

The blood drained from her face, and an icy chill swept up her spine, pricking the hairs on the back of her neck. Darbune and Firfell wanted her dead. The dragonlord mentor she had betrayed still lived in the dungeons beneath her feet. And untold assassin children of the mountain despised her as a traitor.

The threat on her life was no longer simply a fear.

It had come alive.

Semra crumpled the paper in her hands and went to the lantern to burn it. Her hand paused inches from the flame. No, any scrap of evidence that someone else was up to no good was worth keeping. All the evidence so far pointed to her killing Arnevon. She folded it thinly and slipped it through the hidden pocket of her skirt into the free sheath on her trousers.

Her head throbbed and she massaged her temples. She considered taking another dose of tonic, but what would two extra doses before dinner do to her? Better not to risk it. Semra wondered if Coanor would be sent to her, or if all visitors would be kept away.

What if Coanor couldn't get more tonic to her?

Semra knelt on the floor beside the broken crystal and brushed the pieces into a small pile. She pressed a finger to the tip of one of the shards. Sharp and strong. *Waste not,* she thought to herself. She needed more knives.

Semra picked up the three largest shards and stowed them throughout the room – one under the loose floorboard under the bed, one under makeup powders in the bottom drawer of her vanity, and one inside the bottom of a couch cushion. She would need a handle for the shards—something stiff enough to hold firm and protect her hands, but pliable enough to wrap around the broken pieces.

The wardrobe had little to offer. Dresses, more dresses, ribbon, a few girdle belts. The lantern on the side table was low on oil and the wick was nearly out. Semra moved on to the desk. A writing kit held simple reed quills, inks, and parchment. She pulled out the other drawers of the vanity, but the sealing wax and extra candles were missing.

Not that it mattered. The lantern wasn't lit, and she had no way to make a fire. Semra wiped sweat from her forehead with a trembling hand. She was getting hot again. A water pitcher stood next to the lantern, but without any crystal glass to pour into. Semra picked up the pitcher and tilted it back, drinking out of the spout. She dipped her fingers into the cool water and splashed it onto her face, then sank down onto her bed.

If someone was coming to kill her, they'd have to wait an hour or so. She needed to rest. Semra took a deep breath and eased back against the pillows.

Rest had done her body good, but something was still pounding in her ears when she woke. No—no, that wasn't quite right. It was more like a thud. A thud in her ears?

Semra squinted and sat up slowly. The shadows from the sunlight told her it was well into afternoon, and the noisy racket told her someone was hitting her door. Gaulen shoved the door open and glared daggers at her.

"Did you need something, Gaulen?"

"I called for you three times. I won't be so generous next time."

"You probably shouldn't have been so generous *this* time, if I'm really as dangerous as you idiots seem to think I am. I fell asleep. Don't worry, it's hard for me to carry out horrific schemes while unconscious."

"I wouldn't put it past you."

Semra frowned. "You look like you're strategizing my gruesome and untimely death. Annais, is he strategizing my gruesome and untimely death?"

"Probably," Annais said from the hall.

"You're the one who knows a thing or two about gruesomeness," Gaulen bit out. "I still see that little girl's eyes at night, the one you gutted like a fish at the villa."

Semra pulled back, then smoothed her features into perfect nonchalance. "Really? I don't," she lied. She could see the young teenage assassin now, snarling at her from the stolen villa. "I see the surrounding town with living children, surviving governors, safe families. You know, the ones she would have slaughtered for money, like they'd done to the town before when they ransacked it. In my position, you would've killed her too. You would've had no choice. If you didn't, she would've spit you like a pig, and my gutting her like a fish might not seem quite so outlandish as she drained your blood on the floor."

Gaulen's expression hardened, and he turned to look at Annais. "I love it when she says things that make her sound harmless and innocent, don't you?"

"I don't want any part of this picking sides. I'm just here to stand guard."

Gaulen grunted and swung back to Semra. "You've been summoned to an audience with the king."

Semra's stomach soured. "Twice in one day. Lucky me. Any chance it's for a leisurely tea?"

"I wouldn't count on it."

8

Gaulen and Annais took Semra through the keep toward the west wing, then surprised her by leading her out to the courtyard by a small side door. She could sense through the dragon's kiss on her chest that Zez was not nearby, but no one else knew that. It was risky for them to take her outdoors.

Her guards each gripped one of her arms as they progressed into the maze of green gardens, too far from the main courtyard to be seen. Firfell's urgent voice rose from the other side of a row of hedges as they approached.

"The prince must give up his obsession or support for the crown will diminish; there will be no money left to support the war efforts, and the kingdom will fall."

Semra couldn't hear the king's response. They rounded the corner, and Firfell spun toward them with fire in his eyes and a reddened face. Firfell's eyes narrowed to slits. "Gaulen. Search the prisoner."

"Suspect," Turian amended, but Semra knew Firfell's characterization was more accurate. Turian stood in a grove of trees, four more guards posted with an eyeline to the king. Semra spotted an archer hidden in the tower at the edge of the keep, and another along the covered garden wall.

She heaved a heavy sigh. There had been no time to remove her two knives, and Gaulen knew where she preferred to carry them. Better to demonstrate good faith than be caught and look deceptive.

Not that it helped much for someone who knows they're about to be searched. Semra lifted her hands. "May I?"

"Not a chance," Firfell said. "Gaulen can find whatever you have."

Semra held her arms out, and Gaulen patted her down. His face turned red as he encountered the knife hilts on her thigh.

"How about now?" she offered. "Your archers can pick me off if I raise my arms above my waist."

Turian nodded, and Firfell conceded. "Slowly. Drop them on the ground."

Semra pulled up her skirts from the bottom—no need to reveal the hidden slits—and retrieved the two knives from their sheaths. She dropped them on the ground, lifted the skirts to her waist, and turned a slow circle before letting the skirt fall. The threatening note remained undiscovered, tucked inside the sheaths.

Firfell arched an eyebrow at her trousers. "New leaf?"

Semra shrugged. "Old habits."

Turian waved him off. "Semra, you and I will converse in private."

She furrowed her brow. "Private?"

He smiled, but the wrinkles in his face seemed to deepen. "As private as it gets for the likes of me."

Firfell was dismissed, and all the guards hung back—close

enough to secure line of sight and swift access to the king if necessary, and far enough away not to overhear him speak. Turian clasped his hands behind his back and strolled with her through the garden to a stone bench beneath a canopy of fruit trees. He took a seat and patted the space next to him.

Semra sat. She fidgeted. Bit her lip.

"You look like you're waiting for me to kill you," the king observed.

"Shouldn't I be? Aren't you waiting for *me* to kill *you*? If all I am is a contract killer ..." Semra swallowed, and her cheeks flushed. If he wasn't sure he wanted to kill her before, he would be now.

"You often say things you shouldn't. Have you been told that before?" Turian asked.

Semra stared at her toes. "Yes." Ramas had said it when Semra had suggested Brens should not be punished for failing to catch a rabbit for dinner, since skipping a meal was punishment enough. He'd said it again when Semra asked about the targets in her assignments.

"I don't recommend any sudden movements, considering the archers you mentioned, but I see no reason to have you dispatched. Bluntness is not always a vice. Do you remember how we first met?" he asked.

"In the upper courtyard. You were sitting on a bench like this one." The corner of Semra's mouth quirked up. "That's why you brought me here, isn't it?"

Turian nodded. "You asked me for directions. Nobody asks me for directions. It's probably silly, but it was nice." The king stared out over a bed of bright-red poppies, but Semra knew he wasn't really seeing them. "You didn't know who I was, and didn't seem put off by my company, even if you only stayed to avoid angering Garbane. At least, based on what I knew at the time. What were you really doing there? Scouting positions for the gala?"

"Radix—one of the assassins from the mountain; you met him in the throne room with Azi that day—had inserted himself as one of the castle guards and was looking for me. I had just escaped another old colleague trying to kill me and needed someplace to lay low for a minute, and I figured having another witness around would help."

The king ran a thoughtful hand through his beard. "Tactical. Smart. Regardless, I enjoyed the anonymity, for however short a time. Did you really not know who I was?"

"I had no idea. I felt stupid staring at your portrait in Ancestry Hall later, but you just looked so ..." Semra swallowed.

"Human?" Turian offered.

Semra shrugged. "Maybe."

Turian straightened into the monarch she'd seen with Firfell. "I don't think I have to tell you how precarious your position is right now. If you were framed, they did a good job. Everything points to you."

Semra's shoulders drooped, and she stared at the poppies. "I know."

"Pardon my language, but I can't be seen playing favorites with a contract killer. And I'm afraid that so far, it appears that I have."

Semra clenched her jaw at *contract killer,* then steeled herself and relaxed. She was never a contract killer. She had served the Framatar, Turian's brother Azi, when she thought it was her duty. She'd never been paid for her work. It was expected that as part of the twisted Bandaka family, she would kill to purge the world of evil. Semra was provided for in basic ways, with the possibility of greater assignments as time went on.

She hazarded a glance at Turian. He had the same nose and chin as his brother, but there was little resemblance otherwise. When she looked into his eyes, they were not the manipulative dragonlord's, but Zephan's.

Turian was studying her, and she doubted much got past him. Another trait he had passed down to his son. Semra realized she was picking at the cloth on her skirt and dropped her hands in her lap.

"Well? Aren't you going to defend yourself?"

Semra looked up, startled. "What?"

"I told you all evidence points to you assassinating the Belvidorian king, and that the favor you've enjoyed from me so far must come to an end. And you have nothing to say?"

Semra cocked her head. "I ... thought it was a statement of fact. I would agree that the evidence looks bad. Reasonable people would be forced to consider I may have done this, because there's no way for them to know for sure. I don't know who did it, and have no way to prove I didn't do it, since the only people who could vouch for me are as untrustworthy as I am."

Turian let a long pause marinate as he scrutinized her. A smile broke across his face, and he let out a laugh. "You really are different, aren't you?"

Semra's eyes widened. "Did I say something wrong?"

"You said something unexpected, which is not the same as wrong. You're rather terrible at diplomatic presentation."

"Oh." Semra's head hurt. She propped her chin on her hand and let out a sigh. Add it to the list of failures.

The king squinted at her, and she could have sworn she almost saw a twinkle in his eye. He collected himself and continued. "Kings rise and fall every day. If assassins are looking for their next big payout job, I can only assume I'm high on the list. I need to know who is doing this and how to make it stop, or the trail of bodies will never end. It will be a game of chess—each of the pieces killed off from the board until so few are left it can hardly call itself a kingdom."

Semra nodded. "You want me to find out who did this."

"No. You could barely stand this morning, and I'm not sure by what magic you're functional now. Coanor says the tonic is only cloaking what could very well be the brink of death. She doesn't trust it to last. I want you to sit still and let my people figure out how to get you better. And cause no fuss. Stop running off and doing suspicious things. If you're innocent, it'll only make everything worse, and more resources will be wasted guarding you instead of finding the real killer. If you get involved, the evidence is muddied once again."

It made sense. If Semra were isolated, it would be easy to prove her innocence in anything else that happened. The more intwined she was with international issues, the more convoluted the situation became, and the more likelihood that an accomplished framer could set her up again.

"I understand. I'm sorry I left Coanor's. But you're also asking someone to stay in one room when people want her dead. My room is a kill box." Semra thought back to death threat under her pillow. Who had put it there?

"Tell me what security you want on it, and I'll have it done," Turian said. "But it has to be my people, not yours."

"That hardly helps matters. Radix was one of your guards for months."

"I'm afraid we're coming to a standstill, Semra."

Semra bit her lip. Not only was the leader of a vast kingdom giving her the time of day –when everyone else seemed to want her dead—but she was arguing with him. She knew she should apologize, but her next words were out her mouth before she could stop them. "What did you expect when you tried to coop up an assassin? We're used to running for our lives; we hate being cornered, and we're prone to freak out if we're in one place for too long."

The king crossed his arms. "What did *you* expect when you chose to affiliate with royalty and stay in a royal residence?"

Semra's stomach dropped. He had a point.

Turian sighed. "I'm going to assume for the moment that you are innocent. But before I continue, I need you to know that the moment I find out otherwise, everything I am about to say is void and you will discover for the first time what the wrath of a king and the snap of his fingers is truly capable of."

Something in her chest caved in, and a thousand angry butterflies in her gut threatened to consume her from the inside out.

Turian took a deep breath. "I know the sideways glances you get in the halls, the whispers when you pass. You want to prove yourself, but you also want to run away. Don't run. Let them talk. Don't go out of your way to prove them wrong—let them prove themselves wrong when they exhaust themselves chasing you only to find a colossal waste of time.

"Nobles are a necessary unpleasantry at times, though I'd appreciate you not sharing that I said so. Some of them are invaluable, aging like fine wines the longer you know them. Others are a bit like food poisoning—the longer you spend with them, the longer it takes to recover afterward.

"And as disarming and even refreshing as your blunt approach may be at times, watch your mouth. Maybe even make a friend. Practiced politicians are smooth liars, but more than that, they are networkers. And you are low on friends."

Semra grimaced and looked down at her hands. Her bloodstained, violent hands. She glanced at Turian's hands—

strong, bejeweled, capable. Clean. They could not have been a stranger pairing sitting there on the garden bench.

"People don't like being friends with killers," she said.

"Nonsense. People don't like being friends with *murderers.* You and I are both killers. We engaged in that particularly unsavory activity together in the throne room as we fought off my brother and his minions. What you need to do is prove that you may be a killer, but you are a restrained killer with principles. One that serves the crown, that condemns evil and takes life only to protect good in the world.

"The stakes are high with you because not only are you a trained assassin but also you are a dragonlord. I've only ever known two, and the first was not a good experience. Understand the threat you pose if your allegiance could be bought. Especially considering your closeness with my son."

Semra looked up at the king. "I would never hurt him. I don't want to stand in his way. That's why I was planning on leaving before. Before Avaya was taken."

Turian leaned back. "That is generous of you. See, you're already more diplomatic than you think. Zephan told me of Avaya's betrayal, but you protected her reputation in front of the nobles, and you did it again with me just now. You also protected Zephan; I know there is more between you than you described."

Semra's heart lurched into her throat. She swallowed, but the sensation didn't ease. The hairs on her arms stood on end, and she folded them in hopes of concealing it. She shifted uncomfortably. "I don't know what you mean."

The movement didn't escape Turian. He grunted. "Mhmm. I'm sure you don't." He stretched his legs in front of him and crossed his ankles. "You remind me of Sharsi when I first met her."

Semra arched an eyebrow. His beloved wife?

"I am not the first king to wed a commoner. The first Shamaran king did the same, and he named the Nezil Myansara flower after her. The Myansara is not just some flower we slapped on a flag. Nezzi was resilient and beautiful, and a friend to the throne of Jannemar. The prophecy of the architect was written after that time, and the flower has come to symbolize not only strength, but the legacy of the queens of Jannemar."

Semra tried to remember the prophecy ... She remembered some poetry Zephan had recited to her once about a beautiful flower at the high altitudes and harsh conditions of rocky mountains. She'd even seen the coarse white blooms at the top of Mount Hara. But she didn't remember it being a prophecy.

"I fell madly in love with Sharsi and refused to listen to any of my counsel telling me it was unwise to wed. It caused friction with my court at the time, and I'm afraid it's driven a wedge between Avaya and I all these years later. Sharsi was a spitfire, and she didn't care to coddle my gentry sensibilities. It took her some time to adjust to castle life, but she threw herself into it. Despite the court's concerns, she slipped into the role of queen with effortless grace. I needed someone on my side, someone who wasn't just trying to make me feel good or spewing their personal agenda, someone to make me a better human and remind me that I am still human underneath the royal mantle I bear."

Silence stretched between them. Semra tried to imagine the elegant woman she'd seen at the ball as anything less than pristinely perfect, stunning, and poised. Semra thought of King Turian that day in the courtyard, dejected, bereaved of his wife, struggling between the pressures to strengthen international relations, and his desire to protect his daughter from an unkind marriage. Had anyone been there for him then?

When Zephan took his place one day, would he feel that same crushing weight, the sadness she'd seen in Turian, the small relief when asked a simple question? Semra took a breath. "Is it—is it terribly lonely, being king?"

"Anyone who would choose to be king for the fun of it is a fool."

"That's not what I asked."

Turian eyed her, and the corner of his mouth twisted into a sad smile. "Sharsi would have said something like that. She never let me get away with anything either." He pressed his lips together and stared up into the canopy of fruit trees above them. "Sometimes it is. Sometimes it's terribly lonely. But it's not something we can generally talk about."

He snapped his head down to look intently into her eyes, and she drew back in surprise. "Love is not enough for a king. Love is not enough for a prince. I have tried to tell my son this. Anyone who would dare embark on the precious adventure of marriage must be fully sacrificial and supportive, and those traits must go both ways. But in the union of a monarch, the kingdom is a third person in the relationship. It must always come first. A queen is as beholden to the crown as her king, and the stress of that reality will either bind the two together or drive them apart. Semra, look at me."

Semra jerked her gaze back up to the king from where it had slid down to her anxious fingers, feverishly working the material of her skirt.

Turian's face dropped all softness, and his tone became urgent. "The court *must* trust the crown. The king *must* be strong; he *must* earn and keep the allegiance of powerful gentry. We have to play the game in politics, even when we hate it. The castle walls are confining in many ways. It *can* be a lonely life. Having the right people around us is important, but they have to know the risks and be willing to take them on. If they can't do that, *we* have to be strong enough to let them go. And those who love us most must come alongside us or release us to our duty. Entanglements with those incapable of taking on the weight of the kingdom are dangerous. Do you understand what I am saying?"

Semra nodded. Guilt seized her. His son had had his arms around her just hours before. Turian's meaning could not have been clearer. Semra was a dangerous entanglement, and Zephan was not letting her go as he should.

"I want things to go well for you," he continued. "I want to believe good things about you. Stay out of trouble, because if you keep knocking down your already concerning credibility, I will not be able to protect you. You'll be in the dungeons at best, and at worst, you'll be dead."

Semra swallowed. "I understand."

"Good. You may go."

King Turian stood, and Semra followed his lead. She curtsied and turned to go, then paused. "May I ask you one question?"

Turian nodded, and Semra wiped sweaty palms on her skirt. *Will you hate me if I disobey you? Will you understand if I cannot keep my head down? Will you feel guilty if I'm murdered in the rooms you lock me in?*

"If ... if you had to choose between life and betraying the only people who've ever cared about you, which would you choose?"

Turian's eyes narrowed. "I'd think long and hard about whether those two options are a false dichotomy. I would not stop until I found a third option, one that betrays neither my life nor my honor."

Semra considered his words, then dipped her head. "Thank you."

"Stay out of trouble."

"I will," Semra promised.

By Aurin, how she wished it were the truth.

9

─────────

The mark on Semra's chest burned, and her hands trembled. She folded them in front of her as she walked, Annais and Gaulen gripping each arm again like two inescapable shadows as they wound through the gardens back up toward the courtyard. *Not entirely inescapable,* she corrected herself. *But getting away without killing or injuring them? Without being caught?* As much as Gaulen irked her, Semra could never kill him. And Annais was naïve. *Weak,* Ramas' voice reminded her. Semra dismissed the thought. Her old commander's voice no longer held power over her. Naivete was a gift, and it would be taken away from Annais soon enough, serving as a guard to the king. Leaving them alive was both wise and kind. Semra liked being kind.

She just didn't want to end up dead.

The king had chastised her for disappearing from the healer and warned her that he could no longer protect her. He had told her in so many words to disentangle herself from his son and elicited a promise from her to stay out of trouble.

But what if trouble came to her? After all, she didn't kill

the Belvidorian king, but was framed anyway. And she'd never asked for a threatening note to appear in her chambers.

Semra thought of Turian's thoughtful, gentle eyes, and the way they transitioned to intense, calculating, and questioning —and back to gentle again.

"Long live the king, we say, over and over," Gaulen grumbled behind her. "*Long live the king,* and yet we let him inches from someone who could very well have ended his life then and there."

Semra ignored him and focused on her task. *One step in front of the other.* There was nothing to protect herself with in her room except the girdles. They'd do decently for strangling, but so would her arms if it came down to it—and both of those options relied on only one attacker coming for her. The only way Semra could imagine a single person coming to take her out was if that someone was one of her fellow assassins of the mountain.

Who would be sent? Radix? Tymetin? Vix? How much would they be paid? Would they hesitate, or would they rush through it, greedy to rid her from the earth and have their compensation? Tymetin certainly wouldn't. She doubted he had a soul—or if he ever did, it was stolen long ago. He'd smile while he did it, slow things down to enjoy her pain ...

Semra grimaced.

She needed weapons. Any weapons. She'd acted nonchalant when her only two knives were taken from her, but she felt naked without them.

The dragonlady feels unwell; death to come if castle dwell.

The words of the parchment swirled in Semra's mind. Someone wanted her out of the castle. Were they trying to draw her out and kill her beyond the walls of Shamaran Castle? Or were they trying to remove the dragonlady for easier access to harm the royal family?

It was risky, entering the castle in the wake of Arnevon's assassination. Everyone would be on alert. But what if it was one of Azi's sleepers, and she didn't know his face? What if it was someone she knew?

What if it was Annais, and he wasn't as naïve as he seemed? It was the perfect cover.

Semra stiffened, and she felt Annais and Gaulen's grip tighten in response. The king's voice rang in her mind. *You want to run. Don't run …*

Could he really expect her to stay in her room and play house? Trapped rat, more like. The mark on her chest burned hotter. She felt the call within like a beacon in the night.

Stop running off and doing suspicious things. If you're innocent, it'll only make everything worse …

Semra stumbled up a mossy stone step and fell to the ground. Annais dropped to one knee beside her, and Gaulen tried to haul her to her feet, but Semra's knees buckled.

Cries went up from the archers in the towers, and the familiar sound of enormous beating wings filled her ears. An unnatural wind blew the dark hair from Semra's face as she looked up. Dearest Zez. Rats and rot, why did a dragon love her better than any human ever had? Faithful and true, Zezura had never missed a call.

I'm sorry, Your Majesty. You really are the only king I could ever respect enough to serve.

Arrows hit the dragon's hide, and they rained down to clatter harmlessly against the cobbles. Zezura let out a short indignant huff of fire, and Annais threw his arms over his head. Gaulen drew his sword and stood over Semra, who still half-lay, half-sat on the ground. She drew her feet under her in a crouch and looked up at her giant aquamarine saving grace.

Don't land on the grounds, Zez. We will honor the king's request —one of the few we can.

Zezura beat her wings in a hover and stretched her nose down toward Semra. Gaulen thrust his sword forward, but the dragon plucked the blade from his hands and snapped the steel in two with a single crushing force of her jaws. Blue wings, snout, and fire filled the air. Guards split their focus between the dragon and their king, and Zezura took their useless beatings like chaff on her scales as she hovered and wove between them.

The frantic guards cast their eyes to the sky as Zezura ascended into the air and wheeled in a tight circle, releasing a stream of fire well above the heads of the Jannemari men down below. But the dragon left just as it had come —riderless.

And Semra was gone.

***

SEMRA WOVE her way through the underground servants' quarters and glanced back only once to see if anyone had noticed her slip through the garden door. *You could have gone with Zezura,* her thoughts chided her. *You could have been free.* True, but then she never would have gotten more tonic, and the king would be forced to assume she killed Arnevon—and abandon all pursuit of an alternative.

She tried not to think about Turian's disappointment in her running off mere seconds after she'd promised not to. Semra twisted her hair up, snatched a hat off the head of a blacksmith as he bent to adjust his shoe in the crowd, and placed it on her own head as she melted into the throng of workers. The workday was ending for some, and others who lived here beneath the castle were grabbing a quick meal at their quarters before heading out again. Small rooms and even shops lined both sides of the street, illuminated by lanterns and small windows at the very top of the walls before they plunged beneath the surface of the earth.

The burble of moving water caught her ear to the east, and Semra followed the sound. The dimness of the cavern as she moved away from the slight windows of the outer walls reminded her of Mount Hara, but the bustle of the working class and the hum of casual conversation struck a stark contrast to her upbringing. Two women laughed as they walked together with baskets of laundry, and a group of men debated the best horse breeds. From the muck on their boots, Semra guessed they might be stable hands.

Aurin, it was a good thing it was dim down here and she'd chosen to wear the wrap skirt. It made blending in easier. She kept her head down as she picked her way to the river and across the bridge. The river, a branch off the Dezapi, progressed north by the catacombs and spilled over the cliff beneath the castle keep into the Shalladin down below. Semra hoped one day she could return to the cleft on the cliff there with Zezura, hidden behind the wall of water. It was so peaceful and private.

Her plan was wildly risky. There was no reason to believe she wouldn't be tossed in the dungeon immediately upon capture, and for her plan to work, she had to avoid being apprehended until she could make it clear she had no real intention of escape. But she needed to talk to someone first. And she needed weapons.

Zezura's diversion had covered her disappearance and bought her time, but Semra hoped the king understood the third purpose of Zezura's visit: *I have a dragon, and I can leave whenever I want. I am only here because I want to be.* She may have broken her promise to keep her head down, but she also wanted to stay and prove her innocence. Not to mention Zephan might never forgive her if she left without warning now. Semra hoped Turian understood this was as close to a third option as she could manage.

Semra left the river behind and wound through the passageways until she was beneath the east wing, climbed the stair to the exit, slipped into the first floor of the keep, and up to the second floor. Her room was on this floor, but down on the far side. Running feet pounded along the passage overhead. *Bang.* A door slammed open. *Bang.* Another. *Bang.*

She needed to talk to someone. Siler. He would understand, know what to do. But he was in Belvidore, the traitor! Probably preparing his villa ...

Her heart kept time with the frantic search upstairs. Firfell's booming voice floated down the stone stairwell, barking muffled orders to check the third floor, and another set of footsteps echoed up from behind her down below. Semra ducked into the storage room and out of sight, took off her hat, and scanned the shelves. Jams, preserves, sugar ... salt. Semra snatched the salt and dumped a large pile of the tiny sparkling grains into her hat.

"Ahem."

Semra spun and came nose to nose with Saeb, master housekeeper of Shamaran Castle, a stern heavyset woman armed with a rolling pin and the grumpy disposition of a blue jay whose nest has just been invaded.

"Now what in the name of—"

Semra smothered the woman's mouth with her hand and pushed her up against the storage room wall. A jar of pickled herring fell from the shelf behind her, and Saeb's eyes bulged as she watched it fall. Semra cradled a hat full of salt in one hand and ripped the other from Saeb's mouth just in time to snatch the jar out of the air three inches from the floor.

"Not a word," Semra hissed. She pressed the jar into Saeb's free hand and put a finger to her lips. "Has Zezura landed in your courtyard recently? No. Did this jar of pickled herring break? No. All because of me. You're welcome."

"Yes, but you are the one who brought the dragon and knocked over the jar in the first place," Saeb whispered back. "And she did knock over and break an expensive commissioned stone statue in the main courtyard a while back. I haven't forgotten."

"All I need is fifteen minutes. In fifteen minutes, I'll be exactly where I need to be. And I'll make sure Princess Aviama lobbies the king for your raise."

Saeb arched an eyebrow. "They're looking for you everywhere."

"Saeb, someone is *always* looking for me. But you know I didn't do whatever they're claiming. That's why you came after me with a rolling pin—not only because your tireless, unappreciated work organizing this castle is worth protecting but also because you know I would never hurt you."

"Maybe, but that's not my job. I'm a housekeeper, not an investigator. And besides, you can't get Princess Aviama to do anything."

"Please. Since I've been around, has Aviama been harder to clean up after, or easier?"

Saeb's eyes narrowed, but she pursed her lips, considering.

Heavy footsteps flew down the corridor toward them and Semra flattened herself against the wall. Saeb turned to fill the doorframe just in time, blocking the guard's view.

"Move aside, Saeb," Gaulen's voice growled. "We need to find Semra. I need to look in this room."

"Lost your charge, have you? Well, I can tell you that I haven't seen her in a hot minute, and I'll thank you to keep your grubby hands off my preserves, thank you very much!"

"It's the last room I need to search on this floor, so if it's all the same—"

"It is *not* all the same! Out, *out!* Don't think I haven't caught you guardsmen trying to sneak morsels out of my storerooms before. I know your kind, and I don't like it, not one bit! Dragons and daylilies, have you lost your mind? Don't you think I'd notice if a girl were hiding in this tiny room while I were inside it?"

Saeb lunged and Gaulen yelped as the rolling pin made contact with his knee. Semra couldn't help but smile. Aurin, Saeb was good to have on her side!

Gaulen fled down the hall, and Saeb reappeared in the doorway, hands on her hips, rolling pin still gripped in one fist. She lifted one finger and wagged it at Semra's nose. "I expect you to talk to Her Highness Aviama. And keep your dragon off my flowers. And your mouth shut about my involvement in all this. I'm not involved, you hear me?"

Semra held her free hand up defensively. "You were never involved."

"And I will *not* be asking why you're stealing my salt, but you'll never steal from me again, you hear?"

Semra nodded, cradling the hat full of salt against her body. "Of course."

Saeb let out an exasperated huff and gave a curt dip of her head before disappearing toward laundry. Semra took a deep breath and crossed the hall to a room just two doors over. Two large wheels stood to one side, and hot wax filled a huge cauldron in the center of the room over a furnace. Long narrow candles hung upside down over the cauldron from a metal ring suspended from the ceiling, and several simple wooden frames held rows and rows of candles on the opposite end of the room. Metal ladles, flint and iron, and a stack of rags and extra kindling occupied one of the workbenches, and a middle-aged man dipped his ladle into the cauldron of hot wax.

Garbane glanced up from his work as Semra shut the door behind her, and then returned his focus to candle making. He held the metal ring steady with one hand, and slowly poured hot wax over the hanging candles with the other. Garbane's chandlery had become a refuge for Semra over the course of her time in the castle. His prickly exterior kept chattering gossips far away, and his refusal to care about status and drama made her visits peaceful and quiet.

"Feeling better I gather," he said.

"For now," she answered. The doors to Ancestry Hall crashed shut down the corridor and she flinched.

"Keeping up appearances, are you? Making friends?"

Semra gritted her teeth. "Oh, you know. The usual. Trying to stay alive."

Garbane eyed her. He grunted. *"Mmm."*

Semra couldn't help herself. "What?"

"I don't like people. But sometimes we need them."

"What's that supposed to mean?"

"It means you need to trust someone other than you when you find yourself in a pinch."

"I'm here, aren't I?"

Garbane wiped the sweat from his brow with the back of his hand, then dipped the ladle back into the wax.

"Sure you are, kid. Looking guilty as a dog with a shoe in its mouth. Any idiot would deduce you were responsible for the latest atrocity."

Semra's mouth went dry. *"You* don't think I did anything ... evil, do you?"

Garbane poured wax over another candle. "Recently? No. But not everyone is as smart as me."

Semra leaned back against the wall and let herself slide down it to the floor. The heat from the furnace in the little room was making her head swim.

"You pride yourself on being some one-woman show, but you're not," Garbane said. "Mighty dragonlord whatever, but you're still a lonely young girl who hasn't a clue about things outside your childhood. You need people. You need *partners.* Not business partners, not thieves to get you what you want for a price, but people who care about you and are on your team. You need to stop running all the time and pretending you're okay alone."

A deep pang struck her in the gut, but she lifted her chin. "I *am* okay alone. I always have been."

"Sure you are."

A flurry of heavy footsteps ran down the second floor hall just outside Garbane's door. "Guards on every level of every stairwell!" Firfell called out, his voice drifting in from the open stairwell down the hall where she had come. "Close every window! Keep an eye on the skies!"

"I'd say it's certainly going well for you, wouldn't you?" Garbane said.

Semra swore.

Garbane set the ladle down and wiped his hands on his apron. "Do I want to know why you have a hat full of salt?"

"Probably not."

"Are you going to do something stupid?"

"Maybe, but only because this morning I received a death threat under my pillow, and my room is the one place the king thinks I have to stay penned up. Having friends sounds nice, but what I seem to accumulate easiest is enemies."

Garbane sighed. "Do you need anything else? Never mind, never mind." He pulled three dry candles off one of the frames and laid them out next to the rags and other supplies on his workbench. "Don't tell me. Just leave me one of my flint and iron sets." Garbane crossed to the door and opened it a crack.

"Saeb! Belon needs help bringing in the guest room laundry!"

"Belon needs to handle her own problems!" Saeb yelled back from the kitchen.

"Clear out of there and don't be back for a few minutes, or I'll make sure that pitiful oaf Weggil hears you're in love with him."

Something crashed in the kitchen, and Garbane grinned.

"The puppy-eyed fool! Keep him away from me! I'll have your head, you lard!"

He winked at Semra. "She's on her way, and she's dragging the other two staff along with her. You have two minutes."

Semra smiled and scrambled to her feet. She threw on one of the extra aprons, dropped flint and iron and two candles into the left pocket, and dumped the salt from the hat into the right pocket. Garbane took the hat from her hands, shook it out, and fitted it to his own head.

"I've been needing a new hat."

"Thank you," Semra said, and disappeared out the door and across the hall behind Saeb and the two other servants she had in tow. As the group passed by Semra's room, Semra ducked inside, letting the three women ahead of her obstruct the guard's view down by Ancestry Hall.

Shouts rang out as Semra shut the door. Semra felt the adrenaline pull at the edges of the tonic, threatening to pull back the cloaking effect and leave her in the throes of whatever illness plagued her. A wave of nausea rolled through her as she ran to the side table and yanked off the apron. Semra threw the candles, flint, and iron under the bedsheets and dumped the salt into the water pitcher next to the bed.

No sooner had she flung the apron under the bed than the door behind her swung wide and Firfell stalked in with four guards, swords drawn, scowls permanently fixed to their faces.

Semra stepped in front of the pitcher, its water cloudy as salt granules sifted slowly to the bottom. A wicked smile played across Firfell's face.

"What do you think, Gaulen? Should you haul her to the dungeon, or shall I?"

10

AVAYA

"I'm afraid, Axis."

Avaya pressed closer to him on the couch, pressing her hands to his chest as his arms looped around her waist. "It's been … so hard, for me. Locked in my chambers in Jannemar while two enormous dragons tore my home apart. Kidnapped and dragged out of my country. Not that I didn't want to come. I did, I wanted to be yours, ever since the gala. Oh, I'm so grateful to be here now, but if only it hadn't happened this way. And now King Arnevon has been killed." She flicked an imaginary tear from her eye.

"No need to worry, my love. I will keep you safe." Axis planted a kiss on her lips and pulled her close.

"If only I could stay with you forever," she said. "But now you are king. A king has too many responsibilities to be tied to his wife every moment."

Axis pulled back. "Wife?"

Avaya played with the collar of his shirt. "I am your fiancé, aren't I? Beginning your reign with a union to the princess of Jannemar, with hope for the people, would be wise, don't you think? As soon as you think is respectful, of course."

The new king laughed. "So eager to be empress."

"Only with you as my emperor." Avaya handed him his goblet of wine, and he took a drink.

Axis paused, glowered into the goblet, and lifted his eyes to hers. "My father's untimely death was not so untimely, it seems. Your status is soon to be elevated beyond any you would have received in antiquated Jannemar, with their policy that only men can be monarchs. Do I have something to worry about, future wife?"

He thought he was a clever fish, didn't he? Avaya kept her eyes locked onto his, took the goblet from his hands, and drank deeply. "Your only concern need be for the firm establishment of your reign and legacy, my king."

Axis leaned back against the cushions of the sofa, satisfied. Avaya drained the goblet and turned it over, letting a single red drop fall into her palm. "And perhaps my safety, while you are away on more important business. I'm frightened, with so many assassins on the loose. How am I to protect myself, without knowing who to trust?"

"What would you have me do? I can't spare a platoon just on your security."

Scourge, did she have to do everything herself? Avaya painted her features with a soft pleading and turned her green eyes to the man before her. "All of the assassins are terrifying, but most can be bought. My father is too married to idealistic scruples to utilize them, and Jannemar coffers can't afford them all. But Semra is a wildcard. She's good. She can get inside the fortress, take whatever life she wants. She's done it before. And she is vehemently against us.

"We can't afford that kind of liability, not with your reign only just getting off the ground. We need credibility, strength, and control. She undermines all of it. I have just two small requests ..."

Avaya leaned in, running a hand up into Axis's hair and kissing him on the neck. She pulled back just enough to speak softly into his ear. "I want to be trained to defend myself. And I want Semra's head on a platter."

Axis's eyebrows shot up. "How very Belvidorian of you. I thought Jannemari women were better suited to embroidery, whereas ours fill every position of government and are often capable fighters. I wouldn't hold you back, but you're starting training rather late. Are you sure this is the best use of your time?"

She nodded fervently. "Oh, yes. I know most fighters train from a young age. That's why I have to be trained by someone as good as Semra is. Someone who knows how she fights."

Axis pursed his lips. "You want the Raven."

If I can find him. Where did Siler keep running off to?

Avaya pouted. "Don't be cross, my sweet. He's the only one who knows how she thinks. He's beaten her before. He can make me better than her. But only with your blessing."

Axis frowned. "That's the only reason you want to meet with him?"

"Are you jealous? Of a nobody from nowhere? King of nothing?" Avaya set down the goblet and fastened her arms around him, laying her head on his chest. "He's useful, that's all. In keeping me alive long enough to enjoy your rise to power. I want to be there to support you."

"Very well."

Avaya smiled, then paused. "And ... the other request? As a wedding present?"

"For you, my love, anything. There will be a bounty on Semra's head by morning."

11

"I thought my personal chambers the most appropriate place for house arrest," Semra said, crossing her arms. "If I'm going to be held prisoner for something I didn't do, this seemed as good a place as any, wouldn't you say?"

"You broke the king's command."

Semra gasped in mock surprise. "I did no such thing. His Majesty ordered me to remain in my quarters, ordered Zezura not to land on the grounds, and stated dire consequences would come if I were *outside* the castle walls." Semra spread her hands and looked around. "Here I am in my quarters. Zezura did not land on the grounds. She didn't land at all. And I was never once beyond the walls."

Firfell strode into the room and waved a finger at her nose. "Thinly veiled loopholes are not to be borne. You are *always* to remain with your guards, *inside* your quarters. You may have noticed that your window has been upgraded to help you remember that little requirement."

Semra twisted round to take in her window, now outfitted with metal bars on the interior side. Her heart rate ticked up a notch, but she lifted her chin. "How kind of you. And as for remaining with my guard, well, perhaps it would have been easier to keep track of them if they weren't so busy losing their minds and getting distracted by a friendly dragon swinging by to say hello."

Gaulen scowled. "It must have been the flames that gave me pause." His tunic was scorched and tattered at the edges, and he looked positively haggard. Semra bit the inside of her lip to keep from laughing. Gaulen was never in any real danger, but he didn't know that. She would have paid good money to have been able to stick around and watch the show. It would have had to be someone else's money though, of course. She didn't have any.

Firfell straightened and looked her up and down. "You're looking much healthier after your little escapade."

"Thank you. Fresh air is good for the body."

The captain sidestepped to the bed and crouched down. He pulled out the apron and lifted it up. "Taking up baking? Or chandlery?"

"Pottery, actually," Semra drawled. "I acquired the apron before realizing I had neither clay nor wheel to begin. Nor tutor. I had to give up, and in my exasperation, I threw it under the bed."

Firfell's lip curled. "I don't know what you *think* happened between you and the prince in Belvidore, but believe me when I say, your association will not save you. I will find you out, and I will see you hanged for your crimes."

Firfell gave a short whistle and the guards fell in step to follow him out. "No one goes in or out without being searched. *No one!*"

The door swung closed behind him. Semra grabbed a pillow off the bed and screamed into it. Her shoulders heaved from pent-up adrenaline, her body ached, and her head complained about the screaming she'd just done. She put a hand to her head and groaned. Dying was one thing, but did she have to feel so *fragile* while it happened?

Semra reached into the pitcher of saltwater and stirred with her arm, then dried her arm with bedcovers. She retrieved the three glass shards she'd hidden earlier, extracted parchment from the writing kit on the desk, and moved the pitcher of saltwater behind the partition used for bathing. Ever so carefully, Semra dipped the parchment into the pitcher, wrapped it as closely around the base of the first shard of glass as possible, and laid it down to soak in the brine. She repeated this process with the next two shards and sat down to wait.

The parchment-wrapped shards of glass soaked in the salt-water for an hour before Semra patted them off with an old tunic and set them out to dry. Afternoon wore into early evening, and her body aches competed with the pounding in her temples for her attention. Heat roiled beneath clammy skin, and she was grateful to be seated as the weakness returned with a savage ferocity. Semra allowed herself only a moment for dizziness to pass before using the flint and iron from Garbane to light her lantern, melt wax from one of the candles, and drip it along the edges of the parchment to seal it down around the handles of her makeshift knives. The wax cooled quickly, and Semra examined her work.

They wouldn't make reliable throwing knives, but they were sharp, and they'd do in a pinch for hand-to-hand combat or close-range throws. She adjusted her grip and ran through a few of the knife flow exercises she'd learned in training. The soaked parchment had molded well to the base of the shards and dried stiff and firm. The wax strengthened its hold, and her hand was well protected while manipulating the glass.

Semra slipped them into the sheaths of her trousers beneath her skirt. She wasn't leaving the room anytime soon, so she might as well have them handy. When was she supposed to have her second dose of the tonic again?

Scourge. She'd already had it, of course. Hours before she'd been instructed to.

A knock sounded at the door, and Semra lurched forward off the chair behind the bathing partition and lunged for the bed. A woman wanting privacy when she had an unlockable door might not seem suspicious in other circumstances, but all things considered, being found hiding out was probably less than brilliant. Her legs failed to catch her, and Semra saw the wooden floorboards rushing up to meet her as the world toppled.

"Semra?"

"Get her up. Annais, help!"

"What happened?"

The voices swirled in her mind as she felt her body being lifted off the floor and laid on her bed. The rustle of sheets, the smoothness of silk, the crinkle of paper and clink of dishes filled her senses. The smell of beef stew and bread reminded her stomach how long it had been since she'd eaten anything. It growled.

"I'm fine; I'm okay," Semra mumbled. Another dizzy spell hit her. She squeezed her eyes shut tight, then opened them. "I fell, is all."

"My brother told me never to believe you when you say you're fine."

Semra's heart lifted at the sound of the bright young voice. It was tinged with ever-so-slightly disapproving tones, but when Semra followed the sound to the stunning sixteen-year-old princess, she was smiling. Aviama's green eyes, slender figure, and wavy golden tresses were startlingly reminiscent of her older sister. But Aviama hated gossip, and politics, and charade. And most disparate of all, she liked Semra.

Coanor, with unkempt hair and shadows under her eyes, stood beside the princess. The healer looked as though she'd started raking a hairbrush through her gray mop and forgotten to complete the job—after failing to sleep for weeks. Had Semra never noticed, or had she always looked so?

"Thank you, darling, that'll be all," Coanor said, ushering Annais back out the door. "My patient needs her rest now. Goodbye!"

"Firfell has limited the number of visits you can have in a day, so we consolidated and came together. And he's snooping through everything that comes in or out of your room," Aviama said, perching herself on the bed next to Semra. "He actually made Coanor pour your stew through a sieve so he could see everything in it. Can you believe that? I think he's gone totally mental. Or maybe he went there once for holiday and never quite came back, if you know what I mean. Has he always been this unreasonable, or is it a unique effect dragonlords have on people?"

Semra furrowed her brow. "How am I going to research anything with him breathing down my neck? Will he even let me have books?"

"I did request some reading materials for you, but the captain only sent this," Coanor said, pulling a book from a small bag.

Semra squinted at the gold-leaf lettering. *"Mox's Collection of Children's Bedtime Lullabies and Poems.* How thoughtful."

"Monac and Zephan are trying to get actual information on what could be going on, but they haven't had any luck yet," Aviama said. She leaned forward and grabbed one of Semra's hands. Semra jumped at the sudden movement, then rearranged her pillow to cover it up. "Semra, this is all my fault. If I hadn't pushed you to go after Avaya, none of this would have happened. I can't believe Avaya chose to stay in

Belvidore. Doesn't she know how it's tearing our father apart? How could she be so heartless? It's just not like her at all."

Not like the lying, conniving older sister to choreograph her own kidnapping and betray her perfect family? It was better for Semra not to voice her opinions about that. Semra squeezed Aviama's hand. "It's not your fault. And some sort of evil was bound to catch up with me one way or another—it's just the way my life goes."

Aviama worried her lip, and Coanor stirred the stew. The older woman propped Semra up with more pillows and handed her the bowl. "Have you had your evening dose yet?"

"I had my second dose hours ago. It really does help—I was getting in bad shape again before I took it. Were you able to make more?"

"My supplier didn't have enough of what I needed, so I was only able to make one more bottle. But you shouldn't be going through it so fast." The lines of Coanor's face deepened and a shadow passed over her face.

She pulled out a small bottle identical to the tonic she'd given Semra before. Semra reached for it, but Coanor pulled it back. "Half a moment." The older woman walked to the end of the bed and held up the folded clothes Semra had taken from her room.

Scourge! Semra had forgotten all about them. She grimaced.

Coanor pursed her lips. "As much as I appreciate your resetting my room to the way it was, and folding the clothes you stole, I'd very much like to know what you were doing in there."

"You put me in a nightdress. I needed clothes."

"For your adventures off increasing your heart rate instead of resting like I told you."

"Yes."

"Perhaps you wouldn't have needed the extra dose if you'd followed instructions. Clearly staying alive is not a strong enough motivator. Now tell me, darling. About my room."

Semra shrugged. Her head throbbed, and her face flushed hot. Sweat poured from her pores, glistening on her skin. "Does it matter?"

"Indeed it does, because we need to trust one another. I could wait until your fever goes up and see if you answer my questions while delirious. But I'd rather not."

"What's going on?" Aviama asked.

Semra sighed. "Coanor wants me to tell her about the booby-trapped door in her room, the quotes on the wall, and the creepy poems about dragons destroying the kingdom."

"She *what?*" Aviama gasped.

Coanor put her hands on her hips. "They're not creepy poems, and they're not about dragons destroying the kingdom. You thought it was about you, didn't you?"

Semra winced as another dizzy spell set in. "Isn't it? You blame me for the war."

The healer clucked her tongue. "What vast accusations you make. Not everything is about you, darling."

"What is it about, then?"

"I don't think I'll tell you. You did rob me, after all. But I have no plans of killing you, if that's why you felt the need to hightail it out of my humble home."

Something inside Semra wrenched. She'd been too hasty. Aviama dipped a cloth into the pitcher by the bed and placed it on Semra's forehead.

"Your Highness, we really could have used more drinking water in here," Coanor scolded. "No need to ruin the pitcher."

Aviama's face fell. "I'm sorry. I didn't think about it."

"It's okay," Semra said. "The water glass is broken, and I needed fresh drinking water anyway."

Coanor arched an eyebrow.

Idiot, Semra chastised herself. *The fever is getting to you. Watch your tongue.*

Coanor dipped a finger into the water pitcher and touched it to her tongue. Her face screwed up in disgust. "You certainly keep us on our toes. Sit up a bit. Let's get you something to eat."

Semra struggled to sit, but her limbs felt like lead. Aviama pulled her up and adjusted the pillows to prop her in a better sitting position. She stilled, and when she finally pulled away, she held a slip of parchment in her hand. Aviama's gaze swept over it and she looked up, eyes wide.

"Semra?" Her voice quaked.

Semra's stomach dropped. Another note?

Coanor snatched the paper from Aviama's hand and read it aloud:

> *Get out now while still you can*
> *Far from where this mess began*
> *I hate poems but if you stay, you'll die*
> *Don't be an idiot*

"Well, your poet isn't nearly as good as the ones in my books," Coanor said.

"The first one was better." Semra wracked her brain. This one didn't seem threatening. It sounded more like a warning. Who could be warning her, and how were they getting in? What information did they have?

"The first one?" Aviama squeaked. "How many have there been? You're going to be killed!"

Semra fished out her tonic and threw back her third dose of the day. She had to think, and the sickness wasn't helping. Nor was Aviama's careless squawking.

"You've got to calm down and be quiet," Semra said. Aviama's mouth closed, but her face was ashen. Semra took a deep breath. "You really don't get it, do you? You just think I'm reckless and stupid for the fun of it? Do you really think I would run from Coanor, duck my guards, and make myself look more guilty without a reason? I could have been gone by now. I chose to stay. I wanted to give Turian a chance to do things his way, or mostly his way, but ..."

Aviama's chin quivered, and her eyes brimmed with tears. An answering tear escaped down one side of Semra's face, and she glared out her newly barred window. It would have been so easy before. Firfell would have been satisfied to keep her in her room, but anytime she wanted to leave, she could have jumped out the window onto Zezura. She'd waited too long.

"My place was ransacked when I came back today," Coanor said softly. "It's a good thing you got out when you did. After seeing the folded clothes on the end of your bed, I knew it wasn't you. It's not your style to leave such chaos. When you confirmed you'd returned everything to its original state, I knew the other intruder must have come later in the day."

"Your trap—did it go off?" Semra asked hopefully. "Maybe the poison killed them?"

"It's not poison, darling. I work for the king. I can't risk someone more important than me dying in my house, or I'd be as good as dead myself. It's a staining powder, to scare intruders and help me identify who did it. It'll be difficult to wash off, and remnants of the blue should be on their skin for several days."

Semra slipped her hand through the slit in her skirt and retrieved the first message from her pants sheath, laying it out on the bedcover. Coanor placed the new one beside it. The handwriting matched.

"Do you know who's sending the messages?" Aviama asked Semra.

Semra shook her head, then immediately regretted the movement. She groaned. Only one possible culprit for the notes came to mind, but it didn't make sense. Could Siler be in Jannemar?

Aviama spoke in a hush, pained resignation heavy in her voice. "You can't stay."

"No."

"You know my father will send people after you."

Semra sighed. "Yes."

"And you don't have much tonic, and the tonic isn't a cure anyway." Aviama bit her lip.

"Staying here is becoming worse and worse of an option," Coanor said. "I don't think the king would tolerate Firfell keeping Semra from a healer, but someone doesn't want Semra healed. I might never get what I need to make more tonic, and even if I do, our research here will be slow ... and watched. King Turian is doing the best he can, but I fear it is not enough."

Coanor opened her mouth to say more, then paused, flitting a furtive glance at Aviama.

"Oh, out with it," Aviama said. "I already know more than I should, if you're trying to protect me, and I don't care if it's against my father. As king, he's bound by more limitations than I am. Everybody thinks I'm so terrible at secrets, but has anybody tested me out? No! And did I keep Semra's secret when I turned her into glorious Axelia Belinon—"

"Berinon," Semra corrected.

"Whatever. Didn't I keep that secret? I didn't tell a soul. Not even my lady-in-waiting."

Coanor put her hands up. "Calm down, princess, calm down."

"Everybody can stop telling me to calm down too. That would be great."

Semra grinned as Turian's words came back to her. *Maybe even make a friend.* Is this what it felt like? Having friends? A strange warmth spread over her that had nothing to do with fever.

She wondered what the king would think if he knew she'd taken his advice, and that his own daughter had weaseled her way into Semra's heart. Maybe she was low on friends in court, but in the inner workings of the castle ... well, she had a gruff chandler, a reluctant housekeeper, a healer, and a princess.

Not to mention the crown prince. Butterflies sprang to life inside her, and she shoved them back down. She wished he were here, but it would only cause him more problems if he were. It was better for both Turian and Zephan that they stay out of the loop.

Coanor cleared her throat. "Very well, darling, suit yourself. But holding in this secret could place you in danger. The truth of the matter is that going against the king's order may be the only way to preserve Semra's life. But once you leave, your tonic will soon dwindle to nothing and it's only a matter of time before your illness overtakes you. You need to find a cure, or it won't matter whether you stay or go—you'll die ether way."

Semra nodded. "I understand. You've done the best you can for me, and if I don't find a cure, maybe I'll find a mountain somewhere to spend my final moments. No need to bring the Shamarans further into it than necessary."

Coanor swatted her upside the head. "No! Idiot! If you die, the court will stop looking for Arnevon's true killer. If you die, Belvidore will no longer be put off by the protection of the dragon over Shamaran Castle. If you die, not even one of Azi's assassins will be left on our side to tell us who is friend and who is foe, and the army of killers you come from will descend en masse to receive their fortune. Belvidore is not short on money, Semra. And who better to kill for than a rich king bent on revenge?"

Semra's mouth went dry. First the Shamaran family, and then the kingdom. Turian, Zephan, Aviama—they would all be lost. Aviama swallowed.

"Stay safe," she pleaded. "Didn't you say the healers Zephan apprenticed under moved to Camar?"

"Yes, they did." Semra thought for a moment. It was the only reasonable next step. "They escaped there with Lesala after the assassins burned their house down, but they've been quiet about it."

"Quiet is good," Coanor said. "Listen to me. If you put a box over a flower and create a maze for it to get to the sun, it doesn't crumple at the first sign of difficulty. It grows toward the light. We aren't born with the amount of resiliency we will have for our whole lives. Everybody has a past coloring their present, but that doesn't *define* our present. It defines what lessons we have to pull from. The direction we grow is up to us.

"My grandmother used to recite this saying to me: 'we all have roots, down in the ground; strength is made, it isn't found.' No matter how many obstacles you hit, remember the sun is always shining above you. Hope lives. Grow toward hope, even when you don't feel it, even when it hurts, and you will make it out of the darkness.

"Now eat. You're going to need your strength."

12

AVAYA

"Have you been avoiding me, Siler?" Avaya arranged herself on the opulent chair in her sitting room and tilted her head at her bodyguard. Bodyguard, kidnapper for hire, assassin, informant – such a useful man. Her gaze swept over the sharp cut of his jaw, the way his tunic failed to conceal his muscled chest and arms, his dark hair, his indifferent gray eyes. No wonder Semra liked to keep him around. Avaya wondered how many powerful people the man before her had brought to their knees.

Little else in life gave her such a thrill as controlling powerful beasts. And Siler was a lion. He crossed his arms and leaned against the doorframe as if he were the master of Madensig Fortress himself. What would it take to shake that confident demeanor? To see behind the curtain...

"Never, Your Highness. I'm simply a busy man."

"Your responsibilities lie with me, do they not?"

Siler smirked. "You pay me to watch over your interests, which includes your life, and requires me to keep an ear to the ground. If you wanted someone to stand in the hall at your beck and call, you could pay a much lower rate to any brainless goon off the street."

Avaya tossed a perfect golden ringlet over her shoulder. "Open up your schedule a bit. The king has approved your tutoring me in combat."

"Ridiculous. I'm not doing that. My time is better spent elsewhere, and to be frank, your safety is better left to the professionals."

"Do you think so little of yourself as a tutor?"

Siler snorted. "I think too little of you as a student."

Avaya stiffened, then forced herself into relaxed, languid movements as she stood from her chair and sauntered toward him. She wouldn't let him know his little jabs were capable of pricking her spirit.

"Come in, won't you? Let's talk about it."

Siler eyed her suspiciously. "I'd rather not."

"I'm a princess."

"And I'm a poached egg. Do tell me why I should care."

Avaya sidled up to him and walked her fingers up his arm. "You dare defy me?"

Siler gripped her wrist and twisted it behind her back in a smooth motion, pulling her against him and applying pressure. Avaya winced. She tugged to no avail, then leaned into him instead. Siler nearly dropped his grip, then adjusted before she could twist around to see his face. She smiled to herself. He was a man after all.

"I could always get another job if you become too much trouble," he rumbled, his voice low against her ear.

"Oh, I'm not so bad. And I'd love to see you more often. Wouldn't you like seeing me?"

"The most attractive thing about you," he whispered, "is your fat purse and desperation to spend money."

"Are you certain there's *nothing* else you like about me?"

Siler released her and stepped away. "I'm not your lackey. I don't want to play your games."

Avaya pouted. "Please teach me. It might be fun."

"Why do you care?"

She let out a long breath and spread her hands. "I'm scared, okay? I'm a little bit scared. People are dying left and right, Semra hates me, and you—my mighty protector—are frequently disappearing. I don't want to rely on other people anymore. I want to be able to fight. And I want to be better than Semra."

Siler laughed. "You can't be better than Semra."

Bitter ire bubbled up inside her chest. She paused to settle her nerves. No anger could show in her voice. "But you can beat her, can't you?"

"Without her dragon? Sure, *I* can beat her. But *you* can't."

"And why not?"

"Because she spent eleven years training to be an assassin—which she achieved a year earlier than anyone else, by the way—and another three years in practice after reaching mission-ready status. You, on the other hand, spend your days dripping honey into the ears of people you deem important and easily swayed. And as royalty, you're used to instant results, which means you'll probably expect to be a proficient swordswoman by Tuesday."

Avaya lifted her chin. "I can be patient. I am soon-to-be queen of a nation. Jannemar does not respect its women, but here in Belvidore, the women fight. I will lead my people and earn their admiration. And who knows if one day I will be called upon to lead Jannemar? There is only one male heir. Who is left?"

Siler's eyebrows soared, and Avaya grimaced. She'd gone too far. She chewed her nail, then snatched her hand away. Siler strolled into the sitting room and pilfered a pastry off a silver platter on the low table in front of the sofa. He took a bite, chewed, and swallowed before breaking the silent tension.

"There is a man in your dungeons back home who might claim there are two male heirs."

"His rights as heir have already been stripped."

"You know better than that. But even if he were truly out of the way, is your greed so great that you would kill your own brother?"

Avaya bristled. "I'm not saying that! I'm saying that ruling a nation is a dangerous position, and you never know what could happen." She smoothed the fabric of her skirts, but her fingers trembled. "Don't be a fool. I could never kill Zephan."

Siler took another bite and waved the pastry in her direction. "But you could kill other people."

Avaya snatched the pastry from Siler's fingers and shredded it, dropping the crumbs on the floor. "Far fewer than you. A monarch must do difficult things, you know. So little is truly black and white."

The man glowered at the dismantled bakery item and raised his gaze to hers with disdain. "That was the last one."

"It was on *my* table." How could he be more impassioned by the stupid pastry than by her advances? Avaya ground her heel into the remains on the floor and licked cherry filling off her finger to clean it. "In addition to becoming my combat tutor, I have one more request. I would consider it a personal favor, but it also comes with a significant monetary bonus to your retainer fee."

"I'm listening."

"Kill Semra for me."

13

Semra stashed her wrap skirt in her bag and slung it across her back. At last, she wore just her basic tunic and trousers. With weapons. Crappy makeshift ones, but weapons nonetheless.

Her evening dose of tonic had taken the edge off, and her temperature was back down to a manageable level. The pounding in her head receded to a dull roar, and the sweat on her skin dropped back from buckets of clamminess to a mildly uncomfortable glisten. Semra placed her first threatening note on top of her pillow for Firfell to find and hoped Aviama would find the right time to deliver her letters to Zephan and King Turian.

And that they would each burn them afterward, as instructed.

The second note, the one that was more of a warning, she kept with her as a handwriting sample in case she had the chance to compare with any suspects. The two bottles of tonic were wrapped in cloth and set carefully in the bottom of the bag on her back. Semra felt the tingle of the mark on her chest as she reached out to Zezura again.

It is time.

Turian's men were unlikely to get to the bottom of King Arnevon's assassination alone, and if Belvidore really did have Ramas' amulet, Semra's case was as good as closed. And she would be condemned. Not that it mattered, if she couldn't find a cure. She'd be dead either way.

Even so, Semra refused to take down the one good monarch she'd ever heard of by associating too closely with him. She would make a clear escape and let Turian send his soldiers after her. And if she had to go into Belvidore, it would be obvious it was not done under Turian's command. Semra wished she could give Zephan a proper goodbye, but she and Aviama both knew an in-person farewell would make him try to follow her. The letter would have to be enough.

Night had fallen. Semra waited just inside her door. A dizzy spell washed through her, and she closed her eyes as the feeling slowly passed. Shattering glass broke the silence down the hall, and Semra heard running feet as one of her guards sprinted toward the sound.

It would be Gaulen. Prickly, negative, gallant, principled Gaulen. The perfect king's soldier.

Semra eased the door open, jumped on Annais' back, and cinched her arm tight around his throat. A soft gagging sound scraped from his throat. He clawed at her fingers and slammed himself backward against the wall. Semra swallowed a groan as pain exploded in her hips where they were crushed between Annais' body and the castle's stone walls, but she held tight. His grip loosened and he sagged. "I'm sorry," she whispered in his ear. And she was.

Did it make her soft, like the Framatar had always said? Caring? It certainly did make her vulnerable, but maybe it also made her human.

Semra liked the idea of being human. But could she stay human and keep herself alive at the same time?

Her feet hit the ground with a soft *thump* as Annais' body crumpled beneath her. A shout rang out down the hall, and she turned to see Gaulen throw Aviama's lady-in-waiting, Murin, out of one of the rooms before barreling toward Semra. Murin stumbled and caught herself, a bashed in lantern hanging from one hand.

Aurin, bless her. Semra hoped whatever reason Aviama had cooked up for Murin being there was enough to keep her out of any deep trouble.

Semra flew across the hall into an empty guest chamber on the opposite side. Flying glass exploded from the window on the far end of the room and Semra threw her arm over her face to protect it as a massive dragon's head drew back to admire its work. Behind her, Gaulen's shouts caught the attention of the east tower, and she heard a chorus go up in answer. She sprinted forward, planting one foot on a trunk by the foot of the bed and propelling herself over the broken glass and headfirst through the second-story window.

She overshot the jump. Semra hit Zezura's scaly hide hard and tumbled over her back. The courtyard rushed up at her in the dim cast of the moon, and her heart lurched into her throat. She braced herself for impact, but a great force of talons wrapped around her waist and yanked her upward.

Terror gripped her. *It hurts! Mother? Help! I'm sorry, mother. I only wanted the ball ... it didn't roll too far outside ...*

Semra shuddered and shook off the memory. She wasn't four years old anymore, and this wasn't Rotokas. This was Zezura, the dragon whose life she saved, the dragon bound to her for life and better trusted than any human.

The courtyard dropped away, and for an instant Semra was face to face with Gaulen in the open window as she dangled from the dragon's claw. Stupid, stone-faced Gaulen. She could just hear him now. *I love it when she does things that prove she's still a cold-blooded killer, don't you?*

She knew she shouldn't. She knew it only reinforced the guilty narrative. But she blew him a kiss and fluttered her fingers in a wave as Zezura pulled her higher and higher into the sky. He opened his mouth to scream his rage, but the sound was lost to the wind.

Semra refocused on Zezura. *I can't ride like this. Get me on your back.*

A ripple of pleasure from the beast, and—was that amusement?—she surged straight upward. Semra groaned as her body screamed for reprieve against the tight grip of talons and dizziness that overtook her. And then she fell.

Zezura dropped her.

Nausea, weakness, and fear swirled about her like the tumult of air in her ears as Zezura made a swift arc and swung beneath her just in time to catch her, nearly matching Semra's speed to lessen the impact. Semra's forearms caught the brunt of the hit, but she pulled herself up into a seated position and hooked her feet in place behind the more prominent spikes along Zezura's side.

Zezura's mood sobered, sensing Semra's distress, and slowed almost painfully as Semra reoriented herself and let her stomach settle. She closed her eyes and let the night breeze nip at her clammy skin, soothing the fire inside. Her pulse hammered a warning in her chest. It was far too soon for another dose.

The shimmering scales beneath her winked from aquamarine to deep indigo, concealing their gentle glide over Shamaran Castle. Torches cropped up in the gardens below. Guards searching the skies, archers aiming for a dragon they had no hope of bringing down.

How long would it take for Turian to send soldiers into the surrounding area, waiting for her to come looking for supplies or healers? Would he issue an edict in the dead of night, or wait until morning? Semra wondered if Firfell knew about Shafii and Tinat Renab, and where they had settled. She had to get there before anyone else.

She had a dragon. She could travel quickly.

Heat burned like a furnace inside her, creeping through every screaming fiber of her being. Semra felt herself slipping, and Zezura adjusted under her to redistribute her weight and keep her upright. Speed was important, but if she didn't rest soon, she'd never make it at all.

Zezura coasted across the air at a deliberate, cautious pace. They dropped altitude over the river and flew down by the waterfall beneath the castle. Zezura's wing ever so softly grazed the wall of water where the two of them had so often sought refuge. A fitting goodbye. Would they ever see it again?

They left the falls behind and gradually ascended once more, and Semra swept her gaze one last time over the elegant Shamaran Castle. Once foreign, it was now so familiar. She wondered how angry Saeb would be about the broken window, and if she had had a conniption when Firfell installed bars on her beautiful Nezzi Room meant for visiting dignitaries. She wondered if Garbane would miss her popping by to escape judgmental eyes.

She wondered who was climbing up the west wall to King Turian's bedroom window.

Semra tensed and leaned forward. One hand slipped to her thigh to rest on the hilt of her glass blade. A dark figure made a steady climb only ten feet from the king's window.

A lantern winked on inside. Perhaps the guards had woken Turian with news of Semra's escape. She should go while she had the chance. She should stay beyond the range of the archers.

Semra edged closer. The intruder had a small frame, the scant moonlight highlighting defined arms. Form-fitted trousers like Semra's, stocked with all six knives. Semra's brows rose. A woman.

An assassin sent to kill Turian.

Was she hired by Belvidore as revenge? Or was another nation taking advantage of the influx of quality hitmen, and picking off monarchs?

It didn't matter. She couldn't leave the assassin on the wall. The mark on Semra's chest tingled as it always did when she communicated with Zezura. Semra gave the order, and Zez angled in toward the woman on the wall. The shadow of the dragon fell across the king's window, and the intruder yelped as Zezura gripped her in her front feet and wheeled around. Semra glanced back. King Turian stood in the window, holding a lantern, face unreadable.

14

Semra let Zezura fly south for three hours before landing at the fringes of the forest. It took their new captive a full twenty minutes to tire of screaming, first in fear and then in fury. The night still covered them. They were miles from the main road, and Semra had managed another dose as they rode.

It would take a week to travel from Qalea to Camar on horseback. In normal circumstances dragon riding would be faster, but Semra feared her illness would slow the pace. *I won't need this much tonic on normal days,* she told herself. *It's just all the excitement. If I keep my heartrate down, the tonic will manage the fevers.* Semra needed boring travel days to recover.

She drew one of her glass shard knives and slid down Zezura's side just as Zezura deposited the woman on the ground.

"Who hired you?" Semra demanded.

The intruder drew two of her knives and dropped her center of gravity, ready to fight. "You're not the only capable assassin, you know. Is it so hard to believe someone else landed a job?"

Semra knew that voice. She stepped forward and squinted into the darkness. "Pidge?"

"Yeah, what of it?" the girl snapped.

Semra ran through what she knew of Pidge from the mountain where they'd grown up. The program had housed over a hundred people in the mountain before Semra and the task force dismantled it. Since they were in different classes, they'd never sparred, but Semra had seen Pidge practice on occasion. Short and wiry, aggressive but hasty.

Olive skin, straight black hair, brown eyes. Seventeen years old.

It wasn't a guess. None of the children recognized individual birthdays. It wouldn't have been allowed even if they'd remembered them. Everyone in the program simply aged up at the start of the new year. Semra had graduated a year early with the class of 4998, so Pidge was two classes behind her but had aged up to seventeen this year at the same time Semra aged up to eighteen.

Pidge was one of the seven assassins pending graduation when Semra stopped the Framatar's coup. Year 5000 was supposed to be Azi's year, a year to usher in a new era, a new reign: himself at the helm of Jannemar. When Semra turned against him, Azi graduated the upcoming class early to send out as many assassins as possible to kill her. Pidge was one of these.

"Well, dragons and daylilies, the famous Semra's lost her voice!" Pidge chortled. She rotated her wrists and stretched her hamstrings before sinking back into an engagement fighting stance. "Thanks for the ride. I thought dragons were fast. Rotokas was. What's wrong with yours? Is it still sick?"

Semra bristled. How many people knew Zezura had been sick? Did they know it was from konnolan?

Pidge launched herself at Semra, and Semra parried the

blow and thrust her glass blade forward before she could process the attack. Pidge dodged, slashed upward, danced inside Semra's guard, and wove out of range as Semra swung.

Semra leaped back and made a mental note to add data on Pidge: *lightning fast.*

The girl was back before Semra could blink, driving forward again and again, Semra blocking, parrying, striking, blocking. Her head screamed at her with every blow. She clocked Pidge on the temple with her elbow and heat exploded from her chest. Semra kicked Pidge in the stomach, and she landed on her rump, but bounced back an instant later with more fervor than before. Semra cursed and twirled the makeshift blade in her fingers. She was better than Pidge. She should have laid her out already.

Pidge dove for Semra's legs, and she felt herself crash to the ground. Her skin crawled with fire. She tried to move her arms, but Pidge pinned her to the ground, and she had no strength left to fight. A knife blade whistled through the air.

A stream of flame lit up the night, illuminating a mass of indigo scales and black talons as Zezura tossed the girl off Semra's chest. The dragon roared and pounced, her claws pressing the assassin into the earth. Pidge screamed.

Semra still lay on her back several paces away, sucking in gulps of air. Her fists curled around two glass blades. She couldn't uncurl them.

Pidge's piercing voice cut through the air.

"Lunatic! Coward! Face me like a man!"

Semra closed her eyes. *Zezura's got her. Focus. Breathe in, breathe out. Breathe in, breathe out.* She willed herself to experience the rise and fall of her stomach, the expansion and contraction of her rib cage with each breath. She needed tonic.

"We're both women, idiot. And you don't want to face me in any capacity."

"Well, I just did, and you were pathetic. You're not okay. Something's wrong with you."

Semra ignored her and rolled to one side and shrugged out of the bag across her back. She dragged it in front of her and dug her hand inside. Oil, cleaning cloths, bread flattened to a pancake. Her wrap skirt and extra tunic, cushioning the tonic vials. Semra withdrew the ball of cloth and started to unwrap it. Something was wet.

She froze. *No, no, no.*

"What's that?" Pidge asked.

Semra glanced up just long enough to confirm Zezura still held her down, then returned to her work. Her temples throbbed and her chest ached. Semra pulled away the last of the fabric and her breath hitched. The bottle was broken, its contents soaked up by the folds of the skirt.

Where was the other one? She propped herself up on one elbow and plunged her hand to the bottom of the bag. Semra's hand brushed a small cylinder, and she seized it. Her fingers shook as she took out the surviving bottle of tonic and fumbled with the cork.

"It's spirits, isn't it? Are you a drunk?"

Semra let a drop hit her tongue and replaced the cork. Terror gripped her belly. She was taking tonic twice as often as she should, and now was left with half as much—with no means to replenish it. She fitted the small bottle snugly into one of the sheaths on her thigh. There was no reason to think it was safe there, but there was no reason to think it was safe anywhere, so at least this way it was on her body and impossible to lose.

Zezura huffed smoke and laid down, folding her front feet over Pidge's body. Pidge craned her neck.

"It's medicine. You're sick. What have you got? Is it—is it contagious?"

Semra stuffed the skirt under her head and sank into it. "Do you ever shut up?"

"Not really."

"I'm not going to be able to move for at least an hour, maybe two. After that, we're going on a ride. Get comfortable, because if you move, I'm going to let Zezura eat you."

Zezura snapped her jaws. Pidge flinched.

"You're going to let her keep me here? How can I sleep with claws on my chest?"

"*I'm* going to sleep. I really couldn't care less whether you sleep."

"Are you going to tell me what's wrong with you?"

Semra groaned. "You tried to kill me. Why would I tell you anything?"

"You could at least tell me if it's contagious, if you're going to force me to stay here."

"Rats and rot, leave it alone! I could have her kill you now if you prefer."

Pidge's lips tugged downward, and she hesitated. There was a slight quiver in her voice when she spoke again. "Sorry."

Semra glared into the darkness. *Are you seriously feeling guilty? She tried to kill you.* Somewhere in her mind, another part of her would not release her conscience. *She's you. Doing what she was trained to do, what she's good at. She doesn't know what else to do.*

And she had information.

Semra swallowed. "Okay, if you want to talk, we'll talk. Tell me who hired you to kill Turian, and I'll tell you if you're going to get sick and die from fighting with me."

"Axis hired me."

Semra pulled out the oil and cloth from her bag to clean

her knives, stared at them, and put them back. No use cleaning glass shards.

"Axis? Why?"

"Is it customary for kings to explain themselves to contractors?"

Good point. Semra grunted. "So you're just going to answer my question outright, simple as that? No tricks, no baiting, nothing?"

Pidge sighed. "Ehh. I know you could torture me, or have beasty do it for you since you're basically an invalid." Semra blanched, but Pidge continued. "I don't care which one of them dies. I just want a good payout to use for a fresh start. There's a price on your head too. Can you imagine the prestige I would get for killing you and Turian in one fell swoop?"

Semra considered this. "What do you mean there's a price on my head? Was the Turian job a bounty or a contract?"

"Contract. You're the one with a bounty."

Good. That meant no one else should be sent for Turian.

Zezura yawned and laid her head down on Pidge's legs. "Oof! Move over, scaleface!"

Semra ran her fingers along the edge of the parchment and wax handle. "What's the required proof? Somebody needs to haul my body back to Belvidore?"

"Severed head."

"Delightful."

"You asked."

Silence stretched between them. Somewhere a cricket chirped.

"Not all of us wanted to kill you, you know," Pidge said. "Back when you beat up Brens and left. Azi said you betrayed us, and sicced us on you, but it didn't make sense. Didn't seem like you. You were always so committed. But then you and Siler killed Brigg, and Behruz, and Manu, and Pinji."

"It's not like I went on a murder spree for kicks. I did kill Manu, but Brens killed Pinji, once she realized I was right about Azi. Manu and Pinji were trying to kill us in the woods outside Qalea, and we tried to explain, but they refused to listen. After Brigg tried to kill us on the plateau, he got hold of Lesala and was going to drag her back to the mountain. What would you have given, not to have this life? To be normal, to have a family? I thought maybe Lesala was the only one of us who still had that chance.

"Behruz threw a spear in my chest. If it weren't for Zezura, I would be dead by his hand. Zezura killed him and healed my wound with the mark of the dragon's kiss." Semra tugged the edge of her tunic down to show the opal-like mark. The stone glittered in her chest under the moonlight, and Pidge gaped at it.

"Blessed by the gods," she whispered. "It's true."

Semra laughed. "Blessed by the gods? A fairytale created by our dear old dragonlord to keep us all entranced by him, obedient. He and I each saved the life of a dragon. They are bound to us, and us only, for as long as we live."

Two hours passed before Semra felt stable enough to ride again. Pidge stole glances her direction, and Semra pretended not to notice. Over the course of those couple of hours, the edge left Pidge's face, and though the fire remained in her eyes, the feel in the air between them had changed. Semra wondered what she was thinking – and why her shoulders dropped, and she seemed to relax into her place under the dragon's weight. Whatever was going on in that head of hers, and whatever had shifted her mood, Pidge still couldn't be trusted not to make a move for the bounty. Semra took Pidge's knives, filled her own sheaths with them, and tossed her homemade glass ones aside. Pidge stretched and stood, grateful to be free for the moment of Zezura's grasp.

"Aren't you going to kill me?" Pidge asked.

Semra arched an eyebrow. "Why in the name of Aurin would I have listened to you ramble if I were only planning on killing you anyway?"

Pidge shrugged. "I'm a good time. Maybe you're lonely."

"If I'm being honest, I should probably kill you. You'll get money for making your way back to kill Turian, and you'll make money for killing me. I obviously don't want either of those things to happen, so I can't let you go. But the longer you're with me, the more chances you have to put my head in a sack."

"I thought I'd use a bucket, to keep the blood from getting all over my stuff."

"Seriously? A bucket? That's going to be bulky and heavy, and you have to carry it. Better to first drain the ..." Semra stopped. Was she giving an assassin tips on how to more conveniently cut off and transport her head?

Pidge grinned.

Semra frowned. "You're just a girl doing the only thing that feels natural. I get it. But if you don't set your heart on some new life aspirations, there is nowhere safe I can leave you."

Something in Pidge's face glowed with expectation, and Semra's eyes narrowed. Pidge stepped forward, and Semra stepped back.

"I could come with you. You could use some muscle."

Whatever the girl had been thinking the last couple of hours had shifted her mood more drastically than Semra had thought. Semra laughed. "You're barely five foot three. You call yourself muscle?"

Pidge crossed her arms. "You were unable to stand for more than a two-minute fight, on easy terrain. Being more reliable muscle than you is not exactly difficult at the moment."

Semra glared at her.

"And you still haven't told me if you're contagious," Pidge added.

Semra waved her off. "Not contagious."

"Good, good. Okay, so what do you need now?"

"To find a very deep hole to drop you in."

Pidge rolled her eyes and tapped her foot. "I mean *information*. I'll give you some if you let me come with you. I know you didn't kill Arnevon. And I know how you can prove it."

15

AVAYA

Avaya stiffened as she followed Axis through the flap of the large tent and resisted the urge to wrinkle her nose. The iron smell of blood mixed with sweat and body odor and a flurry of healers swarmed the sickbay. Somewhere down the row, a grown man screamed as a broken bone was set. Two men carried a gurney across the aisle, its occupant unconscious. His head was wrapped in strips of cloth, and both legs were missing below the knee.

Belvidore still held control over Seddon, and the Surion River now delineated a tense border between the two kingdoms. The temporary setup they'd just entered stood between the Surion Strip and Seddon, just a three-day journey from Madensig Fortress.

A bedraggled man in a battered uniform with bags under his eyes stepped forward and bowed deeply. "Welcome, most glorious King Axis. I am Captain Zoltan. It is my honor to be with you today." Zoltan's gaze flicked nervously from Axis to Avaya. "Princess Avaya, we were not expecting you."

"Thank you for your welcome, captain," Axis said. "My future bride has sworn her allegiance to Belvidore and has sacrificed much to be here with us. She requested to see the damage her father has caused us, and we will not deny her. Our people will soon be her people."

Avaya conjured a sad smile. "I am grateful for your hospitality in these trying times."

Zoltan dipped his head. "As you say, Your Majesty. Thank you, Your Highness. Please, follow me."

"How many are well enough to travel?" Axis asked.

Zoltan led the royal pair down the first of four long rows of injured men and women warriors and spread his hands. "Those well enough to travel have already been relocated to Horen for healing houses with more resources. All that are left are those warriors who require more care before the journey.

"As you can see, Your Majesty, there are many typical battle wounds. But many of our casualties are from our own explosives."

"I imagine most of those were fatalities rather than injuries," Avaya said, raising her voice just a hair. "The way the ground rocked, and bodies flew ..."

"Your Highness was there?" Zoltan asked, his eyes widening.

Axis slipped his arm around Avaya's waist. "She fought her own brother to save my life."

"We are in your debt!" Zoltan said.

Avaya put a hand on Axis's chest. "It was the very least I could do to minimize the damage Jannemar has done." She exchanged a longing look with her new king before examining Zoltan for his reaction. His face softened as he looked at the couple, and she let the tension in her shoulders release. He bought it. She scanned the nearby beds and caught several of the warriors gaping at her. They all bought it.

Zoltan touched his hand to his heart, then returned to Avaya's earlier statement. "Few survived those blasts. When the dragon ignited the accelerant before we had planned, there was nothing we could do. And then there are the burn victims who took direct hits from the dragon's mouth."

Axis nodded. "You did the best you could. Talk to me about the strategy for holding the line, the numbers we have here, and the resources for transporting the injured as they recover."

Avaya laid a hand on Axis's arm. "My love, would you mind if I spent my time talking to the injured while Zoltan gives you the numbers? I am so grateful you thrive in working through the detailed minutiae, but it's all above my head, and my heart is with the people."

Axis smiled and waved her off, and Avaya glided away down the row. She stopped at the foot of one of the beds. Half of the man's face looked as though the skin melted like wax, rippling, sagging, and pulling at the layers beneath. His right forearm and right leg were both missing, their stubs wrapped heavily in gauze, so that from one side he looked perfectly healthy and from the other, hardly recognizable. The man looked up at her and dropped his gaze immediately to the floor.

"Excuse me, sir," she said. "Why do you look away from me?"

The man pulled back in surprise. "I—I'm not easy to look at. You're rather *too* easy to look at. I didn't want to disturb you."

Avaya sat at the edge of the bed and tilted her head. "I came here for the honor of meeting and hearing from our heroes. No scar earned in the service of one's country could ever be ugly."

He lifted his head and met her gaze, and a smile lit up half of his face. The other half hardly moved, and one eyebrow was missing, but the wonder and hopefulness in his expression was unmistakable. Such beautiful puppies, they were. If she could build them up at the right moment, their loyalty would be hers forever.

"What is your name?" she asked.

"Matyas."

"Tell me your story, Matyas."

It took twenty minutes for Matyas to share his story. He spoke haltingly at first, then faster, then the dam burst, and words and tears poured from him in a flood. A woman in the next bed over interjected bits to the story as their experiences of the battle interwove with one another, and as the conversation grew more animated everyone in earshot was glued to the gorgeous princess in velvet who had eyes only for whichever wounded warrior was currently speaking. Two of the healers stopped to listen, and several of the wounded that could walk moved closer.

Matyas explained how he had been on the eastern flank where a line of explosives had nearly hemmed Jannemar in completely, drawn attention from the approaching western force, and secured victory—nearly. The dragon had risen from the dust of the battle and charged through like a hurricane, setting off barrels of explosives long before they were safely positioned.

He had been driving one of the explosive wagons when a wall of flame descended. The dragon's fire would reach them at any moment, lighting the fuse and killing everyone in the immediate radius. But if the horses were galloping full speed, would the dragon be close enough and the fire sustained over the wagon long enough to burn through the barrel without the fuse?

Avaya gasped, oohed, and aah-ed in all the right places, despite the obvious exaggeration depicted in Matyas' series of inhuman stunts to save the day. He had aimed the horses at the Jannemar line, leaped in the back of his own wagon, and covered the fuse with his body as Zezura scorched him with white-hot flame overhead. Somehow the barrels were not eaten through by the fire, despite an inferno consuming the wagon around him. Not only did he single-handedly manage to tumble out of the wagon with the fuse in tow after losing all function of his right arm and leg, but he still managed to kill three Jannemari soldiers before losing consciousness.

Avaya clapped her hands. "A hero among men!"

Half of Matyas' face flushed pink, and his chest puffed out as he propped himself up on his remaining elbow. Avaya begged for more tales of valor, encouraging their bragging, crooning her admiration and praise all the louder for each death-defying feat. The timing of this tour could not have been better.

Two hours passed by the time Axis returned to collect her. He found her surrounded by his people, laughing, and smiling together, the tent abuzz with life and hope. Axis smiled at her. She smiled back. Axis delivered his curated speech, but it was Avaya they were sad to see go when all was said and done.

They left hand in hand, the perfect visual of union and peace. Of battlefield sacrifices not made in vain. Axis squeezed her hand as they exited the tent, and Avaya squeezed back.

News of me will spread. Your wounded are mine. Soon too, your able-bodied. And you will curse my name as the people chant it.

16

———

Pidge's claim to know how to prove Semra's innocence was enticing, but there was no reason to believe it. The bounty on Semra's head was good motivation for Pidge to stick around and look for opportunities to kill her, and the free ride on Zezura toward Belvidore might behoove her also. Still, Semra couldn't pass up the chance to clear her name and protect Zephan and his family from the real threat.

The decision to take the bait and follow Pidge's lead was dangerous for another reason too. It meant delaying her trip to the Rinat and Shafii Rinab, and letting her illness continue untreated and unresearched. Taking Pidge along to the Rinabs was out of the question. Her knowing where they lived would put them at risk, and Semra wasn't willing to take the chance.

Semra swirled the tonic in the vial and frowned. How long would it last her? She took doses as infrequently as she could manage, but even with Zezura pinning Pidge down to sleep each night, Semra needed to be stable enough to fly.

"You need to tell me where we're starting, specifically," Semra said.

Pidge ripped off a piece of cooked rabbit with her teeth

and cocked her head. "What were you planning on eating on this trip, exactly? If you hadn't found me, I mean. Was Zezura going to snatch a whole sheep for you every night?"

Semra pursed her lips. It would have taken her twice as long to go into villages or cities for food in her weakened condition, and she didn't have any money. Hunting with only a few throwing knives was equally challenging. "It's possible you've been mildly helpful. But I still need to know where we're going."

Pidge grinned. "I think you just complimented me. Did you just compliment me?"

"I acknowledged a basic level of utility."

"You're welcome. And not only have I kept you from starvation, but I *also* haven't skinned you alive or brought back any guards or other assassins. I haven't even sought out a quality sack to dump your head into, after you recommended that much more practical approach to your death. Dragons and daylilies, I think I'll help myself to another roll! I've earned it, wouldn't you say?"

Semra brushed the crumbs from her fingers and sat back, watching as Pidge dove into her third roll. She would die before admitting it out loud, but she'd had no plan for feeding herself on the journey. Her only thoughts were to escape the castle. She'd always been able to provide for herself easily enough on the ground, but her mysterious ailment tossed all normalcy out the window.

"Pidge. A location."

"It's been a week already. I definitely could have figured out how to kill you by now. A little appreciation would be nice, is all."

Semra's mouth twitched. "Excellent work going twenty-four hours without killing anyone—under close supervision and threat of dragon. Speaking of dragon, should I let her eat you, or are you going to tell me what I asked?"

"I don't think your beasty even likes the taste of human. It hasn't done any stalking or eager sniffing or any of the creepy stuff Rotokas used to do."

"Zez, do something creepy."

Zezura bobbed her head up and down and huffed a short puff of fire at Pidge's roll. Pidge yelped and dropped it. She glared at Zezura.

"That was a perfectly good roll!"

Zezura chuffed a great dragon laugh and curled all fifty feet of her in a tight ball. Semra folded her arms and waited. Pidge threw her hands up.

"I can't tell you everything, or you won't let me come," she whined. "But I know who found the amulet."

Semra's eyes widened before she could catch herself. She smoothed her expression, but it was too late.

"You didn't think I knew any of this, did you?" Pidge asked, satisfaction thick in her tone. "Maybe it would be easier if you told *me* what *you* know. Badgers don't care for the work of bees."

"Where did you hear that?"

Pidge shrugged. "Lots of commoners say it. I spent some time in Pillerae. The farmers, lumberjacks, herders—they're the backbone of society, doing the foundational work. The rich just profit off them, often destroying half the work when they do. 'Badgers don't care for the work of bees, but they eat the honey just the same.'"

Semra set her jaw. "I'm not a badger."

"You've been holed up in a badger's den. Information flows differently there than it does in the trenches."

Not if you know enough bees, Semra thought to herself. But being a dragonlord and seen either as a hero or, more commonly, a treacherous threat to kingdom security, was isolating. Even the bees went quiet around her. Saeb was a gossip, which served Semra well, and she'd learned news from Garbane too when he was up to it. But she'd been completely cut off since returning from the battle at the Strip. She only knew what the court had allowed her to know—and what the notes under her pillows had hinted at.

Knots tightened in Semra's stomach, and she pulled out the oil and cloth from her bag. Semra laid out the six throwing knives she'd taken from Pidge and examined them.

"You're the one who wants me to keep you around, so you'll be doing the talking."

"Fine, fine. I have a contact—someone inside Madensig. They have proof it wasn't you, and I can get us a meeting."

Hope leaped inside her, but Semra frowned. "And what do they want in exchange for this meeting?"

"Money, I assume. Don't they all?"

"No. Some people prefer to stay poor and live."

"I'm positive this one likes money."

Semra's eyes narrowed. "Is *this one* also you? We get to the place, they don't show, they don't exist, you take me out?"

Pidge rolled her eyes. "I do like money. But I know you don't have any, and I've actually managed to get some in the last months of freedom I've enjoyed. Which is why I'm going to pay my contact a small fee on your behalf and make a few empty promises."

"Why would you do that?"

Pidge plucked at the grass and ripped the fragile green blades. The motion reminded Semra of Zephan, and a pang struck her heart. Pidge's shoulders drooped.

"I don't like my life."

It sounded dangerously close to vulnerability. Semra furrowed her brow. "What are you talking about?"

Pidge shrugged. "I don't like it. My prospects are nil. I can keep doing what I know how to do, looking over my shoulder for the more experienced of us to take me out as their competition. Nobody would miss me. But I can't spend my days as a farmhand either. Not cut out for it. I'm too old to apprentice under someone, and I've no birth or standing to make some wealthy snoot marry me. Nor would I want to, unless he footed the bill for my private mansion and extensive hobbies."

Semra swallowed. Pidge's reason to follow Semra around was precisely the reason Semra had stayed at Shamaran Castle, accepted the task force position, and hung around after it dissolved. That and Zephan. Her stomach flipped, then soured. Semra cocked her head at Pidge.

"You have extensive hobbies?"

"No, but I would if I had a wealthy snoot."

Semra laughed. "I get it. I'm not good for much either. We didn't get much exposure to real life, growing up in the mountain. The Framatar never meant to give us options away from himself."

"You say that, but you live in a castle surrounded by royals who like you."

Semra picked up another knife and ran the cloth along its smooth edge. "I wouldn't say it's that simple."

"Well, they haven't executed you, and they should have. So you're doing something right."

"Pidge ..." Semra ran a hand over her face and sighed. They were only a year apart, but Semra was more experienced, and the age gap seemed much larger. For all her bravado, the look Pidge was giving Semra now pulled at heartstrings she wished she didn't have. *No, heartstrings are good,* something inside her said. *They would've upset Ramas, which is exactly why you should keep them. They make you human.*

Semra took a breath. "This is why I left the mountain. I

didn't betray you. *Azi* betrayed *us.* I left for myself, but I also left to bring him down. Someone had to stop him, or we would have all gone on being his mindless minions forever, being the evil he promised we were fighting. He lied, Pidge. About everything. Did you know my parents came for me? They climbed Mount Hara. Azi slaughtered them and told me they abandoned me. He stole children too young to know better and sent us out to kill and be killed, all for a chance at the throne."

The younger girl picked up a rock and threw it up in the air. She caught it and tossed it again. Zezura knocked it from the air with her tail, but Pidge hardly noticed. She stared into the distance, lost to a secret inner world.

Semra set down the last knife. She winced as a heat wave from inside rocked her body. They felt like burning fevers, but in strong pulses rather than steady pains. They'd started two days ago. Semra wiped sweat from her forehead and dug out her tonic. She took a dose,

"At this rate it'll take us a few more days to get to Horen. I pick the place. You set the meeting."

17

It took a grand total of thirteen days to reach Horen from Qalea. It should have taken less time to travel by dragon than it did, but Semra's frequent needs to rest prolonged the trip. They had opted to fly at night and sleep in daylight, since Zezura had to ascend and descend the skies multiple times in the space of one travel day. Even a color changing dragon could not conceal itself close to the ground.

They landed close to the fringes of the city in the dead of night, slept until first light, and left Zezura in the foothills to head into the city on foot. The first day, Pidge made contact with her source and set up the meet. The second day, Semra sat tapping her foot incessantly under the table in the back corner of a pub called Back Alley Brews.

Pidge kicked her. "Stop it. You're making me nervous."

Semra twirled a coil of hair around her finger and pulled her shoulders back, adjusting her tunic to make sure her slouching wouldn't reveal the opal mark on her chest. "She's late."

"I know what time it is. She'll be here."

Semra smoothed the worn fabric of her wrap skirt and

picked at the stew in front of her. For all her confident airs, Pidge glanced at the door three times in the next minute.

A surge of heat racked her body, and Semra dropped her head in her hands with a low moan. If Pidge was going to turn on her, she picked a good day for it. Searing pain in her chest consumed her attention like a white-hot iron. The sensation radiated throughout her aching body.

It was too soon. She'd already taken two doses of tonic today, and it was only early afternoon.

"We're too close to Madensig."

"I told you, my source is skittish. They live and work at the castle and need someplace nearby. If you thought you were going to get them outside Horen, to some deserted plot with scaleface beasty looking on, you can think again."

Semra grunted. "That's not ...what ..." She let the sentence drop and winced as the throbbing in her head and heat in her chest grew, swayed in her seat, then opened her eyes again as the worst of it passed.

It never completely goes away. Not anymore. She dipped her fingers into her water and ran it over her face. Her sickness was getting worse, and her limited remaining tonic was losing effectiveness against it.

Two men sat in the corner nearby with tankards, and Semra's ears pricked at their words. "They caught one of Turian's spies yesterday. He was executed right there in the throne room."

"Seems impulsive," the second said.

"Watch your tongue, or you'll be next," the first responded. "If he's anything like his father, a sideways glance is enough to get yourself killed, much less an open criticism."

"I don't think it was impulsive. I think it was strong. He's showing he's not afraid to get his hands dirty and do what needs done. King Axis is nothing like his father."

Pidge stiffened beside her. "She's there. She just passed the window."

Semra snapped her head up. "Why didn't she come in?"

Pidge shook her head. "I don't know."

A woman in modest maroon dress passed by the window again, her brimmed hat pulled low over face, and Pidge frowned. "Something's wrong. Stay here."

Pidge slipped from her chair.

"Pidge!" Semra hissed. But it was too late. She was gone.

Semra gripped the table for support as another wave of heat rocked her body, her chest burning, her head swimming. The ache in her bones had ignited into flame, and her heart pounded in her ears. She couldn't stay here. She slung her bag across her back.

Coanor said to keep your heartrate down, she reminded herself. Yeah, right. Semra took a deep breath and willed herself to stand. Her limbs moved like lead through mud. Either Pidge was telling the truth, that really was her source outside, and she'd been spooked—or Pidge was lying, and someone would be coming to kill Semra instantaneously and splitting the bounty with her.

Semra's elbow knocked her cup over as she passed. She lunged to catch it; she couldn't afford to cause a scene. Her hip rammed into the corner of the table, yanking her tunic askew. She stumbled. The cup fell to the floor with a clatter.

The light caught the mark of the dragon's kiss on her chest as she stooped to recover, sparkling a thousand shades of rainbow. For an instant the only thing louder than her clamoring heart was the sound of gasps rippling through the pub.

Swords rang from sheaths in the table next to her, and she bolted for the door. Her knees buckled and she tucked into a roll. Semra ripped a knife from its sheath and knocked a chair over behind her. Enormous boots appeared in front of her, and she twisted to look up at him. A dark beard, round face, and huge fists greeted her. Semra raised her knife from her position on the floor, but the man evaded her thrust, decked the first of the two attackers with a haymaker, and flipped the second man onto a table in the space of thirty seconds.

Semra's feet left the floor and her stomach dropped as an iron grip hauled her up by the throat and shoved her back against the wall. Semra's feet flailed. There was no foothold to relieve the pressure of her bodyweight against her neck. She gagged. No air came.

Semra pulled at his hand with one of hers and wrapped her legs around his waist. The pressure on her neck did not release. Semra slashed upward with her knife, but the man's second hand overpowered hers just as the tip of the blade met his skin. He stripped the knife from her hand with a smoothness that left her reeling.

Was he that good, or was she really so weak?

She fought against every instinct and abandoned the grip on her neck. Semra snatched her skirt up out of the way, plucked two new knives into her hands, and thrust both at her attacker. The man blocked her right-handed attack but dropped his grip on her throat to defend the left; the knife grazed his torso and she crashed to the floor.

Something gripped her ankles, and she slid beneath a new pair of legs. A dagger cut through the air over her head, and chairs and tables bumped and tumbled into each other as bodies arced and danced in and out of range from blow after blow between the two men. The newcomer ducked under a wide swing from the bearded man, and Semra's fevered blood turned to ice.

She knew those storm-gray eyes. Siler, who helped her escape the mountain. Siler, who'd become her closest confidant. Siler, her only support from childhood. And her deepest betrayal when he took Avaya's money and followed her to Belvidore.

Semra winced against the pain in every fiber of her body and struggled to her feet. Her hair matted damp against her face and sweat dripped off her face to the floor. The bearded man slugged Siler in the gut and dove for her. Siler stuck him through the stomach and kicked him backward, but he only grunted and bounced off the wall.

"What are you doing?" Siler screamed. "Go!"

She tried.

Semra fell into a drunken, weaving flight, a knife in each hand, her vision blurring. Feet slapped on wood slats; onlookers screamed obscenities she could not decipher. Three Belvidorian soldiers burst through the entrance to Back Alley Brew just as Semra approached the door.

Pidge appeared and wrenched her beneath a table and out of sight. "Follow me."

Semra's chest heaved and her heart sank. She rested her forehead on the boards between a puddle of spilled beer and a clump of potato stamped into the floor. Maybe if she lay here, just for a moment, they would all leave her alone...

Pidge let out an exasperated puff of air and dragged her by the wrists under two more tables behind the service bar. She pried one of the knives from Semra's hands and threw it. Semra didn't see where it landed, but something heavy rocked the floor.

Somewhere the manager was shouting. The pub was in uproar, and a server slung a pan at a customer across the bar. Pidge disappeared. Semra's eyelids felt heavy. So heavy. Her eyes opened slowly. Siler slid across the floor toward her, dagger stained red, mouth open in a scream.

This was her last shot. Her last ounce of energy. Semra flicked her wrist and the knife in her hand sailed through the air, missing her target by two inches and flying off to unknown chaos beyond.

Siler hoisted her over his shoulder and tore through the pub kitchen and out a back door.

"Did you just try to kill me?"

Maybe. Semra's matted hair swayed about her face as she hung upside down over Siler's back, catching glimpses through dark curls of buildings, trash strewn in the alley, and Pidge tumbling out the door after them. Semra tried and failed to brace herself against Siler's body, her head pounding and body screaming at every jostle and bounce. Three armed men streamed into the narrow space behind them.

"Where's Zezura? We need her *now.*"

"Not...close," Semra wheezed between bounces.

Pidge fended off the fastest of the men with a sword that seemed to have materialized from nowhere. Siler had one arm hooked around the back of Semra's knees, pinning her legs to his chest, and snatched one of Semra's knives from her trousers with his free hand. He spun and released with beautiful accuracy, and the second man fell with the knife in his carotid.

Semra bumped around the bend as Siler dove into a narrow side street and nearly crashed into a wagon full of flour, sugar, and spices outside the backdoor of a bakery. The door was open; the staff would be back out to unload. Siler dumped Semra into the wagon, yanked the top off an apple crate, and emptied the crate on top of her. Apples cascaded in a red and green waterfall, obscuring her vision.

Hands plunged beneath the sea of fruit and traveled to her waist, loosening her skirt and tugging them over her hips and off her body so she lay in the wagon in her signature tunic and trousers. Her chest heaved from exertion and her skin pricked with sweat. She mustered the strength to push the apples off her face just in time for the emptied crate to block out the afternoon sun as Siler turned it upside down on top of her.

"Call Zez. Do it now. Do it *yesterday*. I'll be back for you. Pidge!"

Quick, light footsteps padded up to the wagon and the rustle of fabric told Semra that Pidge was stepping into the skirt and fastening it around herself.

"You're the decoy," Siler said.

Pidge grunted. "Hey!"

"More are coming. I'll put you down in a minute and circle back for Semra. Run hard. Meet us on the roof of Silver Glory in an hour."

Running footsteps took Siler and Pidge further and further away. Ten seconds later several more sets of heavy footfalls ran by. Someone ricocheted off the corner of the wagon as they ran by, and Semra winced as the wagon rocked.

And then she was alone.

Semra closed her eyes. Her fever was back. Her breaths came ragged, her limbs weak, her chest burning fire. She needed tonic. She'd needed it at the pub, but it had been too soon for a dose, and she had hoped to wait until after meeting Pidge's source. Her pack was still on her back, a canteen jutting through the bag into her ribs as she lay curled in a ball under the apple crate. Apples littered her torso, and one had rolled halfway under an arm and gotten pinned against the box. Semra didn't have the will to move it.

She felt for Zezura. *Where are you?*

Sun beat down on smooth scales, and the long dragon body flattened against the heat of the rocky crag. Mountainous clefts and plateaus were preferred, but foothills would do, in a pinch. Wind whipped against her nostrils, and she lifted her head. Color exploded in Semra's vision, but the shades were wrong. Horen stretched before her, the Surion

River winding down from the mountains on the east, around Madensig Fortress's moat, and off toward Seddon and the Surion Strip. She blinked and flicked out her tongue. Something inside called to her, a small beloved little tug. Distress. Semra was in trouble. A surge of tingling heat filled her dragon chest, and she opened her mouth and let loose a soundless pulse. The mark of the dragon's kiss on her lord's chest answered like a beacon. Her location was locked, and the pulse would only grow stronger as she homed in on her. Zezura unfurled her wings and took to the air.

Semra gasped and lurched back into her own body. Her eyes snapped open, but all she could see through the cracks of the box were the slats of the rough wooden crate, and the red and green apples pooled around her in the wagon. Semra squeezed her eyes tight, then opened them again. Wood crate and apples.

How had she just seen Zezura?

The mark on Semra's chest tingled warm—a mild sensation amid the chaos racking her body. Semra felt herself fading. Someone was screaming from the direction of the bakery.

"Ruffians! I have a business to run! Did you see who busted the crate?"

"Soldiers, Papa. There's nothing we can do."

There was a dragging sound as one of the sacks was pulled off the wagon. The crate over Semra lifted, and a grown man squealed in shock. She grimaced in the light. Her fingers twitched on her knife blade, then fell useless at her sides as dizziness swept through her. But this time it didn't stop there. It knocked her into unconsciousness.

18

"She's drunk. I've had the hardest time keeping her home when she gets like this."

Semra's lids fluttered. Siler stood with the baker and his son in the back room of the establishment. Semra was on the floor, half-propped against a wall.

"She looks unwell. We should get her a healer."

"Oh, we have a healer. He's been with our family for twenty years. I'll get her where she needs to go."

"She still ruined our crate."

Semra groaned. Siler lifted her up, but she leaned heavy on his arm. Her eyelids drooped and her body sagged. Heat boiled her blood. Her eyes glazed over, and she collapsed. Nothing mattered now. Nothing but the raging inferno inside.

"Almost all the apples are still usable, and you're going to throw out the crate anyway."

"She looks familiar. Why do I know her face?"

"Just one of those faces. Look, I'd appreciate it if you didn't tell anyone about this. Our parents would die if they heard she'd embarrassed us again."

The world went black.

"Wake up. I need your help, Semra. I need you to climb."

The voice filtered into her consciousness through red-hot steam, a fog clouding her mind and filling her body with pain. Her vision swam and she squinted out into the light. Her pinpricking, sweat-smothered skin sent no signal to her brain that his arms were around her, but now she saw he cradled her against his chest. They stood in another alley, behind an inn with a silver goblet on a signpost at the back-door. The only foothold options in the alley were a barrel and a broken vase, so the only way up to the roof would be …

Semra shut her eyes again. Siler thought she could suspend her entire weight on her arms and legs and scale a wall to a roof? She would rather die.

Maybe she would.

"Can you stand at all?"

Semra ignored him. Speaking would be too much effort.

"Did you call Zezura?"

Had she? Vaguely she remembered doing so. Was that today? Did it even happen? She had seen through the dragon's eyes. It made no sense. Was it a dream?

"You're on wanted signs all over Horen. The city is alive with hunters, and now that you got yourself seen at Back Alley Brew, half the world is out looking for you. We have to get off the street."

Semra's head lolled back against his arm, and she stared up at him. Her empty eyes connected wearily with his urgent gray ones. "It's okay," she mumbled. Her lips were parched, and she rested two more slow breaths before speaking again. "Take the bounty."

Siler cursed. "Idiot. I'm not taking the bounty. But we need your dragon, or we're both going to die. What happened to you?"

"Tonic," Semra slurred. "Need. Tonic." She closed her eyes. Fire consumed her bones, and a scream filled her mind, trapped in the space between forming the sound and releasing it out the mouth. She was silent.

"What are you talking about? What tonic?"

Something crashed inside the inn, and a bellowing voice rose above the din. "I told you, I haven't seen any girl like that. Get out!"

A dark shadow blocked out the afternoon sun overhead and the alley dimmed. Siler adjusted his grip on Semra and swore again. "Our ride is here, but we'll never get out in time. The alley is too tall and narrow for Zez to fit."

Zezura did another pass, and the beast's anxiety seeped into Semra's chest. For an instant, Semra felt as though she were in the air. The colors were all wrong again, with new shades that Semra had ever imagined existed. The mark of the dragon's kiss pulled at Zez, shining like a beacon through Semra's tunic down below, radiating a pulse for the dragon alone.

A man held Semra in a narrow alley surrounded by cobbled streets, shops, and houses. The dragon recognized his frame and huffed her annoyance. He'd been both friend and enemy. Untrustworthy. But her lord did not look able to ride on her own, so she would have to tolerate him. A weather eye and a flame from her reptilian throat would keep him in check.

Seven men crashed through the door of the large building north of the beacon. Five split off to the east, and two to the west. Zezura circled and did another pass. The east was too narrow; the best she could do there was spew fire down on them from above. The west opened up to a small square.

Semra gasped as her vision and consciousness snapped back to her own body. "West," she rasped. "Move west. Two men. Five coming from the east. No time."

Siler gaped at her only for a second, then pivoted and ran west. Siler and Semra spilled into the alley and pulled up sharp as two men with drawn swords sprinted toward them. Zezura landed in the square between the two parties, unfurled her wings, and roared. The men fell back, one sword clattering to the cobbles, another raised in defense; Siler ran to Zezura and planted a foot on the spines along her side. He hoisted Semra up in front of him and climbed on behind her.

"Go, go, go!" Siler yelled.

Semra furrowed her brow and glanced to her right and left. "Where's Pidge?"

"Doesn't matter. She's a big girl. Go!"

Semra's stomach churned as Zezura lifted into the air, and Siler slung an arm hard around the waist to catch her as her weight shifted sideways. "No, no ... you said ... meet on roof," Semra managed. "She expects ... we need to bring her."

"Don't be ridiculous," Siler snapped. "I don't know what's wrong with you, but by the looks of it, you could die any second. We don't have time."

Semra lurched as the dragon dropped into an air current. "No! She's Lesala!"

It was the only way she could think to make him understand. Lesala, the four-year-old Siler had helped Semra rescue from the mountain when they escaped. Innocent, small, undeserving of the lot she'd been kidnapped for. A girl on the precipice of a bleak life, with hopes of a brighter future. One nudge was all it would take to push her over the edge.

Zezura arced to one side, ignoring Siler's directions, and bending to Semra's will. Siler slammed his hand down on

Zezura's hard scales, then wrung his hand. "We don't even know where she is!"

Zezura dropped altitude and circled back over Silver Glory. Semra felt the change, the dragon's muscles gather, her angle shift, as she zeroed in on a target. They landed on a rooftop two buildings down where Pidge was just pulling herself up.

"Aurin's spear," Siler said. "Good eye, Zez."

Semra relaxed back into the pool of flame as Siler reached a hand down and pulled Pidge up behind them. "Tonic," she mumbled again at Pidge.

"Dragons and daylilies, haven't you had any?" Pidge exclaimed. She reached around Siler to pat down the sheaths of Semra's legs. "Rats and rot, it's gone. You haven't got any."

Semra moaned. She felt worse now than she had when Zephan first brought her back to the castle. At this rate, she'd be dead by morning.

"What's this tonic? What's wrong with her?" Siler asked.

"I don't know exactly. From what she's told me, it's some unknown illness or poison, and the Shamaran's healer cooked up a tonic so she could function through it. It seems to hit her in waves, and when she's on the tonic it's not so bad, but it's been getting worse even when she takes it."

Zezura launched into the air and Pidge yelped. "What do we do now?" she asked.

Semra shut her eyes. "Camar." She was out of time—she had no choice.

"Camar?" Siler sucked in a breath. "Oh, you don't know. The Rinabs moved to a small town in nowheresville in the foothills by Seddon a few months back."

Semra's stomach flopped. They'd nearly wasted precious time traveling to Camar only to find themselves back to square one with nowhere to go. But it wasn't the brightest decision to move toward Belvidore in such unstable times. She sank back against Siler as the wind started to pick up. "Stupid," she managed. "On border."

"He's on the northern side of the river, and armies can't travel the mountain quickly, so I think Shafii felt like he had good natural barriers. It's easy for a healer to find work in war, and I think he wanted to be a part of the effort somehow."

How did Siler know the Rinabs had moved? Had he been keeping tabs on them? Of course, hardly anyone knew the truth about the children of the mountain, and they knew more than most. That put them in danger, either to be extorted for healing by injured assassins or to be exterminated for their knowledge.

Azi had sent assassins to burn down their home in Ryden when Siler, Semra, and Lesala had stayed the night last year in their escape from Mount Hara. That was back when Semra first met Zephan, known to them then as Shafii's apprentice Dahyu. The fires had successfully smoked them out, but Semra, Siler, and Dahyu had escaped on Zezura. Shafii and Tinat Rinab had taken four-year-old Lesala with them on horseback to Camar, in hopes of staying safe off the grid. Maybe it hadn't been as safe as they'd hoped.

Horen dropped away beneath them, and Semra tried to focus on the way the air blew her hair back and wicked the sweat from her skin. Her cold clammy exterior was a welcome contrast to the raging furnace inside. The easy, mission-focused communication and rhythm of the ride almost made Semra feel like they were riding for Qalea those months ago, instead of toward Seddon.

Except Pidge filled Zephan's position as their third passenger. A deep pang struck Semra's heart. Siler's arms around her were strong, but a far cry from the comforting haven Zephan had become to her. She wondered what Zephan was doing now, and how angry he had been when Aviama told him what had happened. Would he ever forgive her? Would it matter, if she never saw him again? And, of course, Siler had betrayed her, chased her down, and watched her be beaten in Belvidore. What was his angle now?

Not that it mattered. She would never have made it without him. And no matter how much he loved money, so far, he'd been more interested in stopping or restraining her than killing her—pushing her off his path to no longer be an obstacle. Semra wondered what secret mission she had interrupted at Back Alley Brew, and if he'd ever tell her.

Alarm bells rang somewhere in her mind, muted by fever, diminished by fatigue, but calling out in a small voice. What if the Rinabs hadn't moved at all? It seemed convenient, didn't it, that Pidge's source was little more than a fast-walking woman with a hat who never showed. Convenient that Pidge left the pub, and Siler entered moments later, following a slew of soldiers and other killers. The large, bearded man fought like an assassin, not a soldier. She hadn't recognized him. Could he be one of Azi's sleepers?

Had Pidge and Siler agreed to split the bounty? Perhaps this time, the money was too great a temptation ...

Or would Siler kill them both and take it all?

The rush of wind, the gentle bend and sway of the dragon, lulled her away from her fears and pulled her into sleep. But even in her dreams, she was on fire. On fire in the house in Ryden, on fire tied to the stake in the Belvidorian tournament, on fire as Ramas' venomous snakes sank their fangs deep into her flesh.

Slowly, every other sense melted away before the heat of the flame. Soon there was no house, no stake, no serpent. Nothing existed in her fitful waking and sleeping but an all-consuming fire. It swallowed her whole.

19

"Bloodletting is my last resort. To be frank, I rarely see any positive effect. But this illness doesn't act like anything I've ever seen."

"Is she going to make it?"

"If you had asked me that last night, I would say no. I would say she wouldn't make it until morning. And yet, here she is."

Semra tried to place the voices. One was mature, soft, and confident. Had they made it to Seddon already? Her chest tightened. She had been in and out at Coanor's for nearly two weeks before coming around. How long had she been out this time?

"Could it be from the konnolan poisoning?" Familiar. Problem-solving. Siler.

"Didn't you say that was weeks ago?" Shafii asked.

Siler paused. "A month, I'd guess."

"Konnolan debilitates magical essence. Because a portion of a dragon's makeup is magical at the granular level, it impacted Zezura's system. She shouldn't have been impacted at all, unless ... well, either way, she started getting better after the initial encounter with konnolan. So there is something else at play."

"And it's not poison. By now she would be recovered or dead, but not hovering in this state."

"Correct."

Semra stirred. Her head throbbed, her muscles screamed, and she was weak as a feather, but some of the heat had dissipated. She furrowed her brow and parted dry lips. "Shafii?" Her eyes opened and Shafii Rinab came into focus in the early morning light spilling through the window. The man was in his late fifties, with more gray hair than brown, and wrinkles at his forehead, eyes, and mouth that had deepened since last she'd last seen him. He jumped at the sound of her voice, then leaned forward on the tree stump he was using for a stool.

"That's been my name, as long as I've had one." Shafii smiled. "Welcome back."

"Semra!" Siler pushed off the doorframe where he'd been leaning and crossed to the foot of the bed. "How are you feeling?"

Semra cleared her throat, and Shafii held a wood cup to her lips. She drank every drop, then turned to Siler. "A little better, I think. I think maybe I can think straight, so that's nice."

Siler smirked. "Good. Maybe we won't hear any more senseless ramblings."

Semra bolted upright. Her head felt like it might split in two, and she winced. "Ramblings?"

Shafii waved her off. "It's a good thing Siler found you. You would have lost days of travel going to Camar, and still not known where to find us. I'd sent word to the king about the move, since Prince Zephan wanted to keep up with us after Ryden, but I guess you didn't have much chance to hear the news when you got back to the castle from the battlefront."

Semra frowned. How did Shafii know what had happened to her after the battlefront? Siler had still been in Belvidore, and Pidge hadn't been there. But another question rose to the forefront of her mind. "The source ... Pidge's source. Is she real? We need her testimony."

Siler crossed his arms. "She's real. Pidge has talked about nothing else since we got here, and we got here the night before last. She ran out of the pub and caught up with her, but the source was paid off—to draw you out and disappear. The source got spooked when she saw your face through the window, and guards on duty just outside. Your face is plastered on wanted posters all over Horen."

"So she doesn't have any real proof of my innocence? Does she have any evidence at all? Who knew I would be there?"

"I don't think they knew for sure, but somebody must have guessed you'd be by," Siler said. "Or that someone would be by on your behalf. When Pidge reached out to set up the meet, the game was up. You were doomed from the start. She did have some real information though. Pidge would kill me if I told you, so I'll let her do the honors. She's in town following up some leads on dragonlord research."

"But we need a plan. We need to get back to Belvidore and find a way to get people to talk. And we don't even know who knows things—*who* to get to talk. We've got nothing."

"Slow down," Shafii said. "Let's make sure your physical body survives this illness first. We'll work on your reputation later."

Semra gritted her teeth. It was about so much more than her reputation. "I need that proof. And we need more. More than one woman's conjecture."

"You're going to be fine," Siler said. "Calm down. Just heal up first."

"If I don't clear my name, Jannemar will be forced into a

standing kill order for me. I'll essentially be banished. They won't ever look for the real killer, so the Shamarans will be in danger once again."

Siler crossed his arms. "They're royals, Semra. Risk is a part of the job. If we don't figure out a cure, you'll die, and who killed who won't matter."

Semra bit her lip and stared down at her lap. She picked at the blanket. "Everyone will think I assassinated King Arnevon."

"I'll be sure to write your tombstone. *'Semra, no last name. Lived from year 4982 to 5000. Killed lots of people, but not King Arnevon of Belvidore.'*"

Semra glared at him. "Was it you?"

Siler pressed his lips in a tight line. "I'm touched. It was fine work, and you're right to think it was one of us. But no."

One of us. Would she never be free of the mountain?

"It's not like I don't have good reason to suspect you."

Shafii glanced between them and poured Semra another glass of water. She ignored it, despite her dry throat. Siler arched an eyebrow.

"You mean the occupational specialty we share?"

Semra's heartrate jumped, and the throbbing in her head returned with a vengeance. She had to push through it. She had to say this. "I'm not a sell-out. You went to the biggest purse strings you could find and abandoned Jannemar and any sense of decency. You have no loyalty."

"Loyalty!" Siler loomed over her, leaning on the bed. "Loyalty to whom or what, exactly? To the evil dragonlord that turned us into the monsters we are, or the latest monarch in a centuries-old tradition of squabbling over power and land? Squabbles, I might add, that are fought with the same currency as the Framatar ... blood and money."

Semra's lip curled. "Tell me, did you tap your wrist before

dragging me into the arena in the tournament? Or perhaps when you threw me into that pit beneath Madensig where you watched Axis's goon beat me? You know the gesture. The two taps you make with these two fingers on your left wrist, for luck before missions. Was I a mission to you?"

"Did you ever consider, for a single second, what I might be giving up to be here right now? How at every turn, you show up while I'm trying to work, and I have to drop everything to keep you alive? And I do mean *everything*. Because you can't do things halfway. And you insist on sticking your nose into every possible crevice, whether or not in belongs there. If you think I enjoyed seeing you beaten, or watching you scream on that pyre, you don't know me at all."

Semra gaped at him. Her chest caved in, and her blood boiled as guilt and rage fought for prominence. Hot tears welled in her eyes, and she glared into the corner of the room. The rough-hewn table and trunk in the corner tilted as the room began to spin. She slipped a hand down to the mattress to stabilize herself and shut her eyes.

"I think that's enough excitement for now," Shafii said. His voice was even, gentle but firm. "The bloodletting seems to have helped, but we can't afford to do it over and over, and her temperature is climbing again. Siler, why don't you go see if Tinat needs help with dinner while we wait for the others to come back."

Semra opened her eyes but did not look at Siler. She felt his cool stare, but at last he turned to the door. At the last moment, he turned.

"You've always been a better person than me. But don't lie to yourself, Semra. Proving your innocence isn't some noble effort to save a kingdom. You don't care about your reputation in Jannemar, about 'everyone' thinking you assassinated Arnevon. You only care about princey. And if you really want him so badly, just ask yourself one thing. Does he know you? Because if he does, you won't have to prove you're innocent. And if he doesn't, no amount of evidence will convince him of the truth."

Siler disappeared and hot tears trailed down Semra's cheeks. She didn't mean to make Siler feel like a bad person. It was just that she knew he was better than this, better than the traitorous actions she'd seen of him. She hadn't thought about the fact that, as exasperating as it was for her to run into Siler while trying to save Avaya, it was equally as distressing for Siler. But he shouldn't have been in those situations to begin with!

Was he right? Did she only care about Zephan's opinion, the man she could never have? The man she'd run from, again and again, when he asked her to stay. The man who flirted when he knew it could only end in hurt.

Images of Zephan flooded her mind. He was fighting back-to-back with her in the throne room, covering her body with his in the face of Azi's black dragon, dancing with her in the loft of Madensig's stables. Carrying her to Coanor. Asking her to stay in Jannemar.

Garbane's gruff face filed in next, and Aviama stuffing her wardrobe with ruffles and silks. Even Saeb. King Turian, who had shown her that not all kings were evil. No, it wasn't just Zephan.

But Zephan would always be the first name coming to her mind. His piercing amber eyes, and the memory of his lips on hers, were as inescapable as the blood on her assassin's hands. They were like a fading tide, a wave upon the sand, doomed forever to be pulled away. The sands belonged to the sun, but the ocean was ruled by the moon.

Even their kiss had only come about during a mission, to explain their presence outside the arena in Belvidore. Semra hadn't dared tell anyone, and Firfell wasn't the only one who had expressed distaste for her closeness with the prince. It was stupid to hold on to. But she couldn't shake it.

And she wasn't sure she would give it up if she could.

"I've got water here for you whenever you feel up to it," Shafii said. "It would do you good. And … well, it's none of my business, but for what it's worth, Siler tipped us off that some of the assassins knew our location in Camar. He had connections near here and helped us get settled."

Hot tears ran down Semra's face. Shafii pressed her back down into the pillows and laid a cool compress on her forehead. "People are complex, but they're also simple. A person is more than their past. That doesn't excuse their actions. But we can't be defined by them, or the past we fear will swallow us forever.

"You could have left us in our house to burn, but you didn't. You have a drive to help people. That's not what you've *done*. That's who you *are*. Looking into the black pit of our past and having someone else look into it with us and truly see our humanity somewhere in that muck —well, those moments have the power to sway us. We can stay in that mire, cycling through paralyzing self-punishment, or we can launch toward something new. Grow to something better.

"When we talk to people, we push them one way or another. And when we listen to people, we accept one voice over another. Speak in a way that frees. And listen to voices that push you along rather than tie you down."

Shafii patted her arm and slipped out the door. At the *click* of the latch Semra was alone, and the floodgates opened. Sobs racked her body. She rolled onto her side on the bed and clutched her knees to her chest. Her body ached, and deep pain seared her through at every sharp movement of her stomach and shoulders as she wept. The dizziness returned, and she hardly noticed when the compress fell from her fore-head to the floor.

She didn't know how long she lay there. She thought of Siler fighting on the plateau of the mountain, giving Semra a chance to escape with Lesala. She thought of him dragging her into the Tabeun Tournament arena over a month ago, but then saving her life and the two of them fighting their way out of Madensig together. For all his mercenary ethics, Siler *had* protected her, in his way. And she chose the moment when he'd saved her life yet again, to accuse him of betrayal.

Unbidden, Zephan filled her mind. His kind, handsome face, soft lips, defined chin, strong arms. He was holding her tight in her chambers at Shamaran Castle, right before he threw the crystal glass. Dancing with her in the woods. Catching her as she leaped off the explosives wagon and carrying her off the battlefield.

What is it he had told her once? *I think you are remarkable ... brilliant ... and stunningly beautiful. You do have a good heart. And I won't be going anywhere anytime soon.* Those amber eyes. Would they ever look at her as tenderly as she saw them now?

"Forgive me," she whispered. "Forgive me."

"For what?"

Semra snapped her eyes open. Zephan sat at her bedside in the flesh, crushing coriander seeds with mortar and pestle.

20

Semra shut her eyes again. Zephan couldn't really be sitting with her. She scanned her body for symptoms. Her head still throbbed, her insides still burned, her body still felt weak. Her mind felt hazy and muddled.

She tried again, opening one eye at a time. There he was. Only, he looked more like Dahyu than Prince Zephan. A thin rough spun beige tunic adorned his muscled chest and shoulders, and she stared just a moment too long before noticing the dirty brown trousers. He must be borrowing Shafii's clothes. Semra frowned.

"Disappointed to see me?" Zephan mixed the coriander powder into a cup of hot water and set it down on the table beside him.

"Maybe if you were real, I wouldn't have to be disappointed," she mumbled.

"I'm not real?"

"No."

"Wow. Well, then, my schedule has really opened up."

Semra's eyes narrowed. The fog in her brain began to lift, and she pursed her lips. Had she been sleeping?

She wiped lingering tears from her face and propped herself up on an elbow with a soft groan. How long would her body punish her for every movement? "How are you ... how are ..."

Semra's voice cracked, and she stopped. *How are you here?* Zephan would have had to set out almost immediately from the castle after she left, traveling on horseback, to make it here by now. He would have had to make a beeline for whatever "nowheresville" town they had found themselves in outside of Seddon. It didn't make sense.

Fresh tears traced rivulets down her face. Semra's stomach turned into sour knots, and caged, anxious butterflies materialized in her gut. She shifted under the blanket, glanced at Zephan's face, then stared down at her fingers. The last time they spoke, she swore she was innocent, and he told her he'd have to keep his distance for the sake of the court while she healed. Zephan wanted her to trust him and Coanor. And then she'd fled without a word. Her chest tightened and she swallowed against the lump in her throat.

Zephan cleared his throat. "I wish you could have come to me first."

"You know I couldn't. It would only have made things worse."

He shrugged. "Maybe. But you keep making decisions on your own."

"Not completely. I had help getting out." Semra bit her lip. A flash of heat rolled through her, and she fell back into the pillow. The world began to tumble, and she forced her eyes to stay open, fixed on Zephan's face. "I didn't do it," she whispered. "I didn't, I didn't. Please."

Zephan shook his head and reached for her hand, then snatched it back and stared at her. Had she offended him?

"Are you here to take me away? Where are the guards?"

"No guards. I'm technically with the army at Kinlock. I do hope I'm doing a good job there. Erm, I think it's time to check in with Shafii. Pidge and the others are back as well, so we might as well have a meeting."

Zephan disappeared and five minutes later a whole troop walked in—Shafii, his wife Tinat, Siler, Zephan, Pidge, and two young children. One was a boy of about twelve, and Semra didn't recognize him; the second was maybe five years old and her blue eyes lit up the second she crossed the threshold.

"Semra!"

The little girl flounced into the room and flung her arms around Semra.

"Lesala?" Semra struggled to free herself from the blankets, but Tinat tugged her off Semra before she could give a proper hug.

"Remember, she's sick," Tinat said. "Keep some distance, dear."

Lesala hopped on one foot and then the other and dropped a small object into Semra's palm. A little straw doll in a green dress stared up at her.

"I made it for you! Mama Tinat said we could come visit after the war was over, but then you came here instead!"

Semra grinned and smoothed the brown strips of cotton hair back from the doll's face. "It's beautiful! Just like you. It's so good to see you."

Lesala beamed and danced around the room. Giving her to Shafii and Tinat was the right decision. They had tried to find her real parents, but to no avail, and the little girl was flourishing here. She was a little girl with a family, who danced and laughed and played with toys. Exactly the childhood Semra had hoped to give her, one she herself had never had.

Semra glanced back down at the doll. Was the dress singed before? Semra touched her hand to her face. It was hot, but so was every part of her. She could no longer tell what was hot and cold. Anything outside the furnace of her body felt cold. She dropped the doll into her lap and stuffed her hands under the blanket. Tinat whispered to the two children, and they scampered out.

Shafii ushered Zephan toward the stump to sit, but Zephan insisted, and the older man took the seat. Tinat perched on the edge of Semra's bed, and Siler, Pidge, and Zephan sat on the floor against the wall.

Tinat smiled at Semra. "It's good to see you."

A soft warmth filled Semra's chest. "You too."

What would it have been like to have a mother? An ache Semra hardly remembered she had pulled itself from the depths of her soul, and she looked away. They had business to attend to. She could blubber about her tragic life later.

Shafii scooped the fallen compress off the floor and pressed a fresh cloth against her forehead. His hands lingered on her forehead for a moment, and the lines of his face deepened. Something was wrong. But the next moment, Shafii straightened and clapped his hands.

"Well, then. The way I see it, we have three matters to discuss: our best guess as to what is happening to our Semra, how to keep her from getting arrested, and plans to clear her name."

Our Semra. Semra sniffed and all heads swiveled her direction. She pressed her lips together.

"I'm sick. I'm allowed to sniffle."

The corner of Zephan's mouth turned up. Was he harboring any bitterness, or did he really feel as normal as he seemed?

"The first order of business is one I will attempt to cover,"

Shafii began. "We have ruled out konnolan as the sole cause of this illness, but after speaking to both Siler and Zephan, and piecing together a decently tight timeline, it seems that it did have some effect. In addition, we believe the snake Ramas used to try to kill you, Semra, was the Syanor viper. Typical progression is total physical paralysis within seconds, and death within two minutes. Not only did you survive, but you were able to overpower Ramas quickly afterward."

Shafii paused and turned to Semra. "You are absolutely *certain* that you were bitten? And the mark of the dragon's kiss expanded at that moment?"

Semra shuddered, remembering. She nodded. "It slithered up my back and bit me beneath the collarbone. The mark didn't use to extend up that high, but it does now, so there's no scar."

"And how quickly were you able to move?"

"I couldn't breathe. I couldn't move. And then I felt hot, all over, like…" Semra stopped. *Like the fire she felt now, all consolidated into a single moment of agony.* "Like white-hot fire."

"If you would. We are all friends here. What did you do next? I want to gauge physical ability at that point to ensure I am not wrong in my assessment."

"The paralysis just sort of lifted, all of a sudden. I chased Ramas out of my cell, knocked him to the ground, and put him in a choke from behind. The lid to the basket of snakes got knocked off, and one of them came out…I grabbed it behind the head, struck him with it and it bit him, fought my way out of the dungeon, and that's when I got caught and dragged in to see General Gresvig. Zezura crashed through the window, and I made my escape."

There was a beat of silence as her words settled over them. Tinat's eyes bulged, and Pidge's jaw dropped. Shafii cleared his throat.

"Mhmm. Right. Okay, well then. You demonstrated unprecedented, complete recovery in the space of about a minute after paralysis set in. You exhibited immediate superb muscle strength, gross and fine motor control, and general physical ability at this point. The only explanation is the dragon's kiss, and this theory is further supported by the way the mark spread at that moment in time.

"As grateful as we are that these events occurred and you survived, these events are unprecedented. I have done some research on dragonlords since you waltzed into our lives in Ryden, and in the limited resources available to me, I have never heard of a dragonlord's mark changing or expanding. The bite occurred close to the mark itself, so it's possible that played a role. Additionally, dragons are immune to venom, so it seems that immunity was bound up somehow in the dragon's kiss.

"My greatest guess, and it is, at best, exactly that, is that somehow when the dragon's kiss expanded to absorb the Syanor venom, the mark was broken up and its makeup escaped into the bloodstream. I am unsure why it remained dormant until the konnolan, but the konnolan kickstarted something else inside of you, and I believe that something has been in your blood since the viper. Something that has not existed in humans since before The Crumbling."

Semra's stomach flopped, and her heart beat faster.

"So what are you saying, exactly?" Pidge asked. "She's part dragon?"

"Not exactly. Dragons are one of the few species in the world that retained magical essence after The Crumbling. I think when the Syanor venom caused the dragon's kiss to expand, the magic within it leaked into her bloodstream and its power flows in Semra's veins. That is why she got sick with the konnolan – because konnolan deadens or dims magical essence, and Semra's makeup now includes some measure of magic. But Zezura recovered.

"Semra started to recover, and then took a turn for the worse. I think perhaps she recovered from the konnolan itself, but somehow the magic in her blood—well, it woke up, as it were. It's not like the elemental magic of the melders, because it's more like the dragon's magic. Which means we have absolutely no clue what progression this sickness will take, and because all human magic died in The Crumbling, we have nothing with which to fight it."

Siler ran a hand over his face. Zephan stared at Shafii, but his face was blank. Semra blinked. Realization filtered over her. "I'm doomed, then. There's no reason to believe my human body can survive the dragon's magic once it takes hold."

"But what about the tonic? It was helping. Can't we make more?" Siler asked.

Shafii sighed. "Coanor is a genius. I don't know how she did it, but the tonic she developed somehow slowed the transformation. But the power of the magic was stronger than the tonic, which is why the tonic became less and less effective, even as Semra took it more and more often. Even if we knew how to make more, it would only be a matter of time."

"There's no reason to believe she can survive whatever the magic is doing to her, but there's also no reason to believe she can't," Zephan said. "So we need a plan. We need to take what we know and give her the best chance possible."

Semra rested her head on the pillow and stared at her fingers. Was the heat she'd felt that day on the dungeon floor the same heat that plagued her now? Did magic really course through her? Ancient, powerful dragon magic. Magic too potent to contain, and potentially too strong to survive.

"I think our cottage is as comfortable and hidden away as

anywhere else you could go," Tinat said. "There are wanted signs all over Seddon, so traveling anywhere populated isn't a good idea. And Semra isn't in a condition to travel."

"There are wanted signs on both sides of the border," Pidge said. "Soldiers of either kingdom would gladly take her if she's found."

Zephan passed a hand over his face. "The court forced my father's hand. Soldiers have been sent out to look for Semra, with permission to kill if capture is not possible. He did allow one concession—Semra can turn herself in and be held in the dungeons awaiting the conclusion of the investigation into Arnevon's assassination. But the investigation has stalled since Belvidore is not cooperating and we've lost communication with several of our spies."

"Someone at the pub in Belvidore said they just executed another Jannemari spy," Semra said. "They're probably all dead, or in hiding. And with the threats I got while in the castle, I am not keen to trap myself there again. Even if I was up for travel, but like Tinat said, I'm not. I get dizzy just sitting up."

Siler grimaced. "The notes were from me. The ones telling you to get out of the castle. Did you like my poetry?"

Semra jolted up, then cursed and lowered herself back into the pillow. She *had* to stop doing that. "I knew it! But you were in Belvidore. How did you ..."

Siler grinned. "I can't share all my secrets. But I knew you were going to be stupid and try to stay there, and that princey would try to keep you in that kill box. You didn't know the bounty had gone out on you. Every assassin in our network knows they'll get a nice payday to start their new life if they bring you down."

Zephan's eyes narrowed. "Axis?"

Siler shook his head. "I heard the first threats as early as three weeks ago. Some of our old colleagues are still angry about Semra's supposed betrayal, and the payout only sweetened the deal. Axis's money is behind the bounty, but two weeks ago it was Avaya who asked me to kill Semra. As a personal favor." His lip curled. "You've got a delightful family, princey boy."

Zephan's face darkened. "Stop calling me that."

"I didn't know Her Highness was so ... erm, well, that she felt that way," Tinat said. She grimaced and put a hand to her lips, as if reminding herself not to say anything so condemning of the Shamarans.

"We can stop calling Avaya that too," Zephan said. He clenched his jaw. "She doesn't deserve the title."

Shafii turned to Pidge. "What did you and our little Voran learn?"

Pidge brightened. "Voran is a fabulous little sneak. We got all the best gossip twelve hours could buy and pieced it together with what Siler and I have heard in Belvidore. They say Axis and Arnevon had a big fight after the battle. Arnevon couldn't sleep and went on a carriage ride in the middle of the night and gorged himself on a huge brunch the next morning. A lot of poisons would've have slowed his appetite, and Semra was gone by then, so that helps. And my source—the one who never came inside the pub—I chased her and got her to tell me that she saw the amulet before it was found, but in a different location. It was moved *after* Semra escaped Madensig with Avaya. I couldn't get her to stay and give me any more details, but if we could get her testimony and maybe get to some cooks and other servants ..."

The strategizing continued, but Semra didn't hear it. The voices in that little room grew distant as she pulled into herself. Turian's voice came to her again. *Maybe even make a friend. You are low on friends.*

Semra had never had people take care of her before, not like this. She never would have allowed it, had she had any choice in the matter. But now, for the second time in the past couple of weeks, she was lying in a bed while others planned on how best to keep her alive. Semra had convinced herself years ago that having a family was nothing but an unrealistic bedtime story. But if having a family felt anything like this, she'd missed out on a lot more than she thought.

Shafii adjusted the pillows behind her as the group spoke, and Tinat stirred some ginger into the coriander tea Zephan had prepared and set it within Semra's reach. Had she made it this far to discover what family felt like, only to die now?

There were worse ways to die. Her breath hitched, and a sob caught in her throat. Semra picked up the little doll Lesala had made for her and turned it in her fingers. Something inside her broke, and she wiped away a tear.

The doll caught fire, and Semra yelped and dropped it. Tinat snatched it and smothered the small flame in blankets, but smoke still poured from Semra's fingertips. The small room in the modest cottage in the mountain foothills filled with black, and her companions yelled to each other in between coughing fits. Tinat cowered on the floor, and Pidge threw open the window, allowing thick ebony smoke to billow up into the sky like a signal of doom.

21

AVAYA

vaya stalked past the training grounds and around the ward to the stables. A young stable boy passed her, and she gripped his arm. "Have you seen the Raven?"

His eyes went round as saucers. "N-no, Your Highness!"

Avaya released him, and he scampered away as quick as his little legs could carry him. Where was he? He'd been gone for three days.

Ever since Semra was spotted in Horen.

Avaya ground her teeth. Was he following her command and finally removing the blight of her presence from the earth? Or was he chasing her like a puppy, hoping for a kiss?

He thinks I'm such a fool. Last month, when he fought his way out of Madensig, he didn't do it for Avaya. He did it for Semra, and it just happened to serve his employment to Avaya at the same time.

But Semra has nothing for him. I have money, status, prestige. Siler was rough around the edges, but at his core, he was a man of taste. Money and status were a language he could appreciate. And that's why, come rain or shine, he always found himself back with her.

Siler grew bored in Shamaran Castle. That is why he'd let her flirt with him in Jannemar and entertained her idle chatter. It was how they'd eventually struck their agreement.

Girls who sat around in castles waiting for men of rank, men they had no business being with, were boring. They were pathetic. Avaya was many things, but she was never boring.

So Siler had taken her up on her offer. He kidnapped her and took her to Belvidore, guarded her, played double agent with Arnevon, and dipped his toe into royalty. He chased Semra after the tournament, but whether for duty or personal reasons, he came back to Madensig. And after the battle at the Strip, it wasn't Semra he ran to, but Avaya.

He'd been noncommittal when she told him to kill Semra. He'd smirked in that careless way of his and told her she didn't have enough money to foot the bill for a kill like that. Avaya had promised she was good for it, but he only wagged a finger. *"Promises are only as good as the gold they are built on. And your gold, dear princess, is across the border."*

It was true. Avaya had managed to bring a surprising amount of money and valuable objects, but she was running low. She needed access to deeper coffers. The timeline would have to be moved up.

She crossed the yard and reentered the keep, slowing just long enough to smile at the head cooks as she walked by. They didn't deserve her time, but Avaya did deserve the loyalty her time would buy. She swept up the stairs and took the hall down to King Axis's receiving room and study, positioned directly behind the throne room. Guards stood sentry on either side of the double doors.

"Tell His Majesty the King that I seek audience."

The guard dipped his head and slipped inside. Avaya

tapped her foot on the polished floors and lifted her chin. He was gone several minutes. She fought the urge to bite a nail or pace, and crossed her arms instead, pinning her fingers down and away from her mouth.

At last the guard reappeared and held the door ajar. "You may enter."

The guard only opened a single door for her entry, and the other guard did nothing at all. Would they snub her so once she was queen? Or would they throw open both doors and bow?

Avaya pulled her shoulders back and glided through the doors. Axis leaned his head on one hand as he poured over a stack of papers. A quill dripped ink from his other hand, and he blotted it with a napkin from the abandoned lunch tray beside him.

"Can you make time for your soon-to-be wife?" Avaya strode across the room in a rustle of silks and leaned over his chair, kissing him on the cheek.

"For you, my love, of course," he said. But his eyes never left the page.

Avaya frowned. She hopped up on the table and swung her legs. "I've been thinking. It takes too long for me to introduce myself."

Axis scanned the document, signed the bottom, and turned it over, then sat back in his chair. "What?"

"Yes. You know, *soon-to-be-wife.* It's entirely too long. I am a simple woman."

Axis snorted. "You are many things, my princess, but simple is not one of them."

Avaya shrugged. "All I want is the world. With you at the helm."

The king's mouth twisted into a wry smile. "Is that all?"

"Well, like I said, my title is too long. *Wife* would be much shorter."

"Once you are queen, your title will be longer, not shorter."

Avaya dismissed him with a wave of her hand. "Commoners may spend their time reciting my royal accolades, but to you, I need only be one thing."

Axis arched an eyebrow. "Empress?"

"That certainly does have a ring to it. But come now, why are you toying with me? After everything I've been through, I'm here to keep my end of the deal our fathers struck. I've been nothing but good to you, despite our nations' rivalry, and the people love us together. It gives them hope. They are griping about their children being sent off to war. Let's give them something to celebrate."

"Am I not enough for you as we are?"

"Enough!" Avaya gasped in mock surprise and lowered herself off the table and into Axis's lap. "More than enough. But I want to be bound to you forever. I want a ring on my finger to remind me of you. And, of course, there would be other nice perks."

Axis wrapped his arm around her waist. "Do tell."

"I wouldn't have to rely on the Raven. He's *so* unreliable. I could have a permanent guard, and I could help you at state functions, talking to all the boring people while you do the important stuff. I could make people feel important while you were off at the front. It would be like being in two places at once, except I would do all the low level, mind-numbing things and you would be able to spend your time doing what you like best."

"It sounds romantic."

Avaya traced the veins of his hand and forearm with her finger. "It is. And did I mention I'm an excellent spy?"

"Is that so? Do you have experience?"

Avaya skipped over the edge to his tone and kept hers light and fluffy. "Oh, yes. I gossip with the best of them. And do you know what gossipers get, my love, aside from dirty looks in the hallways? Information. And if I were queen, no one would dare give me dirty looks while I could catch them. It's the best of both worlds. The castle would rarely be without someone home to listen in on it."

Axis's mouth quirked into a smile. "You want to be my eyes and ears."

"I want to be your everything. But for this particular job, I need the proper access to do it right. Right now, I'm the enemy's daughter and your plaything. Only as queen can I get the respect and freedom to go where I please unquestioned. The people love us, and as your wife ... we would be unstoppable. Jannemar would be yours, and the hearts of both of our peoples would shout our praise."

Axis drummed the fingers of his free hand on the arm of his chair. "I do look fabulous in my formal regalia."

"And I look spectacular in anything."

"How fortunate."

Axis kissed her. "I suppose we have a rather expedited date to set, and a planner to terrify." He poured a second glass of wine and handed one to her. "To my wife, my spy, my queen."

22

———————

Semra fanned away the last of the smoke from the air and stared at her fingertips. They were stained black like soot. Her chin quivered as terror set in. *What is happening to me?* Her pulse skyrocketed; she began to shake, and her field of vision narrowed so that all she could see were her trembling hands.

"She can't stay." Tinat's voice cracked. "We can't put Lesala and Voran in any more danger."

"There's nothing left I can do for her here," Shafii said. "It's taking on a life of its own, and whatever it is seems to need to run its course. This illness is born of magic, but magic does not exist. Not in any meaningful way, not outside rare species like dragons, and ancient buried trinkets. Either she will succumb, or she'll pull through, but it's beyond the abilities of any healer."

"We'll fly somewhere safe then and wait it out," Pidge said.

"We can't fly Zezura." Siler's tone was firm. "We landed at night, but if we lift off now, everyone will know where we are. After the smoke signal, all of Seddon must be looking across the river to this exact spot."

Semra's chest heaved with every breath, and with her elevated heartrate, the fire returned with a vengeance.

"We need some way to stabilize her." Zephan's voice wafted into Semra's hazy consciousness. "She's fading."

"It will only slow what must come. We can send some herbs along, but you'll be bailing out a sinking boat with a spoon."

"Shafii, sweetheart, we can't send her out in that. She's soaked to the skin, poor thing. Do we have time to set her up with something dry? Wash her clothes?"

The suggestion ripped Semra from the brink of unconsciousness. "Nobody takes my trousers," she mumbled. "Not to wash, nothing." After the nightdress incident at Coanor's, she needed her pants with sheaths and knives.

"You'll catch a chill, dear!" Tinat said.

Semra shook her head. "If I don't make it, you can take them off my dead body. I need them."

"Juniper blossoms, let's hope it doesn't come to that," Tinat exclaimed. "I've got a spare dress, and you can just wear it over the pants. I just can't have you going out drenched in sweat. Something on your body should be dry!"

Semra stared listlessly at the wall but said nothing. Zephan and Siler exchanged a look. She didn't have the strength to argue about skirts, and she knew Tinat meant well. Pidge glanced between them, lost to the significance.

Shafii ushered the men out to pack a few food items, and Pidge closed the door behind Tinat when she ran in with the promised dress. Semra was only vaguely aware of a clammy tunic being shrugged over her head and replaced with a commoner's dress. The dress was barely tugged down over her pants when someone banged on the door.

"Soldiers are crossing the river!" Voran yelled. "Time's up!"

The door opened and everyone swarmed inside again.

"Can we take this blanket?" Siler asked. "I'll replace whatever we take. But it might be a while."

Something in Semra's foggy brain registered surprise. Did Siler just think about other people? He wasn't going to just take whatever he needed?

"Take it," Tinat said. "You need a barrier between your skin and hers, and she can't walk."

"Even if she could, she shouldn't," Shafii added. "Her heart rate needs to stay as low and steady as possible. Here are the herbs. I hope they bring some level of comfort."

Siler stepped toward the bed, but Zephan beat him to it. He tucked the blanket around Semra and scooped her up before Siler could say a word.

Semra mustered her waning strength to lift her finger toward the table. "Wait. The doll."

Pidge snatched Lesala's straw gift from the table and pressed it into the folds of the blankets. Semra clutched it in one hand through the fabric and dropped her head back against Zephan's shoulder and chest.

Lesala and Voran stood in the hall, eyes wide, but Lesala smiled when Semra took the doll. Semra whispered her thanks to Tinat and Shafii, and the group said swift farewells on the way out the door. Pidge had Semra's pack slung across her back, with supplies mildly refreshed. Zephan and Siler both wore commoner garb, Siler's more expensive than Zephan's. Siler carried a sword, and a dagger swung from Zephan's belt.

Rocks skittered down the hill as they picked their way up the slope and left the Rinab's cottage behind. The afternoon was waning, but it would be several hours before the sun kissed the mountainside with its setting. Trees dotted the way ahead, but much of the land was grass, rock, and low shrubbery rather than forest.

Fatigue and dizziness set in again, an almost welcome distraction from the heat of her bones.

"Keep up, rookie." Siler's voice.

"I'm *coming,*" Pidge answered. "And I haven't slowed you down once, so you can keep your nicknames!"

"Semra?" Siler sounded close. He must be right beside Zephan. "Semra, stay with me. How good is your communication with Zezura? Can you tell her to stay out of the skies until dark?"

Semra waited three long breaths before answering. It was hard to think past the fever fire throughout her body. Her brows furrowed as she reached out through the mark. Zezura had caught a deer and was devouring her meal from a mountain peak.

"It's not in words, exactly, but I can get the message across."

Zephan stumbled, and Semra's stomach lurched. He caught himself and adjusted his grip on her. "It would help our travel speed if you got to ride when nightfall hits."

"Tired already, princey?" Siler goaded.

Semra felt Zephan take a deep, steadying breath. "Just trying to be practical. It's not that she's heavy, but we're on an incline, and we've got a long way to go."

"I'll take her when you're too tired."

"I've got it."

"How does the beasty feel about being a horse for a while, instead of a dragon?" Pidge asked.

Zezura roared from her place miles away, and the faintest remains of the call drifted over the mountain to where they stood. Pidge jumped.

"She prefers to fly," Semra said. "But she'll do it."

"The soldiers will search the homes and scout the mountains," Zephan said. "We have a head start, but we can't stop until we get some distance behind us."

"Will the Rinabs be okay?" Semra asked. She struggled to keep her eyes open, and his molten amber gaze landed tenderly on her face.

"They'll be fine," he answered. "But the soldiers can't find you here."

"And they can't find *you* here either," Siler added.

Zephan grimaced. "That too."

"So you really are the prince, huh?" Pidge said.

Zephan hesitated, but that ship had sailed. "Yes."

"And nobody knows you're out here?"

Zephan stiffened. "There are people who know I am here."

"You're not sounding good, Pidge," Semra muttered.

"But you're not where you're supposed to be," Pidge pressed.

"He's not allowed near assassins," Siler said. "Ironic, isn't it? He's surrounded by three."

Zephan set his jaw. "Pidge, was it? How did you get here again?"

Siler snorted.

Semra groaned. "Maybe it's better if we don't talk."

The heat in her body ebbed and flowed over the next few hours, and Semra drifted in and out of consciousness. When she was jostled awake, fever and chill alternated in her body, and Zephan and Siler took turns carrying her over rocky terrain. When she slept, she dreamed of never-ending flame.

A cool breeze welcomed the night. Semra didn't remember calling Zezura, but eventually she woke to the dragon landing beside them. Pidge rode with Semra to keep her on the dragon's back, until at last they stopped to rest.

They traveled like that for two days, following the eastern side of the mountain toward Horen. Travel by foot was slow, and Zezura sometimes flew at a low glide to get Semra across narrow spaces. Semra's skin was clammy and feverish, but the group found it only burned them in occasional flares, and otherwise receded to uncomfortably warm. They used the blanket as a precaution whenever picking her up, but each day they were less careful to avoid her touch.

On the third day, the skies opened, and rain cascaded down on them in sheets of icy water. Sweat mingled with rain to run in rivers down Semra's back. Her teeth chattered, and the violent shiver that ran up her spine brought waves of pain through her aching body.

"She's shaking," Pidge called out from their place on Zezura's back. "A lot."

Zephan lifted a hand to shield his eyes and squinted in their direction. All four of them were soaked through. He glanced about at the sparse foliage and occasional tree and nodded. "We need to get her warm."

Siler pointed down the steep ledge to a copse of trees. "There."

Pidge's arms tightened around Semra as Zezura lifted off just high enough to follow Siler's direction to the trees below. Pidge slipped off the dragon's back and pulled Semra down after her. Semra buckled and collapsed, her legs refusing to hold, and Pidge fell with her as she struggled to bear the weight. Even beneath the trees, the rain pelted hard.

Siler and Zephan picked their way down the slope, and Zezura lifted a wing over the two young women as they huddled in the matted-down grass. Semra's blood boiled even as her teeth chattered. Her vision swam and she teetered.

"I'm not saying you should hurry up, but hurry up," Pidge yelled over the din. "I'm freezing to death over here, and I'm not the sick one!"

Semra could feel the fire inside licking at her bones, a

burning, boiling sensation that etched every fiber of her being with agony. She lay motionless on the ground, resting her cheek in the dirt under the shadow of Zezura's wing, but her heart only beat faster. The rain fell only inches from her nose.

Siler and Zephan's feet ran back and forth—the only thing she could focus on from her sideways position in the dirt. Lifting her head would have been far too much. Branches and armfuls of leaves appeared and disappeared, and then Pidge peeled the soggy wet blanket from around Semra's shoulders and ran off to add it to whatever lean-to they were conjuring.

"Zez, can you dry this off a bit?" Siler gestured toward the shelter beyond Semra's vision, and Zezura straightened and puffed slow fire around the area. The rain started to let up, but it was still coming down.

Zephan knelt in the muck in front of Semra. He was breathing hard, and his damp shirt clung to every chiseled line of his body. He pulled her up, wrung out the bottom of his shirt, and wiped the mud off her face with it.

"Come on, let's get you up. Can you put your arm around me?"

Semra steeled herself for the effort and slipped her arm around his neck. Zephan carried her to a crude lean-to topped with branches, leaves, and a wet blanket. It could only properly fit two people, but as Zephan sat beneath it pulled her against his side, Siler and Pidge piled in afterward, facing out to watch the rain.

"I'm still getting rained on!" Pidge said. "Can you move over?"

"We're as far in as we can get, rookie," Siler said. "Have you always been this prissy?"

"Have you always been a doomsday grump?"

Zephan grunted. "Hold on." He scooted back a few more inches and hauled Semra halfway into his lap so her back rested on his chest. Both their arms on one side rubbed against the rough logs and branches of the lean-to. Zephan's head bent and grazed the top, but Semra rested hers on his shoulder.

Siler and Pidge shuffled in further, and Pidge let out a breath. "*Thank* you. See, Siler? Gentlemen exist. Take notes."

"I didn't know women like you were interested in gentlemen," Siler answered. "I figure you're so used to killing them, that it would be dangerous to look like one."

"Please. I don't want a pansy, but I don't want a bully either."

"Takes one to know one."

Semra felt a brief respite from wild extremes as her cold exterior tempered in the damp lean-to away from the driving rain. Soon the fever would flare hot again, and she hoped Zephan wouldn't be burned when it did. Zephan shivered, and his arms cinched tighter around her, his muscles flexing for a moment against the cold. Her gaze lingered on the veins of his arms, the sculpt of his hands. She lifted a finger and lightly traced the lines of his forearm.

What was she doing? The heat inside must be getting to her. She snatched her hand away.

"Ow!"

Semra dropped her hand and grimaced.

"What just happened?" Pidge asked.

"Um, Semra hit me in the face." Was he holding in a laugh?

Siler snorted. "About time."

Semra never thought she would be grateful for the fever, but when heat flew to her cheeks, she knew they couldn't get any redder than they already were. But nobody in the lean-to could see it anyway.

It took three hours for the rain to stop, and Siler and Pidge set to work gathering damp kindling and setting up a safe fire pit for Zezura to work on drying them out and lighting them. Semra felt the dragon's boredom with the task mediated by concern for Semra as her temperature climbed again. Weakness permeated every crevice of her body just as completely the rain had soaked them through. The aching, sweating, and pounding escalated to new heights, and her cramped muscles threatened to fall apart if she dared move them.

The fire finally got going, and the group stretched their limbs and huddled around it to dry. Pidge wrinkled her nose at the disintegrated bread fragments from Semra's bag. She crumbled them in her fingers and dusted them off into the fire.

"No, thank you."

"What a princess you are," Siler observed, smirking.

"I don't see you eating any," Pidge shot back.

"Maybe I'm not hungry."

"We're all hungry," Pidge said. "Except maybe Semra. She looks dead to the world."

Semra stared listlessly into the flickering flame, wondering what it would feel like to have it consume her. Would she even feel the heat of the fire if she stuck her hand in it? Heat bubbled through her blood as though boiling, and she could feel it starting to pull her under.

She barely registered her friends' concerned looks as she faded in and out. Zephan propped her up next to him and brushed sweaty, disheveled hair from her face. Siler and Pidge started talking strategy for Belvidore, and Zephan stoked the fire, letting them talk. He kissed her on the forehead. His touch was a glimmer of distraction, but the heat was too strong.

Semra's chest tightened, and a blazing inferno erupted inside her. Her mouth opened in a wild, uncontrollable wail of tortured anguish. Her back arched and her body tensed as her blood-curdling scream shook the air.

Rich obsidian smoke streamed from her fingertips, enveloping the camp in ink-black swirls until nothing could be seen. Zezura screeched a furious roar and took to the air, the rush from her wings only further dispensing the dark cloud.

Semra saw nothing, heard nothing but her own ringing shriek, until the dark winked out and she was abruptly submerged into the blinding reality of reptilian eyesight. A dark figure perched along the ridge with a bow; his arrow was nocked and drawn back.

His fingers released the string.

23

TYMETIN

Two hundred and fifty yards was an easy shot. Four figures huddled around the fire with not a single functioning brain between them. They were supposed to be on the run, and yet they made a fire. Maybe next time they would send a formal invitation, and he could eat hors d'oeuvres over their bodies when he was done.

Except there'd be no next time.

Tymetin drew the arrow back on the string until his hand touched his face, index finger above the nocking point, next two fingers below. He dropped his shoulders, took a deep breath, and lined up his shot. His target looked half dead already.

He was only paid for one kill, but he could easily kill all four in thirty seconds. Gathering proof of his kill would be much easier without survivors to contend with. There was the matter of the dragon, but once its lord was dead, it would surely have no tie to her. And if it decided to guard the bodies, he could be patient. He just couldn't let it consume all proof of his target's identity.

Tymetin took a moment to glory in the thrill of the hit.

This was his favorite part—the anticipation, the adrenaline, the moment of calm before chaos. It was like a secret. Only he knew what was about to happen.

A shiver of delight went up his spine, and he released the arrow.

Shock and confusion rocked him just as his fingers loosened, and he startled. His targets were gone. So stupidly visible in broad daylight half a second ago, the entire group had now disappeared in thick smoke. And his surprise had compromised the shot.

Tymetin slammed his fist down on the rock outcropping in front of him. The smoke billowed in an enormous, towering mass, and his lip curled. He knew where they were. He had a quiver full of arrows. He should release a dozen into the smoke and hope for a hit.

Tymetin nocked another arrow and tried to re-envision his shot. Did they know he was here, and have a smoke bomb? What type of mixture could create a smoke signal that large? How far would they have moved from their position?

A disturbance shifted the swirling smoke above the trees, and Tymetin's stomach dropped. Fear wasn't an emotion he often experienced. It felt so foreign in his body, but as fifty feet of scales, wings, and teeth bore down on him from above, terror seized his chest and reason left him. Tymetin released his arrow into the shroud and sent another into the sky.

And another.

And another.

The dragon's coloring flashed from deep blue to crimson to violet as it coursed through the air. Light and heat shattered Tymetin's senses as fire blazed from the dragon's mouth. He threw his arms over his face and ducked behind the rock, a shower of sparks following his movement. The skin of his arms tingled and crawled, and his eyes bulged at the angry red welts and peeling skin. The burning sensation would come, and it would be excruciating. Tymetin threw the bow over his back and dropped into a narrow crevice below him. He waited only a moment before rolling out and sprinting down the mountainside.

24

————

Semra's vision snapped back into her body. Darkness swathed her. She could hear the others coughing, and someone was shouting, but she couldn't make it out. The smoke wouldn't stop. The flame inside had found its outlet, and like a drake released from its cage, it would not be restrained.

Sparks flew from her fingers. Her body shook, tremors rolling through her in heat wave after heat wave. She writhed on the ground in torment that words could not express, given over to the power of that furnace, the ancient power of dragons no human vessel was meant to contain.

"She's going to hurt herself!"

"Grab her!"

"Ouch! She's too hot to touch!"

"Someone get the blanket!"

Her body quaked, her chest heaved, every shred of her screamed.

And then she was still.

There had been no deeper dark, no emptiness so barren, as that space. There were no dreams. No nightmares. No discernible thoughts. Only a vacant sense of foreboding that stretched on and on. A rippling glow floated across her closed eyelids and was gone.

Semra opened her eyes. Three pairs of eyes stared back at her, gray, amber, and brown, each set wide as saucers. Zephan, Siler, and Pidge knelt over her on the ground and blinked down at her. A huge serpentine head popped into view above them as Zezura added her blue peepers to the mix.

Semra frowned and tested her limbs. She wiggled her fingers and toes. No heat. No pain. Just exhaustion. Four concerned parties waited breathlessly for her to say something. She shut her eyes.

Pidge could wait no longer. "Well?"

Semra took a deep breath and squinted up at her. "I seem to have survived."

All four heads, three human and one dragon, let out a huff of relief.

Siler tapped her arm. "You feel normal. How do you feel?"

"Normal seems extreme," she said. "I feel like I need to sleep for about a dozen years, and then I'll be okay."

Zephan held out a hand. "Can you stand?"

Semra took his hand, and he pulled her to her feet. Pidge gripped her elbow on the other side as she faltered, then steadied. "I'm stiff. And sore. But I'm stable."

"*Physically* stable," Siler said. "Mentally, I've always had questions." He grinned.

"You're one to talk," she muttered, then hesitated. Semra glanced around at her team, her support. "I never would have made it if not for each of you." She shifted her weight, and her neck cracked as her joints loosened up. She bit her lip. "I'm not great at this sort of thing, but thank you."

Semra turned to Pidge. "You're not exactly who I expected to be there for me, but you have been. You got us food, you fought for me, you fled with me. I'm not sure why you did it, but I'm grateful to you for not putting my head in a bucket. *Or a sack.*"

Pidge's face lit up, and she pressed her lips together to hide a smile. "Dragons and daylilies," she said with a gasp. "You just thanked me for something. Are you smiling? You're smiling. You *like* me." Pidge couldn't help herself. She grinned ear to ear.

Semra laughed at the girl's excitement, then sobered as she looked at Siler. She touched his arm, then withdrew it awkwardly. "I'm sorry. I still feel some of the things I said to you at the Rinabs. But I think you were trying to protect me, that you were doing what you could for me every step of the way. I was too harsh." She stared down at her soggy shoes, then forced herself to look up at him. "Will ... will you ... um, peace?"

Siler sighed. "I'll have to think about it." He pursed his lips and screwed his face up, as if in deep thought. "Okay, fine. I've thought about it. Peace." He stuck out his hand, and Semra shook it.

Semra twisted toward Zephan. Her breath caught. Was he always so beautiful? He ran his hand through rumpled hair and plucked at the mud dried on the hem of his shirt, the mud he'd wiped from her face. Those molten amber eyes bored into her with the intensity of fire but the warmth of a candle at midnight.

"Um. Thank you. You know, for coming after me. I didn't mean to leave like I did; I didn't want to, but I didn't know what else to do." She broke eye contact, accidentally landing on the definition of his arms and chest. Her stomach dropped. She jerked her gaze back to his face, fighting the urge to examine the curve of his lips, to replay the memory of their single kiss. Her breathing quickened. "I'm ... glad you're here."

"I'm glad I'm here too. I always want to be here."

Semra took a short breath and let it out. She gave a curt nod. "Okay then. Enough of that. What's next?"

Siler arched an eyebrow. "Are you ready to admit I was right?"

You don't care about your reputation in Jannemar ... you only care about princey.

Semra's mouth twitched. "Maybe. But never out loud, so keep your trap shut."

Zephan cocked his head. "Right about what?"

Siler laughed. "Nothing, apparently."

Pidge planted her hands on her hips. "Okay, so now that you're not dying, are we going to focus on clearing your name? Because I recently lost out on a big payday, and I need a project."

Zephan's eyes narrowed and flitted from Pidge to Semra and back. "I'm not sure how big a payday you lost out on, but if you help clear Semra's name and give us direction to Arnevon's real assassin, I'll make sure you're compensated."

Pidge smiled. "I like the sound of that. I'll try to get to my source again, and poke around for more information."

"I think I've seen you in Madensig," Siler said. "Kitchens?"

Pidge nodded. "I have a couple of contacts with the cooks and other servants."

Siler folded his arms. "Great. I can chat up some guards on the inside the castle, and then feel out a few of our old colleagues on the outside."

"I can do that too," Pidge said, lifting her chin.

Siler sighed. "Yes, but can you keep a low profile while you do it? Do you have as much clout as I have?"

"Maybe I'm not as experienced as you, but maybe I'm not as naïve as you think I am either. And I haven't been seen flying around on a dragon and fighting back-to-back with our dearly beloved traitor." Pidge glanced at Semra and put her hands up. "Alleged traitor. From their perspective."

Semra rolled her eyes. "I get it."

"Point taken," Siler said. "We'll split the list based on each person we know. It makes more sense for you to reach out to your classmates anyway, and then we'll talk about the rest one by one, for whoever we know is nearby."

Pidge considered the idea, then dipped her head. "Done."

Siler grinned. "Maybe we should come up with signals for you in case you get captured or trapped, and I have to come find you. You know, since you're a rookie. If you ever can't talk, blink once for no, and twice for yes, okay?"

Pidge set her jaw. "I'm not going to get caught."

Semra looked between Siler and Pidge. "Is there anybody outside the castle that I can work on? Anybody that hasn't seen my face? Once I rest up a bit, maybe I could ..."

"*No!*"

The shout was collective, from all three of her friends. Zezura huffed a snort of fire for good measure and nudged her with her nose.

"You are banned from this mission, for obvious reasons," Pidge said. "Just sit back and let us do this for you."

Semra's heartrate picked up, but she swallowed. "I'm too unpredictable. We don't know if the smoke thing will continue."

Pidge threw her hands up. "Duh."

"Not to mention you are completely drained, and we all just thought you were about to die," Zephan added. "You need time to recover."

"There isn't a soul that hasn't seen your face," Siler said. "If they haven't seen it in person, they've seen it in the posters all over town. You're not setting foot in Seddon or Horen."

Semra nodded. "Someone might come here. There was an

archer down the rise, during the smoke. Zezura scared him off."

Zephan blinked and gestured to a tree off to the side. Semra's chest tightened at the sight of two arrows embedded in its trunk. "*We* know that. But how do *you* know that? You were, um, incapacitated, at the time. And nobody could see anything."

Semra looked at the dragon, and Zezura chuffed. "I can sometimes see what she sees."

Siler's jaw dropped. "The alley? In Horen?"

Semra nodded.

He rubbed his chin. "Well, that's an interesting development."

Zephan clapped his hands. "It's decided then."

"Wait." Semra turned to look at the prince. "Don't you need to get back to Kinlock? There's no way you aren't missing right now, and Zez and I can hide out here."

Zephan shook his head. "You aren't leaving my sight."

"Because you don't trust me?"

"No. Because I'm the *only* person who trusts you, and if I can tell the court and my father that I was with you the entire time, that will aid our case."

Warmth flooded her chest. "Oh."

"And because as great as Zezura is, you might want someone with opposable thumbs. In case you need anything while you're recovering. We need to get closer to Horen and away from your latest smoke signal, but stay high enough to hide Zezura and see anybody approaching our position."

Siler slapped his thigh. "Looky there! Good plan. Princey isn't as dumb as he looks."

Semra's jaw dropped. Did he just compliment Zephan? Zephan bent to retrieve Semra's bag from the lean-to, and Siler gave her a quick nod and wink when Zephan wasn't looking. *He believes you,* he seemed to say. *Let him stay.* Semra's mind reeled. She couldn't have imagined this a month ago when the two men were pummeling each other in a Horen courtyard outside the arena.

Zephan straightened and looked at Siler. "You might even be less prickly than you want people to believe."

"Oh, that's just for you, princey."

Pidge snorted. "Because you're such a ray of sunshine for the rest of us."

"I'm hilarious. If you spent more time with me, maybe you would know." Siler stepped away toward the lean-to, and Semra followed to help him dismantle it.

Pidge shook out the blanket. "I guess I'll just have to stick around and see."

Semra snickered, and Zephan grinned. Siler glared at her, and Semra wiggled her eyebrows. She angled her body away from Pidge and mouth edback at Siler, *She'll stick around and see.*

"I hope you do," Semra said out loud. "Somewhere deep down, he's not half bad."

The group made quick work of the lean-to and surrounding area until there was no sign of camp—except for the massive plume of black smoke that had risen from their precise location less than two hours before. Semra cut four slits in Tinat's skirt up almost to the waist so that it flapped about her pants but left her legs free to move, and the group set off. They hiked for another day until they got to Horen, and Semra grudgingly gave two of the three remaining knives from her trousers to Pidge. Siler and Pidge slipped into Horen under cover of night and brought back stolen provisions before heading back into the Belvidorian capital.

Semra alternated between stretching her sore muscles and riding Zezura to rest. By the time they found a new campsite and Siler and Pidge left for Horen the second time, the fatigue was fading, and Semra began to feel like herself again. She sat against Zezura's blue-scaled hide and twirled the knife blade in her hands. Siler and Pidge had only been gone for an hour, and Zephan lay with his head against a clump of dry grass at the mouth to a small cave.

Semra spun the blade into the grass beneath Zephan's neck and sighed. "Can I clean your sword? I've oiled my knife three times and it doesn't look any different."

Zephan shot upright and plucked the knife from the grass. "Hey!"

"Sorry. I'm so *bored.*"

"We could talk."

Semra grimaced. No good could come of that. "I don't feel like it."

"We could spar."

She wrinkled her nose, and Zephan sighed. "We could try to figure out the smoke thing."

"I can't control it."

Zephan slid his sword and scabbard off his belt and tossed it to Semra. "Yet. You're a dragonlord. And you can sometimes see through your dragon's eyes, which is new. Nothing is certain right now. All bets are off. What if you *could* control it?"

Semra removed the sword from its scabbard, poured oil on the cloth, and ran it down the blade. It was gorgeous workmanship and engraved with his name and title. "We don't even know if the smoke is a thing anymore—now that the fevers are gone. It was probably just part of the transition."

"But transition to *what,* exactly? It makes no sense that you would go through all of that, your body absorbing dragon magic, and not have any changes."

Semra cringed at the memory of her last smoke incident. The white-hot blaze had consumed her. She knew nothing but pain. She *was* pain. Semra gasped as the sword nicked her finger, and she shook off the memory.

Zephan crossed to her and knelt beside her. "Let me see."

"It's fine."

"Did you know that's my least favorite phrase now? It's possible you've ruined it for me forever." He held his hand out. Semra sighed but gave him her hand. He inspected it, then pressed a cleaner corner of cloth against the superficial wound and passed her hand back.

"See? It's fine."

"Yes, it is," he said. "But you are tremendously terrible at accepting help."

Semra spread her hands. "What do you think I've been doing this whole past week?"

"Surviving. It's been excellent practice. If you hadn't been half dead, you'd probably never have tried it—the letting people help you thing, that is."

Semra returned her attention to the sword. He was right, of course. "Sorry."

Zephan settled in beside her against the dragon so that their arms and hips touched. A tingle ran up her arm. Zephan nudged her. "You've done a much better job since being forced into it. Thank you for letting us help."

Semra blushed. She gritted her teeth. Why did her face betray her so?

Zephan crossed his arms and ankles, and watched her as she worked. "You were in and out at the cottage. And you talked sometimes, kind of like sleep talking, but you were half awake."

Semra froze. Siler had mentioned it too. She'd been in such a fog; she could only remember snatches of the cottage. But what had Siler said when she'd told Shafii she could finally think straight?

Good. Maybe we won't hear any more senseless ramblings.

She groaned. "Oh no."

Zephan remained silent for a long time, and Semra wondered if she was meant to say something. She flipped over the sword and caressed its every curve. A gold enamel pattern twisted over the pommel, capturing a ruby and a sapphire in the center of the hilt. His beautifully crafted sword was the only princely thing about him in his dirty commoner clothes. It was far too conspicuous to be traveling with. He must have left Kinlock in a hurry. Regardless, it served as a reminder of the chasm between them.

She cleared her throat. "Do I want to know what I said?"

"You said a few things. You said my name, more than once, while you were asleep. Once you were half awake and seemed to know who I was, but I don't think you believed I was really there. You cursed at me and told me I was handsome."

Semra swore. "Rats and rot."

Zephan grinned. "I've dared to tell you you're gorgeous, but you've never told me you thought I was handsome."

Semra bit her lip. She ran the cloth over the gemstones and leaned forward out of Zezura's shadow to tilt them in the sun so they sparkled. As she did, the light caught the opal on her chest, and it was more radiant than any of the extravagant craftmanship in her hands. She leaned back, suddenly self-conscious.

Don't be stupid, Semra, she thought. *Don't tell him how you can't get him out of your head, how you wish he weren't a prince, how you wish you weren't a guilt-ridden assassin. How you can't breathe when you look at him.*

"Well, do you?" Zephan asked.

"Huh?" Semra looked up at him, and instantly regretted it. His eyes sparkled like a thousand suns.

"Do you think I'm handsome?"

"Um … you … you're good looking, yeah." Semra winced.

Zephan beamed. "Why, thank you. I've never been so happy to be so mildly complimented."

Semra tried to glare at him, but she couldn't help but laugh. His obnoxious face was too attractive, and his annoying eyes were too excited. *Ugh.*

Zephan soaked in the moment, and then grew somber. "At the end …" He paused. "At the end, when you were coming out of it and really waking up, you said *forgive me*. Who were you talking to?"

Semra swallowed hard against the lump in her throat. No, that wouldn't do. She'd done enough to ruin things today. She slid the sword back into its scabbard and stood. "I've changed my mind. Let's spar."

25

SILER

Siler took a breath and tapped his wrist with two fingers as he strode across the draw bridge. The moat was too far across to swim and heavily surveilled in the front. The fortress had been perfect for a paranoid king like Arnevon, and Siler wondered if Mauve Madensig himself had been just as suspicious.

The gate dropped closed after him with a defining *clang*, and a chill ran up his spine. He hated the claustrophobia of castles. The square outer walls with its towers, the square keep beyond the outer ward, the portcullis and heavy guard—it was amazing how many things a king could have in place to make him feel safe. How many archers hid behind those slits for windows on every side?

And yet Arnevon was still dead. And Siler had still managed to position himself inside. So had Pidge. Siler wondered how many assassins had been within these walls since Azi's fall.

He ducked into the side door to his immediate left after the portcullis. There was no reason to cross the open yard or chance running into Avaya in the keep until absolutely necessary. She was probably whipped up into an anxious frenzy by now, and he hadn't finalized a story to tell her.

Rookie mistake. He'd make sure not to tell Pidge of his oversight when they reported back.

Siler took the stairs up three floors and down the hall to one of the guard armories and slipped inside. Three men greeted him with a quick nod. Two adjusted their armor and swords and headed out to start their shifts, and the third leaned back in his chair and held out a wooden beer mug.

"You on shift, or got time for a draft?"

Siler recognized the man as Bonan. He was one of the tower guard, but he moonlit as bodyguard to the royal family when the schedule needed filling. He'd frequently been assigned to Avaya in Siler's absence. Siler glanced through to the adjoining meeting room, but it was empty. This could be the perfect opportunity to gain information. He took the mug and sat at the table opposite the guard.

"I've got time."

"What's she got you doing this time? You were gone a while."

Siler shrugged and poured Bonan another mug. The man's beard was already decorated with foam. Siler wondered how many drinks he'd had. "I've been gone longer. What'd I miss?"

Bonan rolled his eyes. "Getting to be insufferable, I'll tell you that much. She came in all sweet and worried when she was first kidnapped. She's the one that first got whiff of a plot against King Axis, back when he was just a prince. She was so upset. I think she saved his life. But you didn't hear that from me."

Several drinks, then. Bonan wasn't typically so loose lipped. Good. Siler took a small sip and let it linger in his mouth as if he'd taken a bigger gulp. "Insufferable?"

"Ever since they moved up the wedding."

Siler coughed. "To when?"

"Three weeks. She's been floating on air, waltzing through the castle like she's already queen. She seems to really care about our king, but she's been less personable to the guard. And twitchy."

Siler tilted his head. "Twitchy?"

"Listen, you didn't hear it from me. She's just ... *off.*"

Siler considered this. Avaya was always nervous when he was out of sight. Her insecurities over Semra knew no bounds. Siler thought about Avaya's demand that he train her to fight and wondered if she'd found a substitute teacher. "Maybe someone scared her. If she's receiving threats we don't know about, that could make her standoffish. There are rumors of killers about that can hide in plain sight. Maybe she doesn't trust the guard as much as she used to."

Bonan wiped his mouth with the back of his hand and set down his mug. He dropped his voice. "I've heard those rumors. But she doesn't say a thing she doesn't want to."

"I think you're right," Siler said. There was no reason to think Avaya didn't have her hand in ten things and keep the secrets of each one to herself. Who had Avaya been talking to? If she'd found out about the plot on Axis's life and foiled it, could she have known about the plot against Arnevon?

Siler leaned forward. "Bonan, we are her protectors. It is our duty to go above and beyond to keep her safe. The hope of two kingdoms rests on this union, and if they moved the wedding up so drastically, it could be because of threats of harm. If she doesn't tell us what we need to know, how can we keep her safe? Tell me. Has she taken any unusual meetings in the last month? Any late-night rendezvous, unsavory characters, even someone very benign that didn't quite belong?"

"I'm not sure I follow. She goes to the king a lot, and talks to everybody, even servants. It's only the guards she's been stiff to. She makes her rounds throughout the castle, and she even still visits Laurel. You know, the old healer that helped her through … ah, helped her through her sickness those weeks ago."

Siler's expression flattened, but he smoothed it before Bonan's inebriated state could register it. He knew her sickness had been fabricated. Somehow Avaya had managed to get the healer under her thumb to go along with the ruse when she was still holed up in her chambers. For a wealthy snoot, as Pidge would say, Avaya had been more resourceful than anyone imagined.

For a moment he wondered if the rookie had made it to the kitchens without incident, but he shook off the thought and refocused on Bonan. Siler put on his best pensive look and stroked his chin. "She does talk to everyone, but in public. Anything that frightened her that badly would have shaken her up after. Has she been nervous about any meetings, or gone outside her routine?"

Bonan shook his head. "No, no, we have enough royals anxious over nothing. I haven't seen …" He paused, and Siler gripped his mug. *This is it.* "Well, now that you mention it, two strange things did happen. I never saw her talk to anyone that made her upset, but she did visit one of the sick house three days in a row, which I thought was odd, since she never visits the same public place twice. On her last day there, she wrote personal notes to quite a lot of them. It was nice, though. Nothing improper. The soldiers all melted into school children when she came in."

Alarm bells went off in Siler's mind. He only knew of one freelance assassin that required written proof of contract. And he was nearly as dangerous to his employer as to his victim. But had Avaya gone that far?

The sick house was a smart location. Anybody could come

and go, and the bandages and other distractions made disguise easy. The multiple notes would keep the contract inconspicuous, as it was passed out along with the other papers. Siler wondered if Avaya ever saw the face of her latest employ or if he sent someone else to meet her.

Bonan continued. "And just a couple days ago she came back from the dovecotes all upset and bothered, but I'm not sure why. She always goes in alone, but we sweep it first, so I'm not sure how anyone could have gotten in there, aside from the keeper."

Siler swallowed. *Avaya knows something.* He took another swig from the mug and set it on the table. "Bonan, you're a good man. We'll keep our lady safe, even if she does turn up her nose at the guards. Perhaps she's getting wedding jitters and isn't herself."

Bonan raised his mug. "Best of luck, Raven. She's been on the hunt for you, and I don't think you'll have an easy time of it."

Siler grimaced and turned back down the hall, leaving the armory behind him. If Avaya had really hired an assassin, which hit was it for? She clearly wanted Axis alive, so did she hire him to kill Arnevon, or Semra? Avaya had already tried to hire Siler for the Semra job, but when he refused, a bounty went out. Why would she also make private contracts?

All Siler knew was that Avaya *probably* hired someone to kill someone else. Considering she'd orchestrated her own kidnapping through Siler, and already tried to commission him to kill Semra, it was unsurprising. But he didn't know who the target was, or if there were any other contracts. And he still didn't know how Ramas' amulet got inside the castle. He could have sworn he'd seen it on Semra's belt when she escaped from Madensig with Avaya, so it must have stayed with her throughout her capture, interrogation, and escape.

Siler nodded at a pair of soldiers coming down the spiral stair from the roof and followed them down to the ground level. He needed to talk to Nimmer, the pigeon keeper, but couldn't risk being seen near the dovecote. Siler glanced at the sky. It was almost noon. Nimmer would be headed to the northeast tower of the keep where he had lunch with his son on the roof every day.

It meant he had to enter the keep itself, but all he could do was stay well away from the residential halls and hope for the best. He strode across the yard of the outer ward and into the keep on the eastern door of the gateway. No need to be out in the open for a moment longer than necessary. Going up a floor would mean being closer to the residences, but staying on the ground meant he'd have to cut through the kitchens and risk running into Pidge.

Siler grimaced. Better not to be seen together at any point. He was at the southeast tower now, so he'd skip the residences level altogether, cross to the northeast end on the top floor, and ascend to the roof from there. Siler took the stairs two at a time and had just passed the guest-residences floor when a sickly sweet call soured his ears.

"Raven!"

Could he pretend he hadn't heard?

"Raven. Come down at once."

Like it or not, Avaya was his reason for being at the castle. Once that bridge was burned, he'd be outcasted or killed. He gritted his teeth, pivoted in the stair, and descended to the landing. Princess Avaya was a vision in flowing violet, wide sleeves that brushed her skirts as she walked, and gemstones sewn into a wide neckline beneath the collarbone. She shifted her long blonde hair behind her shoulder and placed her hands on her hips. More useless, ostentatious jewelry weighed down each hand in rings and bracelets.

Siler dipped his head. "Your Highness. I only just got in and thought not to disturb you until after the midday meal. You look well."

"I always look well, but you've never bothered to comment on it before," she said. "Why didn't you respond when I first called you?"

Siler cocked his head. "I did, as far as I'm concerned. Perhaps you overestimate my hearing. What can I do for you, princess?"

He needed to appear as careless about offending her as he'd always been, and not a mote more. Too compliant, and she'd be suspicious. Too offensive, and she might do something drastic to put him in his place. The balance was delicate.

Avaya tapped her foot. "You've been gone for days. I've been waiting. I don't like to wait."

"I'm happy to see you survived. I've been chasing a dangerous killer for you, and it sometimes takes more than the blink of an eye to get the job done."

Her eyes narrowed to slits. "In that case, I'd love to hear an update on your adventures. Come give me your report."

26

———

SILER

Siler's chest tightened and his gut twisted, but he said nothing and followed Avaya as she turned on her heel and swept down the hall toward her chambers.

"No more personal guard?" Siler asked, as she opened the door and held it wide.

"They still shadow me, but not so close. I get to pretend I have more freedom. I'm not queen yet."

"Congratulations on your expedited nuptials, by the way. It sounds like a lot can change in a few days."

"You've no idea."

There was a dangerous edge to her voice. Going into her chambers was unwise, but defying her now, in sight of the guards at the end of the hall, was worse. Siler steeled himself and plopped down in the overstuffed chair of the familiar sitting room where he'd given reports before. He rolled his shoulders back and laid his arm across the back of the chair, one ankle on the opposite knee, exuding a confidence he far from felt.

"I came back for konnolan. The dragon is an issue."

Avaya arranged herself against the arm of the sofa and

stretched out her legs. Violet fabric draped down the furniture to the floor like a waterfall. She brushed two long ringlets over one shoulder. "Someone with your talents and personal connections couldn't get close?"

"She may be naïve, in some ways, but I did haul her into a pit recently and watch as you and Axis had her beaten. And then I dragged her into an arena after that and tackled your brother to keep them from flying off." Siler winced. He failed to disguise the bitterness in his voice, and Avaya's brows soared.

"And you were well compensated for your troubles, were you not?"

"I'm only saying she would have to be a bumbling moron to let me in again. So she hasn't taken well to my reappearance in her life."

Siler's heart sank as he spoke the lie. The lie was reasonable. What sane person would trust him again after all that? And yet *he* had been angry with *her* at the Rinabs. And *she* had apologized to *him*. Semra may have been raised in the mountain, but something about her was undefiled. Her mastery in the art of death had made her the youngest mission-ready graduate in the program, but her character had always been of a higher caliber. There was nowhere she could have learned it. It was just … there.

No wonder Zephan was obsessed with her. He followed her like a puppy, shirking royal responsibilities to keep her safe, his presence more comforting to her than Siler's had ever been. Siler thought about that first night in the cottage, sitting with her as she faded in and out, asking for him over and over in delirium. Siler had told Semra she didn't belong in a castle, that people like them could never thrive in highbrow life. But maybe it was only Siler that didn't belong.

Avaya passed a hand over her eyes. "Pour me a glass of wine. The decanter is by the bed."

Siler rolled his eyes. "What am I, your valet?"

Avaya straightened and looked him dead in the eyes, her features harsh and cold. "I think what you meant to say was *yes, Your Highness, most excellent of employers, great lady who holds my fate.* A single word from me to the king, and you're as good as dead. Pour. Me. Wine."

Tension filled the room in an agitated silence as the two stared each other down. The mood had shifted. Something was very wrong. Slowly, Siler got up and crossed to the decanter by the bed. His skin crawled as he sensed her rise and follow, and when he turned toward her with glass in hand, he nearly bumped into her.

"You've been using the pigeons."

Siler stiffened. She'd been spying on him, and more effectively than he'd realized. He offered her the wine, but she ignored it. He set it on the table. "I have connections to maintain. Half of my value to you is in my network."

"Is Teriv one of your connections?"

Siler's hand stilled on the cork of the decanter.

Avaya stepped closer. "Semra was in a dragonless hole at Shamaran Castle. She only left as quickly as she did because of mysterious warnings arranged using accomplices at Shamaran. Warnings my old handmaiden thought were part of some elaborate plan to draw Semra out, messages she thought were from me." Avaya's lip curled into a snarl and quivered in the strength of her anger. "But please, go on telling me how hard it has been to get her to trust you. How great an obstacle the dragon has caused."

Fear gripped him in the gullet and his hand slipped on the cork, missing its target and spilling the decanter. His opposite hand twitched at the hilt of his sword, but killing Avaya would only make his own death swifter. The castle was a kill box, and he had no elaborate escape plans. He hadn't had any reason to question his movements to and from Madensig before.

Any moment now, she would call for the guards. She could claim he hurt her, claim he betrayed her—it didn't matter what she claimed. He was the scum contract killer, replaceable in every way, and she was the valuable key to a kingdom's expansion. The king was wrapped around her finger. She was going to have Siler killed.

The likes of him were not to be trusted. No one would take his word over hers.

No one but Semra.

Or maybe even Zephan. He wasn't so bad.

Siler racked his brain. He had to deescalate the situation, but he had stabbed her in the back. He couldn't come back from this.

He froze. Avaya knew he wouldn't kill Semra when she asked him. That wasn't the problem. The problem began when she discovered how little she knew about his activities. If she'd known, Avaya would have used the information to her advantage and continued playing her games, toying with him, using him as she saw fit.

Avaya felt out of control, and she *needed* control. Siler saw it now. That's what this whole thing was about—the anger toward her father, the being looked down on by people who didn't respect her mother. Jannemar's policy never permitting women to hold office in the monarchy. Status and control would solve all her insecurities.

Well, they wouldn't. Siler had been in many wealthy homes before he killed their inhabitants, and he'd heard them behind closed doors, so he knew the truth. But she *thought* they would, and so status and control were what he must give her.

"Please," he whispered. "She makes me crazy. I do stupid things when I'm around her. But Semra Bandaka has manipulated me for the last time. She double-crossed me. I'm done. Give me one more chance."

"It's too late," she said. But there was hesitation in her eyes.

He leaned in. "I'll do anything to take her down. Just don't tell me I have to bring her in alive."

Avaya scoffed. "And I'm to take you at your word, that you've turned a new leaf, now that you've been caught? How do I know you won't turn on me?"

Siler seized her arm at the elbow and lowered his head to hers as she looked up at him. Her breath quickened, and a question darted across her face. "Because," he said, his voice rough. "Because every time I turn around, you're there, waiting. Because there is no power greater than money and revenge, and now I see that partnering with you will give me both. And because I'm finally ready ... I'm ready to give my attention to a more deserving woman. The kind of woman who is strong enough to handle the kind of man I am, who doesn't squirm at the work I do. The kind of woman who draws the eye of every man in the room."

"Is that so?" A small smile played across Avaya's face. Her shoulders settled as confidence oozed back into her body. The fish was on the hook. Avaya ran one hand up into his hair. She scanned his expression, searching for hesitancy. He'd never entertained her advances so readily. She tilted her chin, so that their noses touched, and parted her lips. Her eyes gleamed as she dared him to kiss her.

He would take her bait. Siler covered her mouth with his and snatched her waist up against him. He could taste her sense of victory as their lips moved with fevered passion, and a tremor rocked her body in his arms. She shoved him up against the bedpost and twined her arms around him.

Avaya pulled back just enough for Siler to glimpse the wicked smile that washed over her. She leaned in and whispered in his ear, "I don't believe you."

A soft *click* sounded, and the steel of his sword rang from its scabbard as Avaya sinched a chain around his wrist and ripped his sword from its place. Siler dove for her, but Avaya leaped out of range and the chain yanked him backward. Two feet of chain ran from his wrist to the bedpost.

"I *do* draw the eye of every man in a room," Avaya said, breathing hard. "Except you. Never you. Why is that?"

Siler flipped his wrist to grip the chain and lunged. She jumped back, and he sneered at her. "Because you're revolting."

Injury flitted across her countenance and dissolved into hatred. She slapped him across the face. "You've underestimated me. Don't feel bad—everybody has. Poor baby, did you really think you were the only assassin I was in league with? That's adorable."

Siler clenched his jaw, and Avaya edged closer, careful to stay just out of reach. "I'm glad you came back, you know. I wasn't sure you would. But I hoped for it, as you can see." She gestured toward the chain. "You weren't just sending Semra warnings. You've been with her, and she's nearby. But I've taken your vows to heart, Siler, I really have. And I'm going to give you that last chance. As bait."

27

"I cleaned all the rooms on the guest hall, not two days before Princess Avaya returned to Madensig." The girl tossed a furtive glance behind her and leaned closer to Pidge as Pidge set out the place settings for Princess Blaise' midday meal. The sickly Belvidorian princess would be back any minute, but the chance for Pidge to talk to her contact had been too good to pass up. "The amulet is distinctive. I would have remembered seeing it."

Pidge made no outward acknowledgment of the girl's report. The girl fluffed the down pillows of the princess's bed and smoothed the comforter. Pidge straightened the silverware and poured wine into a jewel-studded goblet.

"And after she returned?" Pidge set the goblet on the bedside tray.

"I didn't realize what it was until I saw it again when they found it in the kitchens," the girl said. She opened the wardrobe and rifled through it to find a fresh nightgown. "The first thing Her Highness Princess Avaya did when she returned from the battlefront was take a scented bath. I came to collect her ruined clothes, which she'd thrown on the floor.

I reached for the dress and saw something green hidden in its folds, but then she screeched at me to get out, and I ran."

"You didn't take the dress with you?"

"She called me insolent and accused me of barging in on her rare moment of privacy. She demanded I leave them and come back. When I returned, there was nothing but the dress." The girl laid out the nightgown and stepped back. "Please don't tell anyone I shared this with you." The girl dipped her head and vanished out into the hall.

Pidge took her time arranging the last portions of the meal and turned to leave—nearly bumping into a pale, scrawny little thing with sunken in cheeks and thin lips. Her hair was in a simple, messy braid down her back, and she was draped in soft green silk. Pidge gasped and her hand flew to her chest in surprise. She dropped into a deep curtsy.

"Your Highness. Forgive me, I was just setting out your meal. Do enjoy."

"Are you often so slow about your duties?" the princess asked. Her voice came out in a high squeak, and Pidge thought she looked and sounded rather like a mouse.

A needling anxiety sprang to her chest. "I aim to please, Your Highness. I suppose I am precise."

"You aren't drawn to throngs of people gossiping about the latest drama?"

Pidge furrowed her brow. "Your Highness?"

Blaise groaned. "The whole of the castle seems to be up on the roof. It seems my dear brother and sister-to-be have found someone new to blame the family's troubles on. It's quite the scene."

The blood drained from her face. Pidge swallowed. *Siler.*

Blaise waved her hand with a sigh. "Go on, be part of the throng. Listen to the latest foolishness. I can tell you want to."

Pidge curtsied low and fled from Blaise's room, past her

guards, down the hall, and into the stairwell. Shouts came from up above, and Pidge leaped into a stream of people rushing up the stairs. The throng spilled out onto the large open space of the castle keep roof and merged with the mass of humanity already congregated. Pidge ducked, weaved, and elbowed through the swarm until she'd positioned herself only several rows away from the spectacle.

No fewer than thirty soldiers stood in a semicircle, pressing the people back as courtiers, staff, and servants alike craned their necks for a better view. King Axis stood in the open space behind the line of soldiers, with Avaya positioned meekly behind him, her hands folded demurely in front of her, gaze trained respectfully on her betrothed.

Pidge stretched on her tiptoes for a better view. Her heart dropped like a stone, and she felt sick. Siler was chained to the battlement, his arms stretched in opposite directions, his restraints taut. He held his head high, but there were dark bruises on his face and on one arm, and Pidge wondered how badly he'd been beaten before being strung up for humiliation on the parapet. Axis's voice boomed over the crowd.

"The Raven, also known as Siler, has been found complicit in the assassination of the late King Arnevon."

Pidge reeled. Avaya had told Axis the Raven's real name, and he was being accused of conspiring to kill a king. No one with such a charge could ever hope to survive. Especially no one who had been successful.

Axis continued. "He will remain on the wall until his compatriots kill him or turn themselves in for reckoning. Anyone who speaks to this man will be hanged. Anyone who touches this man will be hanged. Anyone who feeds him will be gutted. We must purge ourselves of the assassin wretches among us!"

Ah, the purging of evil argument. Pidge was familiar with

it. These must not be Axis's words, but Avaya's. Pidge wondered if Axis knew she'd got the idea from the founder of the Mount Hara program, the creator of the assassin network now threatening Belvidore. The Framatar always told them their work was noble. Would the Belvidorians buy it?

Pidge scanned the crowd, then shrank back. She almost hadn't recognized the well-to-do gentleman mingling with the nobles on the far side. Vix, a broad-shouldered man in his midtwenties, surveyed the chaos from beneath a brimmed hat with a ridiculous plume. He was one of the most experienced assassins from the mountain, class of 4993. Pidge remembered him as one of the dragon wranglers responsible for catching and training drakes. Seeing him like this was a shock to the system.

She angled away from him and looked back at Siler. She was sure he'd seen her. He was intentionally avoiding eye contact. Keeping her safe.

Axis paused for emphasis, then began again. "I have thrown myself into spearheading the investigation into my father's assassination."

Siler blinked once, more exaggerated than usual. For a moment Pidge wondered if something had gotten in his eye, but as she watched again, the exaggeration dropped away but the pattern remained. He was reacting somehow to Axis' statements.

"Many a sleepless night I have tossed and turned, the grief of his passing driving me forward."

One blink.

"I dream of a greater Belvidore, robust, peaceful, unthreatened by enemies hovering next door. Two kingdoms united. And my dearest Princess Avaya"—here he drew her up beside him—"has been more than I bargained for."

Two blinks from Siler. Understanding dawned. What was

the code Siler had suggested when he was picking on her? He said she would get caught, since she was a rookie. *Blink once for no, and twice for yes.* Pidge gasped. He wasn't reacting. He was *responding*, judging Axis's claims. And his messages were for her alone.

Axis carried on. "She has been everything I didn't know I needed in the wake of such tragedy. And together we shall take the tragedy in both of our nations and turn them to peace. And we begin by cleansing ourselves of any who dare put the honor of Belvidore in jeopardy. Rogue assassins running wild, traitors and spies, anyone connected to unsanctioned activities of violence will be put to death. But come forward now, with valuable information, and you may experience my mercy."

Pidge looked hard at Siler's face. He did not blink. His storm-gray eyes were like the sea, mysterious and mesmerizing at once. She studied the lines of his face. Drawn, but resolute. Worn, yet unflinching.

Axis pointed at Siler. "He knows all about who killed my father." Two blinks. Siler glanced at a point just beyond her. Was he watching her? Should she try to narrow down what he knew? Pidge mouthed, *Avaya*. Nothing. Neither yes, nor no? Maybe he wasn't sure. She tried again. *Tymetin*. Two blinks.

That was it. Pidge knew Avaya had the amulet *before* it was planted in the kitchens, and Siler had learned that Tymetin had carried out the hit. She had to get out and tell Semra. She could come back with Zezura and free Siler.

Pidge lingered, pain etched into her face. The pit in her stomach grew the longer she looked at him, but she couldn't tear herself away. He had defied the order of the princess, spurned her money, and protected Semra, Zephan, and Pidge. If he had accepted their bribes and followed orders, he would have remained happily on their payroll.

A lump rose in her throat, and her eyes stung. Siler turned his head ever so slightly, and for a moment their eyes met. The depths in those raging seas ripped her apart. Raw fear flickered across his face in the span of an instant. His chin quivered once and then regained composure. A single tear fled down Pidge's face, and she turned away, pushing back through the bodies in the direction she had come.

28

Zephan threw a jab, and Semra parried with her forearm and burst into close range. Zephan's long arms and legs would have put Semra on the defensive if she didn't break through his defenses to close the distance. She hurled her fist into an uppercut; he deflected, and she spun and swung an elbow down toward his spine.

Semra slowed her strike at the last second to protect Zephan's spinal column, but he rotated toward her, drove his shoulder into her gut, and lifted her feet off the ground so she dangled over his shoulder. Semra gripped his belt, pulled herself downward, and threw her heels over his head. Zephan stumbled and lost his hold, and Semra flipped over and landed on her feet just as Zephan twirled to face her.

His brows shot up and he grinned. "I think your agility is, um, recovered."

Semra laughed. "I feel like myself again."

Zezura lifted her head from the place she was sunning herself and stared hard down the mountain. She gave a short huff and put her head back down. Semra and Zephan followed her gaze and squinted hard to see what the giant lizard could easily decipher: a familiar form climbing the rock to their position in the cleft.

"That didn't take long," Zephan said. "It's only been two days."

It took Pidge several minutes, but shortly she made it up the rocky way and pulled herself up onto the ledge.

"Where's Siler? Is he coming later?" Semra asked.

Pidge shook her head, and for a moment Semra failed to breathe. Pidge's stoic focus crumbled into pain, and her eyes moistened with tears. She sniffled and grimaced, as if disgusted with herself.

Semra felt her fears collide in a vortex of terror as she pictured Siler in her mind's eye, lying on a cool marble floor in a pool of his own blood. Lifeless, flat, slate gray eyes stared up at her—another visual for her nightmares. She didn't get them as often as she used to. Not since Zephan took her from the battlefield. But surely causing the death of her only positive childhood connection would do the trick.

Zephan nudged her, and she gasped for air as Siler's body slipped from view and the mountainside returned. He stepped closer so that their arms touched and turned his hand so the back of his hand brushed hers. A tingle from his touch shot up Semra's arm. She took a shaky breath.

"Pidge." Zephan's voice was soft, but with a stern edge. "Tell us what happened to Siler."

"On the wall, on the roof. They got him." Pidge covered her face with her hands, then sniffed again and looked up. She spoke again, all in a gush. "Chained to the parapet. Axis commanded that no one touch him, talk to him, or feed him, on pain of death. Everyone in the castle was there. Huge crowd. They said he was involved in Arnevon's murder, and they'd leave him there until the rest of the accomplices either kill him or turn themselves in. Vix was there. He looks ridiculous. Thirty soldiers. Chains too thick. We have to save him."

Semra let out an unearthly squeak that was neither a cry nor a gasp and surprised her nearly as much as it surprised Zephan and Pidge. She clenched her hands into fists and took three slow breaths. "Is there a deadline?"

"No. There's no telling how long they'll leave him out there, or how soon they might take him down. And they didn't just say *the Raven*—they used his real name."

Semra's heart thundered in her chest. Zephan leaned against her side, and the slight pressure was somehow calming. Zephan spoke again.

"You said they …"

Pidge nodded. "Avaya was there too."

Zephan tensed beside Semra. He gritted his teeth. "Of course she was."

"Did you learn anything else?" Semra asked. *Was the whole venture for nothing?* And even if it wasn't, was it fair to ask one man to sacrifice his life to save her miserable reputation?

Pidge brightened a shade. "Avaya had the amulet before you were framed. It was in the folds of her dress when she first came back from the Strip, and then it was gone."

"Scourge!" Zephan ran a hand over his face and started pacing. He tugged at the hem of his tunic and turned to Semra. "You said you lost it on the battlefield. She must have lifted it."

"Or it fell, and she snatched it," Semra agreed. "But either way, she's been planning this."

"Tymetin made the hit," Pidge said.

Semra groaned. "Rats and rot. He keeps proof of contracts, and probably blackmail, but he'll never give it to us. And there's no way we could find them without his help."

Zephan cocked his head. "Is he …"

"The one who framed me for murdering your mother, and I took his bait, and got dragged off to the dungeons while he laughed at me? Yes." Semra slipped her single remaining knife from its sheath and started flipping it in her hands. "He's bested me at every turn."

"A startling revelation from someone with a dragon."

The trio on the mountainside jumped at the sound of a newcomer's voice and whirled toward the sound. Wide shoulders, thick forearms, and a cocky smirk greeted them. A thick-brown beard and long matching mane framed the smirk. His skin was tanned, his hands rough, and his eyes mirthless.

Semra snatched her knife from the air, rolled forward and popped up in front of her prince. No sooner had her feet planted in the dirt than Zephan slipped his arm around her waist and swung her behind him again. He drew his sword.

Zezura unfurled her long body from its place and snapped her jaws.

Pidge craned her neck around the pair in front of her. "You're Radix. Class of '98, right? Semra skipped a year and graduated with you, Isra, and Treq. And a few I don't remember."

"Fountain of knowledge, this one," Radix said. "Look at you go." His air was nonchalant, but his gaze slipped upward to keep tabs on the dragon.

Pidge shrugged. "The younger years always know the classes ahead of them. The older classes hardly ever care to know the youngers."

"I remember you," Zephan said. "You were in the throne room that day. You whipped Semra the first time, then you wanted the king to bribe you as a mercenary to switch sides, and in the end, you turned against Azi on your own. Whose side are you on today?"

Radix shrugged. "I haven't decided. Thought I'd do a little

digging of my own, since your little posse up here has all the drama. And little miss doesn't know how to lose a tail."

Pidge's shoulders slumped.

Warning bells sounded in Semra's mind, and her eyes narrowed. "What are you deciding, exactly?"

Radix indicated the sword hilt at his side and the bow on his back, then spread his hands. "First, let's agree to be civilized, shall we? No need for the prince to get his hands dirty."

"It wouldn't be the first time," Zephan said in a low growl.

Radix pursed his lips. "I should think not. You're quite the swordsman from my recollection. Much better than I'd anticipated."

Semra let out an exasperated sigh. "Just tell us what you came for."

"All right, don't get your scales in a twist. Rumor has it some strange things have happened to our dragonlord of late. I won't bother asking if that's true. The truth is, you know about the bounty on your head, but Madensig has several contracts out to kill you. It reeks of desperation, to have a bounty *and* a contract—and multiple, at that. But, alas, desperate men pay fabulously. Or desperate women."

"Are you so quick to give up your employer?" Zephan asked. "Avaya doesn't take kindly to betrayal. She tends to envision extremes wildly beyond reality and let them run away with her."

"Are you so quick to assume I meant your sister?" Radix countered. He laughed at the expression on Zephan's face, then waved him off. "You were right, anyway. That's precisely what I was implying. But the money is coming through the Belvidorian crown, not his pernicious fiancé. They've tried to cloak the funds, but anybody with a brain has already tracked it back to the source.

"I've come to decide whether to collect on my deliciously

expensive contract. Tymetin looks dreadful, and I've no desire to have matching burn scars. I like to keep as few similarities with the man as possible. So you can rest assured I have no plans on killing you now, with your dragon so easily accessible. But if I wanted to kill you, I'm confident I could get the job done. And I am hoping you'll convince me it isn't worth it."

Zephan whirled his sword in a low arc. "You're asking for more bribes."

"Maybe he'll take the bribe, then kill Semra and take the reward money," Pidge said.

Semra put a hand on Zephan's arm and took a seat on the rocky ground. Pidge and Zephan cautiously followed her lead, and Semra felt the tingle of the dragon's kiss as her instructions went out wordlessly to Zezura. Zezura shook her head in delight and bobbed up and down. She loved being in the thick of things. The enormous dragon let out a short puff of flame over their heads and settled in uncomfortably close to their guest. Radix shifted his weight and stepped back.

Semra rested a steadying hand on Zephan and Pidge's knees on either side of her. "Radix might expect killing me will break my bond with Zezura and leave him free to escape, but I frequently prevent Zez from killing people she doesn't like. It's hard to imagine the bloodbath she'd leave behind if not for me. Siler certainly wouldn't have made it this far."

Zezura bobbed her head again and chuffed a serpentine laugh. Semra smiled. "Radix, it seems we have business to attend to. I'd hate to waste our energy standing around feeling anxious while we got around to it, wouldn't you? Take a seat. You have the floor."

29

———

Radix lowered himself to the ground and did his best to retain that unworried look, but Zezura's nearness had shaken his confidence. "Just have her back off, will you? She was close enough to incinerate me as it was. There's no need."

"She's comfortable where she is," Semra said.

Zezura spewed another burst of fire just over Radix' head.

He ducked and brushed stray embers from his hair, then crisscrossed his legs and settled in. "Fine. What marvelous hospitality."

Semra shrugged. "I'm a better host than the Framatar ever was, and you know it. I haven't beaten you silly, had anyone eaten in front of you, or destroyed your view of yourself."

"Only one of you has flogged the other," Zephan said flatly. "As far as hospitality goes, I'd say that ship has sailed. I'd have run you through by now." His eyes were as stony as Semra had ever seen them, and every muscle of his body was tensed.

The scars on Semra's back prickled at the reminder, but Semra shut down the memory. Now was not the time. "Incineration by dragon is far easier. I see why Azi preferred it. But it does leave a burning smell lingering in the air." Semra gestured at Radix. "So we're supposed to persuade you against killing me?"

"Precisely," Radix said. "I have been working out a number of pros and cons, and thought you were just the person to help me iron out the details."

"Though undoubtedly somewhat biased."

"One would assume."

Semra's insides squirmed. She plucked at the stubble of grass at her feet, then pulled out her knife and began spinning it in the air to occupy her hands. Radix adjusted his scabbard beside him to a more comfortable position and clapped his hands together.

"Pros. Excellent payout. Fantastic connections to powerful people in Belvidore. Potential for a significant number of future jobs. Removes possibility of you turning me in to Jannemar for my crimes—the same kind of crimes you've committed—if I'm found there.

"Cons. Too much competition. It's bad for business to encourage such rotten deals, offering both bounty *and* contracts on a single target, and having to fight off colleagues to get to it first. Removes possibility of you helping the kids from the mountain that are currently failing to adjust to their new life. Elongates the war, which makes travel obnoxious." Radix spread his hands. "You see my dilemma."

Semra's chest tightened, and she pressed her lips together. He must not want to kill her, or he wouldn't be here. He wanted something from her. She needed to tip the scales in her favor, and he knew she'd be game to try.

Pidge grunted. "There are too many assassins in the area. It's bad for business."

"True," Radix said.

"Then why not leave?" Zephan asked.

Radix shrugged. "I have my reasons."

"You have your reasons." Semra mulled over the statement, tasting it, testing it, working through his list of pros and cons. He wouldn't care about being found in Jannemar if he planned to disappear far away. And he wouldn't worry that he'd be caught unless he'd be close Qalea, where he assumed she'd been setting up a life for herself. And he wanted her to help kids from the mountain. Since when did he care about humanitarian efforts of any kind? Since when did he serve anyone but himself?

A light dawned. Her lips parted. "You have a Lesala."

"Excuse me?"

Semra straightened, eyes bright, and looked him dead in the eyes. "You have someone you care about. One of the children. And they're in Jannemar, and you want to maintain a relationship with them. Aurin's spear, you have an ounce of selflessness somewhere in your rotten bones."

Radix' face drained of color, and his body went rigid. He swallowed.

Pidge perked up beside Semra and looked up at her hopefully. "It wouldn't be hard to narrow down. You were on the task force."

Semra looked back at her, her own brown eyes looking softly into the expectant, excited face of another daughter of the mountain. Another Lesala. There were so many. Semra's fear at her own impending doom melted away, and she felt every muscle in her body relax. They had stumbled upon a common goal.

She turned to Zephan, and they exchanged a knowing look. A matching smile crept over their faces as they shared the moment. He knew exactly what she was thinking. "We certainly *could*," he said. "The castle has record of where every child was relocated."

"You kill Semra, and we kill your … your young person you care about," Pidge blurted.

Radix's lip curled, and Semra patted her on the knee. "Take it down a notch, Pidge." She took a deep breath and settled into the confidence of tables turned. She had felt it the moment she'd identified his weakness. The real reason Radix hadn't killed her. Maybe even the reason he had turned against Azi in the throne room in favor of a stalwart, faithful king. The kind that keeps promises, the kind that takes care of his people.

Semra looked at Radix. He fidgeted, then stilled as he clung to the shreds of his poise. "We *could* do that, but we won't. You want a different life for this person. A better one than the life you've been forced into. You want to keep them safe and have the freedom to check in on them from time to time, which is of course totally counter to our training. You want an entanglement. An attachment. And it's too late to avoid it because they already have your heart. It's too late not to care. And they are suffering."

His face slackened and his shoulders dropped ever so slightly. There on the mountain, three assassins, a dragon, and a prince sat in the dust hanging on her every word. Every fear, every anxious thought melted to the back of her mind like wax before a flame, and she settled into that space where nothing else existed, nothing but the mission. Today, her mission was her life. Today, her mission was Radix Bandaka, still bound to that identity from which Semra had fought so desperately to break free.

Now was the time to release the most dangerous prisoner —the kind that didn't know they needed saving.

Semra spun the knife in her hands one final time and twirled it into the dirt so it stuck out of the ground half an inch from her toes. "Like I said, we could threaten your loved one, but we won't. Even if you decide to kill me. Zephan, assuming he survives this whole mess, will make sure of it."

Radix passed a skeptical glance from Semra to Zephan and back. "You can't know that. He hasn't made any such promises."

"I can and do know it. He has already made the promise because of the kind of person he is. It would be contrary to his nature to do otherwise." Semra looked at Zephan, and her breath caught as his amber eyes pierced her through. She knew every word was true. "We are together on this."

Radix looked at them skeptically. "You would give up your greatest bargaining chip? That weakness of mine is the best leverage you had."

Semra shook her head. "Caring for people is not a weakness. That was a lie. And I think you still believe a number of other lies we were told. Radix Bandaka, it's time to be free of them."

"Bandaka." Radix said the word slowly, as if exploring it for the first time. "I did some research after that day in the throne room." He looked at Zephan. "Your father was right. It *does* mean bondservant. The Framatar mocked us from the very beginning, even as he manipulated us into doing his will, as we begged for our turn to come. Our turn to proclaim our allegiance and formally become part of his sick, fake family."

Zephan nodded gravely. "You knew it was true. You could feel it."

Pidge opened her mouth, then closed it. She sat very still, and Semra could almost feel the wheels turning in her mind. She hadn't heard that before.

Semra refocused on Radix. "You want me to help you, and you said there are young ones suffering. I believe you, but I'm not sure what you're talking about. What's going on, and how can we help?"

"You'll forgive my skepticism," he said. "I'm not ready to share names. But some of the children are old enough to be apprentices in trades, or to hold jobs, that sort of thing. I know of one that was given a position at Shamaran but is ostracized, watched like a hawk, and not trusted or permitted to move freely. Another was placed in Qalea, was starving and wound up killing someone for food. The promise was to safely relocate them, to offer jobs and security, but the reality is they were dropped off and left to fend for themselves."

Zephan and Semra shared a concerned look. Zephan frowned. "That's not consistent with the program we had in place."

"Well, then your program isn't being followed. These kids are going to kill or be killed, or starve, or fall prey to some other manipulative schemer." Radix leaned forward. "Are they free, or not? Are there looming consequences, a hammer waiting to fall the first time they slip up? There was no trial. There was no acquittal. And yet they are not treated equally. And what are they going to do when they feel confused and like they're failing in everything new they try?"

Pidge stared at the dirt and her face fell. "Go back to what they know."

Semra was convinced in that moment that Pidge had tried to break free of assassin life before getting caught up by the promise of money and a fresh start. She'd gone after Turian because she had nothing else to turn to.

Radix spread his hands. "Exactly. They are lost."

"We need to follow up with the children then, make sure they're being treated well, treated fairly," Zephan said. "We can't give handouts forever, but we can make sure they have all the resources they need and get them on their feet. We want to be understanding, but at the same time we have a responsibility to the rest of our country to uphold justice. If they kill someone and get caught, they aren't going to be let off the hook."

"Which leads to another excellent question," Radix said. "What about me? You know who I am, what I've done. Am I to believe I can really roam free in Jannemar? Can I visit people in Qalea without looking over my shoulder?"

Something in Semra's gut twisted. She glanced at Zephan, suddenly unsure. Zephan caught her glance and took a breath. "We don't have enough evidence connecting most of you to any particular crime. None of you would voluntarily register as having grown up on the mountain, and you'd be fools to confess to the killings. But I'd be lying if I said we weren't nervous about what you all may be doing inside our borders. Or outside, for that matter."

"What would happen to us if … if we were identified in Qalea?" Pidge asked. "As being from Mount Hara?"

"That depends wildly on what we know of you. It's case by case. Some are known to have attempted murder on the royal family, for example. We know who is responsible for my mother's death, for example—or at least one of those responsible. Those who acted under Azi's treasonous orders to trespass our grounds and mercilessly attack our soldiers would have to be brought to justice."

Semra grimaced. It was the wrong thing to say.

Radix' mouth twisted into an unimpressed glower. "That's not confidence inspiring."

"It's honest," Zephan answered. "I'm not sure we even know what exactly we would do in a murky situation like that. We can't give bribes. It's not something Jannemar does."

Radix laughed. "It's what all powerful people do."

"I hope to prove you wrong. I want to do right by all of you and also do right by our people. My family wasn't the only one grieving a loss after Azi's coup attempt. A lot of good people were lost that day. I'm open to suggestions."

A lump lodged in Semra's throat. Sometimes she nearly forgot Zephan had lost his mother. He bore it so well, and most of the time they spent together was spent in high level crisis, which tended to distract from grief. Still, in quiet moments when the distractions died away, sadness sometimes settled.

"Justice for your people is death to all of us from Mount Hara," Radix said.

Semra shook her head. "I think it's more complicated than that. I think we can negotiate."

"Even if we were forgiven, how are we supposed to just … move on?" Pidge asked. "What am I fit for? I can't spend my life gardening or staying home cleaning house for some old snoot. Who'd want me, anyway?"

"Pidge, we're trying to keep Semra alive right now," Zephan said. "But I'm sure we'll find you something you're happy with after she's out of harm's way."

Semra groaned. "*Out of harm's way.* Is that even a thing? Is that possible? I've never lived like that. It sounds weird." Nice-weird, though. She ran her finger along the handle of the knife at her feet. "Finding a new purpose isn't easy. And they aren't required to stay in whatever arrangements we help them make. We're offering a starting point that won't land them in dungeons or nooses, and a way to pay for food while they build their own lives. If they're being mistreated, we can fix that. All the younger ones are innocent, kidnapped children, and nothing in their history is held against them."

"You did that before, and it's not working. Anyway, where does that leave me?" Radix asked.

"Let's come up with an arrangement," Zephan said.

Radix gave a small smile, but his eyes were hard. "Ah, there it is. The bribe."

"Consider it restitution," Zephan corrected. "You already helped save us in the throne room. Whatever evils you've done since then, we have no proof of, and you can help us keep Semra alive and Jannemar safe for you to travel in. I'll wager we can fix the competition issue for you too. But if you kill again within our borders, there will be no further mercy."

Radix pursed his lips. "I have your word this arrangement will allow me to come and go as I please, and my ... entanglement will have your protection?"

Zephan dipped his head. "My word."

"I'm not accustomed to accepting word as bond. You haven't got anything shinier to go with it, have you?"

Zephan lifted his hands, palm up, and gestured to his peasants' clothing. "Afraid not. But again, that would get us into bribe category."

"The sword would do. Looks fancy."

Semra held up a hand. "Let's focus on keeping your little one safe, shall we? Whoever they are, they'll need us all alive to keep our promises and make sure they get what they need. First, your end of the deal. You need to not kill me, obviously, and we need to make sure nobody else kills me."

Radix nodded in mock concern. "Lofty goals."

Pidge rolled her eyes. "Where do we start?"

"Not so fast," Radix said. "We still need to iron out the details of my arrangement. And I want it in writing."

"I need time to think," Zephan said. "I'm on my own out here, and I don't have my father's crown."

An idea was forming in Semra's mind. Radix and Pidge had similar anxieties about how Jannemar would treat them. The other Mount Hara assassins would feel the same. They would assume the worst, and they were trained to kill first—never mind about the questions.

She had to pacify them with real, authoritative answers before they destroyed all hope for themselves and slaughtered Zephan, Semra, and the whole monarchy across Belvidore and Jannemar.

Semra sheathed her knife and jumped to her feet. Zezura straightened with a rustle of wings to look at her lord, and the three humans on the ground gaped up at her. Semra planted her hands on her hips.

"You may not be king," she said to Zephan, "but you are the crown prince, and you *do* carry authority to make a variety of field decisions." Semra turned to Radix and Pidge. "I am one of you, and I will represent you in a private audience with the prince."

"Have I agreed to such a meeting?" Zephan asked. "Sounds dangerous. One on one with an assassin." He grinned.

"You're currently one on three, so the ratio will only get better." Semra licked her lips and surveyed her companions.

"After we negotiate the details of Radix' deal and our offer to all the children of Mount Hara, we are going to host a caucus of assassins. And we are going to go to Siler."

30

Semra and Zephan left Radix and Pidge behind with the dragon and set off for some illusion of privacy. Zephan stared at her the whole time as they clambered up a ledge of the mountain and disappeared around the bend. His amber eyes were wide and sparkling, and he nearly burst the second they were out of earshot.

"You're magnificent, you know that? Magnificent. You have this confidence, just in the moments you need it. It just ... took you over. He came to play games, and you took hold of his heart and ripped it from his chest to do surgery. You cut to the root, found the child or whoever it is, and it worked. You're a master negotiator."

Semra blushed. "I don't know about that. I just knew he was like me. He had a Lesala. And he needed me to save her."

Zephan shook his head, smiling. Something in his face flickered somber, then warm and soft. "You remind me of my mother." She pulled back in surprise, and Zephan laughed. "I didn't expect it either."

Semra waited, unsure of herself, but he didn't expound on his statement. She took a breath. "Pidge wanted to know what she's fit for after all of this. I don't know. I don't know what I'm fit for either. I can't imagine spending my days as a baker or a seamstress. It's bad enough wearing skirts for missions. But spending the rest of my days making leg traps for women whose lives revolve around lace and frills? I think I'd rather die."

"Maybe you'll meet someone." Zephan's tone was light, but his face was hard.

Semra glared at him, longer than she should have. The silence betrayed her, and she looked away. "I think I'd rather die."

"Good. I'm not sure I could stomach watching you with anyone else."

Semra's cheeks blazed red, and she swallowed. His words streamed in like sunlight in a dark, dusty room, when a window is opened after far too long. She didn't want to stop him. She wanted to ask him to tell her more. "You get brave in peasant's clothes," she said softly. "Almost like someone with a peasant's freedom, whose only responsibility is to keep himself and his cattle fed and watered."

Zephan let out an exasperated breath, as if the reminder of his status took all wind out of his sails. "Aurin's spear, you're exhausting. Maybe, if you ever stopped avoiding things and told me what you wanted, we could talk about it."

"I didn't leave Zezura to babysit Radix and Pidge while Siler is chained to a wall so that we could squabble about our feelings," Semra said. She bit her lip. She hadn't meant to be so harsh.

Zephan arched an eyebrow. "So ... you're admitting you *have* feelings."

Semra crossed her arms and steeled herself against the butterflies in her stomach that were refusing to behave themselves. "I'm admitting that you're a very frustrating person.

And that right now, you are not Dahyu. You are His Royal Highness, Crown Prince Zephan of Jannemar." Zephan grimaced, and Semra wrinkled her nose. She continued. "And I am the incredibly reasonable and remarkably convincing representative of the Mount Hara assassins, come to negotiate terms for our treatment and freedom in Jannemar."

It took two hours for Semra and Zephan to work out the details. The two of them batted around ideas, several times nearly coming to an agreement and then one or the other of them bringing up a new concern that threw the whole thing off and made them start over. Once they were agreed, they returned to find Radix and Pidge avoiding eye contact with each other across an expanse of scaly dragon hide. Zezura was half asleep by the time they returned, but she perked up at Semra's voice. Semra and Zephan relayed the arrangement, and Radix and Pidge both found it acceptable.

The sun set over the mountain in a swath of reddish orange, a mesmerizing combination of aggressive color and calming effect. The plan was set, the location chosen for the meet, and Pidge and Radix set off down the mountain into dusk. By the time Zephan and Semra met Pidge at the base of the mountain, it was well into the night. Pidge handed over a massive roll of canvas, a coil of rope, and three large bottles, and receded into the city, where the last of the sparkling lantern light had long since winked out under a crescent moon.

Semra watched until Pidge disappeared, then turned to Zephan.

"Together?"

"I meant it when I said you're not leaving my sight," he said. "Together."

Indigo blue rippled across Zezura's scales, chasing away her usual aquamarine and royal-blue patterning. Semra planted a foot along a row of her spines and took her seat on the dragon's back. Zephan climbed up behind her, and Zezura lifted off into a chill breeze.

The rush of adrenaline was a welcome familiarity as they flew up over the mountain and became one with a clouded expanse of darkness. Goosebumps ran up Semra's arms. The crisp, clean smell of the night sky filled her nostrils. The firm, yet silky smooth plates of Zezura's body were cool to the touch.

It was good for the soul to be up in the clouds.

Nothing but the occasional torch broke up the blackness across Horen and the valley beyond, where the Surion River flowed down from the mountains, filled the extensive moat, and hurried along to the contentious Surion Strip. The Surion originated from the same wellspring as the Dezapi, that same wellspring where it was said Aurin destroyed magic forever.

The moon reflected dimly in the river, and Semra shook her head. He must not have done a particularly thorough job, considering her unexpected smoking. She rubbed her fingers. Most of the black had worn away by now, but the shock of it never quite did.

Zezura angled over the city in a gentle descent, her sights set on Madensig. The fortress loomed out of the night, a bridge leading across the moat to the drawbridge. Semra was grateful for Zezura—it was much too far to swim, and they would need height for this night's feat. The outer walls were just as she expected them, boring old stone dotted with guards and the invisible archers she knew were hidden in the towers. But as they swept over the keep, Semra couldn't help her sharp intake of breath.

A semicircle of torches cast a haunting orange glow on a lone figure chained to the parapet. Thirty guards stood stock still in the fringes of the flickering light, fifteen feet from the prisoner, armed with an assortment of spears and swords.

Zephan's strong arms cinched tight around her, and the security of his presence eased the knot in her stomach. Semra felt Zezura's suspicions match her own as they coursed overhead and arced back to make another pass. The dragon dipped low behind the soldiers, and as she squinted into impenetrable shadow, Semra's vision was pulled into the dragon's kiss. Zezura's night vision was far better than human sight, and Semra's lip curled at the buckets hidden in the pitch, in reach of each soldier.

Konnolan.

She had suspected it would be here. They were baiting her, and they wouldn't do it without proper preparation. Semra took a steadying breath. They'd have to move fast and hope Zezura wasn't hit.

She tapped two fingers to her opposite wrist. *For Siler.*

Zezura swept through in a low *woosh* of wind. In an instant, the gush extinguished all but one of the torches; its lonely final flame was knocked to the ground at Siler's feet, licking the stone. Semra felt the dragon gather herself and they surged forward in another pass, ducking, weaving, and knocking over half the buckets of konnolan.

Shouts and screams erupted and the castle wall sprang to life as soldiers collided, spinning in circles for a glimpse of the invisible intruder. The men clutched their weapons and tightened into half a ring around Siler. Siler's head snapped up to the sky, but they were moving too fast for Semra to see his expression.

Zezura dove down and up, weaving in and out along the top of the wall, then pulling away and dipping out of sight across the wall beneath the battlement where Siler was chained. The dragon pressed close to the wall beneath the soldiers, and Semra and Zephan used the stencil of the canvas and the paints Pidge had provided beneath the soldiers, on the wall facing Horen. Arrows zinged by them from the towers, and they rose up and over the wall. Semra opened one of the bottles of accelerant and Zezura flew in a strange zigzag, hovering pattern as Semra formed letters on the stone from the dragon's back.

The smell of pitch, petroleum, and sulfur filled the air. A sickly sweet smell mingled with the sulfur, and Semra's head swam as fumes wafted upward. Semra glanced down and saw one of the soldiers had plunged the surviving torch into a bucket of konnolan.

She felt herself slipping, but Zephan held her fast. Zezura dipped beneath the parapet and rammed into the stone wall, the beast's mighty shoulder gouging the brick in that place as her wings curled in on themselves. The impact reverberated through all three bodies. Zephan's grip failed.

Semra toppled and fell.

The unforgiving sod of the outer ward raced toward her. How many bones would she break, landing in this position? Deadly talons snatched her out of the air, and her fingertips grazed the grassy doom she'd so nearly suffered.

Up they climbed, floor by floor, past the roof into konnolan's snare. *Push it away, Zez. Change the direction of the wind.*

Zezura opened her mouth and released a deluge of fire as they flew up the wall and crested the battlement. The dragon readjusted her grip on Semra, but she slipped. Semra dropped to the wall and rolled to her feet. Zezura shrank back from the chemical impact of the konnolan and circled overhead.

Thirty men roared to find their prey caught in their midst. Semra could feel the effects taking hold. She needed to lie down. She couldn't face thirty soldiers of any caliber. Siler's lips were chapped and parted, his eyes wide and burdened, his arms outstretched so taut as to leave no room at all for movement. The chains were too thick even for Zezura to break, and certainly not in the fraction of a second Semra had to act.

Siler propped his leg in a ninety-degree angle to the wall and braced; Semra locked eyes with him only for a moment before planting one foot on Siler's thigh and launching herself off the wall into the emptiness beyond.

"We will come for you," she shouted, but her voice was swallowed by the wind.

Her arms and legs flailed hopelessly before crashing into something solid. She landed belly first over the back of the dragon and slid backward into Zephan. He covered her body with his, pinning her to Zezura as they leveled off, then pulled her upright.

"One more pass," she yelled. She didn't know if he heard. She didn't care. Zezura banked hard and drove across the roof one final time. The dragon unleashed a fiery flood on the open roof, and the accelerant powder they'd arranged from the air lit the night. Zezura twirled downward across the wall and smothered the canvas hanging there with a sea of flames.

Zezura bore Semra and Zephan away from Madensig, and Semra breathed in the last pure breaths of night before sunrise. Thirty soldiers cowered from dancing flames spelling out one word: *BOND*. And as dawn kissed a drowsy Horen, the city would wake to strange new artistry on the outward facing wall. A blazing blue dragon was stained on the rampart. The blue dragon's wings unfurled in victory as its body entwined a smaller black wyvern, and its tail wrapped around an emerald-green snake.

31

SILER

A shrill scream rocked the Madensig throne room, and somewhere a door slammed. There was a crash, a *thud,* and a long pause. Siler rolled his shoulders back and cracked his neck. His wrists chafed from the chains binding his arms behind him, and his knees smarted from being tossed on the unforgiving floor. Ankle chains had been added to his restraints, and he faced two empty thrones. A truly laughable number of soldiers stood en masse behind him. Surely no prisoner had ever enjoyed the compliment of so many guards.

A door in the back of the room opened, and King Axis of Belvidore strode across the sparkling floors and took his seat on the throne. He wore all manner of regalia and rapped heavily bejeweled fingers on the arm of his chair.

Siler tilted his head. "Did you get all dressed up for me? No need to primp on my account."

Axis's mouth turned down in a disgusted frown, and he jerked his head at a guard. Pain exploded at the back of Siler's head. Siler winced and recovered. "No jokes today. Got it."

The door along the back wall opened again, and Avaya

floated out. Siler imagined her languid, supple movements were only made possible by her snake-like perniciousness. She wore beauty like the bait of a siren, and her strike was just as lethal. Siler's lip curled as he watched her slither into the seat to Axis's left.

Presumptuous for a daughter of a rival kingdom, yet to be wed to Belvidore.

Axis took no notice. "I'm in no mood, Raven. What is the meaning of the symbol?"

Siler pressed his lips together to suppress a smile. He'd seen the fiery letters, of course. The soldiers had scrambled to put it out, but the accelerant was strong, and the giant bold letters of the word *BOND* had graced the rampart for the better part of an hour. Siler hadn't gotten a glimpse of the wall itself, but it was impossible not to hear the whispers in every hall and guard room they'd passed.

He drew his brows together in false confusion. "What symbol?"

"The *dragon*, you simpleton! The blue dragon, and the black dragon, and the green snake! What is she saying to us? Why didn't she take you with her? Is she threatening us?"

Siler glanced at Avaya and hesitated. There was no question in her eyes, only the endless depths of a stony bitterness. She knew precisely what the symbol meant. It was blatantly obvious to anyone with half a brain and a rudimentary knowledge of the Mount Hara assassins. Why hadn't she told Axis?

"What do I get in exchange for this information?" he asked.

"You're in chains before me," Axis said. "Do you really think you are in a position to negotiate?"

Siler shrugged. "Considering I have information that you want and apparently don't have"—here he tossed a pointed look at Avaya—"I'd say it's my only leverage. Might as well milk it."

"Your life," Axis growled.

Siler grimaced. "No good. I've grown quite accustomed to the idea of dying, and I believe someone else in this room may kill me if you do not."

Axis's eyes narrowed. "I know your kind. You are as manipulative and twisted as Semra. Don't sling accusations you will regret."

Avaya crossed her legs and drilled him with a cold glare to match the king. Axis may have hired a few of the assassins, but he knew nothing about them. He was their purse or their prey.

Siler pursed his lips. "She thinks herself an expert on us, but everything she knows, she first heard from me. Do I strike you as a trustworthy fellow? And on the off chance I do, then consider that neither you nor your father ordered her to be kidnapped, but hired me to do the job and came to you under pretense."

Axis lifted a finger. Siler braced himself as a guard slugged him in the gut. He grunted.

The king lifted his chin. "Do not lie to me again. You are complicit in the assassination of His late Majesty, King Arnevon. Your head belongs in a basket, and then tossed out for the dogs. Tell me what I want to know or I end your miserable life here and now."

Telling the king would only worry him, and paranoia ran in the family. Why hadn't Avaya told him the symbol? How would her life be complicated by him knowing?

Anything that made life difficult for Avaya was a victory for Siler. He dipped his head. "Your city is overrun."

Axis brows shot up. "I beg your pardon?"

"No need to beg, Your Majesty. I said *your city is overrun.* You think you've bought the allegiance of the Mount Hara assassins, but there are too many for that. You think a band of miscreant contractors raised on lies will not see through your empty promises and double dealings? Setting a bounty and a slew of contracts on a single target simply isn't done. It's asinine. The only thing we kill for aside from money is revenge."

Axis's face reddened, and Siler forged ahead before the king could stop him. "You want to know what the symbol meant? A blue dragon—*the* blue dragon—defeating a black wyvern and a green snake."

"The snake is obviously symbolizing Semra," Axis said. "It has been her token since my father's death."

Siler paused. It was a simple explanation from an outsider's perspective. Was there any reason to let him believe this? His eyes flicked to Avaya. She was allowing it. He would meet them in the middle ... with a twist.

"Yes, Your Majesty. An astute observation."

Axis settled back on his throne, satisfied that his captive was telling the truth at last. Siler continued. "The blue dragon represents both Semra's actual dragon, and Jannemar as a kingdom. You're familiar with the three gates of Shamaran Castle? Dragon Gate, Spear Gate, and Nezzi Gate? All based off the flag itself, which incorporates all three elements into its banner."

"Yes, yes of course I'm familiar." The king gripped the arms of his chair, and Avaya straightened, her lips tight. They hung on his every word.

Siler took a slow breath, letting the apprehension of the moment marinate. "In the symbol, Semra links herself with her own dragon *and* with the kingdom of Jannemar. Up until now she has supported the Jannemari crown, but never formally considered herself a subject of any nation. She has declared war on a smaller dragon—a kingdom she views as lesser and already defeated. It is not a message for you, but for the assassins you have both hired and snubbed. A warning for all who aid Belvidore."

"She *is* threatening us, then." Axis stroked his beard. "And yet she left you on the wall."

"I am not as important to her as you think. She is as twisted as you say, and if she leaves me with you, and you kill me, she can circulate to the others what you do with assassins after you hire them."

Axis glared at him. "I have never hired you for a kill."

Siler shrugged. "I've been on your father's payroll for weeks, and now I am on yours. Who's to say?"

Axis rose from his throne, and his lip curled. He marched down the steps and waved off the guards. They stepped back just as the king landed a punch across Siler's jaw. Siler registered the coppery taste of blood as Axis's fist smashed Siler's lip across his teeth. Axis leaned down and yanked Siler's head back by the hair.

"I had thought of killing Arnevon myself," the king said, soft enough that only Siler could hear. "He was a dimwitted oaf, cowering behind his borders, refusing to do what needed done. I just hadn't gotten around to doing it. So you see, I'm not sorry you did it. I just can't have you doing it to *me*."

Siler stilled, and a vague nausea washed over him. Axis didn't order the hit on Arnevon. He didn't even know who was responsible. Siler's gaze shifted over to Avaya, the corners of her mouth contorted in a coy smirk. A tingling sensation swept over him, and he clenched his hands into fists behind his back. There was an uptick in his breathing, and a wave of hatred settled over him like thick fog.

She was behind it all. She organized her kidnapping, gossiped her way to every morsel of information held by every class, and twisted powerful people around her finger in such a way that they begged for her to do it again. It was Avaya who had ordered the hit on Arnevon and moved her prince into the king's coveted position. Someone she could control.

Axis kicked Siler to the ground and returned to his throne with a small, wicked smile. He had no idea that the danger was not in chains before him, but in the throne beside him.

Siler spit blood from his mouth in Axis's direction and ran his tongue across the damage on the inside of his swollen lip. Avaya leaped to her feet, screaming obscenities, and was on him in a flash. She slapped him hard across the face, and Siler's head snapped backward.

"You're pathetic," she shrieked. Quieter, she added, "So many attachments, so many fears. And to think I admired you."

Siler scowled, then smoothed his face into a neutral expression. Nonchalance angered her more than a reaction ever could. Avaya's eyes blazed, and she raised her voice and turned back to her fiancé. "My love, do not speak to him anymore. He isn't worth it."

Siler watched them, the king soaking in every suggestion of the venomous woman before him. The king was a weakling, and Avaya was a masterful schemer. Avaya slapped Siler again, gripped him by the shirt, and crouched down, bringing her lips to his ear.

"You're going to be my puppet," she hissed. "A mural on my wall, a trophy of my influence. She doesn't love you. She never has. But she *will* come for you. And we will be waiting when she does."

32

Zezura banked hard and convulsed. Her body shuddered beneath Semra and Zephan as they plummeted from the sky toward the mountains. Semra groaned, her head spinning, her muscles weak, and her stomach lurched with every jerking movement from the dragon. Zezura's wingtip grazed the trees at the base of the mountain; she pulled up just in time to nick a rocky overhang and tug herself higher up once again. The dragon leveled off, spotted the mouth of a small cavern north of Horen, and tail-spun down to meet it.

Semra's eyes watered against the wind as Zezura slowed their descent and made for a rocky landing. Zephan steadied her around the waist and helped her down. Semra put her hands on her knees and breathed hard until her system regulated. Zezura puffed out two smoky tendrils from her nostrils, coughed, and folded her wings.

Zephan peered at Semra questioningly.

"I'm okay," she said. "I think Zez got the brunt of the fumes, and it's way less than when we got dosed in the bloodstream. I'm already feeling better." Semra put her hand out on

Zezura's side, missed, and tripped over her feet. Zephan caught her.

"One hundred percent recovered," he said.

Semra waved a hand. "It'll pass. I'm *almost* recovered as it is." She scratched her head, ran a hand over her eyes and blinked. "Are we at the same cavern Radix said we'd set the meet for?"

"Location seems about right. I think we are."

Chunks of moss and grass ran up to the yawning cavern mouth. The opening was wider than it was tall, perhaps fifteen feet high and thirty across. Though modest compared to Mount Hara, it was certainly a decent size as far as ominous dark holes went.

"We should check it out," Semra said. "I want to scout the best spot for a meet, and we need to figure out what we're going to tell the Mount Hara assassins once they get here. Supposing they show up."

Semra, Zephan, and Zezura stepped into the entrance to the cavern and found a wide-open space quickly narrowing into two channels, each too narrow for Zezura to follow.

"That's no good," Semra said. "We need her with us."

Semra and Zephan came out of the cave and worked together on a makeshift torch out of a tree branch, tree bark, rope, sap, and Semra's spare tunic. When they were finished, Zephan stuffed extra bark into Semra's pack and slung it over his shoulder, then they returned to the cave for Zezura to light the torch.

"We'll see what other openings we find, Zez," Semra said.

Semra and Zephan chose one of the two tunnels and ducked through a narrow opening leading downward into darkness. Cobwebs clung to the sides of the passage, and Zephan cleared them with the torch. It took several hours to explore the first tunnel and its twists and turns, but there appeared to be no suitable outlets for Zezura, so they eventually returned to the main room and set off down the other tunnel. For a while, nothing could be heard but the sound of their soft footfalls, and the echo of a displaced pebble as it bounced down the slope into some open space further in.

The night's events replayed in Semra's mind as they walked. She thought of the look in Siler's eyes when they'd been so close, so close yet so far from saving him. They were never going to be successful, not yet. Leaving the message on the wall of Madensig was just step one in a much longer rescue attempt with far too many variables to be optimistic.

Siler's rescue, Semra's name being cleared, the contracts to kill her being canceled—all of them hinged on the meeting going well.

"On a scale of one to ten, how stupid is it for a bounty target to invite a group of assassins over for a chat?" Semra asked. It had been ten minutes since anyone had spoken, and Zephan jumped.

"Um ... it's a solid seven, I'd say. Where would you rank a prince who gets in trouble for hanging out with one assassin, choosing to put himself in a room full of them without any backup, and not telling anybody where he is?"

Semra's lips quirked. "Oh, at least an eight. Maybe a nine."

"Scourge. Well, at least I'm doing it with someone more level-headed than me. I wouldn't dare partner with another eight or nine on the scale."

Semra laughed, and the sound bounced along the walls. She sobered. "We couldn't have gotten him free, right?"

Zephan stopped, and she nearly bumped into him. He turned to look at her, and the flickering torch light illuminated their faces in an orange glow. His eyes were soft, that molten amber Semra could get lost in. "No, we couldn't. He was fastened to the wall without any slack. There was nowhere for

Zezura to grip it without ripping through his skin, and if she slowed down, the guards would have killed us *and* Siler. And Zez would've inhaled more konnolan, and none of us would have made it. We did the right thing."

Semra bit her lip and nodded. Zephan turned round and continued leading down the tunnel.

"Zephan?"

"Yes?"

"What if nobody comes? Or what if everybody comes, and they slaughter us all? What if they bring konnolan? What if this is a bad idea?" Semra's throat constricted and she choked on her last words.

Zephan took her hand and pulled her forward into an odd-shaped open area extending upward by twenty feet. Electricity ran up her arm at his touch. He squeezed her hand. "It's a bit late for that now. Radix and Pidge should be here tonight, and we'll feel it out then. Your only other option is to stay away from Jannemar forever. Call me selfish, but I'm willing to roll the dice. We'll have an escape plan. We always do."

"We always have a plan, but they don't always work."

Zephan shrugged. "Life's messy that way. We'll take what comes and face it together."

Semra nodded. She swallowed, but the lump in her throat didn't budge. She felt the sting of oncoming tears and spun away from him, trudging further into the cavern and away from the torch's reach. Suddenly Zephan was there, folding her into his chest, his chin on her head, his free arm wrapped tightly around her shoulders.

Semra couldn't hold it in any longer. Sobs racked her body as all her fears and grief collided in a flood of terror, like a dam breaking after years of holding back raging waters. She clutched him to her, and he held her close.

We'll face it together. Semra had never had a *together*, not really. It wasn't right that Zephan should be here with her, however grateful she was for it. She wept that a true *together* it could never be. She wept for her friend Brens, who had betrayed her for fear of the dragonlord, but returned to her in the end and been slaughtered for it; she wept for Zephan's mother, Queen Sharsi, whom she'd failed to save; she wept for her own mother, whom she barely remembered. She wept for herself, and every other orphan child of the mountain whose life had been pilfered by Azi's hunger for power.

Rivers of tears kept flowing as the ache in her chest shifted. "I don't want to die," she whispered. "I don't want you to die."

Zephan said nothing, but his arm squeezed her tighter against himself. His shirt was damp with her tears.

"You'd think I would be used to people trying to kill me," she said at length. She sniffled and wiped her face with her hands. "I've looked over my shoulder ever since Rotokas stole me from Kalma when I was four."

"It's not something we're meant to get used to," he said. "Even if we do get used to it, we give up a piece of ourselves to lock away our fear. It's not really gone."

"How do you do it? How do you bear everyone's expecta-tions, and demands, and tearing you a thousand different directions? How do you survive being a prince, with all its requirements? Don't you ever feel ... caged?"

Zephan cleared his throat, and Semra almost regretted her questions. His voice was thick with emotion when he spoke. "I often feel caged. It's like I said. I think I lock a piece of myself away, and shove it down, and hope it doesn't rear its head at an incredibly inconvenient time for me to fall apart."

Semra swallowed. She took a shaky breath, then laughed. "We're in such different worlds. We never should have met, you know? You're a prince, and you inherited full time respon-sibilities just by being born. You have to be strong. You have to be just, yet merciful; authoritative, yet listen. You have to look at every scenario from an individual level and then again from a kingdom level.

"I'm just a sheltered girl from a mountain like this one, born to two dead nobodies, raised by a criminal, trying to speak up for the ones that can't, and getting a lot of people killed along the way. I want to be safe. I want Lesala to be safe. I want Pidge to be safe. Scourge, I want Siler to be safe too, despite his every idiotic effort to do stupid things."

She pressed her face into Zephan's shirt, and she felt him catch his breath. She clenched her jaw to keep another round of sobs at bay. "I need you. We all do, but I'm one of the only ones that knows just how much. You are our chance at having a life for the first time. And it's not fair that that's put on you either. We keep you in your cage."

"Is that why you need me? For my influence—the way you think I can keep a kingdom safe?"

Semra grew deadly still. Her fingers tensed against his chest, and she pulled them away. "You know it isn't."

Zephan drew back and slipped his hand around the back of her neck, tilting her head up to meet him. "Do I?"

Semra's mouth went dry. "Needing you in any other way isn't fair."

Zephan swore. "Stop it! I need to know if I'm alone, Semra. Just tell me you don't like me. Tell me you don't feel alive when we touch, or a thrill every time our eyes meet. Because I lie awake at night thinking of you. I dream of you, and when I wake, you're the only one I care to see. I'm useless anywhere else, because whenever you're not there I'm wondering where you are and if you're okay. I'm wondering if you're wondering about me too. And I'm wondering ... I'm wondering if you think about our kiss outside the arena as often as I do."

Semra froze. Her heart skipped a beat, and her eyes drifted

from his intense golden gaze to his lips, and the line of his jaw. She bit her lip. "I ..." Her voice trailed off into nothingness, and her stomach flipped.

Zephan ran his knuckles up her arm in a gentle graze that sent goosebumps across her skin. He took her wrist lightly in his hand and extended her arm under the glimmer of torchlight. Her hair stood on end, every inch of her reactive to his touch. She looked away.

"Tell me," he whispered. "Tell me I'm not alone."

Semra leaned into him a moment, mesmerized by the lull of his presence. She snatched her hand back and punched him in the chest. "I can't do this! You know I can't. I can't!" She pivoted and fled from the cavern.

33

———

Semra flew down the passage, up the incline, and out the mouth of the cave. Zephan let her go, but followed close behind, giving her room to move, but not so much that the torch didn't light her path as she ran. His thoughtfulness irked her.

Daylight assaulted her senses, and she came to a stop at the line of sun and shadow in the cavern opening. Zephan's running footsteps scuffed the dirt behind her, and then halted. Semra winced as he put out the torch and stepped in front of her.

He planted his feet a shoulder width apart and crossed his arms. "Why can't you say it?"

"Because if I say it, it'll be real. And that would be ridiculous."

"As opposed to your current, more rational approach of punching me and running away? You can't even look at me."

Semra snapped her gaze to Zephan's face and stepped forward, eyes blazing. She opened her mouth, but as she looked at him, the bite on her tongue died, and her anger melted to frustration. She took a breath and peered up at him. When she spoke, her voice was soft.

"When I look at you, I see everything I didn't know I needed. When I'm sad, you're the one I want to hold me. When I'm scared, you're the sword I want by my side."

Zephan stared at her, and his lips parted. He'd been begging her to say what she felt, but perhaps he hadn't really believed that she would. But she was still beating around the bush. He slipped an arm around her waist. "So ... does that mean you like me?"

Semra rolled her eyes. "Zephan Shamaran. I like you. A lot. And if you weren't a prince, I'd run away with you the moment you asked me and die happy knowing I'd never have to leave."

Zephan beamed a beautiful smile from ear to ear, and Semra couldn't help but return it. His arms tightened in victory, but Semra gripped his arms and held him at bay.

"But you *are* a prince. So remember us from your marble floors and white halls. Remember when the woods were home, and your clothes were tattered. When your sword drew blood, and you didn't know what tomorrow would bring. Because that's not an excursion for me. That's daily life. A different world."

"Why don't you remind me, every day?" he asked. "What would you do if I told you we could figure it out?"

"I'd say your father has been trying to talk sense into you, and you haven't been listening."

He paused. "What do you know about my conversations with my father?"

"Nothing except what he told me."

Zephan groaned and stepped away. He ran a hand through his hair. "What did he say?"

Semra threw her hands up, half reeling from admitting

her feelings, and half relieved the tension of the moment had lifted. "It was so confusing. He said something good, and something bad, and good, and bad, and then told me if I cared about you, I'd stay away."

Zephan frowned. "Tell me everything he said to you."

"He said he can't be seen playing favorites with someone like me. He said all the evidence pointed at me killing Arnevon, and when I agreed with him, he was surprised, and said I was terrible at diplomacy."

Zephan snorted.

Semra cocked her head at him, but dismissed his reaction and moved on. "He told me to stay sequestered in my room and let him handle things. I'd already received death threats from Siler, but didn't know it was him, or who was threatening me. Turian said he doesn't like having nobles sometimes, but he has to network with them and make friends. And he said I should make some friends, because I don't have many."

Zephan grimaced. "You don't have many in the castle. But outside the castle, I think you've made a few."

Semra lifted her chin and sniffed. "I have more than you'd think. I got help from multiple people on my way out of the castle, thank you very much. I just don't have many *snooty* friends. Your father failed to specify."

Zephan smirked. "Snoots, hmm? You've been around Pidge too long. But what did he say about *you?*"

Semra shifted her weight. "Um ... he said I reminded him of the queen, but then he said she entered royalty gracefully, so the list of our similarities must be pretty short."

"Why?"

Semra arched her eyebrows. "*Why?* Did you just ask *why* I would think your mother, gorgeous, elegant, beloved—prim and proper queen—was different from me? *Look* at me. I'm made of mountain. Dust, and dirt. Rats and rot, I wear *trousers*. With knives. And I constantly say things I shouldn't say."

"I think you're gorgeous. And would be beloved if you let people in more. You might be made of mountain, but that's where Nezil Myansara grows. You're resilient. It's inspiring."

"I don't think there's much about my life for people to emulate," Semra muttered. But when she looked up at him, Zephan's eyes were far away, and something in them glistened.

"What else did he tell you about my mother?" he asked.

A pang struck her heart. "He said she reminded him he was human. She cut through all the political garbage and told him how things really were."

Zephan paused. He seemed to be taking his time soaking in her words. "Anything else?"

"He said being king is lonely. And he said love is not enough for a king, that the kingdom is like a third person in the marriage of monarchs, and the stress of it can tear you apart. He said it's dangerous to be attached to someone who can't take on the crown with you. That if they can't bear that weight, they need to keep a distance and not be a distraction. And then he told me to stay out of trouble, and I lied to him."

Semra's insides squirmed, and when Zephan didn't reply, she crossed to the outside of the cavern and leaned her back wearily against a mossy rock. Zephan followed, seated himself beside her, and took her hand. She resisted the urge to snatch it back, and instead allowed herself to revel in the feel of his touch.

He turned her hand over and drew his thumb lightly across her palm, sending tingles across its surface. "Thank you," he said at length. "He hasn't talked about her much. Not to me."

Semra dipped her head.

Zezura slept in a tight ball twenty feet away. Semra would

never have imagined a dragon of her size in a ball, but there was no other way to describe it. She wondered what it would be like to sleep so fully dead to the world.

She turned her head and stared out over Horen. Madensig Fortress was easy to spot, set apart by the moat and rising over the city—the place where everything always went horribly wrong. Siler was down there somewhere, in chains, because of her. Avaya was there, schmoozing a new enemy king. And Tymetin had framed Semra for murder and gotten away with it.

Zephan squeezed her hand. "So. You like me."

Semra startled at the sound of his voice. She cleared her throat. "Yes."

"What … what do like about me?"

"You're really pushing it now, aren't you?"

"Please."

Semra sighed. "You're kind. You're good to people, regardless of their status. You make me laugh, and you feel like home. That's a big deal for someone who's never had a home."

Zephan twined a curl of her hair behind her ear. "I think we're good together. I think our negotiating a plan for the assassins together proves it. And I think you're a much better diplomat than my father thinks you are—you just need to be in the right frame of mind. Outside the castle walls, you're a phenomenal negotiator. You see all sides of the issue, and you work toward a solution that feels like a win for everyone. You chase down common ground that may seem hard to find, and you build on it.

"I think we could solve any problem we put our mind to. You challenge me. You make me think, and you slow me down. I get so … bogged down by the stress of my position, clouded sometimes by being so caught up in everything. You give me perspective and remind me the *why* behind what I'm doing. You give life a light I never had before. I'd be a better ruler one day, if I had you with me."

Semra's jaw dropped. He was forgetting himself. She searched his eyes and couldn't tear herself away from the earnest tenderness she found there. "Your father would kill you if he heard you talking like that."

"Have I mentioned lately that I think you're beautiful?" Zephan asked, ignoring her statement.

Butterflies erupted in her midsection. "No." Was that a tendril of smoke floating up from her fingers? She tried to look, but Zephan blocked her view and held her gaze.

"You are, without question, the most stunning creature I've ever seen."

"I doubt that," she said. "You've met lots of women."

Zephan shook his head. "No, no. It wasn't a question. It was a statement of fact."

"Ah. My apologies."

"I accept your apology. Now, my question is, what does the beautiful woman think of the snooty prince? How do I ... look to you?"

How did he look? Semra was dumbstruck. *Like a lighthouse on a stormy sea. Like sunshine in a windowless dungeon.* Her eyes swept over him—the definition of his chest and arms, the cut of his chin, the curve of his lips, the molten honey gold of his eyes. She blushed.

"You're ... not terrible to look at," she managed. *Seriously? That's the best you could do?* She licked her lips and tried again. "Strong. Handsome. Um, you're incredibly good looking. I'm pretty sure it isn't fair."

Raw delight lit Zephan's face. He released her hand and inched toward her, leaning over her until their noses touched. She thought he might kiss her, and her heart flipped in an explosion of emotions. But he held back.

"What would you do if I tried to kiss you?" Zephan whispered, his lips grazing hers as he spoke. "Because I've been dreaming about it for weeks."

Semra's heartbeat rose to a thundering roar in her ears. A shiver crept up her spine. She ran her hands up his chest, and a flash of heat rolled from her body and singed his shirt in a dotted pattern where her fingertips had been. She shrieked and pulled back.

Zephan jumped and looked down at her in shock.

Semra flexed her fingers. She could feel the heat, could sense its direction now. She pushed the heat from her hands through her fingertips into a harmless, warm glow. "Sorry."

Zephan glanced at his shirt and grinned. "This just became my favorite shirt."

Semra laughed and reached for him, and they kissed for the first time not as a cover but as themselves—a prince and an assassin, a man and a woman, the mystery and disbelief of their pairing as intoxicating as the notion that every secret hope they'd held inside was now realized.

Great plumes of dark smoke gushed from her fingertips and coiled around them in ebony ribbons. When she opened her eyes, she yelped in surprise, mouth agape.

Zephan pulled back and watched the smoke as it curled about them and dissipated into the air overhead. A soft smile crossed his face. "I wonder if…" He never finished.

Zephan kissed her again, hard, her lips still parted as he took control of her mouth. Semra lost herself to the kiss, and the smoke billowed unchecked until they were utterly enveloped in shadow. Sparks flew from her fingertips, bright pops of fire on a swirling background of deepest gray.

A tug came through the dragon's kiss on her chest, but Semra ignored it. She drank in the passion of Zephan's touch like a desert welcoming its first rain. With one hand his fingers twined through her hair at the nape of her neck, and with the other he drew her into him at the waist. Her heart leaped and warmth flooded her body; she pulled him closer as their lips moved in harmony.

The tug from Zezura came again, more persistently. Demanding. *Not now!* Semra shot back. But the dragon would not be ignored. Semra gasped at the intrusion of bursting color as Zezura's vision cut into her world. But as the jolt wore off, Semra looked down the slope and settled on the reason for Zezura's fear. A figure was coming toward them, and he'd had made it nearly to their position before being detected.

Dread set in.

Tymetin.

34

TYMETIN

Tymetin climbed the side of the mountain, a sword at his side and a shield on his arm. Both forearms were wrapped in linen from elbow to wrist, but if he was in pain, he didn't show it. And he was nearly upon them.

Zezura released Semra's vision, and she was plunged back into darkness. Zephan drew back, and the two of them sat stock still.

"Semra?"

She pressed a finger to his lips and brought her mouth to his ear. "Tymetin is here. Stay down." She released him, then hesitated. "You're my safety."

"You're my smile."

Her stomach dropped, and she turned away and fumbled for Zezura. Semra pulled herself up onto Zezura's back and slipped her knife from its sheath. Zezura stepped out of the smoky cloud already wafting away behind them and stretched her wings on the rim of the rocky ledge. She bobbed her head up and down and flashed her scales purple and crimson before settling back into her typical aquamarine.

Tymetin trudged up the steep slope and scowled up at the

dragon from the cleft below. There was a six-foot drop from the ledge where Zezura and Semra stood and Tymetin's position. Zezura breathed fire down on him, but he lifted his shield just in time. Hatred rolled off Zezura in waves. Semra could feel her hostility burning through the dragon's kiss.

Semra rolled her shoulders back and sat tall. The shield dipped down again, and Zezura restrained herself. Angry red burns stood out on the outside sliver of his face, chin to hairline on one side. Semra had only guessed at the mystery archer who had tried to kill her before, but this removed all doubt.

Tymetin gestured at the smoke arching up into the sky and swaying off into the breeze. "That's a fun trick."

"Get a little burned recently? Looks nasty. You should really do something about that."

Tymetin's lip curled. "I see you've made some strategic connections since betraying all our private business. Did he scurry off into the cavern?"

Semra pursed her lips. "Are you upset you can't add him to your collection of signatures? No blackmail for you. He doesn't bribe for blood."

Tymetin arched an eyebrow. "I wouldn't be too sure. He loves too many people too much. That makes a man vulnerable. And his sister is rather less scrupulous."

Semra gritted her teeth and prayed Zephan was smart enough to stay out of sight. "I know you're not here to kill me —this time—so you might as well tell me what this is about. I'd rather not look at your hideous face a moment longer than necessary, no matter how proud I am of Zezura for improving it."

Tymetin glowered at her, but Zezura chuffed a deep dragon laugh. At least someone appreciated her jokes.

"I'm supposed to tell you that Axis will kill Siler unless you turn yourself in to Madensig and confess to the murder of King Arnevon."

Semra clenched her jaw. "That will be difficult to do, since you're the one who killed Arnevon."

Tymetin shrugged. "That's not my problem. But since we both know you'll never confess, I'll skip to telling you his best offer up front. You have until sunset in three days' time to turn yourself in.

"Anyone entering or exiting Horen in the next three days with weapons of any kind will be arrested. Anyone entering or exiting the castle for any reason will be searched. Anyone seen with you will be shot on sight. Archers are instructed to shoot first, and not bother about asking questions."

Semra's grip on her knife tightened, and her free hand balled into a fist against Zezura's thick scales.

Tymetin continued. "The bottom line is that Siler will be dead in seventy-two hours unless you do this, and so will anyone who attends your little get together. By the way, a nasty rumor is going around that you're going to assemble all your Mount Hara colleagues and then kill them." Tymetin clucked his tongue and shook his head sadly. "Such sad slander."

Semra's pulse ratcheted up, and her nostrils flared. "What's keeping me from killing you where you stand?"

"Ah." Tymetin shook his finger and nodded, as if he had just remembered the answer to a riddle he had very much been looking forward to telling. "I'd hate to threaten only one of you, when we both know your princeling is nearby. If I do not return safely to Madensig, Axis will kill Avaya. And if Turian does not retreat from the Surion Strip, Axis will marry Avaya, and she will live out the rest of her useless marital days under house arrest. Oh, and one more thing—we've got a drawing of Pidge circulating in Horen, and if she is found, she'll be killed without trial."

Semra's gut twisted, and her throat tightened. She squared her shoulders. "Let me get this straight. Axis expects me to turn myself in, confess to the hit, and *then* let him kill Siler and me?"

"Nothing so unreasonable. He's willing to release Siler in exchange for you."

Semra lifted her chin. "If he wants me that bad, my life must be worth more than one assassin."

"How many assassins do you require, precisely?"

"I want Siler and Avaya."

Tymetin scoffed. "Ridiculous. Axis would never let her go, and even if he did, she'd only claw her way back. She wants to be in Belvidore."

Semra raised her eyebrows. "It's not required that she *want* to come. Only that she is delivered out, with Siler, alive."

Tymetin shook his head. "He'll never do it."

"Tell him anyway."

"He won't send me out here again. How would you like to receive his rejection?"

Semra hesitated, drumming her fingers on Zezura's back, then looked down at Tymetin again. "Give us a cage of homing pigeons. We'll let you know."

"They won't be delivered. You'll have to pick them up."

"Fine. No konnolan, no soldiers, no tricks. Leave the pigeons on the roof tonight."

Tymetin's eyes narrowed to slits. "Done."

Tymetin turned to go, then glanced back up at Semra. "You've found another friend."

Semra looked down the mountain and saw two figures at the base, a man and a woman, too far off to identify. She couldn't take the chance of revealing Radix' identity to Tymetin. Semra nudged Zezura and the dragon lurched off the ledge to the landing where Tymetin stood.

Tymetin leaped back, lifting his shield to cover his face.

"Our business is done," Semra said. "Go."

Tymetin scrambled down the incline, and Zezura spewed a burst of fire in his direction to encourage his descent. Tymetin swore, and Semra smiled. Small victories.

As soon as Tymetin was far enough from Zephan to satisfy her, Semra took Zezura in a dive over the mountain and landed in front of Pidge and Radix.

"Wow, you really missed us, huh?" Pidge said.

"Get on. Tymetin is here, and he says there are posters of you all over the city. You're lucky you got out of Horen."

Semra reached down and helped the girl up.

"What service," Radix said. "Girls only?"

"You haven't earned a proper ride," Semra said. "But Tymetin is on his way down, and I can't have you running into him, either."

Zezura beat her wings and Radix's hair blew behind him as the dragon lifted off and the wind rushed over his face.

"What are you—*aughhh!*"

Radix's words cut off as Zezura plucked him off the mountainside and flew them back up to the cavern ledge, Radix clutched tight in her talons. Zezura dropped Radix unceremoniously on the ground and alighted nearby; Semra and Pidge slid down and Zephan stood to greet them.

Radix groaned. "That was unpleasant."

Zephan's glare fixed on Semra. "Are you going to tell me what you think you're doing?"

"Relax, I'm not going to confess to murdering Arnevon," Semra said.

Pidge pulled back. "Dragons and daylilies, what did we miss?"

Zephan's hands rolled into fists. "Tymetin says Semra has three days to turn herself in and confess to killing Arnevon, or they're going to kill Siler. And I noticed you didn't say anything about not turning yourself in, just now."

"I'm not going to. But we *are* going to save Siler. First, we need to hear how our little message went over with our colleagues in Horen."

Pidge lit up. "The symbol was genius. Black and blue dragon images are popping up all over Horen, painted on walls, scratched into doorposts. There must be more assassins here than I thought."

"Moths to a flame," Radix muttered. "But it's not all good news. There are a lot of black dragons alone, or blue ones that are broken and bleeding. That doesn't bode well for their opinion of you."

Semra's heart sank.

"But there are blue dragons too, either alone, or defeating a black dragon or green snake," Pidge added.

"How many?" Semra asked.

"Hard to say," Pidge hedged.

Radix frowned. "More black than blue, I think."

Zephan took a deep breath. "Tymetin said everyone coming in and out of the city was being searched, and there are posters of Pidge everywhere. Was he lying? How did you get out?"

"We, um ... removed a couple guards on the north side." Pidge darted a glance at Radix and looked sheepishly at Semra.

Semra glared at her. "You killed them?"

"Pidge insisted we not kill anybody. You're rubbing off on her in a very questionable way," Radix said. "Don't worry. We commandeered a wagon, chucked a couple of unconscious guards into it, and left them to wake up with a little hike back to the city."

"Unconscious guards?" Zephan asked.

"They were unconscious by the time they made it to the wagon," Pidge said. "What's our next move?"

Semra took a deep breath. "Tymetin is threatening all the assassins. He doesn't want us to meet them in the next three days, and is trying to spook them, but it'll only give us more time to stoke the fire. Spread the word—we're meeting all Mount Hara assassins here in four days. Pidge, I have a new symbol for you to draw. And in the meantime, we need to stall our deadline for Siler. We're going to rile up the king."

35

———

The wind nipped at Semra's face as they flew down over Madensig at dusk. There was no reason to wait for night. She was no longer hiding, and the more people that saw Zezura, the better. Let all of Horen hold its breath and wait for another glimpse of the dragon.

Zephan refused to be left behind. Semra mulled over the words he'd spoken before they'd left the cavern. *"I meant what I said. I'm not letting you out of my sight, and I will tell the court precisely what I saw... and didn't see ... when we go home. You may be a warrior, but you are no longer what they think you are."*

It was eerily similar to what his father had said to Semra back in the courtyard of Shamaran Castle.

"People don't like being friends with killers," she had said.

"Nonsense. People don't like being friends with murderers. *You and I are both killers."*

Soldiers were killers, but not murderers. If even Turian labeled himself a killer, perhaps there was hope for her yet. There was no way to shake the fact that since childhood, she had devoted herself to the taking of life. But perhaps she could prove, like Zephan had said, that she was no longer an assassin.

Semra and Zephan knew the truth. Avaya had hired Tymetin to kill Arnevon. But they had no solid evidence—only rumor, the whispers of people too afraid to give meaningful testimony. But maybe if Semra could show who she really was, she wouldn't need their testimonies. Semra couldn't imagine a life where she never saw Zephan again. Not now.

She blinked hard against tears brimming in her eyes at the thought. *Stop it, Semra. You have a mission.*

Zezura swooped down over the castle once, twice, three times as they surveyed the rampart. A bird cage with four pigeons was set out, and guards lined either end of the wall. There was no sign of konnolan. Zezura let out a blood-curdling screech. The men flinched but stood their ground. Semra could almost feel the eyes of every man and woman in the city turning their gaze to Madensig and the dragonlord swirling over it.

Zez released streams of fire as a warning to the guards, and they pressed themselves backward. *That's right. Give us space.* Zephan's arms tightened around Semra's waist to stabilize her as Zezura flew next to the wall and Semra leaned out and grabbed the bird cage. Zezura lurched upward, and Semra dropped a large rock down to the wall below. The note would reiterate her demands—Siler and Avaya present on the rampart of the south outer wall, rather than the wall of the keep where they had been before, for proof of life. No konnolan, no tricks. In exchange, Semra would provide her confession and they would set up the exchange, Siler for Semra. Tomorrow night.

They returned to the cavern and set the bird cage down. It

was stocked with parchment and writing utensils, and a note pinned to the bottom.

Zephan pulled out the note and read it.

Princess Avaya is safe but will not be returning to Jannemar. In Belvidore we respect the wishes of our women and defer to Her Highness's integrity in keeping to her promise. She declines your invitation, but Siler will be released as soon as the conditions of our agreement are met.

He scowled. "We do respect our women. Idiots."

"But Avaya *does* want to stay in Belvidore," Semra said. "So he's right about that, at least."

Pidge grimaced. "And Jannemar doesn't allow for female-led monarchy, but Belvidore does."

"It's an archaic tradition." Zephan passed a hand over his face, and his features looked worn. "We probably should have changed it long ago. But he's only saying those things to throw low jabs."

"I don't care about your little highbrow offenses," Radix said. "I'm ready to paint some walls."

Semra glanced beyond him at the large stencil they'd created. A blue dragon stood over broken chains and the words *Bandaka is bond.* Semra smiled. "Good, because it's nearly dark. You did great, Pidge."

Pidge beamed.

Semra dropped Pidge and Radix inside Horen under cover of night to scout the city for signs of the children of the mountain and leave their messages. Semra and Zephan took turns catching snatches of sleep or staring anxiously up at the stars, and then they picked up Pidge and Radix before first light.

Being around Zephan was electric. She thought often of their kiss, their conversation, and his belief there could somehow be hope for them. Zephan was constantly at her side, and she was grateful for his nearness, even when nervousness came over her. It was dangerous to hope.

They didn't have a chance to relax together again, between strategizing with Pidge and Radix, scouting the surrounding area for mobilizing troops, and taking shifts to sleep. In the rare moments they were alone together in daylight, Semra was afraid of the enormous smoke signal she could send up from their location again if she and Zephan got too close.

Three nights remained until the deadline. On the first night, Semra and Zephan flew back over Madensig. It was evening by the time two figures emerged, hidden in the shadow of the south tower. The man was dark haired, strong, and in chains, and the woman was richly dressed, with golden curls spilling over her shoulders. Two lines of guards created an aisle as they stood watch on either side. The two guards furthest from the tower held torches along with their swords.

Zezura coursed over the parapet with a burst of fire. *Yes. Let them know we are here,* Semra thought to herself. *Let them all know.* Zezura banked for another pass and breathed out another stream of fire, this time the flames kissing the stone of the battlement.

Light blasted through the darkness, chasing off the shadows and illuminating the two figures. Two strangers blinked back at her. Semra's lip curled and anger seethed in her chest. Axis was playing games. Poorly.

Smoke curled from her fingertips, and suddenly Semra was grateful for the cover of night after all. The city should see the dragon and dragonlord, but not the freakish, uncontrollable smoking. Zephan gripped her hand, and she took a breath, pushing the heat out of her hands, and releasing the last of the smoke. Three sparks popped from her fingers, their embers floating through the night, lost to the sky as the dragon turned away.

"No," Semra hissed aloud. "No, we're not done."

"Semra, what are you doing?" Zephan spoke in her ear, the tone in his voice begging her for caution.

It was too late for that. She gave the order. Zezura would know what to do.

Semra closed her eyes and pushed into the reptile's vision. She felt the shift, the welcome as Zezura acknowledged her presence. The dragon enjoyed the connection, and for the first time, Semra did too.

The definition was impeccable. Where she had only made out dim outlines toward the tower, she could now see the lines of each body stark against the gloom. But it was better that those on the wall could see as little as possible.

Kill the lights.

Zezura surged forward, slinging her wingtip over the torches and extinguished them in the span of an instant. Audible gasps ripped through the breeze. The door to the tower opened, and the troops pushed and shoved toward refuge.

Take one.

The dragon made a final pass, her talons outstretched. A shrill, otherworldly cry shook the air. Guards cowered. Arrows flew. Zezura seized a guard and rocketed off into the sky.

When they reached the mountain, Zezura dumped the unlucky guard at the mouth of the cavern, curled herself into an enormous ball, and went to sleep. Semra slipped off the dragon and her knife was in her hand before her feet hit the ground. The guard put a hand up toward her, palm out in surrender, and then retched over the ledge.

Pidge wrinkled her nose. "Gross."

Radix cocked an eyebrow. "So it went according to plan, hmm?"

"Aside from Axis thinking I'm dumb enough to accept decoys, yes," Semra said. She glared at her new captive.

"I don't mean to complain about your, erm, initiative, but I'm going to venture to say we had too close a call," Zephan said.

Semra whipped her head toward him. "What are you —ohhh!"

Her hand flew to her mouth. The shirt on Zephan's upper arm was torn and stained with blood. She ran to him and squinted at the injury, but it was too dark.

"Zez, I need your eyes," Semra said. An extra curl of steam rose from the dragon's nostrils, but there was no response. Semra sent a pulse through the dragon's kiss, and Zezura huffed discontentedly. She opened one eye, then the other, and lifted her head just enough to be eye level with Zephan's shoulder. Semra pulled the tunic down over Zephan's shoulder, slowing when she heard his sharp intake of breath. She dropped into Zezura's vision. It seemed to be a graze, with no dirt or debris. There was a small divot in his arm, and it was still bleeding.

Semra took back her own vision, and Zezura resettled herself to sleep. "We need to clean it, but you'll be okay."

"I could have told you that."

Radix tossed Semra a small flask of spirits. "I brought my favorite medical treatment."

"You had better not have been drinking," Semra said with a disapproving glare.

Radix rolled his eyes. "Sure, not at all. I had to be on the top of my game for all the excitement I had today with Pidge."

Semra opened the flask and carefully poured it over Zephan's injury. He flinched once, then was still. She ran her fingers over the curve of his shoulder, and he turned toward her in the dimness.

Pidge eyed the guard. "Can we keep it?"

"It probably has a name," Zephan said.

"Fine, whatever. What's your name, puky?"

The guard gaped at her. Pidge lunged at him, and he lifted his hands again. "Puri."

Pidge drew back, and his gaze danced between Pidge, the dragon, and the other three standing around him.

Semra stepped forward and crouched in front of the guard, her knife blade glinting in the scant moonlight. "Have you ever lived in a cave, Puri? Because most of us" —here she swept her hand toward her companions—"grew up in one, and feel as at home in the dark as we do in daylight. You're going to stay out of sight in the cavern, and you're going to tell us everything you know, every rumor, every whisper, or I'm going to flip a coin to decide whether I let Pidge flay you alive or the dragon tear you into manageable bite-sized pieces."

Puri gulped.

"We've had a long night," Semra said. "So we're going to take shifts and get some rest. Think long and hard about what information you may have to share, because your openness might determine how long you live. Your king doesn't mind wasting human life, and he breaks promises daily. I am not like him. If you're reasonable, you'll be released in a few days."

Semra spoke privately with Pidge, Radix, and Zephan about her plans for the guard, and Radix took him into the cavern. Semra sat down against Zezura and leaned into her. The dragon didn't open her eyes, but her tail curled around Semra. They both let out a long, weary breath.

Zephan stretched out on the ground five feet away and stared up at the stars. "You're confident when you need to be, and you get things done. You made me nervous when you took the guard, but you're playing hardball, and Axis needs that. You're doing a great job."

Semra swallowed hard against the lump that sprang up and ached in her throat. *You're doing a great job.* She cleared her throat. "Um, thanks."

The words replayed in her mind over and over until she drifted off into a fitful sleep. By the time she woke, a soft purple haze mingled with pinks and blues over the mountains. Dreamy whisps of cloud overhead heralded the dawn. Semra rubbed her eyes. Radix slept just inside the mouth of the cavern, and Pidge and Puri were out of sight further in. Zephan was feeding bits of roll from Pidge's scavenging the night before to the pigeons.

Semra extracted herself from Zezura's tail and walked over to Zephan. He tore the roll and handed her half, then gestured to the parchment. "Ready?"

Semra took a bite of the bread and nodded. She'd been thinking about what to say. She picked up the pen, dipped it in ink, and touched it to the paper.

Zephan leaned over her shoulder and dipped his head. "I like it."

Semra stared down at what she'd written:

You weren't listening. Proof of life. Siler and Avaya, the rampart of the south outer wall. Tonight.

She let out a breath. "Off it goes, then." She rolled the message up tightly, and Zephan stuffed it into the tiny canister and attached it to one of the pigeon's legs. He released it into the air, and the two of them watched it fly.

Zephan looped his arm around her shoulders, and she leaned into his side.

"Proof of life is even more important after last night," Semra said. "Axis won't be happy. He'll either be so desperate to have me that he keeps his leverage alive, or he'll be so angry that he strings up Siler piece by piece."

"To tonight then," Zephan said, solemnly toasting her with half a bread roll.

Semra tapped his half with hers. "To tonight."

36

AVAYA

Avaya chewed her nail and searched the skies for the hundredth time in the last thirty seconds. When she had agreed to the proof of life, she'd thought the experience would be quick, relatively painless, and unrepeated. The decoys had been a stupid plan, and Avaya had opposed it, but Axis thought the dark and the height from the dragon would be enough to conceal his deception. Semra had stolen a guard along with her blasted pigeons, and insulted the king with her message.

The following night, Axis had agreed to an honest proof of life, on the southern wall as requested, but with well-hidden konnolan. The plan had been impeccable. There was no way Semra and Zephan had seen the chemicals. And yet they had —or perhaps Zezura had sensed it. And again, the dragon had dragged off a guard.

A second homing pigeon had brought in another insulting message:

I said no tricks. Try again.

Avaya licked her lips. It was dusk, the time when Zezura

had made her first pass the last three nights, but there was no sign of Semra and her brother. Why did Zephan insist on coming along, anyway? She couldn't ensure his safety. Only Semra's demise. Avaya sighed and rubbed her wrist where the chain chaffed.

It had been Avaya's idea to chain one wrist and one foot to the castle wall to keep the dragon from carrying her off. She shuddered. No, the ride she'd taken with Semra on the dragon's back had been bad enough. She couldn't imagine those massive claws digging into her perfect skin. And right before the wedding!

She cast a sideways glance at Siler, who was chained safely out of reach. He was watching her. Smirking at her.

"What's your problem?" she demanded.

"You've had that chain on for thirty minutes. It can't possibly be annoying you yet."

"I don't know. You've only been talking for ten seconds, and you already annoy me to no end."

"I can't believe you wanted to learn to fight better than Semra. You wouldn't have lasted one training session with me."

Avaya scowled. "I'd have done better than you think."

Siler gestured to the knife hidden on the inside of her sleeve. "You realize if you ever fought her, she'd be able to take that from you and gut you with it, right?"

"You're quick to compliment the woman who left you here," Avaya said with a sniff.

"You're quick to kill everyone who cares about your family."

Ire burbled up in Avaya's chest and her lip curled into a snarl. "You're lucky I let them chain me. Perhaps I'm tired of hiring people, and I'm ready to take matters into my own hands and kill you myself."

Siler pursed his lips. "Killing isn't the solution to everything. I should know. Besides, I've never seen a more desperate employer than you. And I'm your only leverage."

Avaya gritted her teeth and turned away. He was right, of course. She couldn't shake the hatred she felt for Semra. Her death was the only way to be free of it.

She scanned the rampart. Fifty soldiers packed the wall tonight, twenty-five on each side. They stood in tight formation, expressions neutral, their only nerves showing in a taut muscle or glance at the sky. Which one of them would be next if Semra wasn't satisfied?

Her heart hammered in her chest. Could the archers bring her down? Every slitted window of the towers held an archer, but none could be visible on the wall. Would they get a good shot?

What if they hit Zephan? Her blood ran cold. They certainly had their differences, but before Semra had manipulated him and poisoned him against her, he and Avaya had been close. Well, maybe not *close*, but as close as an older, underestimated sister and a younger, golden boy brother could be.

A rustle and gasp among the guards shook her from her thoughts. A blazing azure dragon broke through a thick cloud much closer than Avaya had expected. Her glare locked onto the flying beast, and terror gripped her chest. *She's going to kill me.* The thought burst through her consciousness like a clanging cymbal. *Idiot, she can't take you off the wall, but she can kill you where you stand with a ball of fire or a stroke of a claw!*

Zezura aimed for twenty feet over their heads, and at the last second dropped low. Avaya was going to be run over. Avaya screamed. She flung her hands over her head and dropped to the ground, her wrist held over her head to its fastening point on the wall. A rush of air pressed her back against the parapet as the dragon swept past where Avaya's head had been just seconds before.

Avaya braced herself for a second pass, but it didn't come. Not a single arrow had left a string. She chanced a glance skyward. Nothing greeted her but swaths of blues and pinks, gently fading into twilight.

She straightened, frowning. That was it? Could she really be so sure of their identities with a haphazard pass quicker than a falcon dive?

"Hey, Avs."

Avaya shrieked and nearly jumped out of her skin at the sudden sound of her brother's voice. She whirled, only to find herself nose to nose with the scaly face of the dragon herself. Avaya froze, eyes wide. She tore her gaze off the dragon and over the wall where the rest of Zezura's body was hiding, clinging to the wall of the fortress, its wings blocking Semra and Zephan on her back from any assault from the towers. Was this how Avaya would die? In chains, while her enemy and her own brother looked on?

Zephan's eyes were ice. He set his jaw. "Give our regards to your fiancé."

The dragon lurched upward one last time, and as Zezura crossed above them, a large rock dropped to the stone walkway. A great roll of parchment half-unfolded from underneath it, and Siler kicked the edge of the paper so it unfurled its full length.

The sign was four feet long and impossible not to read from anyone standing within reasonable distance:

Dearest King Axis:

Good boy. I accept your proof of life. Now for one final request.

You want to kill any assassin that doesn't take jobs for you, and let them kill each other on their way to the same targets. You are not operating in good faith. Free the children of the mountain and make no more contracts. The blood on our hands may fill rivers, but the blood on yours fills the oceans. Do this, and I, Semra, will fulfill our agreement.

37

"Stop worrying about it," Radix said to Pidge as she hopped from one foot to the other, spinning a knife in her hands. "The meet is set. Either they'll show up and try to slaughter us all, or they'll stay away, and that will be that."

Semra grimaced. "Optimistic, I see."

Radix shrugged. "Okay, the third option is that fearless dragonlord Semra gives an epic speech that sways every heart from revenge and violence to warm and fuzzy feelings, and there's a group hug."

"I will not be participating in the hug," Pidge said. She jerked her head to their two hostages, bound and gagged inside the cavern. "What about them?"

"They get to witness it all," Zephan said. "They'll tell what they saw on the wall and take what they hear back to Madensig."

Pidge furrowed her brow. "Speaking of which, I'm surprised they haven't responded to your message yet, Semra."

"It was a big move," Semra said. "Last night was day three, so by adding a demand I missed the deadline. They'll be considering all their options, and they'll probably want their response to be public since my insult was public. That said, though, we should probably swing by again and check."

She stood up and stretched her legs. Zephan sprang to his feet, and Semra laughed. "You're going to get sick of my face."

Zephan grinned. "I am convinced I could never be sick of your face. Distracted by it, yes, but sick of it, never."

"Getting bold, princey!" Pidge said. "I thought you two were committed to being weird and tense and pretending you aren't in love."

Semra froze, and she and Zephan both slowly turned to stare at Pidge.

She frowned. "What?"

Radix guffawed. "They're ready to be flirty-flirts, but not the big *L* word."

Pidge rolled her eyes. "Nothing I've said should come as a surprise. As far as smart people go, you're both awfully stupid."

Zephan cleared his throat and turned to Semra. "Shall we go?"

"Yes, *please.*"

Semra let Zephan help her up onto Zezura, and she offered a hand back down to help him up after her. They took off toward Madensig, and as they neared the south wall, Semra saw Siler still chained to the rampart—and a white flag waving above him. For a moment Siler was still, and Semra feared it was only his head fixed to the top of the wall without his body, or he'd had his throat slit as he stood there, but then he turned to look at her.

She locked onto him, and he returned her gaze. His arms were outstretched as they had been each night, wrists chained on either side of him. The chains were thick, with little slack.

But today, there was a little. Could Zezura rip out the base from the wall without taking Siler's arm off?

"Semra. The flag."

At the sound of Zephan's voice, Semra ripped her attention away from Siler and looked at the flag waving above him. Large black letters declared the king's response:

His Majesty, King Axis of Belvidore, is a great king. Outlaws and crooks do not dictate his clemency. You have until sundown.

The meet for the Mount Hara assassins was set for that afternoon. Semra had no idea if their conference would even be over by sundown. If they could get Siler now ...

Zezura swept past and did another loop. Two arrows bounced off Zezura's shining scales, and the dragon banked left.

"Get going, Semra," Zephan warned. "It can't be done. Not now."

Semra clenched her jaw and wheeled Zezura around for another pass.

"Semra!"

The chains were thick, but if she could get just one of his hands free, and Zezura could pull the other side out of the wall ...

If she could melt the links of the chain, or cut them somehow, with something hotter and more precise than Zezura's flame ...

Siler shook his head. *Don't do it.*

Clink. Whizz. Clink.

"Semra, you're going to get us killed!"

Zephan's scream in her ear yanked her from her trance. Semra turned the dragon on a sharp tilt away from the arrows, the hard scales of her underbelly taking the brunt of a shower of archers' missiles. The children of the mountain were not human. Once they were innocent children, with large, frightened eyes and an abyss of grief and terror inside. How long had it taken for that deep chasm to shut off their emptiness from the surface, to twist their minds into grasping at straws—anything for a semblance of family, the comforting lie of purpose?

How could they be expected to make it out unscathed, to develop normal lives, when they were only passed about from abuser to abuser? No one saw their inner selves. Least of all the children themselves. No, they weren't seen as human at all. The Framatar saw them as free labor, instruments to power. Arnevon and Axis had seen them as tools of power to be pitted against one another, and none of them would bat an eye if the lot of them died after their usefulness was exhausted.

Semra had been part of it all. She had bowed to Azi's will, carried out his missions, believed his lies all her life. And now that she was free, she had no idea what to do with herself except that the next right thing was to save Siler and stop the children of the mountain from destroying the Shamaran family and each other. And she was likely to fail on all accounts, starting right now.

Seething anger and pain ripped through her chest. Sparks flew from her fingers. Smoke poured from their tips, ribbons of smoke streaming behind them as they arced through the air. She fixated on the narrow slitted windows of the towers where the archers haunted the wall. They would pay for their interference.

Zezura rose above the southeast tower and dove down along its curved side, pouring streams of fire through the slits, her open mouth inches from the windows. Screams rewarded Semra on the other side. *Message received.*

Semra whirled toward the southwest tower. Let no one accuse her of favoritism.

"Enough!" Zephan bellowed in her ear and reached around her to grip her hand, hard.

She felt Zezura's hesitation. The dragon would do whatever Semra asked. She had only to say the word ...

"We are at *war!*"

"Even in war we act out of necessity, not anger. Don't be like him."

Semra felt her chest cave in as the crust of fury she'd built around her sadness crumbled. The smoke cleared, and the sparks ceased. The glow in Zezura's throat ebbed, and the southwest tower was saved as the dragon lifted away toward the mountains.

Zephan squeezed her hand and pulled her back against him with his other arm, cradling her against his chest as Zezura flew. He stroked her hand with his thumb, and a tingle ran up her arm. She hadn't realized how tense she was. Every muscle was on edge, clenched for a fight, taut from her rage. She rested her head back against him and let it go.

Tears spilled rivers down her cheeks and her shoulders racked with sobs. Semra didn't know how long she wept, for Siler, for the children of the mountain, for the person she had almost become if Zephan hadn't stopped her.

Don't be like him.

She almost had. She'd almost abused the power she held as a dragonlord and taken her retribution out on mindless men who knew no different than she had when she was in Azi's clutches. Axis wasn't there. He wouldn't be hurt by her display. But Semra would have, and her conscience would forever have been marred.

She was grateful the windows were only archer positions, and not large enough to scorch them completely. They'd have to be treated for severe burns, but they would live. She had to watch herself. She had to be more careful.

By the time they made it back to the mountain, her tears were spent, and Semra was sapped of all energy. For a moment when they landed, neither of them moved.

"I'm sorry," she said softly. "You've already been wounded by coming with me. I never should have put you in that position."

Zephan remained silent, and Semra's gut doubled over in anxious anticipation. When he did speak, his words came slow and deliberate.

"You shouldn't have put either of us in that position. It was dangerous without reason, and the arrow could just as easily have hit you instead of me. You got too close and lost your head. We already knew we couldn't get him off the wall."

"You're right." Semra paused. "Maybe you should have stayed behind."

"I don't think you're hearing me. If I leave you for a single instant, my entire testimony to clear you is destroyed. They will say you carried out your plots—whatever they make up —in those two hours, in those thirty seconds, that I lost visual. If you want any hope at clearing your name, you need me. We just can't take unnecessary risks when you're feeling scared."

Her denial died on her lips, and she looked down at her fingers.

He sighed. "And you need to start caring about your life a little more."

"I'm sorry. I will."

"Good." He tugged her against him one more time and pressed his lips to her neck.

Warmth and butterflies exploded in her chest as he slipped off the dragon and extended a hand up to help her down. She took it, sheepishly, and smiled. "What are you going to do with me when you get back home?" she asked.

"I don't know yet," he admitted. "But maybe we can do some brainstorming between now and then."

Semra pursed her lips. "In the ample free time we have for relaxation."

"Good, you're back," Pidge called from the cavern. Semra arched an eyebrow at Zephan and gestured toward Pidge. *See? So much free time ...*

Pidge bounced from one foot to the other and bit her lip. "Um, our guests are going to be early."

Semra cocked her head. "Why do you say that?"

She gestured down the slope. "Because they're already here."

38

Zephan and Semra turned to look down the steep slope and saw five bodies climbing the mountain. Two moved side by side, and the other three were spread out from one another. Semra figured they had maybe forty minutes until they made it to the cavern ledge.

"Do we have any idea how many are in Belvidore?" Zephan asked.

Pidge shook her head. "No, but we're a lot more concentrated here than anywhere else. A lot of bounties have gone out from Madensig, so there are business opportunities. And with Semra considered a traitor in league with Jannemar, across the border felt safest to most of us. Some of the younger ones have either banded together or made little groups with older ones. But, as expected, there are quite a few mission readies in the wind."

"Let's hope we can change their minds about me," Semra said. "How are our two favorite guards?"

"Bound, but not gagged." Pidge grinned. "Having a dragon around does wonders for a cooperative spirit."

Semra laughed. "Well, then. We're almost out of time, and

we have some writing to do. Zez will stand watch. Zephan, I still really think you should stay out of sight until we have some stability in the meet. If they see you before I've bought their curiosity, all they'll think of is moneybags Axis and what they can buy with your head in a basket."

Zephan rubbed his neck and made a face. "I trust you. I'll wait. But I need to be able to hear everything, and when you get to the part we talked about, I'm going to join you."

Semra dipped her head. "Done. Okay, grab the pigeons and the parchment. We don't have much time."

Semra, Zephan, and Pidge set to work writing out copies of a page Semra had written the previous afternoon, then they retreated into the cavern to wait.

"Five is better than none," Pidge said.

Radix cracked his knuckles. "These are early. There will be more."

"I'd be pleasantly surprised by ten," Semra said. "We don't have any idea how many are in Belvidore, and of those, who would show up after being told they'll be killed for coming?"

"We don't do well with taking orders," Radix answered. "Not anymore. No one is going to appreciate Tymetin's control, and I may or may not have spread word that Tymetin and Axis were trying to keep them from meeting with you. That'll spark their curiosity. Forbidden fruit is always so tasty."

"How long do we wait?" Pidge asked.

Semra worried her lip. "We set the meet for sunset. We begin at sunset." She glanced at their two hostages. "Radix, are you still good to watch them?"

"Pidge and I can alternate. If trouble comes up, I want to be available to jump in. They need to hear you out, and I want our arrangement to work. I need secure travel to and from Jannemar, and I need the younger ones of us taken care of."

"We'll do it," Zephan said. "As promised."

Radix pursed his lips. "Only if you're alive. Which is why I plan to keep you that way. Take the dragon if you need to. Don't be idiots." Radix jerked his head in Semra's direction. "Drag her with you if you need to. She's got a tendency to do stupid things."

Zephan grinned. "I know."

Semra spread her hands. "I'm standing right here!"

Zezura let out a low rumble from the mouth of the cave. Semra came to the opening and looked down. The original five climbers were spaced out on the ledge below, and several more could be seen making their way up the mountain from further down.

The dragon suddenly pushed in front of Semra, blocking her view, and roared. An arrow hit Zezura and fell to the ground. Semra's heart raced. She scooped it up and climbed onto Zezura's back. Where was the archer?

Zez pulled Semra's vision into her own and narrowed in on a rock three hundred yards away. A small movement beyond it confirmed the archer was hiding there. Semra lurched back into her body. It was an excellent shot, even for accomplished archers. Archery wasn't Semra's specialty, but she had only ever gotten comfortable at two hundred yards, in optimal conditions.

Semra lifted the arrow over her head and snapped the shaft in two. To those close enough to hear, she called out, "Welcome! I'm so grateful that you've come. You're more than welcome to keep your weapons with you, but I will not tolerate attacks. We're here to talk, and it's so much harder to talk when one of us is dead."

She leaned forward and Zezura leaped from the ledge. Her heart thundered in her chest. If it weren't for Zezura's keen eye, Semra would have dropped like a stone and never been the wiser. Without a fight, without fanfare, she would so easily have been erased from the world. The way her kind always were.

Invisible.

Semra arced over the mountain and behind the rock where Zez had spied the archer. She threw the broken pieces of the arrow on top of him, and he looked up. Dark eyes glared up at her from beneath thick lashes and long brown hair. His bow was in one hand, a quiver on his back, and a dagger at his side.

"Furis," Semra said in surprise.

He bent in a mock bow, never taking his eyes off her. "So good to see you remember your lowly classmates after your rise to power."

Semra pressed her lips together and reminded herself not to cause more rifts than necessary. She took a breath and steadied herself. "I'm glad you're here. Put your bow on your back, and if you don't touch it again, you'll be welcome to stay."

She didn't wait for his answer, just wheeled about and returned to her place on the ledge. An hour later, streaks of yellow, orange, and red played across the sky. Zephan and Radix had insisted Semra stay out of sight until it was time for the meeting, and she occasionally borrowed the dragon's sight from inside the cavern to check on the progress of their guests.

By the time Semra stepped out again, the sun had sunk low, soon to be hidden against the curve of the mountains in the west. She tapped her fingers along the handle of the knife in her trouser sheath but didn't remove it. Her guests needed to feel safe. If they didn't, most of those present would be dead in an hour.

Semra's throat tightened and her stomach flopped. There were far more in attendance than she'd anticipated. Seventeen, if she wasn't mistaken. She counted again. She wasn't mistaken.

Meeting them out in the open made more sense than the cave, after all. It let them feel in control, and the tremendous spacing between individuals and a few small groups of two or three confirmed their wariness. The ages present ranged from fourteen to midthirties, but most were upper teens and early twenties—the age of program graduates. Anyone else was either an instructor, staff, or student.

"Welcome. I know you've risked a lot to be here, and I don't take your presence lightly." Semra scanned the faces before her, on the ledge below or down the slope. She recognized most of them. There was Furis from her year, Vix from the first year of graduates, and Treq from Radix and Isra's year. Semra had graduated with him when she moved up a class, but considering she and Siler recently captured him with the task force, she couldn't expect any positive feelings. Semra wondered how he got free, then refocused on her task.

"I think the greater risk, by far, would be going on without hearing what I have to say. I'm going to tell you what you stand to gain by working with me, why it benefits you to keep my head attached to my neck and send Axis a message of what you think of his double-dealing bounty, and invite you to an audience with royalty where your voices will be heard and we can put together a solution that offers you freedom and security."

Her gaze swept her little crowd. No one moved. It was deathly silent. Semra glanced at Furis. He was rigid, but his hands were away from his bow. Treq ran a finger along his battle axe. A young girl, maybe fourteen, stood with another boy and girl around the same age, eyes wide. They had no idea what they were into.

Semra opened her mouth to give her planned speech, but

something held her back. Her lips parted, and she searched every face. The speech would come. But it would wait.

"Before we do that, I just want to say that we are used to being talked to. Talked *down* to, to be specific. Our skills have been curated to meet the power-hungry demands of another. But have you thought ... have you thought about what you want most?"

She was met with stares, and a few open glares. One shifted his weight, and another set her hands on her hips.

"Traitors to die appropriate deaths," Furis called out. "Revenge for lives lost."

Semra swallowed, and nodded. "Because traitors—a failure to stay loyal—are the worst scum. The world is better off without them. Or maybe you don't care about the world, but you think revenge will solve the pain you feel. What would it take for you to break loyalty?"

She slipped from the ledge down to the rocky ridge below. Semra could feel the burning gazes of Zephan, Radix, and Pidge from the shadows of the cavern as they burned anxious holes in the back of her skull. She wasn't supposed to leave the ledge.

Semra spread her hands, palms up, in peace as she walked among the children of the mountain. Their collective intake of breath and wide eyes told her she'd had precisely the impact she'd intended. It was a stupid move. It was a *surprising* move. She'd given up a great advantage and safety. What would she do next?

A young man about seventeen years old stumbled backward out of her path as she passed, knocking his sword against a rock in his haste. Every eye was fixed on her.

"Lying once or twice isn't enough, is it?" she said. "What if you were lied to over and over? Would you break trust then? What if you were kidnapped, and your parents tried to save you, but your captor slaughtered them on the mountain and came to wipe your homesick tears with their blood fresh on his hands?

"What if you were reprogrammed to be confident in every skill you possess, the kind of certainty you need to be successful in missions, but so destroyed in your core that when you left the work behind you and came home, you would do anything for the approval of the man responsible for your emptiness?"

Semra stopped and turned, three feet from the young trio. "What class were you in?"

One of the girls lifted her chin, but her voice quivered. "Sabre. Class of 5001."

Semra's stomach tightened. There *was* no class of 5001. Not anymore. That was next year's class. The program was disbanded, and Semra would do anything to keep it that way. "Sabre." Semra eyed the young girl. Her breathing was quick and her shoulders tense. Sabre class would put her at only thirteen or fourteen years old. "Mission support, from distraction and getaway to supply drop. Observation, report, and involvement in planning stages up to execution. I remember being Sabre class. I believed I would be fighting for a purpose, that we were ridding the world of evil. What do you fight for?"

The girl pulled back, mouth agape. She gestured to the boy and girl beside her. "For them, I guess."

Semra tilted her head, considering the girl's words. "For them." Semra took three steps forward, then turned. "Why?"

The girl shrugged. "Who else have I got?"

Semra clenched her jaw against the emotion that threatened to overtake her. She cleared her throat. "Who else have we got, indeed." She raised her voice. "Who else have we got but each other? Who understands our upbringing, if that's what you call it, but each other? What is to become of the younger ones, dragged away from their families, taught to hit a moving target and skin a squirrel, but not old enough to protect themselves? What's to become of the older ones, with nightmares of our kills, and no transferable skills to a more decent life?

"What would you have given, to go back in time and just be a kid? To live in a home with a family, and play with dolls or wooden swords instead of real ones? Our childhoods have been stolen, but the future is ours for the taking. I left the mountain for *you*—to expose the lies, to stop the Framatar from destroying more families. It's too late for me, but not for them. And I ask you, do you want the next ten years of your life to feel like the last ten years? Are you happy, or have you just been waiting around for a mission to go south and take you out? And if you're not happy, and you think happiness is so impossible that it isn't worth pursuing, consider that the only way to absolutely ensure your misery continues is by living the way you always have."

"It's a pipe dream," Vix called out. "Stolen identities are the only versions of us that might be happy. They'll last until they don't, and then we'll move on."

Semra lifted a finger. "What if there were a way for you to move freely in Jannemar, to have real apprenticeships if you want them, to keep connections with each other and not look over your shoulder every second? That if someone found you out, you could admit your past to authorities without fear?"

Furis folded his arms. "I'd say you're lulling us with bedtime stories for children, so we're nice and drowsy when you chop off our heads."

"I get it. It sounds too good to be true, and I'm not going to stand here and tell you there aren't obstacles," Semra said. "You're not children, so I'm going to tell you how things are. Turian is in quite a predicament over us."

The court would fall over dead, hearing her use the king's name so flippantly, bare of titles. But if she used his title here, they would see it as a sign of allegiance. A subordinate. None of them considered themselves subjects, so it would only widen the chasm between them.

She plucked her blade from its sheath and twirled it in the air. A ripple of movement cascaded through her audience, and before she could blink, axes, spears, and swords were in hand and angled her direction.

39

Zezura reared up with a puff of fire and flew from the ledge to land behind Semra. The assassins tensed as her hand moved, watched the glint of her blade in the evening light. One flick of her wrist, and one of them could be dead. She stilled the dragon with a gentle hand, and smiled.

"You see his predicament. We aren't normal. We've killed a lot of people, and no judge could retain his position without acknowledging our violence. No kingdom can survive without order. Turian understands our position and wants to protect us, but without compromising his name or undermining his authority." She spread her hands. "He's in a bind."

A woman in her thirties, whom Semra recognized as an Arrow class leader, readjusted her grip on her dagger.

Semra forged ahead. "He doesn't know what to do with us. He tried, by clearing Mount Hara and only pursuing those assassins actively killing more people. He tried by returning children to their families and finding homes for those without families to return to. He has to protect his people, and if we make ourselves their enemy, he cannot help us.

"I am no Jannemar puppet. I have no country. *You* are my countrymen. We will never be normal. You know things that regular townspeople don't. When a magician entrances a crowd, you see behind the curtain. Like the Tabeun Tournaments that Belvidore holds, you know the magicians are fakes. We see it now with kingdoms. Rulers aren't magnificent figures; they're just people. And people have flaws, fears, weaknesses to exploit. Strengths to play to.

"Turian needs his people to feel safe, his court to continue giving him their money, and his throne to be secure. But security is an illusion. You are behind the curtain. Make magic with me. How do we keep the illusion alive and solve his problem?"

Seventeen pairs of eyes stared back at her. Semra was breathless, her blood rocketing through her veins at top speed.

Treq lifted a hand, and all eyes turned to him. "Brens was your friend, and she's dead. Siler was your friend, and he's up on the wall. He'll be dead soon too, if he isn't already. Word on the street is that we'll all be killed for even being here. Why would we want to align ourselves with you?"

Seventeen heads swiveled back to Semra. Semra reeled, her lips parted. Images of Brens on the marble floor flooded her mind before she could think. Imaginings of Siler, dead on the wall, filed in after. She'd known this question would come. Why did it still sting?

A *thud* sounded behind her, and she spun to see Radix had jumped down off the ledge. "Come on, Treq. We've all seen what kind of world we get when one king gets all the assassins. The price for our services takes a hit when there's so much competition. The war makes travel a nightmare, ties up all the rich people's money—and don't get me started on multiple so-called exclusive contracts put out on Semra. How long did it take Axis to put a bounty on her head after signing those contracts? Semra isn't big on revenge, but I am. I just want it on Arnevon—or in lieu of him, on Axis."

Semra crossed to Radix and held out her hand. "Do you have them?"

Radix nodded and handed her several slips of paper. Semra held them aloft. "These are copies of our correspondence with Axis over the past several days." She passed them out, and let the parchments circulate. "His deadline for me to turn myself in and confess to Arnevon's murder is right now. I'm cutting it close, because I need you. We need each other. And I want us to be free."

"Siler has been on the wall for four days," Radix said. "Tymetin killed Arnevon, and they want Semra as their scapegoat. So Axis puts out multiple contracts, *and* a bounty, *and* uses one of you as bait. Why? Because he doesn't care about you. He makes agreements with you, but he doesn't think twice about breaking them. He has no loyalty. The more of you that die in his service, the better."

Radix strode forward. "Why did he use Siler as bait? Because unlike him, Semra has *loyalty*. Because he knows she can't help but come for him."

Semra stepped up beside Radix, a show of unity. She wasn't alone, and they didn't have to be either. "You all saw the white flag. Surely by now you've heard what it said, as it waved over Siler in broad daylight for anyone to see. *Outlaws and crooks do not dictate his clemency.* You heard it from his own mouth: if you're looking for safety, you won't find it with him. He will use you, then accuse you of anything he wants, and dispose of you. All the better for him, because it'll save him the trouble of paying your fee.

"The Framatar killed so many of us. Xiffin. Koran. Kiar. Brens. How many of us have already been killed by Axis, or by each other at his bidding?" Semra surveyed their faces, and knew she was right—some had already died. "How many of you will survive the year?"

"We'll never be normal," one of the assassins said. "You can't really expect us to be carpenters and seamstresses."

"No, we aren't normal," Semra agreed. "But that's exactly why we can come up with a solution the king hasn't dreamed of. We know things about the world that the normals will never know. We're dangerous, in large part because we know how many dangers are posed to us. We can't unlearn the skills of death. But we can choose whether to put them to use as soldiers, as security, or to start something new."

"Take a few minutes," Radix suggested. "Discuss among yourselves, those of you who dare get within arm's reach of the people you grew up with—that's telling, isn't? —and tell us what you want. If you had an audience with Turian himself, what would make peace with him worth your while? This is not an opportunity the likes of us are ever offered, and it's not one you will ever have again. Use it wisely."

Radix tugged on Semra's arm, and Semra dipped her head and backed away. She climbed up on Zezura's back, and Radix followed her back up to the ledge outside the cavern. Pidge stood with Zephan, her feet apart, arms crossed, over the two bound and gagged guards at the entrance to the cavern. She bobbed her head.

"It's a decent start. Nobody's died yet."

"It's still early," Semra muttered.

"Let them convince each other what they want, force them to talk, and we'll see if this one can pull his weight." Radix jerked his head at Zephan.

Zephan grinned. "I'm ready."

Semra paced back and forth out of view of the slope for a good twenty minutes. She practiced knife flows to calm her nerves and nearly got out her cleaning cloth when the sound of steel and shouting broke the quiet tension down below.

Radix and Semra ran to the end of the ridge. Treq yanked the female instructor back from two younger assassins, and Furis gripped an arm of each of the younger ones. The instructor, Comorrah, threw her elbow into Treq's gut, and he flipped her onto her seat in the blink of an eye.

"We know what we want," Treq called up to them, breathing hard. "And we know which of us is going to live to get it."

"I know you won't all agree," Semra said. "But the offer stands for anyone. If you talk, we'll listen."

The young Sabre class girl from earlier shifted her weight and lifted her voice. "First, we want to know why you renounced the name Bandaka. You renounced it, but now you're saying you're one of us. *Bandaka is bond.*"

Semra nodded. "Yes, that was my message. *Bandaka is bond.* I will be one of the children of the mountain. I care what happens to you because I *am* you. But it's true in another way, too. The word *bandaka* means bondservant. The Framatar was mocking us, and we wore the term with pride. I didn't betray you. I set you free from a man who kidnapped, manipulated, and murdered us. He made us his slaves, and if you let Axis control us with his money, you only serve a new master. I will always be one of you, but I am no one's bondservant."

"We want to visit people in Jannemar. We don't want to get arrested or thrown in prison," a girl said.

Semra dipped her head. "Good. What else?"

"We want a clean slate," another man piped up. "And some of us want job training. At any career we want."

"Done."

Comorrah spat on the ground. "You might prance around in fancy halls, but you have no authority in Jannemar. And how do you set yourself up to represent us? You aren't one of us. No punishment Turian gives will land on you."

"She has no authority," a voice boomed from above them. "But I do."

"Aurin's spear, who are you?" Furis demanded.

Zephan rolled his shoulders back and spoke with deadly confidence. "I am Prince Zephan of Jannemar. And I am here to negotiate."

"You don't look like a prince," someone shouted.

Zephan drew his sword and extended the engraving on its blade for those standing close enough to read. "A prince doesn't always wear silks and furs."

Vix rolled his eyes. "It's him. He's been flying with Semra for days."

"You're no better than us," Furis said. "We picked someone with a fat purse, and so did you. You just don't like the side we picked!"

The assassins erupted, and Semra felt a burning anger rise in her chest.

"Why is she free, and we are being threatened?" one shouted.

"She's as bad as us! If you're really one of us, why are you flying around with him?"

"Doesn't he know what you've done, teacher's pet?"

"You're just like Azi," a man said from the other side of Comorrah. "All you want is power, and to use us to get it."

The last statement tore through the last of her composure. Semra snapped her head toward him. "You think I want power?"

The man spun the axe in his hand and smirked. "I think you betrayed us for a better offer. Maybe you're just not as good as everyone thinks you are, and you need a castle to hide behind. I think you left the Framatar to die in a hole and neglected to tell your royal friends that you should rot right beside him."

"You think I'm drunk with power," Semra growled. "You think I've set myself up as better than you. I'm not. My hands are as thick with blood as any of yours." Semra lunged across the open space, and he leaped back, but she was too fast. Semra hammered him in the stomach with a flying kick that knocked him off balance, and she flipped him over, snatched the axe from his hand, and dropped her knee on his spine. "And my technique is as flawless," she continued. "I respect you, but I am no doormat. Today I demand your respect in return."

Semra backed away, turning the axe over in her hands, and addressed the rest of them. "How many of you stormed the castle? Raise your hands! Don't be afraid ...you're too skilled to be caught, aren't you? What are you afraid of?" Semra circled the group, glaring burning fire. No one responded. Semra curled her lip. "There was a *sea* of you that day. Come on, brainless," she said, waving her hand at the man who she'd just taken down. "What about you? What is your name?"

"Bandaka," he said with a sneer.

"Bandaka," she spat back. "That's right. And how many of us defended the Shamaran Castle? *How many?*"

Silence met her, and Semra looked up at Zephan. He nodded slowly. *They're listening.* She spun back to the assassins.

"*Three!* One of us is dead, one of us is chained to a wall, and yet here I am standing, one against so many, undefeated. You could kill me now where I stand. Go ahead. End my winning streak. But you won't. You won't, because I'm your only hope of getting what you want. I won't push you around, but you won't be pushing me around either."

Semra whirled to the man she'd attacked. He had

collected himself and was glowering at her from a safe distance. "And for the record, you aren't Bandaka to me. I know you; you were in Pidge's class. You are Nomek, and forevermore you are free to be known not as someone else's stolen property or kidnapped bondservant but as yourself. As Nomek. Reclaim your identities. Forge them yourselves."

She threw the axe at his feet and swung herself up to the ledge to stand next to Zephan. Zezura roared, and an eerie wind rustled in the sparse trees.

Zephan slid his sword back in its scabbard and surveyed the men and women—even children—below. How many of them had assaulted his home to kill his family?

"I'm not here to micromanage your lives," he said. "What you do beyond our borders is outside of our control. Come forward now, and you will find mercy. This is our offer: anyone who comes to us in the next six weeks to disclose their identity and commit to peaceful dealings within Jannemar will be given clemency for actions taken under Azi Shamaran's leadership.

"Tell us what you know and help us now, and you will receive identification proving a king's pardon, the option for training in the field of your choice, and freedom to travel within our borders. Stop the contracts. Show Axis what you think of people controlling you and treating you as mindless weapons. Help us, and you can have attachments to each other, to colleagues and younger children of the mountain you may care about, settle them into normal lives without fear.

"But anyone found to have acted against the Jannemar crown since Azi's imprisonment will find no mercy, and no one who strikes out against us now will find no mercy. Actions taken against Jannemar since Azi's imprisonment will go to trial on a case-by-case basis, but that would require hard evidence against you, and I'm not aware that we have any.

Tymetin and anyone who assists him will be punished. To fail to choose a side, is to choose. Now is your chance."

Zephan let his words fall, and thrill ran through Semra as she stood next to him. This was not the boy who danced with her in the woods. This was the royal prince, and even surrounded by assassins, he oozed confidence. He was born for this. He spoke again.

"Bond. Because the Framatar wanted you bound to him, bondservants, slaves, witless servants whose loyalty was both demanded and mocked. And yet, bond, because no one has had the experience you have had. You thought you were a family. And you never really were. Maybe now is the chance to stand together and become that very thing. Jannemar is not afraid of you. We would be honored to have you as citizens, to be the place you call home."

Semra gazed at Zephan, his eyes burning passion for his kingdom, his voice firm, his shoulders relaxed under the weight of the world. He looked at her and her stomach dropped. She clenched her jaw against the warmth that exploded in her chest, and she turned to her colleagues.

"They think they can use and abuse us. They think no one will care. But I care. And it's time you did too. Let's send a message louder than Belvidorian money, in a language they understand. We're going to rise up. We're going to save Siler. And we're going to make them rue the day they ever conned a Bandaka."

For a moment everything was silent.

And then the fight broke out.

40

———

Vix snatched the axe from Nomek's hands as he lifted it to throw, and in an instant the two of them disappeared in a swarm of moving blades and bodies. Comorrah snatched one of the Sabre class girls and cinched her arm tight around the girl's throat from behind, dragging her backward as a human shield. A bow materialized in Furis' hands, and he nocked an arrow to the string. A body tackled Semra and Zephan to the ground.

Semra seized her attacker and reared back to smash her head into her opponent, then stopped. It was Pidge on top of her.

"You were about to get killed," Pidge shouted. "You're welcome!"

Semra rolled to her side and peeked over the ridge.

A hand clawed at her face, and she startled, then twisted and blocked Nomek's second blow in the nick of time as he swung a dagger at her neck. Comorrah was nearly to the edge of the landing, and Semra gasped as she registered the glint of the dagger in her hands. Her human shield was about to be dead weight.

Semra clutched for the knife in its sheath, but the move put her off balance. Nomek captured her neck in a choke, using his body weight to pull her down. Someone gripped her legs from above, so the bottom half of her body was on the ledge and the top half dangled into Nomek's clutches.

Her lungs burned, and blood rushed to her head. She swung at Nomek, but he held fast. Zezura descended just as Radix thrust his sword into Nomek's back. Nomek went rigid, tightened his hold, and then fell to the ground.

"Idiot!" Radix screamed at her. "Stop acting like a bodyguard. You *need* a bodyguard. Stay here."

Semra's jaw dropped. *Stay here?* Nobody was supposed to tell her to stay put. *She* was supposed to tell *other* people to stay put! Semra leaped off the ledge, but an arm circled her waist midair and pulled her back down. An arrow flew through her curls, and her cheek stung from the fletching.

"No," Zephan said into her ear. He pulled her away from the edge and back toward the cavern. "Sometimes it's harder to let others protect you than to do the fighting itself. But if you aren't here to advocate for them, every dream they fight for dies."

He released her. The sounds of the fight beckoned, but she did not move. In a flash, Zephan spun and yanked Puri back from the edge where the two guards had been slipping away. The second Belvidorian guard escaped over the ledge. They'd both gotten their feet free, but their hands were still bound. Puri's eyes bulged as he stared after his friend's getaway.

The other guard screamed. Semra heard a sickening crack and a squelching sound, and the scream was cut off. She grimaced. Zephan had undoubtedly saved Puri's life.

Semra spun to Zephan. "Do you trust me?"

Zephan's eyes narrowed. "Yes. But don't be stupid."

"I have a dragon."

Semra grinned and ran to Zezura. She climbed onto her back and turned to the fight below, but as she whipped her knife out into her palm, the sounds of combat dissipated. Comorrah lay dead on the far side, a spear in her chest. Nomek's crumpled body remained at the base of the ledge where Radix had ended him, and the Belvidorian guard's remains were a brutal cocktail of spilled organs and blood. A quiver and arrows were strewn on the ground, and two silhouettes fled down the mountain into the night. Semra scanned the faces. Furis was missing.

The young Sabre class girl stood holding hands with one of her classmates, shaking like a leaf. Her eyes were red, and her chest was heaving. She would have never seen action up close, and now she'd nearly been choked to death, and three people were dead.

Semra slipped off Zezura's back and opened her arms to the girl. She collapsed into Semra's chest and sobbed her heart out, and Semra held her tight. How long had it been since the horrors of death had impacted her so?

Radix and Pidge appeared on either side of her, weapons drawn. Vix collected his spear from Comorrah's chest, and Semra's gaze was drawn to the blood stained on its tip. An unsurvivable wound. Precisely the fatal blow Semra had been dealt on the plateau of Mount Hara, the day everything changed, the day Zezura sealed her wound with the dragon's kiss and bound them together forever.

Thirteen assassins. Thirteen of seventeen were waiting for her to say something. Radix and Pidge rounded out the number to fifteen. Something between shock and gratitude tangled in her gut at so many willing to stay. How many of them were sincere? How many of them waited for their chance to strike?

Vix wiped the tip of his spear clean in a patch of grass and straightened. "We will fight with you."

Treq looked up at Zephan. "I haven't had the cleanest of hands since the throne room. Do I get clemency?"

Zephan pressed his lips together. Semra was surprised he recognized Treq. Zephan must have encountered him after the task force dragged him to Qalea.

"You can have a commuted sentence by service to the crown, which would start today, and you'll have access to check in on Conet again. I know you want to look out for her. You'll give six months."

"Two months."

"Six was wildly generous, and court will already hate me for this promise."

Treq rolled his eyes, then flourished his sword, and gave an exaggerated bow. "At your service, then. But after we save Siler, I'm going to slug him for how he tied me up and marched me to Qalea for days."

Semra arched an eyebrow. "But I was a part of that too. And to be fair, you were killing people."

He shrugged. "I make a point not to pick fights with dragonlords when I can help it."

"I doubt it, but I accept your terms," Semra said.

"Do I get to steal stuff in Madensig?" he pressed.

Semra quirked a smile. "Don't tell me you took it, and I won't ask questions. But I'm going to make a promise to Horen that we will take no unnecessary human life. Anyone who attacks us is fair game. Anyone peaceable shall remain unharmed."

"So where do we start?" a young man asked, standing with a mace and dagger at the back of the group.

Semra gave the girl in her arms a final squeeze and freed herself.

"We have to weigh the variables that will keep Siler alive longer and play to those, especially since we missed the deadline," Semra said. "And since we plan on making Axis even more angry tonight. We can't have him catapulting Siler's head over the wall to retaliate."

"One moment. Our trusty Belvidorian captive has something to say." Zephan hauled Puri to the rim. "Don't be shy. This is your time to shine."

Puri gaped at his colleague's body on the ground, and the grisly view of death before him where everyone was now standing around chit-chatting strategy as if nothing had just happened. Zephan kneed him in the ribs.

"Erm, Princess Avaya is very upset with the Raven—Siler," the guard stammered. "But she wants him alive. His Majesty the King wants him dead. I overheard them."

"And of course, we have Tymetin to worry about," Pidge added.

Vix cocked his head. "No, we don't. Not in Belvidore. Haven't you sent word back to Qalea?"

Semra turned a quizzical eye on Vix. "What are you talking about?"

"He left days ago. To kill Turian."

Her blood ran cold, and a chill ran up her spine. She looked at Zephan. His face was white. He couldn't lose both parents within six months.

"Send word," Radix said to Zephan. "Now."

He spread his hands. "I don't have anything. Kinlock is the closest, but if Semra goes to Kinlock, she'll be killed. And Tymetin has a four-day head start."

"We have to beat him to Qalea," Semra said. "Zezura is your only chance. I'll have to take you."

"What about Siler?" Pidge asked.

"They'll have taken him off the wall by now," Puri said. "It's after sundown on day four."

"We can't leave him," Pidge squeaked. A tear ran down her cheek.

"No," Semra said. A knot formed in her stomach. "And we won't. But Avaya may be able to keep Siler alive, and there's no way to get to him now. We need time to plan an extraction, time we don't have, and Turian will definitely die if we don't go. And we've promised everyone here that their grievances will be heard and our deal honored."

"The wedding is in less than three weeks," Vix said. "I've only been a nobleman for two months, but I have very convincing invisible money. I can get myself an invitation, and lobby for him to be put on display at the event."

"He'll be dead by morning," Treq said. "Madensig is a kill box. Getting back at Axis will be a big enough task on its own."

Pidge whimpered.

Semra set her jaw. She turned to Zephan. "We need to leave now to beat Tymetin to the castle and warn your father." She put a hand on Pidge. "I need you with us. I'm not sure what will be waiting for me in Qalea, but I need someone I can trust to help us on the way. Zephan and I are too recognizable to go into town for provisions, and we won't have the time for any proper hunting. We will be back for Siler. I swear it."

"We weren't kidding about Semra being loyal," Radix said. "She's often stupid about it. It's a weakness."

Semra crossed to Zezura and pulled herself up. "If caring about people is weakness, you'd better hope I'm downright feeble when I bring your case before the king."

The group spent a few more minutes strategizing, and dispersed—Semra, Pidge, and Zephan on Zezura, and the rest back down the mountainside toward the city. Semra tensed as they flew over Madensig. There was one thing left to do before they changed course to Jannemar.

It was time to give her confession.

Guards waited on the wall to receive her, or whatever message she might bring. Puri had told them how the plan had evolved for tonight. Konnolan would be stored in blow guns and shot into the air, and sacks strung up to be burst with arrows as they approached.

But they wouldn't be going to the wall.

Zezura flew low, up over the outer ward, over the inner courtyard of the keep, and plummeted into a dizzying nose-dive. Semra dropped the rock with its parchment attached, and they were out of range before the rock hit the ground.

As they pulled away and set their sights on Jannemar, two shadowy figures stole into the courtyard. They would not discover until the following morning that the same message was posted all over Horen, outside shops and in town squares. Images of the blue dragon would crop up on walls and doors and streets throughout the city overnight, and some even appeared inside the confines of Madensig Fortress. The two figures unrolled the parchment, and this is what they read:

My name is Semra Bandaka, and this is my confession.

I confess that I did not kill King Arnevon of Belvidore. I confess that I am not so easily controlled as you think. I confess that I have an army of assassins, and I've told them the truth—that the person truly responsible for King Arnevon's murder bears a royal title, and lives inside Madensig.

I confess that King Axis of Belvidore is an idiot. He thinks he can make bad deals with contract killers, and yet expects more contract killers to take out fellow children of the mountain who defy him.

All of Horen has seen a man chained to the rampart of the castle these past several days. His crime was refusing to kill me. I confess that if my colleague dies, bloodshed will fall on Madensig Fortress like you have never seen.

Blood and flame shall rain from the sky.

Your king does not care for your lives. He sent your sons, your daughters, your parents, your siblings to war because he felt insulted. A tantruming toddler is reigning your land.

I care about your families. Therefore, when you see the blue dragon, if you fall back, I will preserve your life. Have no fear to provide for your families if you work in the castle. But if you aid the king against me, if you lift a finger when that day arrives, there will be no mercy.

Lunatics ruling kingdoms are terrifying realities.

Long live the fear of the king.

41

———

It took a week to get to Jannemar by dragon. They stopped only for rest or food, scavenging vegetation or sending Pidge into nearby towns for whatever meals they did manage. They traveled in relative silence for most of the week, Zephan speaking only when necessary, and Semra and Pidge following his lead. Semra wanted to offer her support in her presence, but also felt herself pulling away. The illusion of togetherness, the hope that always seemed to spark in the woods or mountains, would die as it always did in the castle. Finally, Pidge could take the quiet no more and brought up her burning questions.

"Dragons and daylilies, we're two days from Jannemar. Semra is supposed to be killed on sight, she's still assumed guilty for killing Arnevon, and we have no real evidence to prove her innocence. What exactly is the plan?"

The weight on her chest grew as Pidge reminded Semra of precisely what she'd been trying to avoid. "Deliver Zephan back home to save his father."

"Deliver as in drop him in a courtyard from two stories up, like you delivered your confession? Or deliver as in, land, let them kill you, and strand me there in a castle of people who will want to kill me too?"

"They won't kill Semra," Zephan said. He hesitated. "That is, if we can stay alive long enough for them to realize it's me, and they are nervous enough about accidentally hitting me that they don't shoot her, and they listen to me when we land."

Semra's stomach soured. It was only a matter of time. If they didn't kill her immediately, they'd probably toss her in the dungeon and congratulate themselves on how decently they followed their silly prince's whims. Maybe they'd have learned enough by now to line her cell with konnolan and keep her sick. She shuddered.

Zephan glanced at her. He tugged at the hem of his shirt. "Semra, stay close to me when we land. And when I say close ... well, make sure any arrow that goes through you would hit me too. I'll need them to calm down long enough to explain."

"What am I supposed to do?" Pidge asked.

"Stand somewhere behind us. Between us and Zez would be good," Zephan said. "And try not to look threatening."

Pidge tossed her hair over her shoulder. "I'm always threatening."

Zephan drilled her with a cool stare. "Think tiny, harmless kitten thoughts. If you look threatening, you'll be dead before I get a word out."

Pidge gulped and nodded.

Semra looked down at her hands. "They're going to freak out when they find out you were with me again."

Zephan reached out and gripped her hand. Semra started to snatch it back, out of habit, but when Zephan held on, she surrendered her hand to him willingly. His eyes bored into hers, and something inside her squirmed.

"We'll figure it out. All of it. I just need you to trust me. And I need you to help me keep my father alive."

Trust me. Semra ran the words over and over in her mind. *Trust me.* Was it really him she doubted? He certainly seemed less intimidated by the court's opinion than he had in the past. But that didn't mean there was any reasonable way for them to have a relationship. He'd never shake off the crown, and she was born and raised from soot and grime and blood.

The shining white stone of Shamaran Castle sparkled in the broad daylight of early afternoon as they came careening down toward it. Semra's heartbeat ticked up a notch. Three notches. It threatened to burst from her ribcage. What if Zephan's best wasn't enough to keep her alive? What if he kept her alive, but not free?

Semra shut her eyes, remembering what she'd said to him the night before.

"I can't be in a dungeon, Zephan. I won't do it. I won't rot next to him. I would do ... I would do almost anything for you." Her voice had cracked then, and she swallowed a sob. She'd gritted her teeth and tried again. "But I'll jump off the castle before they lock me away."

Zephan's face hardened. "Just trust me. And if I say go, take Zez and Pidge and go."

Pidge yelped, and Semra opened her eyes. Arrows were flying from all directions. Zezura pulled up. The central courtyard wouldn't do. Semra leaned forward and angled Zez around to the carriage road leading up to Dragon Gate. There was a large open space there—room for a dragon, and arrows from two directions instead of four.

"Are they going to recognize you in those rags?" Pidge screeched over the wind. "You should have packed princier clothes!"

"I wasn't expecting to return by dragon," Zephan answered drily. "Hug the southwest wall at the bend of the carriage road.

It's hidden from the bastions, and arrows will only come from above."

Zezura sank into a spin, arrows bouncing off her, swirling wings protecting her three charges. They hit the cobbles and scrambled off the dragon's back. The beast roared as another volley hit her smooth scales and dropped to the ground in a clatter. Zephan ducked out from under Zezura's wing and lifted his hands.

The arrows stopped. An eerie silence followed. Semra squirmed from her place pressed between the cool limestone of the wall and iridescent dragon hide. Invisible archers had hesitated. Did they recognize Zephan, or were they changing their strategy?

Running footsteps approached, and Zephan snatched Semra and pulled her in front of him. He positioned himself in front of Pidge, with the wall to her left and the dragon on her right. Zephan's arms wrapped around her shoulders and held her tight against his body so that as they both faced the castle guards, every inch of Semra was in close contact with Zephan.

Guards surrounded them from thirty feet out, archers filling out their ranks from the rear. Zezura shifted, one minute angry and spewing fire, the next anxiously bobbing her head up and down and prancing in place. Semra's fingers itched as they brushed the hilt of her blade. She flexed her fingers and let it lie. She'd sworn not to draw her knife on the Shamaran guards, and she would keep that promise.

"Stand down," Zephan called. "You all know it's me."

One of the guards shifted uncomfortably. "Your Highness, we are under orders to kill this woman, should she ever show her face again."

"Situations have changed. There's an emergency. Inform the king."

Another man weaseled his way to the front of the guardsmen, tented his fingers, and bowed. "If only we could. The king has asked not to be disturbed."

Semra grimaced. Firfell.

"Let's play a game where everyone guesses how the good captain loses his rank today," Zephan said. "Scenario A: the king is not disturbed but is furious that the prince's life and death emergency was ignored. Scenario B: a mere captain not only disobeys a direct order from the crown prince but is so arrogant he refuses to confirm the appropriate course of action."

Firfell pursed his lips. "I'll be happy to take you to the king— "

"I should hope so, because he's my father and you are out of line," Zephan said.

Semra breathed a sigh of relief at the confirmation that Turian was alive. They'd beaten Tymetin to Qalea.

The captain's mouth curved into a hateful scowl as he continued, "—we'll just have to bind her hand and foot."

Semra heard a gasp behind her, followed by a soft, pained moan. She started to twist toward Pidge for a better view, but Zephan held her fast. "Don't move," he whispered in her ear. "I'll look."

"Pidge?" Semra called.

Pidge grunted. "It didn't hit bone. I'm okay."

Semra twisted toward her, but Zephan gripped her hard around the shoulders and waist. She barely got a glimpse over his shoulder before he pulled her back around. "She got lucky," he grumbled in her ear. "Stop moving. We won't get lucky twice."

Pidge was on the ground, wincing as she inspected the arrow through her calf.

"Leave it in until we can look at it," Semra said.

Pidge let out a low guttural scream and tossed the bloody arrow to the stones at Semra's feet. "I'll run better without it. It didn't hit anything important."

"She's going to bleed," Semra said. "A lot. She'll make it, but we need to stanch the bleeding."

Zephan lifted his voice to the guards. "Stand down now. Lower your weapons and escort us to my father immediately."

Firfell shook his head. "I don't think—"

"Stand. Down."

Zezura punctuated his point with a stream of fire just over the guards' heads, and a roar that left them trembling.

Firfell spread his hands resignedly. "As you wish, Your Highness. You'll understand we must restrain your ... companions."

"They are in my custody."

The captain strode forward. Zezura snapped her jaws, and Semra put her hand out to calm her. Firfell eyed them, then closed the distance and stood close enough for only Zephan and Semra to hear him. "Your Highness, you know I have the greatest respect for you. I would capitulate to your desires at any time, but you are not yet king, and the standing order of the king is to have her killed or apprehended."

42

ZEPHAN

Zephan glared at the captain. "I believe his words were 'apprehended if possible and killed only if necessary.' Lucky you. She's already in custody."

"I'm concerned that when it comes to this particular criminal, you may be compromised, Your Highness. And she has a dragon."

Zephan placed a hand on Zezura's side. "You'll notice the dragon lets me close. It does not offer you the same privileges. The dragon is an extension of its lord, and I'm afraid neither the dragon nor its lord views you positively."

"She would have incinerated you by now if I let her," Semra added. "She hates you more than I do, which I admit is rather challenging."

Zephan tugged at her shoulders. *Hush, now. Let me handle it.* But he coughed to cover a laugh. He cleared his throat, and his tone grew deadly serious. "Listen to me carefully. If you breathe a word of what I'm about to say, I'll relieve you of your duties. The king you claim to protect will not live long enough to be angry with you if you do not take us to him right now.

And if he does not live, who will the king be? And in my grief, I cannot tell you that your consequences will be reasonable."

Firfell swallowed. His gaze swept Pidge on the ground, Semra, Zephan, and the dragon, then circled back to Zephan. "Forgive me. I had no idea." He raised his hand, and the guards lifted their weapons away and stood at attention. "We will escort you. But I'm afraid we must ask that the dragon be removed."

Zephan nodded and eased his hold on Semra's shoulders. "Semra?"

Semra breathed a sigh of relief and looked at the dragon. "Escort us from the air, Zez. Once we're inside, stay close."

Firfell looked nervous, but made no objections, and his tense shoulders relaxed as the dragon took off into the sky. Semra cleared her throat, and Zephan released her. She stepped back to Pidge, and Zephan turned to Firfell. He jerked his head in Pidge's direction. "Give her your shirt for the bleeding."

"Your Highness?"

"We need to wrap her leg. I'd give her mine, but I rather like this shirt."

Semra stifled a smile as Firfell gaped at the prince in his filthy rough spun peasant cotton. Firfell snapped his fingers and called a guard forward. The bewildered man followed orders to remove a leather breastplate and hand over his outer tunic, and it was passed back to Pidge. Semra helped her secure it and stood up, drawing Pidge's arm around her shoulder. "We're in a hurry. Have Coanor meet us at T—at the king."

Firfell's face went ashen, and his eyes bulged at her near slip. No one addressed the king by name. But she'd been doing it with the assassins constantly. She bit her lip and lifted her chin.

Zephan arched an eyebrow at the captain and swept his arm toward the portcullis of the keep. "Lead the way."

Guards swarmed around them as Firfell led them through the gate, across the courtyard, and into the keep. Zephan walked in line with Semra and Pidge, and took Pidge's other arm across his own shoulders to help her up the stairs. They made a quick stop outside Zephan's quarters, a massive group of guards and archers packed into the hallway, while Zephan changed into attire more suitable for an audience with the king and court.

Diplomatic, Semra thought. Unlike her.

Zephan reappeared moments later in a silver tunic outfitted with a breastplate. The breastplate was emblazoned with Jannemar's emblem: a spear with the Nezil Myansara flower at its base and dragon wings spread on either side. He could use a shower, but he looked every bit the warrior prince. It was not the royal cooped up in his castle that they needed today, but the battlefield leader.

They marched through the halls and down a flight of stairs to the lower throne room, Zephan behind Firfell, and Semra and Pidge behind him. They were admitted with little fanfare. Armor and weaponry clinked against each other as forty guards escorted them before the king, creating a bottleneck at the door where they did not all fit inside the smaller room. Turian looked up from his throne, and General Soldan and another adviser rose from their seats at a long table to one side.

Turian set a stack of papers down on the table beside him and rested his arms on the sides of his chair. His face was stern, and Semra's breathing quickened as their eyes met. Guilt flooded her body. The last time they'd spoken, she'd promised to stay out of trouble. She'd broken that promise within seconds.

"Why is there chaos in my house?"

Firfell bowed low. "Your Majesty. His Royal Highness Prince Zephan has returned, and the outlaw Semra has been apprehended."

"I'm not blind, Firfell," Turian snapped.

Firfell shut his mouth and stepped back.

Zephan bowed formally. "Father. I have sensitive information that cannot wait."

"How sensitive?"

"There is nothing more urgent than this. The fewer ears, the better. But Semra stays. Her testimony is important."

Semra glanced between them and adjusted Pidge's arm across her shoulder.

Turian rotated the ring on his finger and studied his son. "Her word has been less than reliable as of late. Give me a good reason to keep Semra out of the dungeons."

Semra stiffened. There were windows along the way to the northwest tower leading to the dungeons. Zezura might be able to get her out, but lives would be lost in the effort. Semra reached for Zezura. *Are you close?*

Zezura sent her response in a flash of her own vision. She was soaring overhead, looping the castle, as close as she could be without landing on the grounds.

"She had a capture or kill order from you, and yet brought me here on a dragon knowing we'd be shot at and knowing she'd end up surrounded. Because a dragon was the only mode of travel that would beat what's coming. Time is running out."

Turian's ice cold glare cut to her heart as he examined her for a long moment. Finally, he dipped his head. "Everyone out. General Soldan, stay."

"Coanor is here," a guard whispered to Firfell, close enough for Zephan and Semra to hear.

"Is the newcomer critical to the meeting?" Turian asked.

"It would be beneficial for Pidge to stay," Zephan said. "Coanor is outside. If you'd allow her, she could fix up the wound as we begin."

"Your Majesty," Firfell began, "I could have restraints brought to—"

The king rose to his feet and pointed at the door. "If I wanted restraints, Firfell, I would have asked for them. Get out before the last shreds of patience leave my body."

Guards tripped over each other making a hasty exit, and Firfell retreated out the double doors. They were nearly shut when the king yelled, "And get Coanor in here now!"

One of the doors opened again, and a familiar gray-haired woman scurried in with a bag over her shoulder and a roll of clean linen under her arm. She bowed to the king. "Your Majesty." She turned to Semra, Zephan, and Pidge, and looked them up and down. "One of you looks better than last I saw you, and one of you looks worse. But I'm here for the new one, I presume."

Turian nodded, dropped back into his chair, and ran a hand over his eyes. He looked much older.

Pidge wrinkled her nose and pulled away from Coanor. "Your bag reeks."

"It smells like not dying of infection, thank you very much. And there's nothing in here that smells the least bit poorly. The alder is my favorite. You're not going to be a wimp about this, are you?"

Pidge lifted her chin in defiance. "I took the arrow out myself."

"An arrogant wimp. Marvelous. Shut up so the big people can talk, and stay still. I'll only be a few minutes."

Pidge's mouth dropped open and she looked to Semra for support. Semra couldn't help but smile at Coanor's pluck, and she gave Pidge a look. *Don't cause problems. Do as she says.*

Semra turned back to the king, and the smile died on her lips. His expression was flint, though his posture was weary.

"What is so urgent," he said slowly, speaking to Zephan, "that my son, who was supposed to be in Kinlock, has rendezvoused yet again with this woman, breaking his word both to me and to his people?" Turian's fingers drummed on the arm of his throne.

Zephan clenched his jaw and pressed his lips in a flat line. Semra wondered how many retorts he was swallowing. When he spoke, his voice was smooth, without a hint of indignation. "Axis hired Tymetin to kill you, and by the time we learned of it he had a four-day head start. Depending on how hard he rides, and if he gets fresh horses, he could be here as soon as tomorrow."

Turian's fingers stilled.

Soldan spilled an inkwell.

"How will he do it?" Turian asked.

"We don't know," Zephan answered.

"What do we know about him?"

Zephan gestured at Semra, and she took a deep breath. "He is responsible for planning your wife's murder. He requires written contracts for his freelance work, and frequently uses blackmail. He specializes in explosives, but Arnevon seems to have been poisoned, and I recently learned Tymetin is also a phenomenal archer. I'm afraid his talents are many, and his conscience does not exist."

"So he was responsible for Arnevon's death also." Turian ran a hand through his beard. "Certainly, it's convenient for an accused person to present a new suspect. How do we know this?"

Zephan shared his side of the story, and invited Semra to share her side, with Pidge interjecting at intervals. They told how Semra's illness manifested and was eventually overcome, how they learned Avaya had the amulet before Arnevon was killed, how Zezura burned Tymetin when he tried to kill Semra, and how his scars would prove their story if he were ever found. They told how Tymetin had practically admitted to working with Avaya when he came to threaten Semra four nights ago, and how trying to save Siler and set up the meeting of assassins had taken their focus, and Tymetin had distracted them from his departure with his threats.

"Coanor can testify to Semra's condition when she left the castle, and the Rinabs can testify to her condition when she arrived there," Zephan said. "Not to mention myself. Obviously, the smoke and sparks from her fingers indicate magical influences rather than any poison she may have been affected by in Belvidore, which was part of the shaky evidence used against her before."

"I had hoped you would understand, when I broke my promise," Semra said. "But I knew it was too much to ask. I can't imagine you could forgive me, but I couldn't find a third option, like the kind you suggested. This was the best I could do."

Turian studied her, then turned to Coanor. "Is it true?"

The woman bobbed her head in jerking movements, and for a moment Semra was reminded comically of Zezura's bobbing gesture. "Yes, Your Majesty. She had limited tonic when she left, and I helped her escape. I saw no alternatives."

"And my youngest daughter. She was involved as well?"

Coanor pursed her lips. "It is possible that Princess Aviama and I encountered each other in the halls a time or two."

"Mmm. Indeed."

Was that a smile? Semra's heart leaped. Perhaps he didn't utterly despise her after all. Or maybe he was only impressed by Aviama's spunk.

"And how did you get connected with Pidge? You said you found her as you were leaving the castle?"

"I ..." Semra looked at Pidge. The girl's color paled, and her chin trembled. She stared at the floor. Semra turned back to the king. "Yes, Zezura and I found her on the outskirts of Qalea."

"Zephan, is she always such a terrible liar?" Turian leaned forward, boring a hole into Pidge's skull. She squirmed. "I know a few things about Semra," he said. "I know she is an accomplished killer. I know she is impulsive. I know she is no diplomat."

"She was incredible with the assassins, Father," Zephan said.

Turian held up his hand, never taking his eyes off Pidge. "And I know she is loyal. To a fault, perhaps. She lies when she is protecting someone. I already know you are one of the Mount Hara assassins, so what could she be protecting you from? She knows she's on thin ice with me. She wants to answer my questions, but she won't betray you, even when she should. Even when it interferes with her loyalty to the Shama-rans. She found you just outside my home. What are you guilty of?"

Semra felt as though a rock plummeted to the pit of her stomach. King Turian was no fool. She'd known it, of course, but to hear how effortlessly he listed her innermost qualities was disconcerting. Semra shifted her weight and clamped her mouth tightly shut.

Pidge shook her head. "Nothing."

Turian straightened, surprised. "You're telling the truth, I think." He furrowed his brow, glancing at Semra. "It isn't what you did, but what you tried to do. She stopped you." He hesitated. "You were on your way to kill me."

43

Zephan spun to Pidge. Pidge shook her head violently, and Semra sidestepped toward her. "You have no evidence that she's done anything but be supportive. All we know for sure is that she is one of the children of the mountain, a kidnapped child with nowhere to go, that chose to aid me and your son as soon as she was given the opportunity. She's been invaluable."

Turian returned her stare for a long time. Semra's stomach flopped, but she kept her face serene. Turian flattened his lips. "And various additional assassins will be traveling here in the next six weeks to receive assurances they are free to travel within our borders."

"Yes," Semra said. "Provided there is no evidence they've killed anyone in Jannemar since Azi's imprisonment, they accept terms never to kill here again, they refuse all contracts with Belvidore, and they assist with sending a message to Axis."

"And saving yet another assassin, who is a captive in Madensig."

"An assassin who fought by your side in the throne room

that day," Semra reminded him. "Yes. Without him your brother would be in that chair instead of you, and everyone you love would be dead or worse."

"I may still wind up dead, if your story is to be believed." Turian stroked his beard and turned to General Soldan. Semra had nearly forgotten he was there. "What do you make of this?"

Soldan paused, then turned to Zephan. "After the Rinabs when you found Semra and she was still severely ill, how long of stretches was she away from you? Could she have rendezvoused with anyone, or sent messages without your knowledge?"

Zephan shook his head. "She never even flew Zezura without me flying with her. Everything from the Rinabs onward I can personally vouch for."

"And this Tymetin, he will know you arrived before him. Will your presence here scare him off? Perhaps he won't want to kill when one of his own kind knows he is coming, knows who he is coming for, and is waiting for him."

Semra blanched at Soldan's word choice. "I am not one if *his* kind. Even when I worked for the Framatar, I thought I was purging the world of evil. I know it sounds crazy, but that's what we grew up believing. But Tymetin is made of something else entirely. He doesn't kill for a cause. He kills for the money, and maybe even for fun. He enjoys it."

"Will your presence be a deterrent?" Turian pressed. "You have a dragon, after all."

Semra shook her head. "His planning is impeccable. He would have prepared for me being here as a variable. I believe he threatened us on the mountain to throw us off course and entrench our focus on Madensig, making it sound like he returned there. I think it's likely he had a horse waiting somewhere and took off straight from the mountain to Jannemar."

"We can't leave the new assassin free," Soldan said. "She's a liability, as someone who attempted to kill the king before. Tymetin could be using her, and even if he isn't, she's not trustworthy."

"I'm not sure you even want me here, considering you'd ordered to have me killed just an hour ago," Semra said. "But if you want me to be any part of this, you will allow Pidge to stay with me."

"You're not in a position to bargain," Turian said.

Semra shrugged. "Maybe I'm not. Kill me then. Let's see how Zezura takes the news that I'm dead. And good luck with Tymetin. He knows this castle like the back of his hand, and he's successfully carried out a hit here before."

A wave of pain and anger flashed across the king's face, and then was gone. Semra winced. Bringing up his dead wife might not have been the best move, but there was no other way to demonstrate how critical the situation was.

Turian leaned forward. "Are you threatening me?"

Semra set her jaw. "With what the dragon will do after I'm dead and have no control over her? Absolutely not. I'm telling you the likelihood that she will act reasonably is low. Your court thinks I'm out of control, that I go on killing sprees like it's my hobby, that I'm dangerous. The truth is, I *am* dangerous, but no matter how you may disagree with my methods, I've never been dangerous to *you*. And my dragon is far more dangerous than I am. She frequently wants to kill people she doesn't like, and I rein her in all the time."

Turian considered her for a long moment. Semra's gut turned sour, and her heart pounded. She forced herself to maintain steady eye contact, to slow her breathing, to project a confidence she did not feel.

"Father. Tymetin has framed Semra twice now," Zephan said. "Once for mother, and once for Arnevon. And both times, his ruse worked. Semra was imprisoned and nearly killed the first time. She lived, no thanks to us. And the second time she fled to escape threats on her life. But here she is, in our hour of need."

Turian barked out a laugh, and Semra jumped. "I was wrong. You certainly haven't won over my court, but you know a thing or two about negotiation."

"Someone I respect once told me nobles were necessary unpleasantries," Semra said. "But if they hate me for things I cannot change, and hold biases I cannot break, I find it more productive to focus elsewhere. You once told me I was low on friends. The only friend I ever dared to have in the mountain was murdered in front of me in your throne room."

Semra thought of Garbane and Saeb covering for her, of Aviama and Coanor getting her out of the castle, of Shafii and Tinat Rinab, taking her in. She thought of Siler, Pidge, and Zephan, going to bat for her against all odds. Semra fought back a surge of emotion and continued. "I've recently learned I have far more friends than I ever dreamed possible."

The king studied her again, and his expression softened. "If Pidge can prove herself in service to the crown—*this* crown, mind you—and you vouch for her with your life, then she can remain. I'll chain her to you if I have to, but she will not leave your presence. Keep her out of the way as much as possible, or my court will never let me hear the end of this. And she has to blend in.

"Pidge, at the end of all this, each assassin will be put on trial with any evidence that they have broken our laws since my brother's imprisonment. I will honor my son's negotiations, and everyone who is cleared will be free to travel and select a new life."

Pidge went rigid at the mention of a trial. Semra felt the knot in her stomach tighten, but it was a good offer. It was unreasonably merciful, and Semra was the best suited assassin to understand that.

"Your Majesty, if I may," Semra said. "The assassins think I'm treated with favoritism. I'd like to be put on trial first, submitting my plea for an identification card. My only request is that I have no last name. I have not been a Bandaka for quite some time."

Zephan snapped his head toward her, but she didn't look at him. The truth was, she didn't know what a trial would bring. Was she still in danger for defying the king's direct order?

Turian nodded slowly. "I think we can arrange that. I suggest you think long and hard about how your next actions will look when it's time to present your case for formal trial. Now, down to more urgent business. Tymetin is cocky. We can use that." The king clapped his hands. "I think it's time we order food and drink. No need to strategize over my life on an empty stomach."

44

"Ooooh, how about this one?"

It was the next morning, and Princess Aviama had rapped on Semra's door early to put Pidge in *blending-in* clothes. Aviama reached into the wardrobe and pulled out a velvet lilac dress with a slim sleeve to the wrist and billowing sleeves overtop, draping down from the elbow. Pidge wrinkled her nose. "Are you serious?"

Aviama clucked her tongue. "*Please* tell me you aren't as bad as Semra. Look at all these beautiful clothes, being absolutely *wasted* in Semra's wardrobe! Did you see the detail on the neckline? And the color will be perfect for you."

"These sleeves are better with this dress than the yellow one," Semra said. "If you're not practiced with quickly accessing your knives with a skirt, you can strap them to your forearms, and no one will know."

Aviama rolled her eyes. "Will I ever get to play dress up with someone who appreciates my glorious taste?"

Pidge moaned. "Fine, I'll wear the purple thing."

Aviama beamed. "The sweetheart neckline, brocade trim lilac it is! Semra, would you *ever* wear an off the shoulder dress? It would show off the dragon's kiss, and I think it's gorgeous."

Semra snorted. "Does *off the shoulder* mean I have a tunic and pants on underneath, and it's easier to rip off and abandon?"

Aviama gasped. "Unbelievable."

"How come Semra doesn't have to wear dresses?" Pidge whined.

"Because people know me here, and if I were wearing a dress, they'd wonder what was wrong with me," Semra said. "I already make people uncomfortable, but if there were two of us, they'd lose their minds even more."

Pidge scowled, took the dress, and stepped behind the screen. "Are you really going to go on trial?"

Semra pulled a fresh tunic from the drawer and changed into it. "Yes."

"Do you think ... I mean, wouldn't that make us weak? Depending on someone else for our freedom, accepting training for free?"

Semra considered this. Six months ago, she would have said yes. "Did you think I was weak when I let you get supplies for me when I was sick? Or when the Rinabs worked to heal me, or Zephan and Siler carried me over the mountain?"

"Well, you were objectively weak," Pidge said. "You couldn't do those things yourself. You would have been stupid not to let me help."

"You're the strongest person I know." Aviama's voice was earnest, her face eager. A gentle warmth and an awkward squirmy feeling squabbled for prominence in Semra's stomach. Why did the princess's admiration scare her?

"I think there is a whiny way to accept help, a parasitic way. And there is another way that is strong. I think sometimes we need to recognize we need help and d be grown up enough to take it when the right person offers. If Coanor and Aviama hadn't helped me, I never would have gotten out of the castle. If Siler and Zephan didn't carry me when I was so sick, I never would have escaped the soldiers. They can't prove you did anything. You need help. Take it. Start a new life."

"What are you going to do next?"

Semra's heart sank, and she looked away. "I don't know."

What *was* she going to do? Visions of Zephan and their kiss ran through her mind. His words, beautifully believable with that intense amber gaze, played across her memory. *Life's messy ...we'll take what comes and face it together.* Zephan in rags, with the singed marks of her fingertips on his shirt, was a man she could long for. But Zephan in royal military regalia?

She would never be his mistress, so what was left for her? Maybe she could pick a profession and get job training like she had encouraged her colleagues to do. The idea made her stomach churn. But she had a dragon. Dragonlords couldn't be bakers or carpenters. Surely they couldn't live normal lives. She would always be a target, more so than the other assassins. Try as she might, she would always be high profile.

The only thing she knew for sure was she wasn't going to ghost Zephan. After everything settled down, she'd talk to him about things like an adult, and they'd have to face reality.

Pidge stepped out from behind the screen and Aviama gasped. "You're *beautiful!* Oh, look at you!" She clapped her hands.

Semra blinked. It was strange seeing Pidge in a dress, and it was obvious she wasn't used to it, but the girl blushed pink at Aviama's encouragement. And Aviama was right. She looked positively regal.

Semra stepped forward, pulled Pidge's sleeves back, and wrapped her forearms with strips of linen. Semra secured the ends and slipped a knife onto each of the girl's arms, then pulled the sleeves back down over them.

"We're meeting in the library, right?" Pidge asked.

Semra nodded. "We should get going. It's best to be early than leave a king waiting, especially if you aren't sure you're on good terms."

"I'll walk you down," Aviama said. She fiddled with a soft blond ringlet of her hair and bit her lip. She'd seemed very much herself this morning, but now her anxiety was seeping through.

"We should have at least until this evening, right?" Pidge said. "And more than likely, a few more days?"

Aviama froze, and Semra cut Pidge a warning glare. She didn't know how much, if anything, Aviama knew about the threat on her father's life. And it wasn't their place to share anything the king had not. The princess glanced between them, and Pidge grimaced.

Aviama's shoulders slumped. "It's okay. You know, I think I'll head back to my room for breakfast. I'm starving."

Boom.

The room shook, and the pitcher on the side table crashed to the floor. Semra stumbled into the bedpost, and Aviama and Pidge collided as they lost their balance. Screams echoed down the hall, followed by a deathly silence. Semra felt her heart pounding in her ears, and the hairs on the back of her neck stood on end.

"What was that?" Aviama whispered.

Boom. The sound was low and deep, as if far away, smothered—and yet it shook the castle. Semra's mouth went dry.

She spun to Aviama. "Where is Zephan?"

"I don't know!" she said, tears brimming her eyes. "He was with father long into the night. He might still be there, in the sitting room."

Semra tore out of the room and took off down the hall. Where were the explosions coming from? Everything looked intact ...

A glimpse out the window tore Semra's heart in two. Smoke was pouring from the king's window on the third floor. She flew down the corridor, through Ancestry Hall, and up the stairs to the walkway toward the king's residence, Pidge and Aviama hot on her heels. A mass of guards swarmed the narrow walkway. Semra swore.

She whirled and flew back down the spiral staircase.

Boom. The third explosion knocked her three stairs down and she rammed into the stone staircase wall. Screams filled the air. Pidge yanked her to her feet, and they crashed down the remaining stairs passed the second floor and to ground level. No, the explosions weren't coming from the king's chambers. They were coming from underground.

The river. A branch of the Dezapi ran under the castle, through the web of servant's quarters, and out over the catacombs to the cleft where Zezura was hiding. "The tunnels," Semra yelled. "He's making it unsafe to take the king underground. We don't know how many more explosives he has."

"Was the king in his room? Did he ... is he ..." Pidge's eyes were wide as saucers. Semra ran to a window looking into the courtyard. Guards were everywhere, but the king was nowhere to be seen. Good.

"We should go outside," Aviama said. "If the tunnels are blown, they'll take him to the cellar. Or maybe the courtyard."

Aviama lurched for the door to the courtyard, and Semra's heart flew to her throat. Semra lunged after her, looped her arm around the princess's waist, and yanked her backward. "Don't let him flush us out. He can't have explosives everywhere, and he couldn't have had much time to set them.

Underground is easier to set without getting caught. Neither of you goes out without me, you hear me?"

Pidge and Aviama nodded. Semra took an unsteady breath to still the tremor in her voice. She dipped her head in a curt nod. "Stay close. Let's go."

Three servants fled past them down the hall, and two guards burst through the door into the courtyard. Hordes of people were pouring out of the feasting hall and guard tower, faces set as flint, or streamed with tears, quiet and focused, or screaming their heads off as if by sheer volume they could keep the explosions at bay.

The mark on Semra's chest tingled as she sent out the call to Zezura. *I'm searching inside, but I need your eyes. I need the sky. Find the king. Find Zephan. Find Tymetin.*

And if you see Tymetin, kill him.

Semra gripped Aviama's wrist, glanced over her shoulder to see Pidge right behind her, and forged ahead against the mass of bodies fleeing the feasting hall. Any of these guards could be Tymetin in guard dress. He would be completely invisible in the chaos.

A flash of movement at the far end of the room caught her eye. Six bodyguards separated Zephan from his father. They pushed Zephan toward the stairs to the cellar, and Turian toward the doors to the courtyard.

Semra screamed and ran forward, but her voice was lost in the din. Turian was swept into the courtyard, and Zephan caught sight of her across the room. She saw her own panic registered in his eyes. He fought off his bodyguards and leaped for the open door.

Windows lined the feasting hall. Semra watched in horror as a small object cut through the air from above. One of the guards caught a glimpse of it in the last second. Semra reeled.

It was Annais. He tackled Turian to the ground and shielded the king's body with his own.

Pop.

Hssssssssss.

Fire burst from the casing and a cloud of dust and smoky fog enveloped the courtyard. Semra lost all visual of the king.

45

Semra threw her arms around Aviama and hauled her away from the door, then reached for Zezura and was rewarded with the dragon's vision. The feasting hall and foggy courtyard before her disappeared in exchange for an aerial view of the castle, in vibrant reptilian color. The cloud was impenetrable. The dragon huffed in displeasure at the rotten smell of burning sulfur mixed with lime. The greenery of the curated grounds near the blast had caught fire, and snatches of flame were occasionally visible through the billowing gray.

Guards swarmed like ants toward the courtyard. The streaming smoke from the king's third floor bedroom had begun to dissipate. There had been no more underground explosions after the first three. A disheveled gray-haired woman threw a bag over her shoulder and ran from a small building on the east side of the outer ward. Servants and staff ran every conceivable direction, often colliding into one another.

Confusion.

Hysteria.

An excellent foray into mayhem.

Guards in the outer wards, towers, and walls retained their posts or moved into reasonable defensive positions. No one seemed to make any unusual movements. Where could the missile have been thrown from? Semra cycled through the options. The walkway on the third floor. The northeast tower. The Grand Hall on the second floor. No, the angle was wrong. It was the tower.

Zezura flew by the tower and looped again. Nothing. The windows were narrow, visibility poor.

Semra snapped back into her body. She didn't know if Turian was alive, but there was nothing she could do for him now. Only one name assaulted her mind.

Tymetin.

She couldn't let him get away. Not again.

Where would his exit be? He would have needed an accomplice, maybe some blackmailed castle servant, to throw the smoke bomb or set off the first underground charge. He couldn't have done both of those things at once. But he would have been in the tower to throw the missile himself.

It was the perfect location. The narrow windows kept Zezura out. The confusion would hide him. His distractions were effective. He loved to watch the pain he caused unfold, and from there he could see it all. Would he dare exit the same way he came in? He likely came through some little-known underground entrance.

He would want out of the trap of the upper floors as soon as possible. And the northeast tower was near the stairs leading down to ...

Semra clenched her jaw and spun.

"Stay with the king!" she shouted back at Pidge. "If he's alive, make sure he stays that way!"

Semra sprinted back through the feasting hall and across

to the staircase leading underground, down to the level where she'd fought Manu months ago, and through the open door.

Why is it open? Tymetin was already here. Semra pulled the knives from her trousers and peered around the doorframe. Dim catacombs stretched in a huge room before her, pillars lining the sides and rising to engraved archways over the dead. Kings of old were buried here, row after row of royalty come and gone.

It was the end of all kings. They had the privilege of being remembered in old paintings and dusty stone sarcophagi, while everyone else simply faded away. But what did it matter? None of them knew the difference.

Was it Turian's turn to trade in his throne for a coffin? How long before Zephan shared his fate?

Semra stole along the shadows toward the small door hidden away on the far side. It led out to the cleft—Tymetin must have climbing gear and a boat. It was smart. Semra hadn't anticipated him to take a river exit.

Movement caught the corner of her eye as she rounded the corner of a sarcophagus. Semra ducked just in time and pain exploded in her shoulder where her head had been half a second before. Semra slashed upward and Tymetin parried before she danced out of range.

He was dressed in guard attire, but the bow across his back wasn't typical of castle archers. Tymetin blocked her second strike and threw an uppercut; Semra nicked his forearm with her blade and thrust into his gut. Her knife clinked uselessly against chain mail under his outer clothing, and Tymetin curled his lips into a sickening smile.

"You're so predictable." His hand shot out and gripped her throat, and stone cut into her back as he shoved her up against the sarcophagus.

Semra gagged. His chokehold tightened, and her heart

rate leaped in panic. She pulled at the meat of his hand, but his grip was iron. She swung her arm down hard on the joint of his arm, but it did not bend. Semra hooked her legs around his waist, trapping his body to hers, and her left hand sent its knife spiraling down into his foot.

Tymetin dropped her with a grunt. She swung her elbow into his jaw and followed through with a strike with the knife in her right hand, but Tymetin deflected and threw her backward into the stone.

Semra tumbled to the ground and rolled, coughing. Tymetin ripped the blade from his foot with a snarl as she sprang to her feet.

"You just attempted to assassinate Turian using all your favorite tricks," Semra said. "No proper frame job, nothing—you practically plastered your name all over it. And you call *me* predictable?"

Tymetin flipped the bloodied knife in his hands. "First, I didn't *attempt* it. I succeeded. If he's not dead yet, he'll die of his injuries. I could have poisoned his tea, or his bath soap, or something elementary like that. But it's no fun, and ever since Arnevon, I'm so *tired* of boring kills."

Bile rose in Semra's throat, but she laughed. "You're punishing Axis—fulfilling the contract, but with a loophole. You'll collect your fee, and you want him to know if he doesn't behave, he'll be next."

Tymetin shrugged. "He was a moron. If you want a rival monarch dead, you don't pinch pennies hiring a rookie. Pinch pennies in war, not on linchpins." He paused. "And I'm no one's lackey."

Semra snorted. "You were the Framatar's *slave*."

Tymetin thrust the knife at Semra's neck; she blocked the blow and barreled into him. He fell backward, and she rolled to one side, the bloodstained blade in his hand missing her by a hair. They danced apart.

"I wasn't a mindless idiot like the rest of you. The Framatar and I had an agreement. And I believe he would enjoy your artful demise just as much as I will."

A chill ran up her spine. She bounced on the balls of her feet. "You think you have time to play before you run away like a scared rabbit?"

Tymetin twirled the knife over his head and caught it. "You know that scream rabbits make? The one that makes the Bow class kids cry at night. They're such quiet creatures, rabbits. Right up until the threat of death. Until it's too late. By the time you scream, no one will be able to save you."

Semra lunged, and Tymetin sidestepped behind the sarcophagus. He threw his weight against the stone top, and to Semra's surprise it slid willingly off its base. Semra ran backward and raised her knife, but she didn't have a clear shot in the vulnerable areas exposed from the chainmail. And she couldn't lose her last knife on a failed throw.

Tymetin dropped out of view and Semra gave the sarcophagus a large berth and crept around the corner. He was gone. Semra circled the coffin twice, checking the surrounding pillars and sarcophagi. Could he still be hiding?

She stopped. *The open coffin.* The lid had moved too easily – like it was accustomed to being opened. Because it wasn't a tomb. It was a tunnel.

Semra crept forward. A tunnel here was genius. Tymetin wouldn't have had time to create it. It must be ancient, but the Framatar hadn't used it in his original plans. How had Tymetin learned of it?

Something solid crashed into Semra and her feet were ripped from the ground. Tymetin threw her inside the sarcophagus, and she landed with a *crunch* and *snap* on something hard and knobby. Bones.

Nausea and heat rolled through her body, and her muscles felt weak. Her mind grew foggy, and she was faintly aware of a distinct smell she'd come to recognize. Konnolan.

A scraping noise sounded above her, and the dimness began to turn to black.

46

The tunnel in the sarcophagus did not exist. Only the coffin—*her* coffin—and the burning powder filling it with fumes of death. Zezura was coming. She couldn't fit inside, but she could make it through the waterfall to the cleft. *Konnolan. He has konnolan.*

Semra hoped Zezura got the message. Her head was swirling. Her vision went black.

No, no, it wasn't her vision—it was her *field* of vision. The lid. It was almost shut. What would Zephan say if she didn't try? *You'll never know what he'd say. You'd be dead.*

Semra mustered every ounce of strength in her body to flip the knife in her hands, holding it by the blade and shoving the handle upward. The lid halted, with only the width of the knife handle to go until her entombment was complete.

She wormed her fingers into the narrow space and braced against the inside of the coffin to push back against the lid. It slid backward just enough; Semra gripped the knife handle again and pushed her elbows up over the lid so that her body beneath the armpits was encased in the sarcophagus, and the top portion of her body clung to the stone statue of a long dead king chiseled into dignified rest.

His remains were less than dignified now, as her feet scrambled to for leverage against the opposite wall of the coffin. A rattling sound echoed in the catacombs as Semra kicked the ancient monarch's femurs and kneecaps out of the way. Tymetin let out a roar of rage and threw himself against the lid. Semra's ribs burned as the stone edges pinned her to the coffin. Dizziness swept over her, and she wavered.

"Youuuu wern gerterbay middis," she drawled. Her mouth was dry, her mind fuzzy. Gentle tendrils of smoke wafted lazily from her fingers. She furrowed her brow.

"I've already gotten away with it," he said. "Meanwhile, I've framed you twice for murder, successfully, and the family you keep leeching onto will never accept you. You're an orphan, and it's time you died like one. Alone."

Tymetin raised the knife in his hand, but a sound from other side of the catacombs gave him pause. Semra threw hers. She watched it spin as if in slow motion, rotating through the air in perfect precision.

Almost perfect. It plunged into his face just beneath the cheekbone. She'd been aiming for his eye. A ghoulish scream filled the air, and Tymetin flew from the catacombs and out the narrow door to the cliff with her blade still sunk in his face.

Semra slumped against the lid of the sarcophagus, too weak to move, still trapped between it and the coffin. One clear thought rang through her mind as she laid her head against the coolness of the stone. Tymetin sounded a trifle like a rabbit giving its death cry.

The king was dead, or nearly dead. Semra hadn't gotten to go on trial and officially clear her name. Siler was captured or dead in Belvidore. The Jannemari court despised her; she had no future, and Tymetin had gotten away.

Again.

For the first time in weeks, her old commander's voice echoed through her mind.

Oh, but don't worry. No one will remember your failings. No one will think of you at all. The only thing you were ever good at was killing. And now you can't even do that.

Semra's head swam, and her body ached. Nausea rolled over her, but she didn't have the energy to lift her head. Dying here was just as well. She would never have cut it as a dragonlord seamstress anyway.

I tried, Zephan. Please know that I tried.

Axis would dispatch Zephan next and sweep through to claim an empire. Unless Tymetin killed him. Then who would reign in Belvidore?

A tear rolled down her cheek. It didn't matter now. How long would it take for the konnolan fumes to kill her? If death must come, she hoped it would be quick. She closed her eyes.

Voices pulled at her consciousness. Why did they disturb her? Couldn't they see she was trying to die in peace?

A scraping sound irritated her, and she tried to open her eyes, but they were so ... heavy ...

The pressure on Semra's ribcage lessened, and without its support, she sagged inside the coffin. Hands pulled at her arms, and her head lolled to one side.

"I've got her." It was a woman's voice. "Go, go!"

Running feet receded toward the door to the cleft, and Semra struggled to open her eyes again. Aviama's face peered down at her, her face pale, her eyes red, half-propping Semra against the side of the coffin.

"Semra?" Her voice trembled. "Stay with me, please. Stay, stay ..."

She leaned over the opening of the sarcophagus and gagged. "I've got to get you out of there. Ugh, it smells so bad. How do you stand it? I guess you didn't have much choice, but I feel like you didn't even notice, and I would have died of shock just from the smell. You're so much stronger than me. You can do this; stay with me." Aviama pulled at Semra's arms and grunted. "Maybe Gaulen will kill Tymetin really quick and come help me pull you out."

Semra moaned. "No, no, he'll die; he'll die ..."

"That's the idea, isn't it? For Tymetin to die?"

Semra's lips parted, but it was a moment before sound came out. "Gaulen."

The little remaining blood in Aviama's face drained. "Tymetin beat you. He can beat anyone."

Semra tried to focus on her breathing. She wanted to nod, but the answer was obvious, so she didn't bother. Maybe Tymetin was already headed down the cliff, and Gaulen would miss him. That would keep him safe.

"He has a knife sticking out of his face, though," Aviama said. "It was so grizzly! You got him, Semra. You did, I saw it. It was a good throw."

"Was aiming ... for his eye."

Gaulen ran back from the cleft and lifted Semra from the coffin. "Okay, crazy, let's get you out of here." His voice was gruff but less cold than she'd expected. The last time she'd seen Gaulen, she'd been hanging upside down from a dragon claw and taunting him through the castle window.

He carried her through the catacombs, out the door, and into the stairwell, with Aviama close behind. The fog on Semra's brain began to clear as they left the konnolan behind.

"Did you see him?" Aviama asked.

"No. And Prince Zephan was explicit that his priority was

Semra, not Tymetin, so when I didn't see him right away, I had to return."

"He's gone," Semra said. She tested her feet, wiggling her toes. Good. Strength was coming back. "How did you know where I was?"

"Pidge ran to my father, like you told her," Aviama said. "She and Zephan are with him now. Zephan told Gaulen to go after you."

Gaulen reached the ground level and crossed the anteroom of the feasting hall to the stairs leading up to the Nezzi Room. "They told me you were running toward the northeast tower. The missile trajectory indicated the throw came from that tower, and I had same thought you did. The catacombs made sense."

"The king," Semra said. "Is he ..."

"Coanor and her team are with him, but it doesn't look good," Gaulen said.

"Aviama, you should be there. Not chasing assassins."

Aviama lifted her chin. "One of those assassins was my friend. And they wouldn't have let me in anyway. They were trying to limit the number of people in there. I couldn't just sit in a hallway and cry."

Semra pressed her lips together. "I get that."

"I'll go now though. Are you sure you're okay?"

Semra nodded. "I'll be fine. I just need some fresh air, and in a couple hours I'll be back to normal. It didn't get in my bloodstream."

Aviama gave her an awkward half hug with Semra still in Gaulen's arms, and ran off. Gaulen reached the second floor and Semra gasped as all the fear and anger Zezura had pent up finally made it through the haze the konnolan had created, and suddenly hit her like a ton of bricks. Zezura was screaming through the air along the cliff face on the north side of the castle.

The castle halls melted away and were replaced by the Shalladin sparkling below, the Dezapi river pouring out into a waterfall over the cliff from beneath the castle, and a figure rapelling down the rocky side.

The dragon's anger burned, and she zeroed in on her prey. She'd gotten Semra's message about the konnolan. And she'd waited anxiously while her lord fought for her life inside. She'd waited for her prey to leave the cleft and descend toward his useless little boat.

Her last instructions from her lord had been precisely what she wanted to hear.

If you see Tymetin, kill him.

At last, Zezura's time had come. She had no restrictions. She would give no quarter. She would have no mercy.

Blazing inferno ignited in Zezura's throat, and she welcomed the heat of her fire as a trusted friend. This human was a monster. And he would not go quietly into death.

A knife protruded from the man's face, the same side sporting burns from Zezura's last encounter with him. She had heard his scream as he fled the catacombs. Satisfaction filled her reptilian chest. *Justice. Death. Death.*

Zezura flew down beneath the cleft and the faint smell of konnolan and let out a stream of fire on her victim. He was a strong one. Tymetin dropped ten feet down the rope before regaining a controlled grip and continuing down the cliff.

Semra could feel Zezura's rage, her hunter's drive to kill. She knew even now if she gave the word, Zezura would turn away. But it wasn't right to take this from the dragon. Tymetin would never end the fight. He would kill and kill, every monarch, every assassin, every soul who breathed. He lived only to kill, and only one consequence was fitting.

Semra answered Zezura's call. *I'm here. I'm alive.* Semra

hesitated, then gave a single condition. *He's yours. Only, leave proof he existed. We need recognizable proof of him.*

Pleasure rippled through all fifty feet of the giant flying reptile as she wheeled in the air for a second pass. Zezura sank her talons into his flesh, the chain mail punctured, and snatched him off the cliff. She flew higher, higher, over the castle, and dropped him.

In a flash he was in her teeth, shaken like a mouse in the mouth of a lion, tenderized by fire, tossed and impaled again and again by razor dragon's teeth and talons. A blood-curdling scream like Semra had never heard rang from the sky, echoed only by the roar of the beast whose bloodlust was at last given rein.

Moments later Zezura rounded the castle and doused Tymetin's body in the waterfall, depositing her gift on the cleft for her lord. Semra's stomach soured at the sight of her enemy — the top half of Tymetin's body, metal chain mail melded to his scorched skin, a terrified expression frozen on his face, Semra's knife blade still protruding from his cheek. The bottom half of him was missing. Zezura roared and flew from the cleft.

"Semra! Semra!"

Semra lurched back to herself. She was laying on the couch inside her chambers, and Gaulen was beside her. She rubbed her eyes and blinked at him.

"There, you're back. You're back, right? You went into some sort of trance."

"I'm connected to Zezura more now," Semra said. "I can see what she sees. Tymetin is dead. You'll find him on the cleft outside the catacombs. He's recognizable, mostly, and Pidge and any other Mount Hara assassin can confirm his identity. It's um ... it's not for the weak of stomach."

Gaulen's eyebrows soared.

Semra watched him for a moment, then swallowed. "Thanks. For bringing me here."

He shrugged. "Didn't have a choice."

"I know. But I haven't made it easy. You're an excellent soldier. And I'm everything you hate."

Gaulen stilled. He studied her. "Some people think you're unhinged."

"Thanks."

"I wasn't finished. They think you're unpredictable and dangerous. But being dangerous only means you are capable. What matters is if you are trustworthy. If you're loyal. I don't always love your methods, but I think ..." He cleared his throat, and his surly exterior softened. "I think you do stupid things in the service of people you care for. And what I saw today made it obvious where your loyalty lies. You expected to die today in the catacombs."

Semra bit her lip and eyed him. She looked down at her fingers, then back at Gaulen. "Don't tell Aviama."

"I wouldn't dream of it."

Semra nodded. "Or Zephan."

"Let's hope he doesn't ask. Because if he does, my loyalty is to him, not you."

Semra grimaced and smiled. "As it should be."

Gaulen stood. "I'll be posted outside your door, but this time, it's not to keep you in. It's to keep you safe. As soon as I hear an update on the king, I'll let you know. But ... prepare yourself. He was severely injured by the blast."

The image of Annais throwing himself over Turian replayed in her mind. The courtyard had been flooded with people, and a blast like that could have killed anyone standing too close.

"Is ... is Annais ...?"

Gaulen stopped and swallowed. He shook his head. "He's

gone. Let's hope it's not in vain. Get some rest."

47

Semra gazed off into the nothingness of her room. Exquisite details surrounded her in the carved canopy of the bed, the workmanship of the desk and chair, the sitting furniture and wardrobe stuffed with expensive clothing Semra would never wear. It was all nothingness.

What good was any of it when it didn't protect a person from death? Semra had been in a hundred fancy halls and residences of the rich. In all her eavesdropping, they'd never struck Semra as happier people than the lower classes she'd observed. Desperation lined an empty stomach, but beyond met needs, the amassing of the trappings of wealth was utterly meaningless.

The master of the house would die, and the walls of the house would go on standing without him. The house would eventually crumble or be torn down, and another would take its place. Just as Tymetin was dead, so too Turian might be dead, and neither would know the difference.

Yet how different were those two men!

Semra thought of the first time she'd met the king. He was so unassuming, so acutely human. But it was his vulnerability that had made him so shocking to her. He was a father afraid for his daughter, and yet responsible for thousands of families with their own sons and daughters, with the two juxtaposed against one another in the bid for marriage between Jannemar and Belvidore.

He had seemed strong yet gentle, caring yet principled. Semra thought of him fighting in the throne room, and again with his head in his hands in the meeting rooms after Avaya's self-imposed kidnapping. She thought of his intimidating intensity when warning Semra to be wise. No one would question King Turian's masculinity.

And yet Tymetin, for all his physical strength and prowess in the arena of death, was not a man. He was an animal. He was vile.

The konnolan wore off as the hours passed, and its effects lifted, but Semra's emotional energy was spent, and she felt sapped and numb all the same. A knock came at the door. Semra sat up, and Gaulen entered. His chin quivered once before he regained his composure. She knew the truth before he spoke.

"The king has succumbed to his injuries. His son and daughter were both with him when he passed."

Semra nodded. "Thanks for letting me know."

Gaulen hesitated at the door, then turned away, closing the door behind him.

Semra sat motionless in her chair, staring at the door where Gaulen had exited. Nothing. She felt nothing. *You're a monster. Turian is the kindest man you've ever known. He deserves a thousand lifetimes.* Feel *something!*

Semra crossed to the vanity and leaned her hands on the desk. Her blank, numb, stupid face stared back at her from the polished bronze mirror. Zephan was truly an orphan now, having lost both parents in less than a year. So was Aviama.

Sorrow for them leaked into her chest, but she felt somehow disconnected from it.

She sank into the chair at the vanity, staring into the corner as a spider spun a dead fly into its silky coffin. The spider was a graceful killer, endlessly patient, utterly silent, perfectly balanced on its own web.

Every day, castle servants destroyed the spider's work, and every day, undeterred, it built a new one. It never got discouraged, never tired, never wavered ... and today was rewarded for its perseverance. The hunter earned its prey.

What would killing look like without the need for reconnaissance, for framing jobs, for chase? The spider had only one trick—letting its prey walk itself into danger. But time and again, the tactic delivered.

She watched the spider until it finished its work and receded into shadows. Her eyes glazed over in the direction of the web until the sunlight from the window no longer glinted off its silken strings.

A knock at the door startled her, and she jumped. Semra shook her head and slapped herself in the face. *What's wrong with you?*

The knock came again, and she blinked in the dim light. Semra crossed to the door. How long ago had the afternoon light faded to dusk? She tugged the door open.

"Garbane?"

The older man arched an eyebrow. "That's me. Long as I can remember."

"You hate the residence halls."

"True enough."

Semra furrowed her brow and cocked her head. Garbane pressed his lips together. He shifted his weight. "Figured I'd see how you were doing."

Semra sighed and dropped the door, gesturing him to

come in and walking to the bedside table. Her throat was dry. She poured herself a glass of water, took a sip, and glared into its boring colorless liquid. She set it back down. "Fine."

Garbane stepped inside, leaving the door open, and crossed his arms.

Semra picked up the water glass again, grimaced, and returned it to the table. Her shoulders sagged and fatigue descended on her like a cloud. "I'm fine, okay? More than fine. I don't feel anything. Maybe Azi really did destroy me. Maybe I don't have a soul."

Garbane took a deep breath in and let it out. "You aren't fine."

"I don't feel anything."

Garbane took two long strides and planted himself directly in front of her. He looked down at her intently, searching her face with an intensity that was at once sharp and uncompromising, yet soft. He spoke again, firmer this time. "You. Are not. Fine."

His words hit Semra like a sledgehammer on glass, shattering to pieces what she had thought was heartless stone. Her stomach turned to knots, and a lump the size of her fist lodged itself in her throat. She blinked hard and shook her head. Her chest tightened and her breathing quickened. She squeezed her eyes shut.

And then she was sobbing.

Tears poured like rivers down her face. She clutched at Garbane, and he tucked her under his chin, stroking her hair and patting her back in wordless affirmation. *I know.*

"Semra?" Zephan's voice broke from the doorway, and Garbane lifted his chin from Semra's head to acknowledge him.

Semra sniffled and wiped her face with both hands, blinking back fresh tears as she turned in his direction.

Garbane took her elbow and gently guided her to Zephan, passing her into Zephan's arms and patting her on the back before wordlessly disappearing out into the hall.

Zephan wrapped his arms around her and buried his face in her shoulder. His body shook with sobs, and they embraced, weeping, for several minutes. Untold time passed, and her tears ran out. She rubbed his back and let his run their course.

They stood together, clinging to one another, for a long time. Semra's body relaxed against him, and she felt the tension in his shoulders ease. Zephan pulled back from her shoulder and leaned his forehead against hers. They breathed in deep, soaking up the quiet of the moment. A welcome reprieve to the chaos.

"I don't think I can do this," Zephan whispered.

"You can. You are the most incredible man I know." Semra bit her lip. The words had slipped out so easily. She realized in that moment she meant every word. "I mean, to be fair, I haven't been exposed to particularly wonderful men. But of the ones I've met, you win by a landslide."

Zephan laughed and wiped his eyes. "I'm a better man than Azi?"

"Definitely. And Tymetin isn't half the man you are." Semra grinned stupidly, and Zephan snorted. Semra raised her eyebrows. "You already know about Tymetin?"

Zephan nodded. "They also searched the catacombs and found a spare meal and another explosive hidden there. A backup plan, I imagine. I'm ... I'm sort of the king now. If anything important happens, I hear about it."

Semra froze at the sound of that word. *King.* "Oh." She pulled her arms in toward herself, and Zephan gently gripped her wrists and pulled her back.

"I already hate this job," he said. "But if I knew that not

only did my father have to die, and I had to give up the remaining shreds of my freedom, but I *also* wasn't allowed hugs, I think I would have refused the monarchy outright."

Semra leaned into him. "I'm sorry."

"I need something normal. Humor me."

Semra's heart broke at the plea in his voice. She avoided his eyes. Smoke curled from her fingertips, and he brushed them with his thumb. Her lip trembled, and she snatched her hands away. "We aren't normal."

"No."

A knock came at the door, and Semra stepped away from Zephan, batting at the smoke and tucking her hands behind her back. The door opened. Gaulen stood at attention to one side, and a guard Semra didn't recognize stood in the opening to the Nezzi Room and bowed.

"Your Majesty. The generals have requested an urgent audience."

Zephan nodded, and Semra could almost feel the weight of the crown's burden as it pinned him to the castle with fetters of bloodline and grief.

"Shall I send them to the throne room?"

"The lower meeting rooms will be fine."

"It is your first military appointment."

Zephan gritted his teeth, and Semra marveled at how swiftly he regained himself. Somehow, despite the bags under his eyes, he looked regal. Zephan straightened. "My father's body is not yet cold. I will not sit on his seat mere hours after his passing, out of respect for his many years of faithful leadership. Send the generals to the lower meeting rooms and spread the word that I do not need the throne room suggested to me at any point this week."

The guard dropped into a hasty bow. "Forgive me, Your Majesty. Of course, Your Majesty."

The door to her chambers stood open in the wake of the guard's departure, and several more pretended not to watch them from the hall outside. Inexplicably, in full sight of the men through the door, the king of Jannemar dipped his head in a gesture of respect to the guttersnipe woman assassin with tattered, filthy clothes. He stepped toward her, took her hand in his, and kissed it.

Goosebumps ran up her arm, and her heart flopped. And then he was gone. Heavy footfalls of the king's bodyguard accentuated his every step as the call of duty took him further and further away from her.

Semra stood rooted to the spot. Her lips parted as the significance of what Zephan had just done sunk in. He was teaching his guardsmen how to treat her. Their open glares and derision would not be welcome in his reign.

Every moment, every gesture, every breath he made would now be fraught with meaning. Semra remembered her conversation with Turian, only a few weeks ago.

Is it—is it terribly lonely, being king?

Sometimes it is. Sometimes it's terribly lonely.

48

Five minutes later, Pidge flew into the room. Her hair streamed haphazardly behind her, her eyes were red, and every muscle twitched with nervous energy.

"They wouldn't let me in the hall until he left," she said. "I need to talk to you."

Semra walked to the couch and fell into it with a groan. "Close the door and tell me."

Pidge shut the door and strode to the chair opposite Semra. She sat down and leaned forward. She opened her mouth. And closed it again.

Weariness descended on Semra like a wave. She ran a hand over her face. "Pidge. Just say it, whatever it is."

Pidge took a breath and sat on her hands. "I know it's not exactly a good time, but Turian is dead, and Siler may still be alive. Also, being in the castle freaks me out."

Semra grimaced. She counted the days since they'd left Belvidore. "The wedding is in just over a week. And it takes a week to get there on Zezura."

"If there's any chance of Siler being kept alive, it will be until the wedding," Pidge said. "After that, all bets are off. If he's even still alive." Tears spilled down Pidge's face. "We can't leave him."

Semra slowly shook her head. "No. And we won't." She dropped her head in her hands and gave herself over to the ache in her throat and chest, where the tears had run dry but the well of pain never would.

Turian was dead. Tymetin had assassinated both of Zephan's parents, and having the culprit dead would never bring them back. His older sister was malicious and causing trouble in Belvidore. His younger sister, just sixteen, was alone in the world without him. The same event that brought Zephan his deepest grief, also caused the weight of the crown to come crashing down on his shoulders.

She couldn't leave him now.

But leaving Siler went against every promise she'd made to herself, to Siler, to Pidge, and to the Mount Hara assassins she'd promised to represent.

"I'll talk to Zephan first thing in the morning."

"If they let you in to see him," Pidge grumbled. "Or we could just go now. Leave him a letter or something. Isn't that what you did last time?"

"I left letters last time, yes," Semra said, "and I won't do it again. I will speak to him face to face. I'm no good to travel right now. You might think you are, but you probably aren't either. We'll rest for the night and make good time in the morning."

Pidge leaned back and crossed her arms. "Why? Because you have to obey him now?"

Semra bristled. "No. Because he matters to me, and we trust each other, and friends don't disappear on friends—especially in their hour of need. I've done it wrong plenty of times. This time I'm going to get it right. And because we're being strategic rather than impulsive, we'll also get to replenish traveling provisions and weapons."

Pidge stayed in Semra's room that night. Sometime in the middle of the night, Semra heard pattering feet pacing up and down in the hall. When she finally opened the door, Semra found Aviama crying, and debating with herself about whether to wake up her friend or go back to her room.

"I'm sorry, I just really don't want to be alone," she said. "I can't. I can't do it. I slept in Avaya's room for two weeks after Mother ... but she isn't here ..."

Semra ushered the princess into her room, and the three of them piled in for the rest of the night. A year ago, Semra would never have dreamed a princess would be begging for a sleepover with an assassin under any circumstances, let alone two of them. But she wasn't about to turn away a friend either.

When Semra had been kidnapped from her village at age four, she had at least had Adis, the kindly induction specialist in the mountain. She was older, working for Azi, and an important part of early indoctrination. But in those moments of deep grief, she was also a shoulder to cry on, a hug, another human body filling the emptiness. And being royal meant that Aviama was limited in who she could comfortably go to for support.

It was a long time before Semra fell asleep, but when exhaustion took over at last, she slept hard until morning. Semra spoke briefly to Aviama about her plans, gave her a hug, and promised to return from Belvidore as soon as possible. Gaulen had just begun his shift and was waiting for her outside when Semra emerged and sent word that she was requesting a time-sensitive audience with the king.

Two hours later, Semra was led into the lower meeting room to speak with Zephan. He nodded solemnly, told her he understood, but that he had something she needed to take with her when she left. He told her to wait in the courtyard for him, and she waited there with Pidge and Zezura for another hour before Zephan appeared wearing armor and a sword, flanked by four bodyguards and trailed by Captain Firfell and General Soldan.

Semra jumped off the bench where she'd been sitting. "What's all this?"

"A terrible, terrible idea," Firfell grouched.

Semra turned to Zephan. "What could you possibly be sending with us that makes Firfell even more miserable than usual?"

The corner of Zephan's mouth quirked upward. "Me."

Her mouth dropped open. "No."

Soldan sighed. "That's what I said. I suggested to His Majesty that this is unwise in every respect and begged him repeatedly to reconsider."

Semra shook her head at the young king. "Zephan. Don't be an idiot." Two of the guards physically flinched at her failure to call him *Your Majesty*. Semra scowled. She wasn't sure she'd ever be able to call him that.

Zephan slapped a sealed envelope into Soldan's hand and strode forward. "I'll be whatever I want. I'm the king."

"You sound like a child," Semra hissed, dropping her voice so the guards couldn't hear. "If you're king, you'd better act like it. You have a terrified kingdom to run, your court is going to lose trust in you, and ... well, is it possible you're running away?"

Pidge sucked in a shocked breath and gaped between them. Zezura puffed out a curl of smoke from her nostrils. Zephan crossed his arms. "The kingdom is in good hands. Obviously, I have no heirs, so I've named Soldan both my steward and my successor, should that need arise."

Semra folded her arms to mirror Zephan. "It had better not. It won't."

"I need to come, Sem. I *need* to."

Semra's heart wrenched in two. She understood the feeling, but any simpleton could see how horrible of an idea this was. He was grieving, and he was reckless, and he had responsibilities beyond all imagining. And Semra couldn't bear the thought of putting him at such risk.

"I have often felt that way," she said. "Like I *needed* to do something bold and brash and passionate. Those are the moments I'm most likely to have a brush with death."

"Better to brush it than to collide with it."

"I'm being serious."

"So am I."

Tears sprang to her eyes, and she blinked them back. *What if I live, and you die? What am I to do then?* "I think you're being stupid," she said.

"I think you're lovely."

He grinned. He knew he'd won. Perfect amber pools stared her down, tender and warm, but resolute. And somehow, behind that veil of confidence, they were sorrowful, too.

Semra threw up her hands. "Now I know you've lost your mind. Here, in your courtyard, in Shamaran's walls."

Pidge laid a hand on her arm. "Just let him come. If he were Siler, you'd let him. If he were anybody else, you would let him. So let him."

Zephan nodded at Pidge. "I've always liked you."

Pidge rolled her eyes. "No, you haven't."

"Well, I like you now."

"Good. Because you made us promises I expect you to keep." Pidge cleared her throat. "Semra?"

Semra worried her lip and stroked Zezura's smooth scales.

Pidge gestured at Zephan. "Just get on. She wants you to

come. Dragons and daylilies, she's at *least* as dumb as you are sometimes."

Zephan smiled. Semra couldn't help but smile back, and for a brief moment they forgot their grief. Zephan swept his hand toward the dragon, and Semra climbed on. Pidge and Zephan clambered up after her, and the dragon took to the skies.

It was time to break up a wedding.

49

───────

Midday sun beat down on the three dragon riders as they glided into Horen. Madensig bustled with activity, extravagant carriages packing the outer wards where they'd been parked outside the stables, ribbons and flowers spilling out into an empty courtyard. Zezura had made good time, and they'd arrived in a week, but they were still behind.

"Will we make it before the ceremony ends?" Pidge asked, yelling against the wind.

Semra shook her head. "I don't know. Vix's message said they won't kill Siler until the feasting begins. They're making him a spectacle—part of the festivities of the day—so we can expect him to be the center of attention as soon as the ceremony is over."

Her stomach turned, and Zephan's arms tightened around her waist. They had made a quick stop over the mountains at the mouth of the cavern and picked up a message Vix had left for them with the information he'd gathered and an update on the plans. Knowing Siler was alive had soothed her soul, but coming up on Madensig now, Semra wondered how a handful of assassins could really take on the Belvidorian army and escape unscathed.

Unlike Shamaran's long windows and stunning aesthetic, few rooms had large glass windows in Madensig. The great hall was the exception, and the only appropriate venue for a wedding at the fortress.

Semra leaned back against Zephan and turned her head so he could hear her voice, and the chainmail shirt he'd insisted she wear clinked against his armor.

"Are you ready for Tymetin's wedding gift?"

"Scourge, yes!"

Ah, the dignified words of the king. Semra grinned and Zezura dropped low along the moat, her wingtip dipping in the water. It was time to announce their presence.

Madensig was truly a remarkable fortress. There were only two ways in, and visibility was excellent. No one came in uninvited. The moat was massive, and the carriage road across it narrowed as it reached the drawbridge. Guards stood in every window, and archers in every tower.

Whizz. Whizz.

Arrows flew as soon as they were in range. Zezura angled her body to protect her three human charges and let out a stream of fire as Zephan threw Tymetin's spare explosive.

Boom.

The wooden drawbridge tore apart, the blast blowing debris high into the air. Semra flinched at the ringing in her ears as they shot up into the air and over the battlement. Madensig's greatest strength was also its greatest weakness. And keeping enemies out was just as easy as keeping residents in.

Fortress exits now cut down to one, Semra leaned low over the dragon's neck toward their next target. The massive, ornamented windows of the great wedding hall. That beautiful, wonderfully fragile glass.

At least, it was fragile to a dragon.

The windows rushed toward them. Somewhere in the back of her mind, a questioning thought nagged. *What if this isn't a good idea?*

Zezura lowered her head like a battering ram. Hundreds of women in gowns and men in embroidered jackets clutched at their pearls or downed a swig of wine to face whatever menace had caused the explosion at the front of the fortress.

Crash.

Glass shattered. Fire blazed from the dragon's mouth. Women screamed.

In the middle of the dance floor, a striking blonde woman stood in a flowing crimson gown. Luxurious gold lace detailed the entire bodice from hips to neckline, and a filmy cape gathered at her throat with the same intricate lace. A silver crown graced the top of her head.

Next to her stood a broad-shouldered giant in a gold-plaited red jacket with an ornamented ceremonial sword and golden crown. Semra had no doubt the sword was sharpened, despite its primary use as a showoff piece. Axis drew his sword and swept his bride behind him.

Avaya's eyes turned to ice as they locked onto Semra. But as Semra landed on the cool floors, all she could focus on was the man chained to the back wall. His filthy rags were hanging off him, revealing a body black and blue with bruises. His lip and cheek were split open, and he was set on a pedestal four feet off the ground. Nothing about his defeated, broken posture was familiar to Semra. But those storm-gray eyes...

They pierced her through. And she would have them find their light again.

Semra ran to meet the first of the guards pouring into the

open space, her knives arcing and spinning like dancing cobras. The first man fell and was replaced by three more. Zezura snapped at an unlucky soldier, her wings too bulky to fit inside the window, her head and neck swinging this way and that.

Zephan skewered a man closing in behind them, and the dragon blew a fountain of flame into the room. Pidge ducked behind her adversary and sent him sprawling.

Whizz. Thud.

Semra's head jerked up, but the arrows were in her opponents. They dropped to the ground.

Whizz. Thud. Thud.

And suddenly the room was alive with combat. Nobles sliced their neighbors through, and servants attacked honored guests. Semra's knife sliced through a brachial artery like butter and shoved aside her latest enemy.

She smiled at the ridiculous plumed hat bobbing across the room on the far side. Vix had done his work. The assassins had all secured their places, hidden in plain sight. And now it was time for the king of Belvidore to learn what they were made of.

Pidge swung for a guard to Semra's right and disappeared under a table in the chaos. Zephan kicked another man back toward the open window, and Semra heard a sickening scream and *crunch* as Zezura made quick work of him. No one dared approach them from behind, though a few brave souls attacked Zezura. Their courage was rewarded by fire.

Wedding guests ran screaming this way and that, an ever-shifting obstacle course for the soldiers making their way toward Semra and Zephan. Semra threw her knife into a guard's throat and yanked it free as he fell. She felt a slash against her side and spun, crashing her elbow into the face of her newest adversary and slugging him with the knuckles of her left knife hand. She slashed his torso, and he doubled over, then she reached toward the sky for momentum and drove her elbow down on his spinal column at the base of his neck. He dropped like a stone.

She hated to admit it, but it was a good thing Zephan had insisted on the chain mail. She'd exposed her abdomen, and her injury would have been severe.

Beside her, Zephan downed another man, and when she lifted her head from her latest opponent, she felt the change in him as he locked eyes with Axis. The new king of Belvidore. The new king of Jannemar.

Vix and an assassin from Pidge's class named Gidyn flanked Semra and Zephan as they cut through the center of the room. A soldier ran at Zephan, but Zephan's gaze was only for Axis. Panic gripped Semra's chest, and she threw her knife. It sailed true to its target, but she was running out of blades.

Up on the platform, Pidge was picking the lock to Siler's chains. A soldier crept up behind her and raised his sword. Siler yelled for Pidge to turn.

But blades fly faster than brains can take instruction. Semra's last knife sank in the soldier's eye and Pidge redoubled her efforts on the lock. Gidyn flipped a guard over his shoulder and snatched the sword from the ground. He tossed it to Semra.

Red-hot anger seized her chest as she looked at Avaya, standing between Axis and Siler with a fallen dagger in her hands. The Jannemari princess, now the young queen of Belvidore. The woman who threw fuel on the fire of it all.

Zephan and Axis clashed steel against steel. Zephan's lip curled and he lifted his voice over the din of the fight. "Is this what you wanted, Avaya? Tearing the kingdom apart was not enough, so you had to destroy the last shreds of our family?"

Avaya whirled the dagger in her hands, and the dexterity of the move did not escape Semra. She'd been practicing.

"Father is weak! This union was *his* idea, not mine. Well, you're welcome, Father! I'll keep the deal you broke!"

"He did *everything* for you. *Everything!* You've always been an ungrateful brat, but now" —Zephan ducked under Axis' swing and drove forward, nicking Axis on the neck before Axis shoved him back—"I don't know you at all."

"No, you don't! Neither of you know me! Father has never respected me, never appreciated me. He never overturned the old laws against women rulers. He married selfishly, and then demands we do what he did not?"

Semra rolled past Axis and sprang to her feet on the far side, three feet from Avaya. Avaya let out a cry and leaped back. Semra's lips pulled back and a guttural roar ripped from her throat as four guards filled the gap between her and Avaya. Giddy leaped up beside her and they struck forward together.

"Is that why you killed him?" Zephan snarled. "For marrying a commoner, and not making you heir to the throne?"

Avaya froze. Her chest heaved, and her face paled. Fear, anger, and hurt flitted across her features and finally settled on a violent rage. Vix spun six feet away to block an oncoming soldier, and a guard surged into the open space, knocking Zephan off balance. Axis brought his sword to bear on Zephan, and Radix appeared just in time to block it.

Semra glanced between Avaya and Axis. Avaya's eyes darkened, and her movements dropped into a fluid, confident strength. Not erratic. Not shaking.

Purposeful.

Resolute.

Semra knew that tunnel vision aggression. She'd seen it in

Tymetin. She'd seen it in Manu, and Pinji, and every set of eyes that had bored into her with intent to kill. She'd felt it herself.

"Axis, my love, what is he talking about?" Honey dripped from her sing-song voice, and Semra wondered if poison ever tasted as sweet.

Axis deflected a blow from Zephan and rotated into a strike at Radix. He sneered. "Darling, did you really think you were the only one who could hire an assassin? Did you expect to keep the best of your assassin pets to yourself and leave me with the dregs?"

Behind the kings, Pidge helped Siler down off the platform. "I need a sword."

Pidge turned and sliced the neck of a passing guard, catching his sword as he fell and spinning the handle to offer it to Siler. He grinned. "Not bad, rookie." Pidge beamed, and Siler blocked an oncoming assault. "Now where's our exit out of this kill box?"

"You murdered my father," Avaya said, her voice so soft Semra could only barely make out the words.

"You're welcome," Axis said. Semra grunted as she collided with a fresh guard. Axis retreated toward Avaya as Radix and Zephan pushed him back. "You're in the business of killing fathers, aren't you? It was only a matter of time until you got to your own. He wasn't doing you any favors."

Reinforcements rushed into the room. "To the king! To the king!"

Zephan let out a roar and flew at Axis with the untenable force of unbridled hatred. The callous confession was more than he could take. Axis stumbled back against the fury of Zephan's sword. He parried and struck forward, but Zephan pushed in, hardly giving him time to recover for an offensive move.

Semra's body ached. She felt the adrenaline coursing through her body, but she'd long lost count of how many men she'd killed, and her strength was fading. She shoved another guard aside and stepped over him, striding for Avaya. Avaya clutched Axis's arm and he turned to look. Radix saw his opportunity. Avaya glanced at Radix, gripped Axis's wrist, and pulled it across her body as if it were outstretched to protect her.

In the same moment, Radix and Zephan's swords each plunged into Axis. Avaya screeched from behind her husband as the blades penetrated through his stomach and out his back.

A new wave of guards poured in from all directions. Semra lunged and her fingers wrapped like iron around Avaya's wrist. Avaya's body ran into the sword still in Axis's torso, then fell forward as Radix planted a foot on the Belvidorian king's trunk and withdrew his blade with a grunt.

Shouts rang across the great hall.

"The king is down!"

"Protect your king!"

"The king is dead!"

"To the queen! To the queen!"

There were too many, and the band of assassins were pushed back, Zephan among them. Semra doubled Avaya's arm behind her back and forced her forward.

A gentle mist hit Semra's face, and her muscles failed her. Dizziness overtook her, and she stumbled. A sickly sweet aroma filled her nostrils. It didn't smell like konnolan. Her sword clattered to the floor.

50

New guards surrounded Avaya and Semra, and Avaya locked both hands around Semra's neck. Her lips peeled back in a wicked snarl. For the first time, Semra noticed a locket hanging from a chain around Avaya's neck—a seashell and a pearl, the pearl cracked open, sizzling with some effervescent mixture.

Zezura was releasing volleys of fire toward them, stream after stream of flame, but the distance was too great. Voices shouted from every direction, but Semra could hear only one.

"You're the one that showed me it could be done," Avaya hissed into Semra's ear. "Taking on the world, destroying your enemies, the power of life and death in your own two hands. You were exactly who I wanted to be, before you crumbled into the pathetic worm I was, under a man's boot."

Semra's lungs burned. It should have been easy to break the grasp of an inexperienced person. If Semra had had her strength, Avaya would be dead on the floor; as it was, she was helpless to stop the chokehold of the queen. A ring of soldiers formed around Avaya and Semra, every weapon was lifted toward the people Semra loved most in the world.

The children of the mountain, whom Semra had brought here with promises of freedom. Siler. Pidge.

Zephan.

Avaya threw Semra to the floor and stood over her body. She raised her voice over the clamor of the room. "Assassins of Mount Hara! Do you leave the slavery of Azi Shamaran for more of the same from Semra? I do not wish to control you. I wish to partner with you. Follow me now or die, just as you watch your leader die."

The young queen leaned down to Semra, disappearing from the crowd behind the wall of soldiers. "You failed my mother. You turned my brother and sister against me. And you bring more assassin trash and death with you wherever you go. As far as I'm concerned, *you* murdered both my parents. And it's time you paid for it."

Avaya held out her hand to one of the Belvidorian soldiers, and he handed over his sword without hesitation. Semra wiggled her fingers and toes. Sensation was returning. Whatever Avaya had used, she'd gotten the dose wrong. But even if she escaped Avaya, she was surrounded by far more guards than she could take on. And Zezura was too far away.

Semra steeled herself, lying on the floor as helpless as she could manage. The timing had to be just right. And afterward, she'd probably die anyway.

One step at a time.

Avaya plunged the sword toward Semra's chest. Semra rolled to the side, and the sword hit the marble floors. Semra gripped the blade with her hands and pulled hard; Avaya stumbled forward, and Semra leaped to her feet and flipped the queen over onto her seat. Semra cinched her elbow tight around Avaya's throat and used Avaya as a human shield on one side, while sword fighting soldiers on the other.

The mark of the dragon's kiss burned on her chest. *There are too many windows intact, Zez.*

Eight assassins crashed against the soldiers, and the circle broke where Zezura engulfed the outer ring in flame before disappearing from her position in the window. Zephan was missing.

And then he was there, launched off a table and flying through the air over the heads of the soldiers. Semra's heart soared at the sight of him. He'd never looked more handsome in all his life. Zephan rolled on impact, sprang to his feet beside Semra, and attacked the soldiers from her side.

"We need some smoke," he said, parrying a blow and nicking a guard on the neck.

Semra winced as Avaya dropped her weight to the floor and forced Semra to lose focus on the guards and bear her up. She tried to concentrate on her fingers, on the heat inside her chest. Nothing.

A shadow passed over the north side of the room, and Semra was vaguely aware of the dragon bashing through another perfectly good window. Shattering glass skittered across the floor in all directions, and Zezura's fire filled the room.

Pidge and Siler cut through the wall of soldiers, narrowly blocking an attack on Semra. Siler groaned as he pushed his wounded body to the limit, slashing at another Belvidorian defender. "Semra! If we're ever getting out of here, we need the smoke *now!*"

She tried again. *I can do this. Where is the heat? Push it out, out to my fingers ...*

Her heart pounded, and her fingertips tingled. She could feel the heat swirling in her chest, but it did not bend to her will. Semra's breathing came in short gasps as panic set in.

"I can't!"

Zephan ducked under an enemy blow, ripped his sister from Semra's arms, and shoved her at Siler. He lowered his sword. "Cover us," he yelled, and the next moment Zephan's mouth was on hers, his free hand at the nape of her neck, drawing her in.

Against all reason, Semra gave herself over to the pull of his presence, drinking him in as the battle raged. For a moment, the passion of their kiss blotted out all else, and she felt only the softness of his lips and the warmth of his hands. Smoke surged from her fingers like a great body of water broken free of its dam.

Inky blackness wrapped around them in long ebony coils. Sparks flew from her hands, the only light in a consuming, swirling dark. Zephan gripped her hand on one side, and Siler snatched her wrist on the other as Zephan pulled them toward the window on the opposite side of the room where Siler had been chained.

"I can't see anything," Siler hissed.

"That's the idea," Semra said.

"Is the idea also to walk straight out the broken window and fall to our deaths?"

Semra rolled her eyes, though no one could appreciate it. She sent the message: *Zezura. Light.*

A plume of fire made a beacon through the thick smoke, and they ran toward it. Vix and Radix materialized with a thick rope. Zezura put her head on the floor inside the great hall, and Semra climbed up her neck, out the broken window, and onto the dragon's back.

Darkness had enveloped them again, but the soldiers knew where they were now. The clamor of footsteps and swords and people bumping into one another filled their ears. Somewhere, Avaya was barking orders. Zephan followed Semra, and Siler gestured for Pidge to go next.

"I'll take the rope. You're injured. Get on."

"I'm fine, rookie. Get out of here before I throw you."

Vix tossed the rope to Semra, and she looped it around Zezura's neck and back to Vix.

"Now or never," Radix shouted. "Let's go!"

Zezura blasted a final torrent of fire into the great hall and withdrew from the window. Semra blinked in the brightness of afternoon and turned to look back at Madensig Fortress as they pulled away. Smoke billowed from its two smashed windows, and Avaya stood in the opening, surrounded by guards.

Zezura clutched two assassins in her talons, carried three on her back, and six more hung from the rope around her neck. Even as strong as she was, the dragon couldn't bear her burdens far. They soared off to the outskirts of Horen in a gradual, steady descent where the two practicum students and several Sabre class students were waiting with horses and supplies.

With the drawbridge out, Madensig would be forced to take the rear exit, to the north, which bought them time. Belvidore's king was dead, and the fortress would be in an uproar. Soldiers would be sent after them, but the Mount Hara assassins had a head start. They would make it.

Semra smiled. Mission support at its finest. And the last mission these young ones would ever need.

They made a quick stop, and Siler shook Zephan's hand and gave Semra and Pidge a quick hug before electing to take a horse and go his own way. Semra caught the corners of Pidge's mouth turning down at the news, but when Semra asked if Pidge wanted to stay behind, she insisted on returning to Shamaran with Semra.

"I always see a mission to the end. And my mission doesn't end until we get you back where you belong."

Where you belong.

Semra didn't know what to make of that. She didn't know that she belonged in any particular location. But she did know she wanted to be wherever Zephan was. It made less sense and was more impossible than ever before, but he was home to her now.

His arms wrapped around her, and the breeze caressed her face with the gentle reminder of life on the other side of every storm. The rain may pour, but good things grow from its water, even in the harshest of conditions.

A lump lodged in her throat. Gratitude. Grief. Uncertainty.

Turian was dead and would need a funeral. Zephan was king and would need a coronation. Semra was free and would need a future.

She would stand by Zephan and Aviama through the grief of their father and the transition of power. Beyond that, Semra could only hope her future and Zephan's had room in them somehow for each other—and a dragon.

51

———

Semra's fingers tapped incessantly on the handle of the knife in its sheath as she passed Ancestry Hall and crossed the long walkway over the great hall to the conservatory. Pidge ran toward her on the walkway and gripped her arms.

"He pardoned me! I can go anywhere, do anything. Nobody will come for me. I'm free!"

Semra hugged her and smiled, but her mind was in the room beyond. "Congratulations. I'm happy for you."

Pidge bit her lip. "They're ready for you. You've done a lot more good things than me. I'm sure he'll pardon you too."

Semra nodded and took a deep breath. No sooner had they arrived back at Shamaran Castle and Zephan was swept off for debriefing and answering before the court and military advisers. Soldan had begun funeral preparations in Zephan's absence and had a thousand questions to raise regarding the ceremony and anticipation of the public mourning period. Semra and Pidge gave statements about what happened over the two and a half weeks they were missing traveling to and from Belvidore the day after Turian was killed, and then awaited further instructions in their quarters. Coanor checked them for physical health, and Semra spent her time comforting a distraught Aviama, sitting with Pidge, taking Zezura for a ride, and escaping to the chandlery to sit with Garbane.

And then the summons came.

A formal, before-the-court summons by the king.

The conservatory was a strange choice for a place to meet. It was adjacent to the king's chambers, which Zephan had reluctantly begun to occupy at his advisers' insistence. But one of the throne rooms or official meeting rooms would have been expected. Semra wondered if perhaps that was exactly why he had done it—to stay out of the throne rooms where his father had sat, or to break the mold and set the tone that things would not always be how they had been before.

Two guards opened the doors for her at the end of the walkway, and she swallowed. She wiped the sweat from her hands on her trousers and stepped inside. The lofted ceiling and tall glass surrounding them with the light, airy optimism of morning. Four pillars stood sentry in the corners of the room, a flowering vine delicately climbing the marble. Various plants lined the walls and filled a stone table in the center of the room, designed with a miniature garden living inside it weaving through chiseled stone patterns. The balcony sat to her right, overlooking the outer ward on the north side.

She'd once flung herself over the railing of that balcony to hide from guards, and Zephan had found her there and hauled her up. He hadn't been a prince then. Just a healer's apprentice with a father who worked in the castle. Or so she'd thought. Semra shook her head. What a long way they'd come.

Zephan sat at the table, dressed in the traditional riches of his station. Select members of the court filled a row of chairs lined the far side of the room. Semra recognized General Soldan, General Tallem, Count Darbune, Duke Villir, and Earl Lundoon. Two other men she did not recognize sat on the end. An empty chair sat across the table from Zephan, where the king and his courtiers could examine her.

"Semra!" Zephan stood when she entered, and his nobles hurriedly followed suit. Zephan gestured toward the chair. "Have a seat."

Formal. Stiff. Weird. Her stomach twisted into a thousand anxious ribbons. She sat.

Zephan shuffled through several papers and pulled a document to the top of the stack before him. It was a hand-written letter, with the king's signature and royal seal at the bottom.

"As you know, I have granted Pidge Bandaka a registered certificate of pardon, and she is officially cleared and free." Zephan glanced up from the documents before him and observed his audience. His air was solemn, but when he looked at Semra, mischief lit his eyes. She cocked her head and squinted at him. *What are you up to?*

"Distinguished members of court, I have heard many of your grievances over my short reign as king thus far. Semra is repeatedly the center of a variety of issues, and each of those concerns will be addressed today.

"Semra's involvement at Shamaran Castle has been ques-tioned, and rightly so, seeing as she has no position at court. She does not come from nobility, and therefore the closeness between Semra and me has been criticized. Her loyalty has also been questioned, but after recent events, standing by our side despite being framed *twice* for assassinations she did not commit, I cannot imagine any of you would dare doubt her allegiance now."

Zephan squared his shoulders and took a deep breath.

"Semra has operated as consultant, military strategist, and invaluable ally. Nevertheless, I am *not* going to grant Semra a pardon."

Semra's stomach dropped like a stone. Her chest caved in, and she couldn't breathe. Hurt and betrayal rocked her. How could he do this?

A low murmur rolled through the nobles, and a sly smile played across Darbune's face. Zephan held up a hand, and his gaze held her fast. It was steady, firm yet reassuring. Those amber pools drew her in, and she couldn't look away.

"I am not going to grant Semra a pardon," he said again, never taking his eyes off Semra, "because my father already made a determination prior to his death. His ruling is written, signed, sealed, and final."

Semra's jaw dropped. Her breathing quickened, and a single curl of smoke escaped from her fingertips. She folded her hands in her lap.

Zephan lifted the document in his hands. "This is the last official document of King Turian of Jannemar, written by his own hand and sealed on the night before his death, in General Soldan's presence."

"Lest any of you think this was my idea, please speak to General Soldan who was with my father the night he wrote this letter and signed the decree with his own hand. I am going to read his determination, and you are free to read the document in its entirety at your leisure on your own time. Copies will be delivered to you this afternoon."

Semra bit her lip. Zephan glanced up at her, cleared his throat, and skimmed the document.

"As a result of Semra's heroics, her enduring loyalty to the throne of Jannemar and commitment to the Shamaran royal family, and actions to repeatedly reveal malicious, murderous plots and at her own great peril fighting against them, I, King

Turian of Jannemar, Sovereign of the Shamaran dynasty, hereby pardon the woman formerly known as Semra Bandaka for all assassin-related activity carried out under the manipulation of the traitor Azi Shamaran.

"Semra is hereby cleared of all charges against her and free to pursue whatever remarkable life she so chooses, and the crown of Jannemar is honored to call her a friend. However, I, King Turian of Jannemar, do not believe a pardon is enough of an appropriate reward for the extreme personal risk, great integrity, and exceptional gallantry Semra has executed on behalf of this kingdom.

"Because Semra has revoked the name *Bandaka,* and because a surname is required for the legal possession of property, I declare her to be known from this point onward as Semra Myansara, and I do hope the name is amenable to her. It certainly is becoming.

"Semra Myansara is awarded the earldom of Pilall and declared Lady Myansara, earl of the same."

Something like a squeak escaped Semra's lips, and she clapped a hand over her mouth. Her eyes bulged and her face flushed. She swayed on the chair and gripped the seat. *Lady Myansara!* King Turian had not only pardoned her but also named her after one of the symbols of Jannemar—the flower Nezil Myansara, the same one painted across the walls of her guest room. Not to mention he gave her an earldom.

Shouts filled the room, and the nobles were on their feet. Semra didn't hear a word.

How did one run an earldom? Why would anyone *want* to run an earldom? What did it all mean? Was any of this even real?

She was free!

"Your Majesty, forgive me," Count Darbune said, chest

heaving, "but you have misread the document! Surely at the very least, she has been named *countess* of Pilall."

A smile crept across Zephan's face, and he did nothing to hide his delight. "No, Count Darbune, my father declared Semra earl. As such, she is not only in possession of and responsible for the earldom of Pilall, but a military leader in her own right."

More grumbling, arguing, shouts.

Semra blinked back at Zephan, and all the flush of her cheeks drained to a ghostly pallor. Her lips parted, but no sound came. Zephan winked at her.

Zephan clapped once, and the attention of the room snapped back to the king. "I know this news comes as a shock, and it will take some adjustment. Under more favorable circumstances, you would have the time to gradually come to terms with the change, but we are not afforded that luxury today. We have a funeral to plan, a coronation to set up, and our own grieving to grapple with. The next few weeks will reveal whether Belvidorian forces withdraw from the Surion Strip, and if the war effort will continue. But there's more.

"According to our sources, in the last few weeks King Axis signed a decree that if no children of the union have yet been born, a ruler's spouse would ascend the throne upon the ruler's death. As a result, my sister Avaya is now the reigning monarch of Belvidore. And she has the support of the people."

The room fell deadly silent.

"You have one hour to accept Semra as your peer before we reconvene. And Semra ..." Zephan grinned. "Welcome to the nobility."

BOOK #4: CRIMSON QUEEN

Continue the adventure with Noble Claims...

Magic is dead, but her enemies are using it. And a prophecy dooms her to fail.

THANK YOU FOR READING!

Thank you so much for reading *Noble Claims,* book 3 of *The Blood and Flame Saga*! I hope you enjoyed reading it as much as I enjoyed writing it.

If you did, would you be willing to leave a review? Reviews help enable authors to continue doing what they do, and help other readers to find books best suited to them.

If you'd like to leave a review on Amazon, **click here.**

ABOUT THE AUTHOR

Author of *The Forgotten Stone* and the *Blood and Flame Saga*, E.A. Winters loves pouring herself a cup of hot chocolate with a mountain of marshmallows and delving into creating epic fantasy worlds for you to enjoy.

Erin lives in Virginia with her husband and two boys. When she's not writing, Erin is spending her time with her family. She loves playing board games and reading, whenever the elusive "free time" opportunity arises.

ALSO BY E.A. WINTERS

Blood & Flame Saga

Book 1: Dragon's Kiss

Book 2: Broken Bonds

Book 3: Noble Claims

Book 4: Crimson Queen

Stand Alones

The Forgotten Stone